Crossing into the Mystic

DL Koontz

Brimstone
Fiction

PRAISE FOR *CROSSING INTO THE MYSTIC*

Crossing into the Mystic is an engaging, page-turning read. Grace's pain, confusion, and desire for freedom to be herself are feelings most of us can identify with. As if that isn't enough, D.L. Koontz deftly paints pictures with her words by showing us the landscape, both beautiful and haunting, where her story takes place. Her historical research is evident, and the rich descriptions of days gone by serve as another magnetic draw. I'm waiting impatiently to read book number two.

~Anita Agers Brooks
Author, International Speaker, Inspirational Coach

DL Koontz' writing is incredibly compelling! I started *Crossing into the Mystic* yesterday afternoon, read as late as I could last night - had to talk myself out of calling in sick to work in order to finish it this morning - and missed my favorite show to keep reading. I finished it just as soon as I got home from work this evening after spending the day more focused on these characters than the ones I spent the day with. If you enjoy a good mystery, and don't mind the hairs on your neck standing up a bit, you will love this page-turner!

The vivid language and descriptions, the deep characterization, the powerful verbs...Koontz' craft is superb! The story is complex and unexpected, and I enjoyed the surprising twists of plot. The author masterfully weaves in the heroine's background and the history of the Civil War to create a marvelous tale.

~Felicia Bowen Bridges
HR Manager, Pastor's Wife and Mother of Four

Thoroughly enjoyed reading Koontz' book, *Crossing into the Mystic*. Intriguing storyline that pulled me right into Grace's life. Loved Koontz' voice as well as her way of describing people, places, and events. Looking forward to hearing more from this author.

~Beth Fortune
Inspirational Speaker and Writer

Crossing into the Mystic captured my attention with its strong, emotional character descriptions from the first page, as Grace, an orphaned teen, plans her escape from her temperamental aunt and wrestles with the death of her parents and sister. As Grace begins her extraordinary journey from her chaotic Boston environment to her inheritance, a mysterious ancestral estate in the Blue Ridge Mountains of West Virginia, the intricate descriptive scenes set the mood for an imaginative, gripping storyline. A romantic triangle and the supernatural invade Grace's incredible pilgrimage as the narrative develops, creating an engaging paranormal romantic suspense novel.

~**Karen Jordan**
Author, Speaker, Writing Instructor, Blogger

A hefty trust fund, an SUV, and an ancestral estate – all for Grace, a 16-year-old orphan anxious to leave Boston, alone, to live three months in the ancient manor home nestled in the Blue Ridge mountains. No one has been in the mansion for centuries except for Grace's stepfather – something has prevented the intrusions. The feisty heroine develops extraordinary relationships – both with the living and the dead. Grace, as well as the reader, must delve into her own belief system as the author creates an interweaving tale of suspense; a tale tossed with paranormal phenomena, geography, history, religious, and love elements – topped with a bit of humor. Vivid descriptions engage the senses as Grace explores the beautiful mountain areas, the Shenandoah Valley, and the abandoned estate house; experiences life during the Civil War era and the Battle of Antietam through the eyes of the soldiers; feels the turmoil and joy of real-life young love; struggles to understand death and the life thereafter; and learns that life is defined by the decisions one makes. Koontz has created a gripping story with a few unanswered details that entice the reader to yearn for a sequel.

~**Darlene Reighard**
Educator and Consultant

Crossing into the Mystic takes one girl's struggle with fear and loss and creates a world where death isn't so final, and love isn't so far away.

From the first few pages, I cared about Grace. Her spunk and bravado and ability to conjure up tons of quotes on facing fear kept me wanting the best for her and reflecting on how I often let my anxiety determine too much for me. So many of her struggles are familiar to most of us at some point or another (except for the scary ghost part), and Koontz artfully crafted a paranormal world around a mostly normal girl.

A story painted inside another story bringing two worlds to light, *Mystic* takes a good look at death and life, exploring the spirit world in a fresh and trustworthy way. Koontz handles the unknowns carefully and keeps the story moving. Her description and wit are refreshing, and she maintains the pace planting little gems along the way. Great job!

~M B Dahl
Author of *Through the Balustrade*

Crossing into the Mystic is a fascinating and engrossing story. D.L Koontz has created a unique tale of life, death, ghosts, other dimensions and mystery. From the beginning of the book, I found myself taken in and I read it in a short number of days. While many other things were demanding my attention, I wanted to get back to it.

In *Crossing into the Mystic*, D.L. Koontz makes a very different world real. Her rich characters, through fascinating discussions and experiences, bring us into a world of life and after-life with ease. As I read, I let my mind ponder the mysteries of life and grew in the process. We witness the main character, Grace's journey towards faith as she experiences great tragedy and asks questions of life and death and mystery. The book takes the reader into a vivid history of the Civil War, and you feel you are there. The book has many unexpected twists and turns, keeping you engaged.

The book ends with words of wisdom on the meaning of life and death and what is unknown to us here. You want more, and I believe D.L. Koontz has left some doors open, so we may have just that.

~Ann Vanino
Career Coach and Blogger at MovingForward.Net

Mystery and historical fictions lovers rejoice! *Crossing into the Mystic* deftly weaves the hauntingly beautiful West Virginia landscape with complex (sometimes supernatural) characters and spiritual truths to create an irresistible plot.

Merging well-researched Civil War history with a modern-day heroine's search for love and self, D.L. Koontz keeps us anxiously turning the pages. Grace inspires us as readers to assess our own reactions to fear and change, and to question our encounters with the supernatural.

Needless to say, the next book in the trilogy cannot come soon enough!

~Alden Cayse
REALTOR® and blogger, www.austinhomestead.net

Crossing into the Mystic drew me in from the start and wouldn't let me go until I'd consumed the entire story in one sitting. Whew! An incredible ride that captivated me and left me thinking about love that is stronger than death. I'm already hungry for the sequel.

~Lori Roeleveld
Author of the Blog, Deeper with Jesus in Rhode Island

Just finished *Crossing into the Mystic*...I was mesmerized from the first word. It touched me on so many levels. Would love to have coffee with the author to discuss the places, in my own life, that her words allowed me to experience. Beautifully written and anxiously awaiting Koontz's next treasure!!

~Joanne L. Stiffler
Entertainer, Mother of Two, Controller for Real Estate Investor

CROSSING INTO THE MYSTIC BY D.L. KOONTZ
Published by Brimstone Fiction
1440 W. Taylor Street, Suite 449, Chicago, IL 60607

ISBN 978-1-946758-03-3
Copyright © 2017 by D.L. KOONTZ
Cover image by Urosh Bizjak, http://uroshb.prosite.com.
Cover design by Ted Ruybal, www.wisdomhousebooks.com.
Interior design by Sherry Heinitz.

Available in print from your local bookstore, online, or from the publisher at:
www.brimstonefiction.com

For more information on this book and the author visit: www.dlkoontz.com

Brought to you by the creative team at Lighthouse Publishing of the Carolinas and Brimstone Fiction: Rowena Kuo, Eddie Jones, Meaghan Burnett, and Brian Cross.

Library of Congress Cataloging-in-Publication Data
Koontz, D.L.
Crossing into the Mystic / D.L. Koontz 1st ed.

Printed in the United States of America

Acknowledgements

For helping me bring *Crossing into the Mystic* into the world, I owe thanks to so many:

I'm grateful first to my husband, Joseph Roberson, and my son, Matthew Traverso. Joe always seems to know when I need his encouragement and strength the most, and he never fails. My son Matt patiently heard every sentence of this book read aloud, offering, as usual, a keen insight that startles me. To my lovely step-daughter, Megan Roberson, for many hugs and words of encouragement.

To my parents, R. Clair and (the late) Mary Koontz, together they built a life farming and doing their share to feed America. They are/were courageous and steadfast, and taught me the joys and rewards of hard work, and an appreciation for history and wide open spaces.

To my cousins, Brenda Orndorff and Darlene Reighard, whom I must daily remind myself are not my sisters; thanks for clearing my head with laughter when I need it the most. And, to Charlie Stanley, for encouragement and goading that I hurry up and write more.

To Mandy Feight, Beth Mende Conny, Cheryl Burgwald, Anita Agers Brooks, and Johanna Doebling, for loving me, inspiring me, helping me grow, and believing in me, each in her own way.

To my late Uncle, Jake Koontz, the most crackerjack storyteller I've ever known, for proving that the Koontzes have stories worth telling.

To Dean Koontz for reminding me that even kids from the boonies in Bedford County, Pennsylvania can develop wild imaginations and capture them with ink. I aspire to your level of masterful storytelling and sky-high talent.

To Michael McGowan, Eva Marie Everson, Kristin Procter, Keiki Hendrix, and Reverend Dale Seley for delivering encouragement in a way that you probably didn't even realize at the time. To Torry Martin, for making me laugh and reminding me that laughter is an amazing gift, Divinely given.

To the amazing writers in my writing group, the Light Brigade, a collection of future Pulitzer Prize winners, *New York Times* bestselling authors, and some of the most inspiring writers I've met. You each have spent time with me on this tortured and thrilling walk called the writing life, continually offering praise and prayer, as we've stumbled down the path together. Thanks for kvetching with me when I needed it most.

To Dale Hansen, for first chances. To Eddie Jones, for bigger and better second chances. To my incredible editor, Rowena Kuo, for removing chance and replacing it with exactitude. And thanks to the other extraordinary people at Lighthouse Publishing and Brimstone Fiction who provided tireless expertise and support: Brian Cross and Meaghan Burnett.

To all the American soldiers and wounded warriors for giving me freedom, particularly the freedom to live my life—the writing life—the way I choose. God bless each of you.

And, thank you, Lord, for the blessings of the journey and all you've taught me along the way.

Visit the author's website at www.dlkoontz.com

Crossing into the Mystic is a work of pure fiction. While there are elements some might find open to interpretation, it should not be misconstrued as hindering Biblical truths. Instead, its storyline is intended to open a door of dialogue and an exploration of God's word. Isaiah 8:19-22 says to look to God for answers, not to the dead, and that God will judge those who pursue the occult.

DEDICATION

To my mother, Mary Audrey Stanley Koontz, who moved on to live in heaven, as I was writing this book. All that I am is because of the foundation, love, and encouragement you provided. I miss you every day.

PART I

Valley of the Shadow

Chapter 1

All of it became mine that day: the hefty trust fund, my mother's red SUV, and my stepfather's ancestral estate isolated amidst the caverns of the Blue Ridge Mountains. I was embarking on a 500-mile journey to make solo use of all three.

As long as I remained in Boston, I would continue to live my life backward—dwelling on the past and longing for the parents and sister who were dead. Buried. Gone. There was no way I could have known that by turning away from death I would be running into it.

That day seemed like the perfect time to launch my escape. The rising sun shot beguiling streaks of crimson through the divisions of the massive brownstones on Boston's Beacon Hill, teasing away any threat of "Red sky at morning, sailor take warning."

In the stillness of the morning, I heard a house door latch, then a husky voice grumble. "Ouch ... ouch ... dang!"

My cousin, Michael, barefoot and clad only in gym trunks and a T-shirt, pranced between stones as he hurried up the steep three-block incline toward me. He was carrying travel snacks, but what I hoped he was bringing me was reassurance of our individual escapes.

"Grace, go! Go! Go! Click your heels and get the Sam Hill out of Oz before she changes her mind!"

Though Michael's words echoed my resolve, I laughed. He was four inches taller and eight years older, but a million times more sociable and often reminded me of an oversized little boy.

"Auck, Dorothy." He reached my car, glanced back toward our house, and handed me a zip-locked bag stuffed with trail mix. "You're too late. You'll never get to Kansas now."

I turned to see the subject of his wicked witch allusion exit through the oversized front door of our ivy-covered brownstone and begin her march up the sidewalk with Uncle Phil dawdling behind. Aunt Tish wasn't toting a flying broom, but she was storming along, face scowling, hands fisted.

Michael grinned. "I guess she's saving the flying monkeys for me."

"Maybe. She wasn't very happy about you leaving tonight for Chile. You sure you're tough enough to stand up to her?" I elbowed him, knowing he wouldn't feel the jab. Despite his baby face and wire-rimmed glasses, he had the abs of a bodybuilder.

"No problem. She can't control me anymore. It's you who better leave quickly."

"I'm going. Don't worry about that." I tossed the trail mix on the back seat. From the front, my dog, Tramp, watched it land and turned back to the front window, more excited about going somewhere than the goodies. He barked twice. *Let's go.*

"Good. It will be two years before you'll get another chance," Michael warned in a whisper. "I won't be here this summer to save you like I have before."

"Which is exactly why I'm leaving today. Thanks for coming home to see me off. She's not that bad you know." Maybe voicing such hope would make it so.

Eyes wide, he said, "What? She's an unstable, soul-sucking—"

"Shush." I stifled laughter. "She'll hear you."

He sobered and leaned against my car, crossing his arms. "You're sure about this?"

"The trip? Of course."

He shook his head. "The house. It sounds … weird. Like Norman Bates lives there."

I looked at him, startled. Michael was generally carefree and titillated by the unknown. He loved the notion that people held secrets within themselves.

"That's crazy," I affirmed, lest his uncharacteristic concern unnerve me.

"Is it? Jack was so close-mouthed about the place."

"Michael, stop it! It's only a house. Jack was there three years ago. How bad could it be?"

"Remember. I'm only a phone call away. You have to live there what—three months?"

"That's what the will says. Then it's mine to do what I want. Including selling it. And, of course, that's exactly what Aunt Tish expects me to do."

"We'll work that out later. Stick with this charade that you're fixing it for your senior project, then selling it and moving back to Boston. By the end of summer, my new company will transfer me back to the states, and you can live with me. Just don't come back here."

"I know, I know."

"And keep Tramp close by."

I shook my head to indicate his concern was unnecessary. But inside, I couldn't help but wonder if Tramp would be able to stop *all* threats that I might encounter.

* * *

After stopping to assess her own vehicle and bark orders at my Uncle Phil to take it to the car wash, Aunt Tish reached us. As her eyes scanned my car, Uncle Phil plodded up behind.

Beside me, Michael murmured, "Shoulda' tied garlic around our necks," then he donned a Cheshire grin and bellowed, "Good morning, Mother dearest."

"Nice of you to grace us with your company, darling," Aunt Tish clucked with saccharin sarcasm and crossed her arms. Her face was stern, her eyes leveled. "If I didn't know better, I'd think you were trying to sleep your way through the day until your flight leaves."

"Got in late, Mom."

She arched a skeptical brow. "If you're turning right around and leaving for that ridiculous job in Chile, why did you even bother coming home? You could have been working at MacGruder's, you know. They *are* the most prestigious firm in Boston."

"Yeah, Mom, I know."

"They certainly would have paid better. Must be nice to have no concerns about money."

"I haven't cost you a cent since I turned twenty-one. And if you're so worried about money, why do you live in this pretentious place? How can you afford it anyway?" He clicked his thumb and middle finger. "Oh, that's right. You used Grace's education fund."

She exhaled into a pout. "You kids are so disrespectful. Why do you do these things to me? Haven't I suffered enough?"

"Here we go." Michael rubbed his forehead.

"And look at you. Go put on some clothes. What will the neighbors think?" Her eyes darted to the windows of the lofty brownstones shadowing the street.

"Yeah, Mom. They'll probably think I feed nails to little children since I don't wear shoes." He turned his back to her and smiled at me, then withdrew to the back of the car and shook my bike as though to make sure it was tethered securely. I could see his grin from the corner of my eye.

"We'll talk later about you arriving home one day just to leave the next."

She turned to me, swapping irritation with sadness as easily as if she'd replaced a straw hat with a ball cap. Wiping at invisible tears, she sniffled and brushed back a lock of frizzled hair, causing her peace sign earrings to sway to and fro. With characteristic dramatic flourish, she took one of my hands and pressed an object into my palm.

"Your keys. Why your mother insisted you keep this atrocious gas-guzzler, I'll never know. I never did understand her."

I wrapped my fingers around the keys, feeling the shape of independence. "Thank you."

It was expected of me to treat this as a heart-rending gesture on her part, even though she had readily agreed to the trip because she wanted the house to be sold as quickly as possible, thereby placing more money into my accounts, to which *she* had access.

Aunt Tish pouted. "You selfish kids are breaking my heart with these trips."

I kept quiet. Best not to acknowledge her fabricated sadness or her varnished insult.

Receiving no response from her selfish kids, she turned to my uncle. "Philip, I must be crazy. I'm going to be thrown in jail for letting a 16-year-old live by herself ... in some creepy house in a ... a ... redneck wilderness."

From the back of the car, Michael groaned.

"Aunt Tish—" I began.

Uncle Phil cleared his throat and stood tall, looking for a moment more like the commanding professor he was when teaching Chaucer at Boston College than the ventriloquist's dummy he played at home for his formidable wife. "Tish, she'll be fine. It's only for the summer."

"But it's so far away from Beacon Hill and civilized society, for bloody sake," she responded stiffly. "She won't be around our kind. Those people are so provincial. What will my friends think? And that house ..."

Uncle Phil sighed. "The house is fine. The management company said so."

"Yeah, Mom," Michael scolded from his retreat, "just because the place is old doesn't make it creepy. Heck, our house is old."

Uncle Phil shot his son a quelling look. "Jack loved the place. He spent a lot of time there. It must be in good shape. And if it's not, then Grace will fix it up. That's the whole point of this trip anyway." He frowned. "Besides, by the time you were sixteen, you had already been arrested for disturbing the peace and indecent exposure."

"Oh gawd, Pops." Michael cringed and reached up to rub his temples. "Too much information."

Uncle Phil continued. "You already set up a bank account for her. She has a credit card. She's got everything she needs. If anyone can take care of herself, it's Grace."

"Yeah, Mom," Michael chimed from behind the car. "Crimeny, she's been taking care of you for the past three years."

Aunt Tish pushed her tangled hair behind her ears and huffed. "Fine. Obviously no one cares what I think. Just go, Grace. But stay out of trouble. I don't want any calls from the police."

I mouthed a "thank you," to Uncle Phil, shoved my backpack on the heap of boxes lining my back seat, and shut the door. Tramp sat waiting on the passenger seat. On the floor, my cat Chubbs crouched in his carrier, obviously annoyed. On the console sat an envelope containing $5,000 in cash, covered with road maps graphing my way from Massachusetts to West Virginia.

"Aunt Tish, I'll be fine." I pulled her into a sideways embrace as I rounded to the driver's side and opened the door. She was my only aunt and despite her opinions of me, I wanted to believe her capable of feeling genuine concern. "I promise to call every day."

"Be careful. If something goes wrong, it's a reflection on me." As she pulled away, she flicked at my hair. "And for pity's sake, Grace, do something with that ridiculous hair while you're there."

I ignored her. "Remember your dentist appointment tomorrow. I left a note on the fridge."

She waved that away with a *Yes, yes, I know all this* dismissal, but I knew she would forget.

Then, because I felt it was expected of me, I looked back toward the house and lied, "I'll miss this place."

I voiced some inane comment about what I'd miss, but my thoughts were on the excitement of being *me*, rather than a dead couple's orphaned child or Tish Rosenburg's ungrateful niece.

The goodbyes complete, I climbed into my car and pulled away. I could see Michael standing behind my aunt and uncle, flailing his arms in a dramatic *don't-stop-keep-going wave*.

"Call your Grandma Sadie, she's not doing so well," was the last thing I heard Aunt Tish bark as I descended the hill and rounded the corner onto Beacon Street, took a final glance at Boston Common, and headed toward I-95 South.

The trip underway, I exhaled deeply. I'd loved to have driven into the future without looking back, to have fast-forwarded to summer's end when Michael and I could plant roots somewhere together. But, there was no shortcut to that time, and I felt dread press in on me as if each accumulated mile were adding a hole to the safety net I hadn't yet hung in place.

Chapter 2

I was scheduled to meet that evening with an agent from the management company that was caretaker of my stepfather's estate. My appointment to meet Ling Ma was at 7:30 p.m. at a café in Williamsport, Maryland. According to Internet maps, that was the town across the river from Jack's house in rural Marlowe, West Virginia. I had hoped to arrive early, find the house, get my bearings, and make a list of questions for Ling.

My plans changed.

Besides encountering road construction in Connecticut and rush hour traffic around Philadelphia, I had to make countless stops to accommodate my pets. Tramp seemed to think he needed to meet every dog on the roadside walking trails, and Chubbs—in true catlike obstinacy—meowed his complaints about sleeping accommodations until I stopped and rearranged boxes and duffle bags to create the perfect cozy sleeping nook, twice. I didn't arrive in Williamsport until 7:00 p.m.

It looked like a honeysuckle and iced tea kind of town: clean streets, huge elms, and tidy houses with enticing front porches decorated with American flags and hanging flowerpots. There were no exhaust fumes, shrieking horns, or street punks with bolts through their lips.

With only a half-hour to spare, I opted to go to the café and get something to eat. The house would have to wait.

A block past a small brick library, I found the *Time Out* on Canal Street, flanked by a small music shop and a drug store. Various other businesses ran in both directions—curio shops, a bank, an old-fashioned ice cream parlor.

Canal Street seemed to be aptly named because the road sloped down a hill toward the river and the C&O Canal, which ran parallel to the river. From there, the street ushered vehicles across a long bridge spanning the wide Potomac River into West Virginia. I judged that to be about a half-mile away for a bird, but more than a mile by car. The land rose dramatically on the other side of the river and, judging by the backdrop of blue mountains in the distance, kept rising as one traveled south into the state. Little wonder West Virginia was nicknamed "The Mountain State."

After setting out water for Chubbs and Tramp, I stepped inside the *Time Out*.

Despite the universal look of my jeans, plain white T-shirt, and backpack, every one of the dozen or so faces in the café gave me a suspicious once-over, as though I'd arrived by spaceship rather than car. Did this mean everyone else in the place knew one another? I immediately longed for the aloofness for which urbanites—particularly Bostonians—are so well known.

Still, the aroma of the coffee and the sound of light jazz mixed together to create an enticing "come-on-in-and-stay-awhile" sensation. I knew immediately that if I could come to terms with the stares and the typical small-town expectations that I be friendly and make an effort to fit in, then this would be one of my favorite escapes.

A tall bottle-blonde with big hair and a bigger smile tossed me a question from behind the counter: "What'll it be, hon?"

"I'll have a chicken salad sandwich on wheat and coffee ... a grande ... or large," I added, scanning the blackboard to determine how this shop described its varied sizes.

"Hon, we've only got one size. Ya' get all the free refills you want, and it's easier to use mugs. Styrofoam clogs the landfills, ya' know."

"Oh ... sure," I muttered. There didn't seem to be anything else to say to that unexpected "go green" reminder.

After I paid, the blonde gestured to a row of large coffee brewers. "Clean mugs to the left. I'll be right back with your sandwich." She disappeared through a set of swinging doors.

Coffee and seat secured, I turned my attention to the shop and was pleasantly surprised. But then, what had I expected? Velvet Elvises? The place had a quaintness that many designers tried to artificially create in urban shops. Here, the motif had obviously evolved, and it worked. Weathered-looking brick walls, burlap coffee bags, and wood floors gave the long, narrow space a rustic feel, while glass-topped tables and metal chairs added a metropolitan touch. The sloping ceiling over the counter featured a large blackboard listing menu options. Another blackboard to the left boasted that the coffee was roasted fresh each day.

Generally, by five minutes into a new environment, I would have mentally identified at least three things that, as an aspiring designer, I would change. Begrudgingly, I realized that the only thing I would change in this shop was the eclectic collection of mugs on the right front wall. Hung on a pegboard, the couple dozen ceramic cups were identified as "Customers' mugs," each sporting a Sharpie-inscripted name. I wasn't sure why the board unnerved me; I guess it was because that little touch of too-much-familiarity and homespun convenience only served to make me feel that much more like an outsider. But what did I care? With names like "Bells," "Cougar," "Big Fred," and "Chester," I figured I was better off remaining a stranger.

The blonde returned with my sandwich and a full carafe of coffee. Instead of the greasy potato chips that I had assumed would line the edge of the plate, there were a few fresh grapes, blueberries, and kiwi slices.

"My name's Cassandra. Folks 'round here call me Cassie," she offered, a look of expectation on her face. For the first time, I noted her Southern drawl and her physique. She stood ramrod straight, as if on guard against any surprises that might walk through the door. Her tight jeans and sleeveless top revealed a toned, strong body somewhere between 35 and 50 years of age, and I had no doubt she could handle whatever the sidewalk ushered in.

"Oh ... hi ... I'm Grace ... Grace MacKenna," I reciprocated dutifully.

"Thought so," she declared. "But I didn't expect to see ya' for a couple a' years yet. You're only what—sixteen?"

If the woman noticed I was startled, she didn't show it. In fact, she didn't wait for my reply before she continued.

"You're as pretty as your momma. Tall, green eyes, golden-red hair. 'Course your momma wore her hair a lot shorter than you. I guess we all do that as we get older." She sighed, absently touching her hair. "Whatever it takes to look younger."

She caught herself and refilled my coffee cup, her bicep rippling as she tilted the carafe. "I was real sorry to hear about your momma and your sister." Then, with more wistfulness in her voice, she added, "Jack too. By the time we heard, the funerals were over."

"You knew my mother?" I could understand that she had known Jack since he had frequented the area, but I didn't remember my mother ever accompanying him on those trips.

"Goodness, no, hon. Jack showed me pictures of her."

She must have read the confusion on my face, because she smiled. "Jack and I grew up together ... dated a little ... but that was long before he moved to New England and met your momma. He'd stop in and show me pictures every time he came back to *Crossings*."

I had forgotten that the house was called *Crossings*—something to do with it being situated near a wide, shallow point in the river where settlers crossed between states, ages ago before bridges were built.

"You knew who I was from seeing some photographs? That had to be more than three years ago." I felt a wistful pang between my ribs, both awed and pleased to think that I looked so much like my mother. My biological father, Anthony Carlotti, had been full Italian and my sister Julie had inherited his raven hair and olive skin. Prior to now, I had always been envious of those dark features since I took after my mother's fairer Scots-Irish side of the family, the Gallaghers.

"Yes and no." She winked. "I saw your license plate, and Ling mentioned she was meeting clients from Massachusetts. But you do look a lot like your momma."

"You know Ling too? This *is* a small town." I cringed at the annoyance in my voice. As I picked up my sandwich, I made a mental note to stay across the river in Marlowe and avoid Williamsport. The fewer people who knew I was living alone and without adult supervision, the better.

If she was fazed at my reaction, she didn't let it show. "Well, I only know Ling because she's a customer. She'll tell you just about anything, bless her heart. But you're right about the town. My son calls it Smallport. Ling often meets people here because it's the only café in town. As for Jack, we lived two blocks apart when we were growing up."

"I thought *Crossings* was secluded on the side of a mountain?"

"It is. I meant his boyhood home in town."

"His boyhood home?"

"Hon, after the war, Jack's ancestors moved into the town of Marlowe, and as far as I know, they never returned to that creepy old house. Fact is, no one ever lived there again until several years ago when Jack started visitin'. Didn't that rascal ever tell you?"

Before I could answer or even process her too-familiar *"that rascal"* descriptor, she must have surmised my situation. "Hon, you weren't planning on *staying* at *Crossings* were you?"

It wasn't that she spoke loudly; rather, it was that she spoke with such shock that every face in the café turned to look at me.

A million questions rushed through my mind: Why was it hard to believe I would want to live at *Crossings*? Did she realize I would be there alone? Did the whole café realize? How could I close this conversation without blowing my cover?

I mumbled, "Uh ... well ... yes ... for the summer ... *we* are going to fix it up ..." It sounded lame even to me.

At that moment, the rattling bells attached to the shop's front door announced the arrival of another customer. A perfectly coiffed Asian-American woman stepped in, and I breathed a sigh of relief.

* * *

Unfortunately, five minutes with Ling made me wish I were still talking with Cassie.

After placing a set of keys on the table, Ling began to fish for information, without a bit of finesse.

"Are you alone?" Her eyes flittered around the shop. Her frame was frail, her face brown and desiccated like a ginger root.

"At the moment, yes." I tried to sound confident.

"When will your aunt be here?" She fidgeted with a pinkie ring, which matched her tailored blue suit.

"A little later," I answered with as much conviction as I could muster. I hated lying, even to this woman who was of no consequence to me. Thirteen years of Sunday school had taught me that lying was wrong, but I rationalized that *a little later* could mean a few minutes or a few weeks, depending on the timeframe of reference. Therefore, a month—by when I actually *did* expect Aunt Tish to pay a visit—truly was *a little later*. "I thought she closed the account over the phone." I tried to make it a statement and not a question. I wondered if an unfinished legal glitch would stand in my way.

"She did, but I would feel better turning the keys over to her." She continued spinning her ring.

It struck me that Ling was nervous. But, I had never met the woman, so perhaps she was a bit high-strung.

She probed, "How old are you?" It was more accusation than question.

My first reaction was to retort with a question of my own: *Why is everyone in this town so nosy?* I decided there was no sense being rude or lying about my age because a request to see my driver's license would uncover the truth anyway. I lifted my chin the way I'd seen Aunt Tish do whenever she wanted to indicate superiority over a situation. "I'm sixteen—so you see, you can trust that my aunt will be along shortly. In fact, she will be meeting me at the house." *Another half-truth: "shortly" and "meeting me at the house"—all true, just not for another month.* I was careful not to let my eye contact falter.

"Well ..." she let her gaze drop to the napkin she was now twisting; apparently the ring wasn't compliant enough for transferring her tension. "I guess it will be alright, if you're sure she'll be joining you soon."

"She will." I needed to steer the conversation away from myself, so I grabbed the keys, placed a tip on the table, and gathered my things so as to tell Ling that we were done here.

As we departed, Cassie yelled a perfunctory "Take care," but out of the corner of my eye, I saw her bite her lower lip and shoot me a concerned look. As I crossed the threshold I heard, "Grace, I could send my son over to check on you."

I pretended not to hear.

Once Ling and I were on the street, I decided the best defense was a good offense, so I began my questions. "Anything special I need to know? I assume the water and electricity are on. Do you know if there's a phone in the house?"

She looked away as though she was trying to find an answer in the distance. I realized she had no idea what the house looked like on the inside. I was beginning to feel as distressed as she looked. "Has *anyone* in your company ever been inside the house?"

A thin black eyebrow hoisted itself up on her forehead. "Yes." Immediately, she back-pedaled with a "No. Yes. On the outside, yes."

I stared down at her. She was at least a foot and a half shorter than me, which didn't help in trying to secure her elusive eye contact.

She squared her shoulders. "We ... felt it was in the best interest of our employees ... and the house, of course ... not to go inside ..."

I felt the seconds tick off as I waited for clarification.

"We regularly checked the grounds, of course," she added defensively, "but we ... we didn't want to disturb anything." She seemed to grow paler as she talked.

Frustrated, I turned toward my car. "I guess we'll find out what shape it's in once we get there. Where are you parked?"

"I'm in the black Mercedes, but you won't have trouble finding it. Follow Canal Street across the Cushwa Basin Bridge." She pointed across the river at a distant and obviously abandoned white structure. "Once you pass that farmhouse, you'll see Whistle Ridge Road on the right. It will take you directly to the house."

Before I could wrap my brain around the realization that she was sending me off to an empty house, alone, at dusk, with little direction, she turned the tables on me again, demanding, "You're sure your aunt will join you soon?"

"Yes." I mustered a huge smile to hide my discomfort. I had to stick with my story even if it meant proceeding to the house alone. "Uncle Phil too," I added for good measure. *I was getting too good at these half-truths.*

As Ling pulled away, I looked across the river. The trees were laced with the final purple and gray vestiges of a setting sun. Darkness was moving in, and the canyons in the sides of the mountains gaped like dark open mouths.

My anxiety leaped, and goose bumps rushed across my arms.

A few minutes away lay ... what? For all the bravado I had flaunted in the past several weeks, I was now scared of what I had gotten myself into. I felt my knees begin to shake. I realized that I had to get to my car; otherwise the locals might watch me drop on the street.

Once tucked into the driver's seat, I wrapped my arms around Chubbs and Tramp, hoping their nearness would steady my nerves.

My mind raced, thinking about my conversations with Cassie and Ling. My stomach tightened as though someone was clenching it like a ball. My body's reaction was all too familiar, and I began to panic. I was thirteen years old again and had just been told that my family was gone forever. The fear of being alone in the world came rushing back.

Six months of therapy had taught me to recognize the signs of distress. I caught myself, took several deep breaths, and exhaled slowly, just as I had at the funeral, just as I had when I was removed from my beloved home, just as I had every holiday, birthday, and countless times in between.

My therapist eventually had impressed upon me that to indulge in fear, one had to relinquish all logic. Then he had, somehow, magically, re-hardwired my fear to my stubbornness and my stubbornness to action. When he finally convinced me that thinking won't conquer fear and that action will, I decided I had my solution and never returned.

In the interim, and probably as double reinforcement, I immersed myself in what great thinkers had to say about fear. I reasoned that I could carry their wisdom with me anywhere I went. Almost trancelike, I began to recite: *"The thing I fear most is fear ... All fear is bondage ... Only your mind can produce fear ... To live with fear and not be afraid is the final test of maturity."*

It helped. The moment I verbalized the word "maturity," I thought of Aunt Tish. I was here because I had convinced her that I was mature enough to undertake this venture on my own. If I were to acknowledge any fear, or to admit defeat, she would make me return to Boston.

There was no way to turn back the clock. I had to go to *Crossings*. And I had to go *now*, before my anxiety returned, and before the sun disappeared for the night.

Chapter 3

I'm not sure I breathed at all during the drive from the café to *Crossings*. What struck me most was the steady immersion into elevated darkness. With the evening fade of Williamsport in my rearview mirror, I pulled onto the long stretch of the unlit Cushwa Basin Bridge, which ushered me across the Potomac River into West Virginia.

The terrain instantly changed as my car began its incline. The mountains beyond blocked the receding sun, so the contrast from one side of the river to the other was startling. Light changed to shadow. Civilization turned to wilderness.

Once past the bridge, I spotted a lopsided sign to my right announcing Whistle Ridge Road. I wasn't surprised to find that the road was unpaved. The gravel seemed to groan beneath my tires.

For a long, bumpy half-mile or so, Whistle Ridge ran parallel to the river. To my left, overgrown trees arched thick over the lane, further weakening the fading sun. On my right, Williamsport's distant lights appeared in my passenger window, prompting a peculiar relief, much like a convicted man must feel upon learning his execution has been delayed.

The contentment was short-lived, however, as Whistle Ridge faded away into patches of tall weeds. I saw a crude lane rising off to my left through a thicket of frowning trees. To call it a "lane" was a gracious stretch of language, because it consisted of two rutted tire paths. By the looks of it, the lane had not been tended for several years—no doubt, not since Jack had traveled it or the management company had done a drive-by.

After another eighth of a mile incline, a building appeared in the headlights, and I slowed to a stop. When I gazed at the full extent of what was obviously *Crossings*, I realized I was breathing heavily, as though I had been deprived of air.

Inexplicably, the thought struck that this was where my past and my future were going to collide.

I don't know what I had expected, but certainly not this. The house loomed like a dark, gray mass, crouched into the curve of a hill, a hulking presence set amidst weeds and wildness. Made of stone, it looked strong, heavy, almost vile, as though the walls were there merely to encase the darkness within. It appeared to be deserted and probably neglected for years. The windows, flanked by deteriorating black shutters barely holding on by their hinges, made the house look as though its dark eyes were tired and defeated.

At three stories tall and the collective width of five Boston brownstones, the house was massive. Most of the lowest level disappeared into the hill on either side. The second level—which appeared to be the main living floor—was fronted by a huge covered porch that spanned from side to side and disappeared around the right side of the house, out of view.

The top-most level, barely rising above the crest of the hill behind it, seemed to be the darkest of the three as thick-trunked trees crushed in, many gnarled branches and limbs pressing against the upstairs windows.

Immediately, my brain raced back and pulled out a few memories of Jack referring to *Crossings* as "quaint," "comfortable," and "my oasis." This was the first time I ever questioned Jack's opinion. I thought of Aunt Tish's use of the word "creepy" to describe the house, and I wondered if *Crossings* could ever be an oasis for me.

Tramp must have sensed my tension. He barked, breaking my paralysis, and began prancing on the seat as though to say, "We're here! Let's go, let's go."

"Hold on Tramp." I exhaled and scruffed the top of his head. Thank goodness he and Chubbs were with me.

As I neared the estate, I discovered that the crude driveway led to the right side of the house. About half way toward the back, a mismatched one-story structure bumped out from the right side of the house at the main level, sitting atop a swell jutting out from the curve of the hill. It was fronted with a porch attached to the one on the old house. A long stairway on the right led from the driveway to the porch. The architecture and the aluminum siding suggested that the structure had been added in the last twenty years or so.

This was obviously the addition that Jack had once talked about. Aesthetically, this crude addition did a disservice to the grandeur the main house must have had in its heyday, but I was never so glad to see an architectural mistake in my life. At least this portion of the house looked as though it was created in the same century in which I was born. And, its "creep factor" was extremely low, compared to the main house.

Still, I wondered why Jack had added an addition when the house was so large to begin with. It flicked through my mind that I would never know the answer to that.

"Tramp, Chubbs, we're home." Was it my imagination or had my voice cracked on that last word?

I felt as though the house were waiting, watching my every move. Despite my apprehension, I sensed a strange pull to the house, and my desire to be in Jack's old location became as strong as my fear.

Only your mind can produce fear.

"Come on, you two. Let's get moved in before we lose the sun … *and our nerve … entirely.*"

As I stepped out of the car, a raven complained in the distance.

The light was fading so quickly that I felt like I had been stricken blind. I decided everything could remain in the car except Tramp, Chubbs, the litter box, and my backpack into which I threw a flashlight and my CD case.

I found a switch inside the door and breathed a sigh of relief when a table lamp lit up, its dim sixty watts revealing a furnished apartment. I set Chubbs and the litter box on the floor, parked his carrier on the porch, and plunked my backpack on the nearest table, scattering dust.

The space was basic and architecturally unimpressive, but I was pleased to see that the furnishings, rugs and window coverings were of high quality. It had an efficient kitchen, a dining table by the front window, a sitting area complete with couch, a few chairs and an entertainment center hosting a television and stereo system. A stacked washer and dryer stood in the corner behind the front door. Another door led to a furnished bedroom and utilitarian bathroom, each with one lamp, equally dim. I made a mental note to pick up about a dozen 100-watt light bulbs.

I spotted a few reminders of Jack—a pair of Wellies my mother had given him one Christmas, a fishing pole hung above a chest of drawers, a rifle parked by the coat rack, and a picture of the four of us, taken when I had graduated junior high. Jack must have lived solely in this apartment when he stayed here. But why? Why had he never fixed up the main house? He had been an executive vice president for a telecommunications firm, and my mother was a pharmacist, so money wasn't an obstacle.

With no answers, I looked back at the picture and picked it up. A million conflicting emotions surfaced, and the memories came rushing back: the smell of the vanilla candles my mother had loved, the clack of a keyboard which sounded like Julie endlessly updating her Facebook profile, the sheen of a freshly waxed car which was Jack's pride.

But it was pictures like this—blatant recollections of happiness that hurt the most. The picture represented my life *before*, and it would never be available to me again.

I had grown up in an instant. From one second to the next I achieved a maturity that neither age nor milestones could provide. I hadn't reached age twenty-one, owned a credit card, or voted in an election, but my childhood was over.

I put the picture back and turned to study the room. I don't know what I thought I would find here, whether it was *remnants* of Jack or the *energy* of Jack or some combination of the two.

Aunt Tish had spent three years trying to instill her ultra-atheistic views into me, among them—when you're dead, you're dead. In contrast, my parents—perennially more optimistic and content than Aunt Tish and Uncle Phil—taught me about ascension into heaven immediately upon death, a reward you achieved if you had faith in God. In either case, how could I have hoped to *feel* Jack here?

Or, was I here simply to put a tourniquet on my memories so that I could finally heal?

With thoughts of my mother and Jack and the confidence they had in their beliefs, I focused on the door that connected the apartment to the old house. Perhaps I would find answers beyond that barrier.

Only your mind can produce fear.

* * *

It took four hard tugs to pry the door open, and on the final yank, the door crunched as it separated from the frame. A loud, hollow moaning sound escaped, as though a pressure valve had been released, and a force of air burst through, slamming into me with such intensity that I gripped the door handle to keep from falling. Chubbs leaped to his feet, hissed, arched his back, and streaked into the bedroom. Tramp merely looked up from his perch on the kitchen rug.

In the next second, the house was quiet. Despairingly quiet. My heart was the only thing I could hear.

Beyond the threshold was blackness. Creepy, inky blackness. It was like looking into a bat cave at night; you knew there was something in there, but you didn't know what or where.

Despite my resolve, I felt a spurt of fear so strong that I froze, unable to move, unable to think. After a few seconds, I rationalized that the house had simply released a built-up vacuum of air. I ignored the more practical voice which argued that the main house was not airtight enough to have produced such a strong exhale.

The desire to step into the main house returned with such intensity that it surprised me. I inched backward to retrieve the rifle, never turning my back on the darkened doorway. Not surprisingly, the rifle was still loaded. I would be as comfortable handling a gun as I would a tube of mascara; Jack had made sure that all three women in his life could protect themselves. With the flashlight in one hand and the rifle hooked over my shoulder, I headed into the main house.

Stepping through the threshold was like stepping into another century. The flashlight's limited beam was bright enough to reveal the shapes of period furniture covered in dusty, gray cloths, but not so bright that it could remove the moroseness the stillness evoked—a feeling of deep anguish mixed with an eerie anticipation, as though the place was endlessly waiting, expecting. I'd felt that same sensation when I had been forced to shop in the dimly lit casket room at the funeral home that had handled the final services of my family.

Forcing myself to focus on the here and now, I directed the light around the room. It must have been one of those old-time parlors as it seemed to center around both music and books. To my left was a grand piano, topped with a candelabrum. Topping the candelabrum, as with everything else in the room, was an endless highway of cobwebs.

The room emptied through a wide archway into a foyer, but the beam of my flashlight was too weak to reach beyond that. I noted carved sofas, ladder-back chairs, and a slant-top desk. Heavy draperies flanked the narrow windows. Faded wallpaper featured panoramic landscapes.

Across the room and to the right, hundreds of books were stacked on shelves, from the floor to the elevated ceiling. The multi-colored spines looked like an oasis in a desert of gray. Before I realized what I was doing, I found myself stepping through the room to get closer to them.

The air was different in the old house. It was heavy and dry in a way that had nothing to do with temperature or barometric pressure. With each step, the wood floor creaked, despite being covered with thick wool carpets. I could hear a faint whish of air as my hand lifted the flashlight higher. There was no other sound. It was like walking through a museum at night—or worse, a mausoleum.

Suddenly I felt something. Something to my right. Then behind me. Something like the heaviness of a presence. A presence watching me. Something colder than the room. I froze for an instant. I couldn't breathe. When I felt my heart beat again—*was it a hundred years or a second?*—I grabbed the rifle and, cradling it with the flashlight, whirled a half circle. No one was there. The heaviness, the something, continued moving around me. I spun with it. Just as quickly, I felt it leave.

I waited, but heard nothing, felt nothing.

I stood as still as a statue, scanning the room, staring into the shadowed corners, wondering if there could be things in those shadows waiting for me to move. *Courage faces fear and thereby masters it.*

Collecting my wits, I applied logic again and decided I merely had felt a strong—albeit, *strange*—draft. It raced through my mind that no draft had ever before left the hairs on my arms standing straight up, but I would think about that later.

I would surrender to stubbornness, but not fear.

Taking a deep breath, I moved to the bookcase and scanned the titles. Each was a choice that a scholar would want on his shelves. No subject was left out: science, anthropology, geology, philosophy, art, architecture, politics, history—most on the Civil War. I recognized a few books that we'd had in our home several years ago. Perhaps Jack had brought them here.

Interspersed with the books were several daguerreotypes and photographs, some encased in tarnished silver frames, others in wood. One in particular caught my eye—a photo of a young man and woman standing on the steps of an old church. Other young people were standing to their right and left, but the focus of the picture was clearly on the couple. The man in the center could have been Jack when he was in his 20s. I recognized the eyes, the jaw, the shape of his cheeks. Judging by the clothing and the hairstyle, the picture must have been taken in the 1800s. On the man's left stood a young woman wearing a long, white, hooped dress. A wedding picture perhaps.

I'm not sure how long I stood there staring. Seconds? Minutes? The silence was broken when, from the direction of the apartment, came a crash, then a deep moan. It happened so quickly I couldn't tell if the sound had come from a person, an animal, the weather, or something I didn't want to imagine. By the time I reached the apartment, Tramp was in full frantic mode—growling, barking, and leaping at the door.

I tossed the flashlight on the sofa, stormed to the door, and whipped it open. I expected to experience a cold presence of air again. Instead, a face—dirty, edged with a scruffy beard, and topped with a blue bandana corralling long hair—stared back at me.

I screamed and lifted my rifle. The man ducked behind the outside wall. I felt dizzy. I had practiced this same scenario in gun safety classes, but always in simulations where the threats were imitations. I was stunned into inaction. My voice wouldn't come, so I couldn't call a warning to him. My arm faltered. The man somehow knew I was briefly paralyzed because he reappeared, and with a guttural yell, he leaped straight at me.

Chapter 4

I t should come as no surprise that two hundred pounds of determination would overpower a hundred and twenty pounds of fright. He won instantly. Despite my flailing and kicking, he pinned me down, my back to the floor in seconds. No time to go for the groin, eyes or carotid artery, as I'd been taught in self-defense classes. The rifle had fallen about two feet from my right hand. In skilled, warrior-like fashion, he adroitly kicked it away using his left leg. I was aware of strength and agility, and yet he never lost his grip. His chest pressed against me, his hands gripped my wrists, and his face was mere inches from mine.

"What the devil's the matter with you?" he demanded. "You could have killed me."

"Get off of me!" I sounded far braver than I felt.

He leaned back. His jaw tightened, and his wolf eyes widened. He seemed startled, almost embarrassed. He loosened his grip. I took advantage of the movement and shoved him hard. He fell easily to the side, offering no resistance. I tried to scramble from him toward the gun, but he grabbed my ankles and pulled me back.

"Whoa, we'll let that alone for now." He parked a leg over both of mine to disable me again. Breathing heavily, but not breaking eye contact, we both eased into an upright sitting position, him leaning against a chair, me against the dining table, his leg still over mine.

I tried to assess the threat. Besides a dirty face and bandana, he wore a short-sleeved, button-down white shirt smudged with random wisps of blue paint, white jeans and heavy, tattered work boots. He looked like the kind of guy you'd find standing on a tall platform brushing a new billboard sign into place. The kind of guy who spent more than his share of nights in jail for busting up a bar.

I looked around for Tramp. *Where was my trusty watchdog when I needed him?* Before I could call for him, the man began to laugh. My head snapped up. His gaze was on my hair.

"You look good in cobwebs."

Great, I thought, *a scruffy redneck wacko with a demented sense of humor.*

Impulsively, I reached up to find the source of his amusement. I pulled down layers of aged cobwebs. My hair must have brushed against them in the main house. As I clawed a second layer from my hair, I discovered a spider still attached to it.

"Augh," I screamed and began frantically flailing my fingers through my hair.

His laughter elevated. "You were ready to shoot me, yet you're worried about a spider?"

Fury took over. This man had trespassed, scared and tackled me, and now he was using me for amusement. "Who are you, and what do you want?"

He flinched at the anger in my voice. His smile dropped, but it was still there, lurking, as though he was fighting to keep it from returning.

"Clay Baxter. I stopped by to check on you, but before I could knock on your door in the *gentlemanly* fashion and call on you *properly*, I fell over that blasted cat carrier and into the porch glider." He chortled. "You need a light out there."

Thrown off guard by his lighthearted admission of fallibility, I reminded myself that this man was still an intruder. "And what makes you think I wouldn't be just fine?" I snapped. "What's it to you anyway?"

He glared. "Well it's nothing to *me*, but it matters to my mother. *She* was worried about you." He climbed to his feet and retrieved the rifle.

"Your mother?"

"Cassandra Baxter," he replied walking back to me. Seeing my confused look, he added, "Cassie? From the café? You met this evening, so she sent me over. She was worried about you."

"Worried?" I quipped. "Or nosy?"

He pursed his lips into one of those "I'll-ignore-that-snide-comment" type of smiles. "Don't flatter yourself. She worries about everybody. She hears all the gossip in that place, but she doesn't spread it."

"Sorry," I muttered, wondering how he had turned the tables on me. "It's odd that a total stranger would be concerned."

"Yeah, well, you're new. People around here can seem a little odd at first."

"Oh," was all I could think of to say.

"After you've been here longer, they get even odder." He emptied the rifle and, with mocked flourish and the hint of a bow, handed me both the rifle and the bullets.

I stared at him, waiting for the trick. Seeing none, I grabbed his peace offering, feeling like the angry child who grabs her ball and goes home when no one lets her play. I started to climb up off the floor, but my grasp of the rifle and bullets made it difficult. Instinctively, he grabbed my arm to assist. This man was ruffian and gentleman all in one package.

Once on my feet, I realized how tall he was. At least six-two, six-three. He was broad-shouldered and reminded me of a professional athlete. "You can't be Cassie's son," I eyed him suspiciously. "She's too young to have a child your age."

"Well, she'd love to hear you say that, but she *is* my mother," he drawled, brushing the dust off his pants. "She's a health and exercise nut. Some would say a nut, period."

It was obvious that his comments were only half-hearted. This was a man who thought quite highly of the woman. If he truly was Cassie's son, then that meant he probably had known Jack. If I kept treating him like a suspicious intruder, then the details of this encounter could be all over Williamsport by morning. I couldn't risk any more curiosity about me and my stag presence here this summer.

"I guess I have no choice but to trust you are who you say you are." That sounded more childlike than what I intended.

I had the brief satisfaction of watching his neck muscle flex before he crossed his arms and shifted his stance. "Let's see ... I'm twenty years old. I have a mother, a fiancé, one sister, a brother-in-law, two nephews, lots of friends. I live in Williamsport. Graduated Williamsport High. I know all the words to *The Wreck of the Edmund Fitzgerald,* I break an 80 in golf, hold the record for largest trout caught at the annual sportsmen's fish outing, and I hate anchovies," he spewed, as if he were answering questions at an interrogation which he wasn't taking seriously. At the same time, I couldn't help but notice the fluent articulation of his words. His polished delivery seemed at odds coming from such a roughneck. Certainly nothing in his delivery reminded me of Cassie's drawl.

He continued: "I'd just finished a painting job in Smithsburg when Mom called and asked me to check on you ... Anything else you want to know?" He grinned. "I can give you my Social Security number and Zodiac sign if it would make you feel better."

"Very funny," I grumbled. *A painter? And getting married so young? Great, a scruffy redneck **blue collar** wacko with a demented sense of humor. Still, he might come in handy around here.* I hated the dirty white on the walls in this room.

"Oh, before I forget," he sobered, pointing outside. "I think I broke the door on that cat contraption. I hope you didn't plan on using it soon. I'll have to fix it."

"No ... I'm here to stay for a while." I then remembered my cover story. "*With my aunt ... She'll be joining me ... later ...*" I looked at my watch, hoping he would interpret the gesture to mean "later tonight"..."We'll be here for the summer."

The seconds ticked by until he responded. "Right." It was a simple word, but the insolence in his voice spoke volumes.

I groaned inwardly. If I didn't get better with my story, I'd end up with the police questioning me.

At that moment, Tramp walked sheepishly in from the bedroom. In the blur of the action, he had dashed there for safekeeping.

"Some protection you are," I scolded.

"Hey there, boy." Clay smiled. He crouched down to rough up Tramp's fur and stroke his head. Tramp basked in the attention, licking Clay's face and practically sitting on the man's feet.

"Lab?" Clay asked.

"More like a Heinz 57."

"What's his name?"

"Tramp ... but I'm thinking of changing it to 'Traitor.'" I crossed my arms in disgust at my dog's zeal toward this stranger.

Clay raised his eyebrows. "Tramp?"

"He looked like a grungy beggar when he showed up in our yard, so we adopted him." With a harsher tone and a glare at Tramp, I added, "And up until now he's been a great guard dog."

"What about him?" Clay pointed to the corner.

I followed his gaze to see Chubbs, peacefully lying on a makeshift bed of folded towels beside the washer-dryer unit, giving himself a bath.

"That's Chubbs. He's only afraid of things that *aren't* there." Irritated, I remembered how he had jumped at the air but not at the man outside my door.

"Chubbs?" Clay grinned. As he spoke, Tramp leaned in closer and burrowed his nose on Clay's shoulder, as though he knew he was no longer the focus of conversation.

"It's short for chubby," I responded defiantly, almost daring him to laugh again.

To my surprise, Clay simply responded, "I like it. It fits him."

Why was I pleased that this scruffy redneck blue-collar wacko with a demented sense of humor liked my cat's name?

Feeling annoyance return, I straightened my shoulders. "Assuming you are who you say you are, it's still no reason to come barging in here and knocking me to the ground."

"I wasn't expecting to see you point a gun at me, and you didn't look receptive to conversation at that moment," he countered, still stroking Tramp's fur. Then as if talking to himself he added, "It's been a long time since anyone's tried to shoot me."

*Great. A scruffy redneck blue-collar wacko **fugitive** with a demented sense of humor.*

I shook my head. I wasn't going to apologize. I reminded myself not to get too comfortable with this man. His presence here remained questionable. Still, I figured an explanation for the rifle was in order since many people had unwarranted fears about weapons. "I was in *there*." I pointed to the open door to the main house, assuming that would explain everything. "And it was a little ...unnerving."

He glanced at the open door and stood. "Mind if I have a look?"

Actually, I was glad he wanted to look, but I wasn't about to tell him that. I would feel safer searching the rest of the house with a wacko fugitive than by myself. I knew I wouldn't be able to sleep that night unless I knew what lie in the house beside me.

"I guess not," I replied, trying to sound indifferent. I started to reload the rifle. "But I'm taking this with me."

He cocked his eyebrows. "You plan to shoot *me* or things that go bump in the night?"

I ignored his question *and* his sarcasm, but realized how childish I must have sounded. I propped the rifle against the couch, but couldn't stop from voicing my fear. "Jack once told me that the locals think this place is haunted. Do you believe in ... well ..."

"Ghosts?" Clay finished for me. He had turned to head toward the connecting door, but now stopped and turned back to me. "Well, Grace ... may I call you Grace?" At my nod, he continued. "According to Soren Kierkegaard, there are two ways to be fooled. One is to believe what isn't true. The other is to refuse to believe what is true. I suppose that applies to ghosts too."

At my dumbfounded look, he continued. "Kierkegaard was—"

"I *know* who he was. I wanted to know what *you* believe."

Without hesitation, he told me: "I believe in God, and life after death, and that how you live determines what happens to you."

"But then what?" My voice sounded strained, unfamiliar.

He seemed to ponder his own words. "I know that one day my physical body will shut down, and that will be the end of it. But not the end of me. Do I think souls could remain on earth?" He shrugged. "I guess it's possible."

I folded my arms across my stomach and stared at the floor, thinking a million thoughts in the span of a second. Before I could decide if I wanted him to continue with his perturbing thoughts, he did.

"No one knows how long it takes a soul to move on. Science has already proven the existence of phenomenon or energy in old places like this." As he talked, he spotted the flashlight and retrieved it. "Energy can't be lost at death. It merely transforms. But to the best of my recollection, no one has ever proven that the energy is harmful to humans."

The descriptors were adding up—*scruffy redneck blue-collar wacko fugitive with a demented sense of humor **from the Bible Belt who watches the Science Channel.***

"What about you?" he asked. "What do you believe?"

"Me? The jury's still out." I wasn't about to talk about my unstable beliefs with this guy.

Clay waited, perhaps for me to say more, then changed focus. "Come on, let's check it out." He motioned with the flashlight. As if pulled by an invisible rope, I followed.

For the first time, I noticed that he limped. It was barely recognizable, revealing itself only through the slight rigidness with which he moved his left leg. But still, it was there. He hadn't mentioned getting hurt when he fell. The thought struck that here was another stereotype—a typical rural rube with no gumption to have his condition corrected.

"This place is amazing." He stepped through the threshold into the darkness. "Cold. Sterile. But amazing."

"And disturbingly quiet," I complained, inching closer to him.

He chuckled lightly. "Some would call that tranquil, serene. But yeah, I guess Poe could write some rather macabre poems here. I don't think anything's been touched in a hundred years." He stopped so abruptly that I bumped into him. "Then again, it's odd that the cobwebs are limited to the furniture and not obstructing any paths."

He ran the beam over the bookcase and spotted the same picture I had studied earlier. "That must be one of Jack's ancestors. Looks just like him."

"You knew Jack?" I asked, realizing for the first time that we were speaking in hushed tones. The darkness, the quiet of the house, all seemed to dictate that we tread slowly and speak softly.

Despite the limited visibility, I could tell he considered my question. "I guess you could say I knew him better than most folks around here. Except my mom, of course. He was a great guy. Taught me to fish and golf. Remembered our birthdays. Stuff like that. Mostly he kept to himself, here, at this place." He continued flashing the light around. "We always thought he was refurbishing the place ... 'Course, he was only here occasionally, so I guess the work went slowly."

We had moved into the foyer. The darkness served to work like a magnet, pulling us closer together as we proceeded. Well, okay, it pulled me closer to him, certainly much closer than I would have allowed in the bright light of day. As for Clay, he seemed undaunted by both the darkness and my proximity.

"Jack always stopped in at the café to visit." He stopped walking and turned to look at me. "We were all shocked about the accident." His tone had softened. "I miss him. I understand you lost your mom and sister too."

"Yes."

"What about your dad? He's dead, right?"

"He died when I was two. Cancer. Julie, that's my sister, was five. She remembers—" I caught myself. "*Remembered* him."

"We have something in common." He turned and continued into the next room. "My father wasn't around either."

"I'm sorry." I didn't know what else to say. I wasn't used to being on this side of sorrow.

* * *

We found the house to be full of architectural details, dark corners and frightening places to hide—all of which seemed to activate the imagination. We also admired the many flawless antiques, including the treasure troves of crystal, silver, and gold accessories. Five expansive rooms and a butler's pantry made up the first floor. Besides being fully furnished, the rooms were carpeted with exquisite Oriental rugs. Each room possessed a large fireplace with a distinctively carved mantel and was separated from the others with wide-open archways or ornate French doors.

Architecturally, no details had been spared, from the carved moldings on the crowns and bases of the walls, to detailed medallions on the ceilings and inlaid wood in the scattered window seats. The last room we entered was a formal dining room with a table that would seat sixteen and a chandelier I was sure would secure about $10,000 at auction.

Clay whistled. "This stuff must be worth a fortune. It's in mint condition. Like someone left for the night and never came back."

The staircase to the second floor was huge. It ascended at least a dozen steps before it emptied onto a wide landing, then turned and ascended a dozen more. Each tread could have accommodated at least five people standing shoulder to shoulder.

Upstairs were six bedrooms, and I marveled that each was the size of a modern-day "master bedroom" found in contemporary homes. Every bedroom sported elevated feather beds with intricately carved headboards and medallions of fruits and foliage. The black walnut furniture with marble tops would have been considered the height of elegance in the 1800s.

When we returned to the parlor, Clay scanned it with the flashlight again. Something lying on the table nearest the door to the apartment caught my eye. I grabbed his arm and directed the light back. It was a slightly wrinkled piece of lined yellow paper from a legal pad, much like that found in modern-day offices.

"Funny we didn't see that before. Do you remember it?"

I shook my head and managed a weak, "No."

He moved closer and picked it up. "It's some kind of a timeline. Do you recognize it?"

My stomach quickly knotting, I took the paper from him and held it under the light. I did recognize one thing. "That's Jack's writing."

The name "William Alan Kavanaugh" was written at the top. Below it was a series of dates and events that must have occurred in Kavanaugh's life.

Clay, now reading over my shoulder, whispered, "Whoa," and pointed to the last line.

It read: "1863—Will dies at *Crossings*."

Chapter 5

D ies. At Crossings. The words seared my mind as Clay grabbed my arm. "Come on, you'll spook yourself."

I wanted to say it was too late to prevent that, but I couldn't speak.

Clay led me back into the apartment, closed the door, and locked it before turning to me.

He took the list back. "Look, it's late. There's obviously nothing in there." He gestured toward the main house. "You'll be fine. This is probably not true." He waved the paper in his hand. "Forget about it." With that, he parked the flashlight, crumpled the paper into a ball, and did a smooth long-range dunk into the garbage can by the sink.

I stood there, feeling numb. It was hard to concentrate. The list, its sudden appearance, Jack's writing, the presence I felt earlier—none of it made sense. I tried to breathe normally.

"Come on." He took my arm again and led me to the kitchen table.

"I'm all right," I winced at the tremor in my voice. "Really. I'm fine."

"Of course you are." He nodded. "We'll put some music on."

Once we were seated, he began leafing through my CD case. "Light rock, jazz, classic, hard metal, country. Eclectic collection you've got here."

When I didn't respond to his observation, he took a more direct approach. "Best album ever made." He lifted the Eagles' *Greatest Hits* album. "What do you like about them?"

"I don't know," I muttered.

"Try."

"Same thing I like about all recorded music. It's constant. No surprises. Everything else in life changes, but not the music."

I could have counted the moments tick by as he stared at me. I doubted that my comment rendered him speechless, and I was certain I hadn't sounded too mushy, so all I could conclude was that one of his own memories had been sparked. "You're right. It can take you from where you are to where you want to be." He shifted in his chair, as though to put an end to the nostalgia. Dropping the Eagles back into the case, he picked up an Eminem CD, then one by Kenny G and studied its contents. "We'll listen to music until your aunt gets here."

My aunt!

I had forgotten that I needed to follow through on my story. Much as I was oddly comforted by his presence, I needed him to leave so that the story about my aunt's impending arrival would still seem plausible.

"No, you don't have to wait." I didn't recognize my voice. It sounded high, nervous. I took on a voice I hoped sounded more convincing. "She'll be here soon."

"I don't mind waiting." He replaced the CD and scanned further. "Who's your favorite?"

"What? I don't know ... Eva Cassidy, I guess." I needed time to think. I had to get rid of him, even if it meant being rude. I felt vulnerable, and although his intrusion was unnerving, his kindness was even more of a threat. My moxie was faltering.

I stood. "Look, you need to go. You act like I'm some helpless little kid, but I'm not. Let's not forget that you came here uninvited, so I'd like you to leave. You can assure Cassie I'm fine."

He stared at me, a look of suspicious confusion, then irritation, crossing his face. I cringed, imagining what he must be thinking at that moment. I braced myself for an angry retort that never came. Instead, he drawled the same "Right," as earlier—same tone, same sarcasm, same disbelief. "Whatever you want. I'll leave you alone to enjoy your ... solitude."

I'd never heard anybody pack so much meaning into one word.

With that, he stood and walked out the door without a backward glance. As the door closed, deep bewilderment consumed me. The silence was so pervasive, it seemed almost sinister.

I had the horrible urge to scream for him to come back, to apologize, to tell him not to let me alone. But I didn't. I reined myself in. When I was sure he was gone, I turned to stare at the wastebasket. I willed my weakened legs to carry me forward to retrieve the list, so that I could make sense of it all. Instead, weariness overcame me, and my legs veered right, carrying me to the exterior door through which Clay had departed. After securing the deadbolt, I turned, almost trance-like, and walked into the bedroom. In five minutes I changed my clothes and climbed into bed, exhausted and anchored by my pets—Tramp sprawled to my right, Chubbs to my left.

Physically, my body felt like dead weight, but my mind continued to race, reviewing the day. I was both glad and sorry that Clay was gone. I needed to preserve my cover story, but I missed the comfort of having another living being nearby—even if that person was a stranger. A peculiar, complex stranger.

I thought about calling Michael but then decided against it, no sense alarming him. My other option was my best friend Kate, but she was in France starting her student exchange experience. I calculated the time difference—four o'clock in the morning for her. Best to forget that idea. Still, I wished she were here with me. We'd probably have been scared together, but we'd have laughed about it.

Suddenly, I felt another concentrated mass of air, as though an invisible body was passing by. Chubbs leaped to his feet, hissed, and dashed into the kitchen.

The nightlight from the bathroom cast enough shadowy illumination into the bedroom that I was able to see the drapes move slightly as if caught by a momentary breeze. Not wanting to feel that insensible—*delusional?*—presence again, I scooched closer to Tramp and pulled the tattered quilt over my head. Then I added the pillow.

Only your mind can produce fear.

Okay, I admit it: I begged God to bring morning quickly ...

... and to let me live to see it.

* * *

In mid-June, morning comes early to West Virginia. By 6:00 a.m., the sun's rays had chased away the blackness of the night. With no dark blinds and no neighboring structures to block the sun, the light intensified at a steady pace. I turned from it, intending only to change my position and go back to sleep. The moment I moved, Tramp began pestering me to let him outside.

With eyes half open, I padded into the kitchen. I wasn't used to the furniture arrangement, so I scanned the room to make sure I wouldn't trip. That's when I saw the crumpled list from the night before, opened full, lying on the table.

I had not retrieved it from the garbage can.

Before my brain could clear, Tramp began springing at the door. He didn't care about the paper; he wanted to go outside.

"Hold on, boy." I opened the door to let him out and then turned back toward the kitchen, intent on using the teakettle Jack had long ago left on the stove. Surely there would be teabags or instant coffee in the cupboards somewhere.

I didn't make it two steps before Tramp barked. A male voice yelled, "Down, boy ... whoa ..." Next came a crash, the screeching of metal against metal, a beleaguered "Blast it," then a low moan.

There was no time to retrieve the rifle, so I grabbed a heavy cast iron skillet off the counter and hurried outside.

I found Clay lying on his back, shirt half-unbuttoned, shoes in one hand, bandana gone and long brown hair sticking in all directions. He was wearing the same clothes he'd had on last night. Tramp was on his chest, licking his face.

"What are you doing here?" I demanded.

At my voice, Tramp turned and dashed back to me.

"Go," I commanded, pointing to the yard. He obeyed.

"Impressive." Clay watched Tramp, moving to sit up further but jerked to the side. "Awww," he groaned and reached for his left leg.

"You spent the night on my porch?" I was startled at the anger in my voice.

"The glider." He smiled, despite his face being slightly scrunched in pain.

"What, are you crazy?"

"Nah. I've slept on worse." He grunted in amusement, then sat upright again and massaged his leg. "Besides, you missed some great stars. It's amazing out here."

"That's not what I meant, and you know it. You were here the entire night like ... like some watchdog." *Or prowler!* I remembered the paper on the table. "You!" I sputtered. "You did it."

He looked at me like I had lost my sanity. "Okay, I'll bite ... what is it that you think I've done?"

"You were in my house last night!"

"Yes." The word had two syllables as though he were talking to a simpleton. "Right after you tried to shoot me."

"No, after that." I walked into the kitchen and retrieved Jack's list. When I returned, he had climbed to his feet, still nursing his leg.

"You came in and put this on my table. Why? To scare me?"

He didn't look at what I held in my hand. "Grace, did you lock your door last night?" His voice was calm, his question pointed.

"Of course I did! In the city, we—" Reality hit. I had unlocked the door from the inside in order to let Tramp out. There was no way Clay could have gotten in. What's more, I recalled him locking the door between the house and the apartment. Someone, or something, from the inside had placed that paper on the counter.

I dropped onto the glider, which then finished crashing onto the porch.

"Ah, I didn't get a chance to tell you that the glider is broken now too. But this time it's Tramp's fault, not mine."

My head stayed still, but my eyes darted up, giving him one of those "just-shut-up" looks.

He pulled the paper from my hand. "You found this on the table?"

I nodded, and he handed the paper back. His eyes flicked over me before he turned away.

"Tell you what, why don't we figure this out after you put some clothes on?" He moved toward the steps that led from the porch to the lawn.

I looked down. In my haste the night before, I'd donned only a large pink T-shirt that stopped about mid-thigh level. Self-consciously, I tugged down on it as I felt a warm blush cover my face.

"After that, we can chat about why your aunt never showed up." He clumsily dropped onto the top step, his leg obviously still sore. Instead of watching for my reaction to his words, he proceeded to put on his shoes.

It was clear from the way he perched himself that he was deliberately looking anywhere but at me. I raced back into the house, although I'm not sure what prompted me to do so—anger, embarrassment, the need to think, or all of those. I slapped the paper on the table and disappeared into the bedroom.

* * *

By the time I changed into jeans and a shirt, Clay was sitting at the kitchen table with Tramp at his feet. Two cups laced with instant coffee were awaiting the water that was now heating on the stove.

Ignoring the liberties he'd taken in my kitchen and his intentions to hold a little coffee klatch, I focused instead on squelching potential questions about my aunt before he had a chance to ask them. Then I would dive into the more pressing irritation of why he was still here.

"For your information, Aunt Tish couldn't make it after all. She's arriving later." I held up my cell phone as though to suggest that I had gotten a call from her.

Clay glanced away, but not before I saw a spasm of irritation cross his face. I could tell he was steadying himself. "I look forward to meeting her."

"Oh, she'll love meeting you too," I replied with equal impudence. Despite my irritation, I couldn't help but chuckle at the thought of my uber-citified, elitist Aunt Tish meeting this roughneck. I could see her now dismissing Clay as "boorish," "uneducated," and "not our kind." Still, when she finally made an appearance in the area, I'd have to usher her around town so everyone could see her. Until then, I needed to start laying the foundation for why she would be so elusive in the weeks ahead.

"You probably won't see her out much." I pretended to search for my sandals, wanting to avoid eye contact while I stretched the truth. "She's an artist, so she loves seclusion. She—"

"What kind?"

His question startled me, and I looked up. "What kind of what?"

"What kind of artist?"

"She works in mixed media." *Ugh*. I made a mental note to work on my cover story. I needed to change the subject so I *found* my sandals. "Oh, here they are."

Thankfully, he let it drop. "About this paper—"

"Yeah," I interrupted, "about that. I don't know what I was thinking. I had forgotten that I woke up last night. Couldn't sleep. So ... I dug it out and must have left it on the table."

He looked at me intently, like he was going to be asked to draw me from memory. "Good. I wouldn't want you to be afraid of things that aren't there."

His voice had changed. It was gentle, almost reassuring. I weakened, forgetting that I was supposed to be angry. He had an uncanny way of catching me off guard with his kindness.

A need for human interaction overcame me, and I sat down, opposite him at the table.

"Are *you*?"

The kettle whistled. He stood and retrieved it. "Am I what?" he asked, pouring water for us both.

"Ever scared? Of things that aren't there?"

He raised an eyebrow. "I used to be. I was a kid when my dad took off. After that, I was convinced there were monsters under my bed." He returned the kettle to the stove and sat again at the table. "I kept a rubber ball in my room. Every night I'd roll it under the bed to make sure it rolled the whole way through."

The vision of a little boy rolling a ball to dispel his fear tugged at my heart.

"Now?" he continued, stirring his coffee and stretching his legs to full length under the table. "No, I'm not afraid of what's not there." His voice trailed away. "Not too long ago, I would have told you that the only thing worth fearing was anything that walked on two legs. It took me a while to learn that fear makes the wolf—"

"Bigger than he is," I finished.

He grinned. "That's right."

"German proverb."

He eyed me quizzically. "Fear is the most damnable, damaging …"

"… thing to human personality in the whole world." To rub it in, I added, "William Faulkner."

He smiled again.

"Want to keep going?" I challenged.

"Something tells me you have a whole repertoire."

I shrugged. "They come in handy."

"Like when your family died," he said almost caressingly.

I pulled my shoulders back. I recognized the sounds of pity coming on, and I didn't want it. "I didn't learn the quotes until after that. As part of therapy. Prior to that, I had no need. Everything was perfect."

"It must have been tough." He spoke to his coffee mug. "I remember being angry right after my dad left. I found his golf clubs in the garage. I got mad that he took off, but left us his clubs. It was years before I decided to pick up those clubs and use them." He cleared his throat and looked away, as though embarrassed that he had shared so much.

"I was angry too," I admitted. "At the dishwasher."

He made eye contact. "The dishwasher?"

"My mom's best friend stepped in to be with me until my aunt could arrive. We came back from the morgue so that I could change clothes. I walked in the kitchen and saw the door open on the dishwasher. Mom used to open it so the steam would come out and the dishes would dry faster. I got mad that the dishwasher still needed to be emptied. People are so much more precious than things, yet my family died, and the stupid dishes remained. And the dirty laundry was piled up. And the mail arrived. And the garbage had to be taken to the curb. And all these things still needed to be tended to even though my whole world had just crumbled." I didn't realize I'd been raising my voice and flailing my arms during my little prattle until my fist hit the table, making the coffee spill onto the table.

Embarrassed, I looked down and shrugged. "There just seems to be some kind of cosmic disconnect about that."

I took a deep breath and lapsed into silence. I needed to get control. I hadn't had these thoughts in a long time. Fortunately, he recognized my need to redirect.

"How old were you when your mom married Jack?" He never broke eye contact as he picked up his mug and took a sip. His grimace told me the coffee was not worth the effort.

"I was eight. It had been Mom, Julie, and me for about six years. Once in a while, Aunt Tish and Uncle Phil would visit or we'd visit my grandma Sadie. That's my mom's mom. But it was hard to talk with her because she'd had a stroke. She's partially paralyzed. So, I never got to know her well." I realized I was rambling again, so I stopped.

"Sadie." He nodded, as though he had heard it before.

"The visits always left my mom feeling sad. I began to hate going there. And then I hated myself for feeling that way. Eventually Elizabeth, that's my grandmother's sister, moved her to an assisted-living facility in Philadelphia so that they could be closer. I thought that would be for the best, but it seemed to make my mom sadder. I just wanted her to be happy."

"I can relate to that. And then Jack came along?"

"He was amazing. He made me feel loved and safe for the first time that I could remember." My voice cracked. "He adopted us, and I became a MacKenna. For the next five years my world was perfect, although I didn't realize it at the time."

"We rarely do," Clay sighed, talking again to his mug. He shifted in his chair and looked up. "Well, your gain was my loss."

I must have looked confused because he continued, "For a couple years I had hoped that my mom and Jack would pick up where they left off in high school, but my mom never got over my dad leaving."

It was my turn to offer empathy. "Sorry."

"I was going on twelve when Jack told us he was getting married. He promised he'd still come to visit ... which he did ... but the visits went from once each month to once every other month, to once every three months." He chuckled. "You must have kept him busy."

I didn't know what to say. I was still reeling from the knowledge that Jack had another life here, without the three of us. I'd had so much of Jack, yet I still felt hurt that Clay seemed to know details about Jack's life that I did not. I remember my mom saying that Jack had asked us to accompany him on his long drives to check on the house, but now I wondered if that was true. I wondered if my mother knew about Cassie. For that matter, did Clay know everything about Cassie and Jack's relationship, whatever it had been? Jack's desire to be at this house made no sense.

"Look, I'm sorry I startled you this morning. You were important to Jack, and I owe him a lot. He used to talk about you and Julie all the time. I feel like I grew up knowing you. I wanted to make sure you were alright, so I slept on your porch." He looked at his watch. "I've got a job in Hancock, and it'll take me a half hour to get there. I have to get a shower and a *real* cup of coffee." Pain crossed his face as he stood.

"Your leg?"

"Tramp caught me by surprise out there."

"How did you get that limp?" I asked before I realized how callous it would sound.

If Clay was insulted, he didn't let it show. He winked. "An ol' war wound."

Typical guy—has to make a joke to cover his weakness.

"Whatever," I mumbled. If he didn't want me to know, I would respect his privacy. Hopefully, he would extend the same courtesy to me.

With a pledge to return the next day to make repairs, Clay was gone.

My eyes shifted from the door through which Clay had departed to the paper on the table, then around the room. With the natural light of the sun coming through the windows, the room seemed innocent, ordinary. I still had no explanation as to how the paper got moved to the table, but in the tranquility of the room, it almost seemed ridiculous to be concerned.

I studied the list. It was a chronology of William Kavanaugh's life, suggesting that Jack had been doing research on the man.

William Alan Kavanaugh
May 1844 – Born in Alexandria, Virginia; best friend is Asa
November 1858 – Crossings is built
August 1860 – Parents leave for ambassadorship in Brazil
September 1860 – Begins University of Virginia; meets Braxton, Fergus, and Jubal
April 1861 – Virginia secedes from Union
June 1861 – Joins 17th Virginia Infantry, Manassas Junction
June 1861 – Becomes engaged to Naomi Weston
April 1862 – Cousin Edmund loses arm at Pittsburg Landing
May 1862 – Commissioned as 2nd lieutenant; Asa wounded at Seven Pines
June 1862 – Fergus Lowe reported missing
July 1862 – Commissioned as captain; marries Naomi
September 1862 – Friends die at Antietam; Will is wounded, captured at Sharpsburg, taken to Johnson's Island
February 1863 – Finds Fergus at Johnson's Island
March 1863 – Will and Fergus escape
May 1863 – Will dies at Crossings

I did the math. William Kavanaugh was only nineteen years old when he died. I knew enough American history to know that the 1860s was during the time of the Civil War and that hundreds of thousands of young men had died in the conflict. Yet Jack had described "Will" as dying *here*. At *Crossings*. Not on a battlefield. How did he die? And why? Was his wife with him when he died?

I remembered the picture in the parlor. Jack and William had looked so much alike. William must have been Jack's ancestor. Perhaps that's why Jack had an interest in him. How much more had Jack known about William?

I kept re-reading the list, searching for answers between the lines. It was hard to believe that a young man's life was summed up here on one side of a sheet of paper. I wondered if *my* life would consist of more than one page of events. Had Jack sat here wondering the same thing? He was only forty-five when he died—barely half way through his life. When he wrote this, he probably thought he had many more years ahead of him.

With these thoughts swirling through my head, I began to feel claustrophobic.

* * *

When I stepped onto the porch to unload my car, I was startled by the view.

I had researched this part of West Virginia on the Internet. Marlowe was the northern entrance into the Shenandoah Valley, which stretches for about 200 miles to the south. The valley varies between 25 to 40 miles wide, and is bound to the east by the Blue Ridge Mountains, to the west by the Appalachian Mountains, to the south by the James River, and to the north by the Potomac River. Countless hits on my search engine turned up descriptors such as "pastoral solitude," "majestic mountain vistas," and "woodsy retreats."

The valley, however, was south of *Crossings*. The porch faced north, probably to take advantage of the scenic river. This meant that my view was merely the entrance to the valley, and yet it was breathtaking. Again the contrast of the two sides of the river surprised me, but this time in a satisfying way. I'd had no idea that all this beauty was hidden under the mask of darkness when I arrived.

Once beyond the immediate perimeter of the house, the ground was green and lush, and it sloped down to the river, about a quarter mile away. Boaters were already out enjoying the day. Children floated in inner tubes. A family of squawking geese rippled the water. Williamsport spanned the landscape on the opposite side of the river.

Just then, a long whistle sounded, and I realized how Whistle Ridge Road had gotten its name. On Maryland's edge, a black freight train snaked through the trees, running parallel to the river. I turned my ear toward the river to hear the familiar soothing rhythm of the train clicking on its rails, but the low lament of the whistle was all that reached the ridge on this side of the river, and I understood the isolation of my location.

With an unexpected feeling of foreboding, it struck me how sadly apropos my new situation was. I was like the house: settling for a comfortable, distant view of life without having to be part of it.

I wondered if this same detachment had contributed to William Kavanaugh's death, here, within the same walls where I now lived.

Chapter 6

I knew from Internet research that I'd never find breakfast in rural Marlowe, so I headed across the river into Williamsport. I had seen a 24/7 diner north of town, and I wanted to avoid the *Time Out* for a while.

After breakfast, the waitress gave me directions to a shopping center about eight miles north in Hagerstown. Besides groceries, I picked up a coffeemaker, light bulbs, door locks, several hurricane lamps, and kerosene.

Back at *Crossings*, I decided to take pictures of the main house before eating lunch. I would need the "before" pictures for my alleged senior project. May as well get the ruse underway.

Reflexively, a shiver ran down my spine as I opened the door to the main house. To my surprise, it opened easily. I stepped into the silent room, waiting for something to happen.

Nothing did. The place felt dead. There was stillness in the air that had nothing to do with the fact that the old house had no aeration. No dust danced in the air; no particles surrendered to gravity. It was as if the motes had long ago come to their final resting place on the sheets. And the air! I had not noticed its stench and stagnancy the night before, as though it had been overused by too many people for too many years and had finally been exhaled in a last belabored breath that was caught between these walls.

As I continued through the room, my footfalls echoed and rebounded throughout the house.

The light of day revealed so much more that had been lost in the flashlight's weak beam. The furniture seemed heavier, the cobwebs thicker. A brass stand by the door still held two umbrellas. A top hat hung from a peg. The shelves were full, and every flat surface was topped with various everyday items that lifted up the sheets.

I was anxious to uncover the furniture, but that would have to wait. I needed to take pictures first, and letting the sheets remain intact seemed like the best way to capture true "before" shots.

After finishing the first floor, I headed upstairs. Halfway up, I felt a faint pocket of cool air, but this time I was rather sure my mind was playing tricks on me. Perhaps the house was prone to odd drafts.

When I returned downstairs and walked through the parlor, I noticed the piano's legs protruding under the sheet. Overcome with curiosity, I removed the candelabrum; it must have weighed twenty pounds. I rolled the sheet back onto itself so that the dust stayed within its folds.

The piano was a work of art, made of solid walnut, intricate scrollwork, and genuine ivory keys. I played a few chords and was surprised that it sounded in tune. In the deadness of the room, the chords echoed hauntingly off the walls as though desperately rebounding in search of some form of life that would appreciate them. Overcome with the desire to play complete songs, I decided to visit the music shop in Williamsport.

* * *

An hour later I was back in Williamsport and headed toward the music store when a bedraggled man trudged up the sidewalk from my right. He looked out of place in the unsoiled little town: unkempt beard, layered dirty clothing, red leathery skin like that of a homeless person. The bicycle he pushed was weighted down with makeshift baskets that carried the same weather-beaten, discarded items that I had seen vagrants pushing around in shopping carts in Boston.

A young woman emerged from the music store. I recognized her as the pretty girl that had been talking to Cassie in the café. Her Pradas and suit had been replaced with sandals and jeans. The man accosted her, requesting money "for some food" because he had not "eaten in days." His voice sounded raspy, tired. I could see apprehension on her face. As I reached the sidewalk, she gave me a pleading look, reached into her hip pocket, and pulled out paper money.

I gently touched her on the back to let her know I was friend not foe. With my other hand, I took her money.

"Tell you what …" I shot the man a direct gaze, but tried to keep my voice light. "I'll match my friend's money, and we'll go in the café and buy you enough food for three days."

The man glared back, stood straighter, and instantly looked healthier. He muttered a few colorful obscenities at me as he turned his bike across the street, continuing on his way.

The young woman stared at me, incredulous. "How did you know he didn't actually want food?"

I shrugged, relieved that she hadn't taken offense at my intrusion. "I didn't, but it's one way to find out. He probably wants booze or drugs. Sometimes giving money only contributes to their delinquency."

"Wow." She practically whispered.

"Here, keep some of these handy like I do." I reached into my backpack to pull out a booklet of ten-dollar coupons to a large fast-food chain. I tore off a couple and handed them to her. "The food's not the greatest, but they can only use them for food, and those restaurants are everywhere."

"Thanks. I'm embarrassed. He startled me ... but I also felt so bad for him."

"He knew you would."

"Where'd you learn that?"

"It's a city thing, I guess. You learn to be tough."

"Uh-uh." She shook her head. "It's not a city thing. I spend most of my year in New York City, and I never learned to be tough like that. It must be a 'you' thing. I saw you in the café last night." She threw out her hand to shake mine. "I'm Adriana Barrone. Thanks for helping me."

"Grace MacKenna. And you're welcome. Thanks for reminding me I can be a little too abrupt sometimes."

"Are you kidding? You were great."

"Do you work here?" I asked, looking up to read the shop name, *Perfect Rhythm*.

"Yeah, I'm a music major in college. I work here during the summer. You coming in?"

I followed her. The store was narrow and long, like the café next door, but every inch of wall was covered with instruments, sheet music, and songbooks.

"Where do you go to school?" I asked, looking around.

"The Conservatory of Music in Brooklyn. My emphasis is music performance ... for flute. Someday I hope to play for the National Symphony Orchestra."

I couldn't imagine how this cultured, bubbly ingénue could be content spending her summers in Williamsport.

"I bet you can't wait to move back to the city." I paused at a rack that held anthologies of classic American songs. "What do people do here? Memorize the train schedule?"

"I love it here, and there's lots to do. New York is great, but I've never been around so many people in my life yet felt so lonely. I always want to live here."

I was startled by her succinct summary of what I'd been spending years trying to understand about myself, that loneliness was a state of mind more than a product of aloneness. I felt drawn to Adriana and safe in her company.

"That's why I targeted the orchestra in D.C. It's an hour by train. I just pray that I'll get a chance to audition and that I'll be selected. It's so competitive. But I can't imagine living away from my family. I'd miss them too much."

"That's great." I was envious that she seemed to know exactly what she wanted, but I was downright jealous that she had a family she *could* be near.

"Yeah, but I wish I was tougher, like you."

I looked at her, surprised. She was such a kind, gentle soul. I found it almost funny that we each wanted to be more like the other.

She flourished a hand toward the racks. "So, what can I do for you?"

* * *

Two hours later, I left the music store with a spiral-bound anthology for piano entitled, "Best Loved Songs of the 1800s" and an agreement to meet Adriana at the canal when she got off work.

When she invited me for a bike ride, I instinctively started forming excuses. Then I realized that if I accompanied her, I could report a social outing to Aunt Tish who would be less likely to worry about me being unsupervised, *and more likely to let me alone.* What's more, I enjoyed Adriana, and there is only so much talking two people can do while they're riding. It seemed like the perfect pressure-free activity.

Besides biking and music, Adriana and I had discovered at the shop that we shared a passion for old movies and impressionist art. Plus, we both had suffered through ballet class, loved Girl Scouts but hated selling cookies. She had graduated high school a year early as I would be doing. At twenty years of age, Adriana was entering her senior year in college. She was intrigued to hear about my senior-year project, but startled to learn that I was only sixteen and declared me "very mature for my age." I ignored the compliment, having heard it dozens of times over the past several years.

I must admit being happy to learn that my new friend practiced her flute for at least three hours every day. This meant she would probably not encroach on my preferred solitude. She didn't ask about my living arrangements or my aunt, and for that I was especially grateful.

Still, I couldn't help but wonder if it was a safe move to embrace isolation while keeping friends at bay.

* * *

Back at *Crossings*, I took Tramp out for a run, then entered the main house, determined to use my new music book.

As before, the house was still, no sound, no movement.

I played a few songs that I recognized from summer camps—*Jeannie with the Light Brown Hair, Camptown Races, Jimmy Crack Corn*. Just as I found *The Battle Hymn of the Republic*, my cell phone rang, and I returned to the apartment to answer it.

Aunt Tish talked for about twenty minutes: Grandma Sadie was no better, Michael was still in transit, and she'd forgotten her dental appointment. She instructed me to email pictures of the house, and reiterated that my social skills were "pitiful" and that I should make an extra effort to meet the right kind of people.

After I hung up, Aunt Tish's comments about Grandma Sadie were still on my mind. I decided to head to Philadelphia in a few weeks to visit her. As for the pictures, I would go through them now and select what to send. I'd have to find a coffee shop or library with WiFi.

I stuck the flash drive in my laptop and opened the file. None of the pictures were usable except the shot of the modern books. Without the three-dimensional effect that real-life offered, the flat images seemed to be nothing more than an endless display of white sheets. I continued scanning. I would have to uncover the furniture and retake the pictures, or only show my aunt shots of the apartment instead.

As I scrolled through the pictures, something caught my eye. In a shot of the foyer, about half-way up the grand staircase, it looked as though a fog had poured into the picture as I took it. A haze—*or apparition?*—flowed from off the top of the picture down to the third step. It was white, thick, and vaporous-looking. With a tinge of anxiety, I realized the form would be about the same size as a human being if one were to stand at this same location.

My mind raced. Maybe I had kicked up a swirl of dust; but I knew I had moved too slowly through the house for that to have happened. Sunlight? No, the house was so dark that I had used a flash.

For an instant, I wondered if I should go online and search for a psychic or medium. I could probably afford one, but word might get back to Aunt Tish. It struck me that facing the unknown was the lesser of my two unnerving options.

My cell phone rang again, and I shot upright in my chair. Adriana wanted to know if I could meet her in a half-hour. Numbly, I agreed.

* * *

The C&O Canal towpath was a pleasant surprise. It runs parallel to the Potomac River, between Washington, D.C. and Cumberland, Maryland, a stretch of about 185 miles, with Williamsport at its midway point.

As we rode northwest, the beauty of the countryside enthralled me. To my left, forested islands appeared in the purling river. To my right were thick woods, rock cliffs, and occasional wildlife—a black snake, a turtle, several squirrels, countless birds. From summer camps, I recognized the sounds of hawks, doves, geese.

Every few miles we passed crumbling fieldstone walls and the remains of locks and aqueducts from the canal's heyday. The trees formed a lacy canopy that only occasionally let the sun peak through. As a result, the trail was shrouded in swiftly changing patterns of light and shadow. At times, I could see the track of the train that I had heard earlier. It traveled about twenty yards to my right and ran parallel to the river and canal.

The scenery, fresh air, natural light, and the steady roar of the rapid river—all made me forget *Crossings*, until we stopped at a wooded picnic area to hydrate and stretch.

Adriana didn't mean to destroy the mood. She merely asked who was accompanying me this summer and why we came. My heart sank. The lies, the hedging. I wasn't sure I could do it indefinitely. I hadn't anticipated meeting so many curious people.

"It's just my aunt and me. For a bunch of reasons." *Ugh—Another dodge of the truth.*

She laughed.

My head snapped up. From her perch atop a picnic table, legs pretzeled beneath her, she grinned at me. *"That's* half an answer. Look, Grace, when you want to talk about it, just let me know."

I swallowed. Incredible. I'd never had such an accepting friend. It struck me that I needed to be the same in return. I felt I could trust her, so I told her about Boston, my overbearing aunt, and the plans that Michael and I had formulated. I didn't mention Clay's visit or the oddness at *Crossings*.

When I finished, Adriana asked: "Is your aunt really that bad?"

I'd already told her about the jewelry and photo albums that disappeared in month one, so I told her about month two.

"I came home from school and found my dog Tramp, my cat Chubbs, and my parakeet Weisenheimer missing. This time—"

"Weisenheimer?"

"Our bird. Julie had taught it to say all kinds of insults—"

"Like what?"

"Like, 'She's a fool,' 'He lies,' and 'You smell.'"

Adriana giggled.

"After a while, 'Polly' no longer seemed like an appropriate name. Anyway, this time Michael was home from college for a friend's wedding, so he came to my rescue. On that day he seemed to assume the role of my protector and has been at it ever since. We never did find Weisenheimer, but Michael tracked Tramp and Chubbs to the local pound. I confronted Aunt Tish, and she pointed out that she was willing to take care of me but not my pets, claiming she already had a dog, she was allergic to cats, and she hated birds."

"Wow."

"Unfortunately, she was right. It was her house. So, I asked if I could live with my mom's best friend and her family. In the time that you could say 'badda-bing,' her allergy disappeared. She even began admiring Tramp's ability to obey orders."

"What did Michael say about all that?"

"It brought us closer. He said that having me under her roof provided Aunt Tish with bragging rights for use with her friends and martyr status to lord over me. And, of course, a generous stipend from my trust fund."

"Thank goodness you got away."

I took a swig of water. I hated pity in any form.

Adriana sobered. "I've lived around here for about eight years. My dad was Army, so we lived in five countries before he retired here. So it was only a few years ago that I met—"

"And yet you want to stay here?" It was rude to interrupt, I know. She had obviously been leading to a different point, but I was intrigued by her desire to stay in the area, particularly since she'd already seen so much of the world.

A momentary perplexity crossed her face. "Well, naturally, I'll have to travel some with the orchestra, but no, I have no desire to live anywhere else. Grace, everything that happens out there, happens here. Just on a smaller scale. A kinder, gentler kind of scale. When I want some of the world, I can go to it."

Again I felt envy wash over me. I wished I could feel her contentment.

"'Course," she added, a grim look on her face, "if I don't get in the National Symphony, I'm not sure what I'll do. And then there's my boyfriend, Darius. He lives in New York City. I'm not sure he'd ever be able to adjust to small-town life." She gathered her arms around herself. "Anyway ..." She shook her head and sat taller. "I was saying that was until I met Jack."

She stopped, assessing my reaction. I wanted her to continue, so I smiled.

"Seemed like a nice guy." She dropped to a bench, making our eye contact level. "I didn't know him well. I remember him in the café showing pictures of his daughters to anyone who would look at them."

"Thanks." I didn't know what else to say, but hoped that she understood how much her words had meant to me.

"So, you weren't in the car when it ..." She seemed to struggle for words.

"No." I swallowed. "I was home. My sister Julie had an early morning soccer game that Saturday. As we were getting ready to go, the air conditioning died. We decided I would stay behind to let the repairman in because it was Parents' Day for the team. The accident occurred about fifteen minutes after they left. They were on a deserted road, so nobody saw it happen. Somehow the car went off the road, hit a ditch, and flipped. The police assumed that something either ran out in front of them or that the car malfunctioned. I think they took pity on me and concluded the latter so the car manufacturer would have to pay a hefty amount. All three of them died instantly. And poof, I became an orphan and moved in with my wacky aunt and uncle. They lived only an hour and six million philosophical differences away."

In three years, I'd learned to end the story with a light-hearted voice to help people ease out of the heaviness of the tragedy and to deflect their attention away from me.

When Adriana responded, her words surprised me. "There's a reason things happen the way they do. I hope I'm around when you learn what that reason is."

"You say that like it's a good thing." I smirked.

"Maybe not a good thing, but it doesn't have to be a bad thing. It can be a good thing. It will be. It can help you discover who you are. What you want."

I gave her one of those "yeah, right" looks. I'd heard the pep talk before: *When something is taken away, something new will take its place.*

"My dad says that heartaches are not stop signs. Instead, they're detours pointing you in a new direction, trying to show you an alternate way to do things. He would know. He's seen a lot of pain and loss in the military."

An alternate way to do things. I smiled at her new spin on the lost/found theory. "Your dad must have been a motivator in the Army." Mr. Barrone sounded like the kind of guy who would take a tape measure and camera with him to go fishing. His daughter must have inherited his optimistic outlook.

"Yeah, he's full of a lot of useless euphemisms, but this one's right. It took me a long time to learn that. You *will* have a happy life."

I looked away, and we lapsed into silence. Her words were nonsensical, yet she was the first person who had ever put a positive spin on my circumstances *and* actually believed it.

A moment later, a group of bikers passed by, and one was wearing a blue T-shirt that read, "Take Time Out for the *Time Out*." On the back of the shirt was a picture of the café. I noticed that Adriana saw the shirt go by too.

"That place seems to be popular. Probably good for gossip, huh?" What I wanted to know was more about Cassie, but I didn't want Adriana to know that.

Somehow she knew anyway. "You concerned about Cassie keeping your secrets? Don't be. She's a good person. If she asked you too many questions last night, it's only because she cared about Jack."

"How *much* did she care about Jack?" I asked, wary.

Adriana tilted her head like a curious cat. She seemed to be considering my question. "I don't know. I doubt if there was anything beyond friendship, if that's what you mean. She's never gotten over Mason. He broke her heart. Maybe Jack helped her deal with that."

"Mason?"

"Her husband. He left one day when Clay and Reaghan were still young. Those are her kids. I didn't live here then, but the story is that he told her one day that if anything ever happened to him, that she was supposed to go see a friend of his. Two days later Mason was gone. I guess he had planned to leave all along. Before she could talk to Mason's friend ... what was his name ... Clyde something-or-other ... he worked at the bank ... anyway, before she could talk to him, he died. Slipped and hit his head when he was sledding with his daughter on Chocton Bluff. Some people wondered if Mason had anything to do with his death, but the guy's daughter reported it was an accident. Besides, Mason had already left by then."

"That's terrible. Poor Clay."

She chuckled. "You've met Clay? Cute isn't he?"

"Cute?" I had assumed Adriana and I would agree on what constituted a handsome man. "I guess, if you like that type."

Her face blossomed with amazement. "You're the first girl I've ever met who doesn't like his *type*. Doesn't matter anyway. That fiancé of his won't let anyone near enough to appreciate his good looks. Such a waste. 'Course Reaghan is pretty protective too. She's six years older than Clay. She treats him like one of her kids." She sighed, looked up, and exclaimed, "We better head back!"

I followed her gaze to the sky. It was barely visible between the thick plumage of the trees, but it had darkened in the last few minutes. A summer rainstorm was brewing—I could smell it in the air.

I collected my helmet and bike.

"Grace, two things before I forget."

I turned to her. She looked somber, uncomfortable.

"Lock your doors. I'm not trying to scare you, but people are aware that someone is living in the old *Crossings* place. A lot of people have been curious about that house for a long time. Some say it has bad vibes, bad karma. They're afraid to go near it. They might think it's safe to go there now."

"Why are they afraid? It's just a house." I laughed nervously. *Crossings* didn't look *that* foreboding in the daylight, but her discomfort was rubbing off on me.

"I've never been there, but people say that they can't get in the place. Sometimes can't even get near it. That something stops them."

"*Something* stops them? Something like what?"

"Like a force. Or an invisible wall. I know that sounds weird."

"That makes no sense, because I'm there. And—" I was about to say that Clay had visited without incident but decided there was no need to bring him into the conversation. "Jack lived there."

"That's kind of odd too, don't you think? That only the two of you can go there, but then Jack died? Anyway, gossip spreads quickly. You know how people are."

"But, how will they *know*? Cassie wouldn't respect my privacy?"

"She will. But ..." She looked down, as though she had to say something uncomfortable. "I can't say the same about Ling. My dad says her idea of keeping a secret is to refuse to tell who told it to her."

I'd have to think about that later—it was too much to process at the moment, and the rain was threatening. "You said two things?"

"Oh yeah." She brightened. "My church is having a huge picnic on Sunday with games and stuff. The food is incredible. We have a lot of good cooks around here. Why don't you come with us? It will give you a chance to meet more people."

I suppose I should have acted like I was at least considering the idea, but I immediately blurted, "No, thanks. I'm not sure about the whole God thing. I'm not much into organized religion." I cringed at my own words—the term was practically a cliché these days. If I hadn't heard myself say it, I'd swear it was Aunt Tish talking.

Adriana furrowed her brow. "So you're saying that disorganized people praying is better than organized people praying?"

When I didn't respond, she continued. "Oh, pah-lease." She crossed her arms. "I am so tired of that phrase 'organized religion.' First off, God is *not* a religion. Second, church is nothing more than a bunch of people who are trying to do the best they can. If they didn't organize their gatherings, there'd be complete chaos in trying to get things done. And third, every valuable thing in life happens because of our bond with others. People give God such a bad rap."

She had a good point. I hadn't thought of it that way. When my family died, everyone kept saying they were in a better place, as though to reassure me that they were better off and that I'd see them again. Yet those same people seemed to fret their days away without any comfort about tomorrow or the hereafter. Overt faith and life after death seemed to be something pulled out of a crisis file for funerals.

"Think about it. Come on. Let's try to beat the rain."

We made it back to our cars, but scattered raindrops hit us as we loaded our bikes. As I crossed the Cushwa Basin Bridge into West Virginia, rippling films of water rolled down the windshield, and trees swayed in the wind. By the time I reached *Crossings*, angry black clouds had shifted into grotesque shapes and chased me into the house.

Chapter 7

The rain continued slashing against the windowpanes, picking up speed as the evening wore on. The gloom outside mirrored my mood. I couldn't get my mind off my conversations with Adriana and Clay, nor could I stop thinking about William Kavanaugh, as questions surrounding his death played over and over again in my head like a dominant chord in a dirge. He had died so young, a war raging around him.

Thoughts of the war reminded me of the song I had left on the piano. *Battle Hymn of the Republic* had been popular during the Civil War.

I lit one of the hurricane lamps and headed into the old house. As with the other times, neither Tramp nor Chubbs followed. The lamp illuminated a larger part of the room than the flashlight had the night before, but whereas there were dark corners and shadows then, now the flickering flame of the lamp gave these same shadows life and movement. I sat on the creaky bench, placed my hands on the keys, and glanced at the song.

Instead of the *Battle Hymn of the Republic*, the song was entitled, *Lorena*.

Goose bumps popped up all along my arms. I swallowed hard but didn't move. There was no draft, no air, no explanation for the book being open to a different page. It was spiral bound and perched firmly on the ledge above the keys. Some-one—or something—had changed the page.

My eyes scanned the room.

Nothing.

I read the lyrics, and grief washed over me like a tide; they were the saddest words I think I'd ever read and described a man separated from his fiancé by death.

Coldness hit me from my left, as though someone had opened an invisible refrigerator door. Inexplicably, the back of my neck prickled, and a chill chased down my spine.

Then I felt the heavy presence again, but it didn't move. It just hovered beside me, like it was watching, waiting, expecting.

Horror struck like a padded fist, and I felt my courage unravel itself from a durable cord to a fraying, hair-like thread.

This might sound bereft of all reason, but somehow, I sensed that it was *waiting* on me.

Waiting for me to play the song.

The icy comprehension of what it was willing me to do grew so strong that I was incapable of experiencing my own thoughts or emotions. It was a frightening sensation, like being cut off from time and space and the rest of the world.

I looked down at my hands. In my stupor, I hadn't moved them from the keys, although now they gripped the piano's edge like claws. From somewhere deep inside, I summoned the strength to loosen my hold and stretch my fingers out. They trembled, and I panicked, wondering if I'd be able to play. For a moment I was paralyzed.

It was then I felt coldness brush over my hands. Immediately, as though capable of their own mental separation, my fingers calmed, and I felt as though they had been infused with their own power.

I began to play.

I sensed an emanation of calmness, although it was slight, as though a lock had been loosened on chains that still remained. A dizzying serenity coursed through my limbs, and I had enough presence of mind to know that this was not natural. I had the uncanny feeling that the presence was reaching through me toward a memory.

Startled, I stopped playing.

The calmness quickly turned to despair, and my body again reacted, sending a prickling sensation down my spine. Somehow the presence—the phenomenon, the energy—was communicating distress to me.

I began to play again. The peacefulness returned but was joined by sadness. I willed myself to focus on the song and not the presence, but it was a futile effort. As the echo of the last chord died away, I worried about what would happen next. The air in the room held a sense of loss, of life plucked away, of love turned to dust.

After several seconds, the presence moved, and I sensed it was leaving. Oddly, I found that I was mesmerized by the trust it had placed in me to play the song, but its departure brought apathy and loneliness. I experienced hollowness, like we had met at some preordained, mystic junction point that had failed to accomplish its purpose.

"Wait!"

The presence seemed to hesitate. I could feel it lingering, as though wondering, considering.

Then it was gone.

I waited, sitting as still as possible, wondering if I'd ever move again.

In the next heartbeat, thunder broke the silence, reminding me of life beyond the room. There would be nothing more. Not this night. There was only silence and stillness. I picked up my lamp and staggered back to the apartment.

Through the night, the storm grew worse. Thunder rolled over the valley. Lightning blazed by the windows; the wind creaked in the eaves. I was beyond tired, beyond logical reasoning. I lay in bed, unable to think.

When a huge clap of thunder rocked the apartment and made it moan, I pulled open the table drawer beside my bed, shoved the paper about William Kavanaugh aside, and pulled out my iPod. With a light-rock group crooning in my ears, I covered my head with the quilt, desperate for morning to come.

* * *

The next morning was one of déjà vu: Tramp woke me, I found the Kavanaugh paper on the kitchen table, I discovered Clay on my porch, and I scrambled back behind the door, once again conscious of how little I was wearing.

"I didn't hear your car pull up," I yelled over the steady flow of the pouring rain, all the while wondering why I needed to explain myself. It was, after all, my house. And he was, after all, engaged to be married. And I was, *most* of all, sure that I didn't care what this man thought of me.

"Rain must have drowned it out." Distracted, Clay worked on the glider.

By the time I returned with two cups of freshly brewed coffee, he had abandoned the glider and was perched on the porch floor, fixing the cat carrier.

At the sight of the coffee, he raised his eyebrows.

"I threw out the instant."

"Thanks." He reached for the mug and smiled, a gesture that made me wish I were holding the mug differently so that our fingers would touch during the transfer.

What was I thinking? The guy was night to my day, truck to my Volvo, grease to my silk, bedroll to my eggroll.

"You finished?" I asked, pointing to the glider.

"For now, but be gentle. I have to pick up new springs and clips."

There was an awkward pause as we sipped our coffee.

"This is why I love porches." He stared toward the river. He wore the same bandana, different shirt, and different jeans.

"So you can sit out here and fix things you broke?"

71

"Funny. No, I meant the view. Even when it's raining you can sit outside and enjoy it."

I followed his gaze. The scene didn't look as appealing as it had yesterday. The rain was pouring from a low, brooding sky, and the river—much higher in depth—had turned a light brown coffee-with-cream color. Still, I could smell the rain and feel its dampness on my skin. My eyes were disappointed, but my other senses were kicked into high gear.

"I know what you mean." I sat down gingerly on the glider and pushed gently with my feet to test it. "My family used to sit on the porch on rainy Sunday afternoons and play Scrabble and Clue. Mom would make iced tea, and Julie and I would make brownies. Jack would cart everything to the porch."

Clay looked up as he continued his work. "Sounds nice."

"It was. Funny how you don't realize it at the time."

He nodded, a faraway look in his eyes.

"Still," I continued strolling down memory lane, "I miss the songbirds. They don't sing when it rains."

"Songbirds?" He lifted his head as though listening. "Yeah, I guess you're right."

"After my family died, I always felt the worst in the mornings. I'd remember where I was and that I'd never see them again. But if it were summer, I'd hear a songbird outside my bedroom window. It always made the sadness a little more bearable." Feeling awkward that I probably sounded like I was babbling, I changed the subject. "Have you always lived around here?"

He seemed so polished, despite his ruffian exterior. I was curious as to how much this hometown boy had been out of the area.

"Mostly. Spent a little time elsewhere, but I was happy to come back." He shifted his eyes to the distant horizon. "Those mountains always seem to bring me home again. Besides," he looked at me and smiled, "I missed the songbirds too."

He wasn't the least bit embarrassed about sounding poetic, and I was impressed. "I know what you mean about the mountains. Mom and Jack used to take us camping, and I was never as happy as when we were there."

"I lift my eyes unto the hills, from whence cometh my strength." He recited the verse as though that explained it all, and he locked eyes with me. For a moment, an intense and indefinable undercurrent ran between us.

And those eyes! Hadn't they looked like "wolf" eyes yesterday? Now they were more like the brilliant blue-green you see in tropic waters, the kind you long to fall into to escape harsh reality.

When he looked away, I rubbed my temples with my free hand, hoping to dislodge clearer thinking. I couldn't deny there was an odd—okay, *very* odd—connection between the two of us. And a comfort. Yes, that's what it was, a comfort. He knew Jack, so he wasn't a stranger. He was engaged, so he wasn't boyfriend material. He'd chosen a far different lifestyle than mine, so he meant nothing to my future, except perhaps mere acquaintance. With these rationalizations, I relaxed and enjoyed the moment.

It was easy to lose perspective with this man.

The moment ended, however, when my dog came trouncing up the steps, soggy as a used dishrag. At the same instant, Clay and I could tell that Tramp was about to shake his shaggy coat dry. We had enough time to yell "No!" before Tramp showered us both.

We clamored to our feet, drenched but laughing, both of us spilling coffee on our clothing. For a moment it was very comfortable, like we were old friends.

"I'll go get us some—" my breath caught in my throat. He had started pulling off his wet shirt while I spoke. His slim waist and well-defined muscles were hard to ignore.

"Towels?" He finished for me, oblivious to my stare.

I looked away, my face embarrassingly hot.

"That'd be great. I'll throw this in your dryer." He turned and walked toward the door.

"Wait! You can't go in there."

He spun around to look at me, as though waiting for an explanation. I couldn't let him go inside because he would see no signs of an aunt. But then, he must have wondered where her car was. With no time to formulate a plausible excuse, I blurted, "The dryer's broken."

"Oh." He relaxed. "Let me look at it. Maybe I can fix it."

"You think you can do everything, don't you?"

He stiffened, looking mildly astonished. Even I thought I sounded rude.

"No. I thought I could help."

"Well you can't help this time. Besides, there's no hurry for these things to be fixed. Can't you go home and get a dry shirt?"

He stared at me, like he was looking at someone he'd never met.

I cringed.

He held his response for a smoldering moment, giving birth to a pause that resembled the lull in a battle where both sides took stock of their positions.

"Yeah." His voice was edged with irritation. "I'll do that." He turned to collect his tools. "But these won't get fixed until much later. I need to get a haircut and do some errands." With that, he tossed his wet shirt onto his left shoulder and walked toward the stairs.

I felt a dull ache gnawing inside. Great. *Another underwhelming performance of the continuing Grace-is-so-mature-for-her-age saga.*

At the top of the steps, he turned. "You know, I don't know if you're trying to hide from life, or if you're hiding a guy in there, but one thing I do know is that there's no aunt in the picture. When you grow up and learn that your choices define you ... and that also means the situations you get into ... let me know, and *then* we can be friends. For Jack's sake."

With that, he descended the stairs and disappeared into the drench.

His words hung in the air, thick and heavy like the rain. I dropped onto the glider. It issued a metal-like groan and crashed to the floor.

* * *

Morning slipped into afternoon seamlessly, and afternoon into evening. Without the sun going through its changes, it was hard to gauge time.

Pushing aside concerns about both Clay and the presence, I focused on restoration of the old house. I measured and figured, then sketched and planned. Dividing the rooms would be the easy part. The challenging task would be fitting the entire house with piping, wiring, and insulation. No doubt it would need a new roof, and the foundation would have to be checked too.

I leaned back from my sketches at the kitchen table and stretched. For the first time, I noticed it was night. I'd had the lights on all day due to the grayness of the outside, so I hadn't noticed the sun going down. I checked my cell phone—9:10 p.m.

Clay had never returned. My mind again wandered back to his parting words. *When you grow up and learn that your choices define you ...*

He was right: My white lies were still lies. Lies that he could see right through. I felt like a little dog trying to hide behind its bark.

To change focus, I retrieved the hurricane lamp and headed toward the old house. I'd only ever encountered the presence when it was dark, so I was curious to see if I would experience it again. At this point, I wasn't sure if I wanted the presence to stay away or to return. For that matter, I half suspected that the entire paranormal encounter had been my imagination. I needed to know.

Once again the door opened without fanfare.

A few steps into the parlor, I called out, "Are you there?"

The only answer was a dead echo. I strained to hear, but nothing.

"It's me ... Grace." How ridiculous I sounded—as if the presence would answer merely because I identified myself.

Disappointment flooded through me. I walked closer to the bookcases and stopped. It dawned on me that I'd been anticipating another encounter all day; in fact, I'd almost become obsessed with the need to have another encounter, to make sense of what I had experienced earlier. The discovery brought a chaotic mix of emotions, both disturbing and exciting.

I turned and looked at the piano. As I sat on the bench, I wasn't surprised to see that the book remained open to *Lorena*. The anxiety and the expectation spurred me to play.

Nothing happened; *Lorena* produced no results, so I moved onto *All's Quiet Along the Potomac*. About midway through, Tramp began to snarl and bark. Annoyed, I assumed that Clay had returned to finish the glider, the rain again drowning out his arrival. I hurried through the apartment, to the exterior door, wishing I'd come up with both a plausible cover story to explain my missing aunt and a polite way to tell him that I didn't want him to come here anymore.

The doorknob rattled as I reached for it. Annoyed at his impertinence by trying to enter without knocking, I whipped the door open. "What the heck are you doing—"

Two of the greasiest, grimiest men I had ever seen stood there, smiling wickedly. One man had a squat, ugly body, receding grey hair and heavy jowls like those of an obese bulldog. The other man was taller with a frail blow-away body and hair so greasy that it shined off the light from the lamp by the door. Both were covered in whiskers and filthy clothes.

"Dang, Henry," the scrawny one sneered to the squat one, "we struck gold."

Chapter 8

In one heartbeat I realized the fragile nature of my situation, and an inexplicable sense of danger washed over me. I was a mile or more away from anyone else, so screaming would do no good. The rifle was now under the couch. The cast-iron skillet was in the cupboard. Even if I could get to my cell phone to dial 9-1-1, the police would take too long to get here.

The full horror of my circumstances began to be obscured, almost cushioned, as adrenaline coursed through my veins. Panic turned to fury, and my body responded.

In the next heartbeat, I threw my full frame into the door, hoping to lock out these strangers.

The squat one, Henry, thrust his foot in the pathway of the door and laughed. Tramp sensed my fear and growled at the men. As Henry pushed the door open, the greasy one pulled pepper spray from his pocket and fired it at Tramp.

Poor Tramp whimpered and fell. He staggered back up and tried to get away, but he seemed so panicked and clumsy from the effects of the spray that his paws kept slipping on the cheap flooring. I screamed and thrashed out to grab the pepper spray away from the greasy man, but the squat man lurched and grabbed me. In seconds, he twisted my arms behind my back. Tramp was on the floor, rolling and yelping in misery.

"Don't hurt him!" I screamed.

The greasy man grabbed Tramp by the collar, shoved him into the bedroom, and slammed the door shut.

Henry began to laugh so hard that I could feel his stomach shaking against my hands, held in a tight grip behind my back. Despite his blubber, he was extremely strong. It would be almost impossible from this angle to get the leverage I needed to break loose, but I kept trying. My efforts were met with a tightened grip and a "Calm down, girlie."

The greasy one returned, licked his crooked, yellow teeth, and began sniggering too. "Dang, Henry, I always wanted to do that. Didja' see that dawg fall?" He sounded like a cross between the raspy crow of a heavy smoker and the cackle of a witch who had just placed Hansel and Gretel in a stew pot.

Henry kept shaking and laughing. The man was all ditz, no brains.

The greasy man began to appraise me. I shivered a little under the impact of his forthright gaze.

"Ain't she a looker, Jim?" I felt my skin crawl where he gripped my wrists together.

Greasy Jim smiled. "She sure is." He moved in close to me, so close that I could smell the liquor on his breath. "You behave, and we'll let you stay that way." He touched a knife to my neck. It was sharp, cold. I shivered. There was no way I could kick him in the groin with that knife so close to me. He laughed and stepped back, his eyes darting around the room.

"What do you want?" I snapped, trying to sound brave. "I don't have any money if that's what you're after." I hoped they wouldn't look in the freezer where I'd hidden almost $5,000. Then again, losing my money might be the least of several horrific options at the hands of these two.

"Well now, that ain't true." Greasy Jim licked his ugly teeth again. "We figure you're here for the same reason we been tryin' to git in this place—the gold."

"I don't know what you're talking about." I wondered if my hands were close enough to Henry's manhood that I could hit it hard, cripple him, and get to my gun.

At my words, Greasy Jim stepped forward and slapped my face with the back of his hand. The force of the blow would have sent me reeling if Henry hadn't been holding onto me from behind. I wailed, and Greasy Jim grabbed me away from Henry. He lifted the knife to my neck again, and started dragging me, roughly, into the main house. Collecting my flashlight from the table, Henry followed us.

"You show us where the gold is, and maybe we'll be real nice to you. Lie, and I'll cut you right here." Greasy Jim sneered as though the idea gave him extreme pleasure.

By now, we had reached the archway between the parlor and the foyer of the main house. Suddenly, the walls seemed to move as a huge gust of air, like a frightening wind, burst through as if someone had thrown a window open in the midst of a tornado. The wind felt cruel, merciless.

The force of the air was so great that Greasy Jim let go of me, reaching out desperately to steady himself. Likewise, Henry faltered and dropped the flashlight. It rolled to a halt and—along with the hurricane lamp—cast enough indirect light that I was able to see the scene before me. I shrank back against the wall, speechless, too shocked to do anything but stare. The wind, or whatever it was, seemed to be concentrated on the other two.

The dimwits, caught in the middle of this invisible storm, hurled choice epithets as they swung to one side, then to the other, then in circles, frantically trying to figure out what was happening. Their words sounded like the snarls of trapped animals.

Stunned, I watched as the front door banged open, and Greasy Jim was thrown onto his back. He screamed, his head flinging to one side, as though someone smashed him hard in the face, and he dropped the knife. The invisible tornado picked him up horizontally and spun him.

In those fractions of a second, his eyes bulged out, and his veins swelled. He flailed his arms, a desperate attempt to find an anchor, anything to release him from this frenzied twister, all the while making fearful incoherent wails and squawking sounds. He was forced higher into the air and hurled out through the doorway into the rainstorm. From his scream, I could tell that he had soared over the porch and had dropped two stories to the ground below.

Henry came out of his stupor, shrieking, and began slashing the air wildly with his hands. He looked like a blind man trying to fight off an attacker as he was racing toward the open door, trying to escape. Once there, he too was whisked into the air, spun horizontally, swirled around several times, and hurled out the door. Above the roar of the pouring rain, his scream, and his thud, were much louder than Greasy Jim's had been.

Almost as quickly, the door slammed shut, and the house was still, as though the incident had never occurred.

Seconds ticked by. I stared into the darkness, willing my breathing to slow down and my heart to stop racing.

I didn't know what to do, what to think.

This was beyond belief, beyond comprehension, beyond reason. Was I part of an unfolding nightmare, or was I on the threshold of an extraordinary understanding?

Then, in one paralyzing moment of sudden insight, it dawned on me that I was safe, not *from* the presence, but *because* of it. That final, icy comprehension spread through me as the integrity of my reality crumbled. I felt drawn to the presence, lured by some irresistible appeal—an appeal that struck both a responsive *and* a hideous chord in me.

The entire foundation of the beliefs I had been taught my whole life about death was about to change forever. Like a derailed train destined to crash, there was no way I could escape the inevitability of this moment.

With the few ounces of bravado I could muster, I whispered, "Where are you?"

There was no response. The room remained quiet, dead.

"Please ... I need to see you."

And just when I thought I would never get an answer, from the wall a few feet in front of me, a dark silhouette emerged.

PART II

Place of Deepest Night

Chapter 9

At that moment, I learned it is possible for the body to stop functioning, for the heart to skip a beat or two, for blinking and breathing to cease.

I also discovered that the fight or flight response is just conjecture; that there is a third option. That fear can be so paralyzing you cease to feel human.

I stood as if frozen, my back ramrod-straight against the wall as this incredible, paranormal experience unfolded before my eyes and all I could do was wonder, "Why me?"

As I watched, the image became clearer. To my relief, it seemed that the more I willed it to, the more human-like it became.

Its features became more pronounced as the facial structure and the outline of clothing emerged. The figure was that of a man. His color turned from a gauzy white, like a thick fog, to a washed-out yellowish brown. I couldn't tell if he was young or old. His face looked ghastly, deteriorated and pale. His eyes were invisible in the pits of shadow beneath his brows.

Still, I couldn't move, as though I had no control over my limbs. From somewhere, a chilling understanding spread through me that I was meant to be there at that moment and would never again be the person I was before. My brain had been imprinted with a new truth, a new reality.

I took a breath as my body began to function again.

But, the vague, disquieting feeling remained that I would forever be different.

As the figure continued to transform, his clothing became more definite too—tattered pants with a stripe down the sides that disappeared inside knee-high boots and a jacket with epaulets on the shoulders.

An outline of scraggly, shoulder-length hair appeared. A mustache hid his upper lip. His eyes became more pronounced, but at best, they were still dull, diseased.

A wisp of disappointment hit me that the figure was not Jack.

He stood still, facing me, no trace of emotion at all on his withered face.

I inhaled hesitantly, the need to communicate overwhelming. "Can …" *Was that me talking?* "… can you understand me?" My voice was a trembling whisper.

Were it not for the light of the hurricane lamp I had left on the piano earlier, I doubt that I would have seen him nod.

Startled, I found it hard to breathe. How could I be talking to someone who walked the earth at the same time as my great, great, great, great grandparents—assuming it was who I thought it was?

"You're ...William Kavanaugh." I was staring at the ghost of a man who had been dead for 150 years.

Again, he nodded, but otherwise did not move. I exhaled, feeling oddly more comfortable that I had identified this figure that had been related to Jack.

As my comfort advanced, so too did the definition of his features. His eyes came into focus, but brought with it a blurred sadness that stared back at me.

"Why did you save me?"

What a ridiculous question. *What was I thinking?* This was a ghost. He couldn't give me explanations. Best to stick with yes and no questions. How crazy this thought seemed too, because until five minutes ago, who would have thought you could converse with a ghost, let alone receive yes and no answers? What if I was losing my sanity?

What if I wasn't?

"Thank you," I fumbled, trying to breathe normally as I spoke, "for saving me."

He just stood there, staring.

"May I stay here?" My question surprised even me, because it revealed that I believed this inhuman form to be so real that he actually had first rights to the house, but I needed to know.

My heart began pounding again when, along with a nod, he mouthed what I believed to be a "yes," although it sounded more like a drawn-out groan, his voice harsh and rusty, as if from disuse.

Seeing *and* hearing this apparition was just too overwhelming. I panicked, wondering if I was losing hold of that precious division between imagination and reality.

"This can't be happening," I blurted in frustration. "You can't be real. I don't understand."

He looked at me, and I could swear I saw the edges of his lips drop. Then he turned and disappeared, almost as if he dissolved back into the shadows from where he had come.

"No, wait!" I pleaded. "I'm sorry. Please come back."

There was no answer, just the muted sound of Tramp bumping a chair as he tried to recover from the effects of the pepper spray. I waited.

Nothing.

Minutes passed.

Still nothing.

William Kavanaugh had left when I had suggested he couldn't be real. Perhaps that had been logic talking, in an effort to restore me to reality.

From the lawn, the screeching cries of retreat from Henry and Greasy Jim broke my stupor. Content that they were both alive and gone, I retrieved the flashlight, extinguished the hurricane lamp, and stumbled toward the apartment, anxious to get to Tramp.

I found him spread out on the floor beside my bed. I wet a washcloth and cleaned his face. He thumped his tail and nestled his head on my lap. Although he reacted with the unabashed love that all dogs offer, I imagined him communicating to me, "We survived." I grabbed my pillow, stretched out beside him on the floor, and wrapped my arms around him. I wasn't sure which of us needed the other more that night.

* * *

I awoke just after seven the next morning, in the same position as when I had dropped onto the floor the night before. I couldn't recall ever having slept that soundly. The sun blazed, drowning the room in a shower of golden warmth.

As had become their routine, Tramp and Chubbs flanked me, despite being on the floor. Chubbs stretched when I stirred, and Tramp stood and began his prance to go outside, the effects of last night's assault now gone.

"You okay, boy?" I frowned as I stroked his fur. He licked my face as though nothing had ever happened.

His coat seemed coarse, shaggy. I felt guilty—I'd been so busy with the house that I had been ignoring him. Chubbs too, although he spent the majority of his time sleeping or grooming. Still, he deserved more attention than what he'd been getting.

I accompanied Tramp outside this time; the poor thing needed a long run, and I needed to stretch away the kinks from sleeping on the hard floor.

As I changed my clothes, thoughts of William Kavanaugh swirled through my head, and I questioned my sanity. I couldn't deny that Henry and Greasy Jim had been real, and something had removed them from the house.

When Tramp and I reached the lawn, I scoured the area where I deduced the two had fallen. I found a fresh patch of flattened weeds and, about a yard away, an indentation in the earth. No doubt the latter had been Henry's landing pad. Searching the area, I found thirty-seven cents in change and spots of muddy soil that looked as though someone had clawed at it in an effort to make a frantic retreat. I smirked as I pictured them falling over one another to get away.

The thought flicked through my mind that I should call 9-1-1, but opted not to. Besides the fact that I didn't want to explain why there was no adult in the house, I assumed I would never see those two scoundrels again.

As Tramp and I headed toward the river, I planned my day. Almost everything on my mental to-do list was designed to prepare me for another meeting with William Kavanaugh. I needed William to show me how I could communicate with my family.

Much as I dreaded the thought, my errands today had to include a visit with Cassie to find out how much she knew about Jack's activities at the house. Perhaps I'd collect some insight into communicating with William. I also needed to visit the library to send Aunt Tish pictures of the apartment and to do some research.

The first order of business, however, was to search the apartment for more messages or lists from Jack, combined with the task of taking new pictures. I just hoped it wouldn't scare away my ghost.

My ghost? Where had that come from? I almost laughed out loud thinking about what my therapist's reaction would be if I were to tell him I had my own ghost.

Tramp's bark brought me back to the moment. Bikers on the canal towpath threaded through the trees, and the thought crossed my mind to invite Adriana to go biking with me later that day.

* * *

With breakfast, picture-taking, and two animal groomings behind me, I searched the drawers and cupboards at *Crossings* for anything that would tell me more about Jack or William. The effort proved futile, so a few hours later I arrived at the small library in Williamsport.

A metal nameplate announced the woman behind the front desk to be Gwendolyn Bealle. She was short, late 60s, and caked in make-up, with several layers of bangle bracelets on her right wrist. When I requested assistance, she cast me a scrutinizing look, as though assessing my trustworthiness with the library's books. It struck me that the only noise this librarian would tolerate was the incessant clang of her bracelets.

Despite her stern demeanor, Ms. Bealle—as she informed me she should be addressed—proved to be quite helpful and acclimated me to the library.

I logged onto the Internet, and after sending the pictures of the apartment to Aunt Tish, I began my research.

Two hours later, I called defeat. Neither the Internet nor the library's holdings gave me any insight into William Alan Kavanaugh. For that, my answers would probably come from court records for the town of Marlowe at the county office in West Virginia.

As for the song *Lorena*, it originated just prior to the Civil War. Legend has it that Confederate soldiers became so homesick after hearing it that many deserted.

Between 1861 and 1865, the Civil War—also known as the War Between the States—claimed the sad distinction as the deadliest war in American history. The library books were rife with stories of homes and farms destroyed, families ripped apart, neighbors battling one another, even brothers fighting on opposite sides. Antietam, just 20 minutes from *Crossings*, suffered the bloodiest single-day battle in American history.

I grabbed the two thickest books on the shelves to read on the porch at home.

Finding information on the topic I was most interested in—ghosts—proved to be a futile effort. Surely I wasn't the first to have held a two-way conversation with a ghost. I suspected that Jack had communicated with William Kavanaugh too. I had no choice but to visit Cassie and learn what she knew.

As I checked out, Ms. Bealle suggested talking to Holland Greer whom she described as a local writer and historian.

"He could answer all your questions about anything that happened in this area during the Civil War. He consults at the battlefield parks around here, and he's written books." Her tone indicated obvious admiration. "He's an expert on the battle at Antietam. And he re-enacts and lectures too. He's quite brilliant, you know."

She looked left and right then leaned in closer so she could whisper—as though a hushed tone with no one in sight was not quiet enough. "And quite persnickety about things."

That needed to be whispered? Something told me that Ms. Bealle found Holland Greer rather appealing, and she whispered lest anyone overhear her calling him "persnickety."

It being a Saturday morning, Holland Greer was in town, and she happened to have seen him go into the bank a few minutes ago.

Remembering the $5,000 in my backpack that I had brought to deposit into my new account, I thanked her and headed to the bank.

* * *

The First Potomac Bank and Trust was two blocks away. Aunt Tish had arranged in writing for me to open a checking account complete with a debit card. Well, truth be told, *I* had arranged it for her, so that all she'd had to do was sign the paperwork.

The only teller at the counter—a mousy-haired gum-chewer wearing a ring on each of eight fingers—directed me to Nidhi Michelson, the branch manager, who stood at the entrance to a partitioned office talking to a gentleman I deduced to be Holland Greer. His scholarly look would be an attraction to Ms. Bealle. Despite the hot June weather, he wore khakis and a British green blazer with patches of tan suede on the elbows—the quintessential "uniform" of collegiate individuals who grew up in the 70s and 80s. He had a blank, distant stare as he talked, as though he were looking for profound ideas in the atmosphere, all the while stroking his white goatee.

The branch manager, a dark-skinned, short, plump woman of about 40 with black hair piled atop her head, straightened and cocked her head at me, her eyebrows rising.

Mr. Greer was startled at the interruption. He stepped back with a sigh as though to move away from our conversation.

"I want to open a checking account. My aunt told me to bring in this card, and it could be arranged." I handed her the card.

With one glance at the signature card, the woman smiled. "Oh, you're Grace MacKenna. I'm Nidhi Michelson, but please call me Nidhi."

Holland Greer's demeanor changed. He stepped closer, into the reaches of our conversation. I could feel the curiosity in his gaze, understandable since I was probably the subject of curiosity around town.

"I'm afraid Tanya gave you incorrect information." Nidhi frowned, almost embarrassed. "Since you're a minor, I have to witness a signature in person from a legal adult in order to open this account. You'll have to have your aunt come in."

"She's rather busy. It's hard for her to get away from her work," I stammered, wishing Nidhi wasn't holding this conversation in front of Mr. Greer.

Nidhi sighed. "I'm sorry. Bank policy. I've been here twenty years, and I haven't seen a year yet where some kind of policy wasn't changed. This year it's signature authorizations. Lord knows what it'll be next year."

Just then a voice came from behind us. "I know the family. I'll sign if it's alright with the bank."

All three of us turned to see Cassie standing there, wearing running gear and sneakers. She shifted a gym bag higher up onto her right shoulder.

Before I could say anything, Nidhi broke into a smile, happy that she didn't have to deal with an awkward situation. "Oh, Cassie, that's great, then we can get this taken care of right away, if that's alright with you, Grace?"

She didn't wait for an answer, but I mumbled, "Sure," anyway. I also noticed that Holland Greer had disappeared.

Cassie and I finished our banking at about the same time. Once in the street, I thanked her.

"No problem, honey. Jack would have done the same for my children." She looked away, as though she were about to say something delicate or uncomfortable. My guess was right. "Look, Grace, Clay told me about your living situation."

I waited, wondering what she—as an adult—would announce she had to do with the knowledge.

"It's none of my business ... and I can't say I approve, but if ya' ever need anything, just let me know. I wouldn't want ya' to be scared out there alone. Now, come on, let me buy ya' a cup of coffee, hon, before I go home and shower." With that, she walked off in the direction of her café.

"Cassie, wait," I called after her. "I need to meet Holland Greer."

She halted and spun toward me. For a moment, I saw an odd look on her face. Then she dismissed Holland with a comment that made me wonder whether she was hoping or dreading her words would come true: "Don't worry. Keep coming to the café, and he'll show up." She turned and walked ahead, her body perfectly erect, determined, like a tall mast against the wind.

Chapter 10

Ten minutes later, Cassie and I tucked ourselves in at a window table to enjoy muffin tops while I relished the best Mocha Java I had ever tasted. Despite specializing in a wide array of coffees, Cassie instead drank from a cup of herbal green tea.

"This is delicious." I savored the coffee and hoped the compliment would serve as the requisite small talk to launch a cordial conversation.

She smiled, leaned in on an elbow, and reached up to wind a short lock of hair around her index finger. I couldn't help but be impressed with the muscle tone in her arm. "That was Jack's favorite."

I looked down at my coffee. Another tidbit about Jack that I never knew. Why did this woman's knowledge of intimate details about Jack bother me so much? "I miss him."

She reached across the table and squeezed my hand. "I'm sure you do. He was a good man, and he loved you like his own. He'd be pleased you seem to like that old place."

"I hope so. From his will, it sure seemed like he wanted me to be there." A shaky clatter as I settled my cup upon its saucer caused her to raise her gaze from my hands to my eyes. "Did he ever tell you much about the house?"

I watched for her reaction. Nothing. Unruffled, as if I had asked her the population of Williamsport.

"You know, about its history," I prompted.

"What d'ya mean?" She took a sip of her tea, her coral lipstick imprinting the cup.

"About William Kavanaugh."

"That guy who lived there during the War?"

"I already know that William Kavanaugh died in the house. We ... *I* found a sheet of paper, a list Jack compiled, noting important dates in William Kavanaugh's life. The last entry said Kavanaugh had died. I've been told there's activity in the house."

She exhaled and sat back in her chair. "I don't know 'bout nothing in particular that Jack experienced there. The only time I ever saw him was here at the café. There were always people around, so we never talked much about his house."

Something didn't mesh. Clay had mentioned doing things with Jack, but Jack could have picked him up at the café. Cassie had no reason to lie to me, unless there *was* something between the two of them.

"Then why were you so concerned when you learned that I was staying at *Crossings?*"

Her face paled, and she looked down at her tea, as though deciding what she could—or should—tell me.

"Cassie, please. I can take care of myself."

Her shoulders slumped. "Last time I saw Jack, he came to get a cup of coffee for the road, like he always did. It was pretty late." She pushed her silverware to the side and leaned forward over the table. "The place was filled with tourists. They were tellin' stories they'd heard the night before at one of them ghost tours in Gettysburg. Jack sure was interested. I had to leave to go into the back room to get more coffee filters, and it took me a while to find them. By the time I got back, the whole place was real quiet, 'cept for Jack. Everyone was staring at him with big ol' eyes and listening to every word he said."

Just like I'm listening to you now.

"Jack was sayin' that the stories of the ghosts were probably true. Then he went off talkin' 'bout how ghosts do exist and what you have to do to see 'em. Stuff like that."

"What did he say? Exactly?"

"He was real convincing. I'd never heard him talk like that. Like he knew firsthand all about ghosts. When a person dies, his physical body is all that stops. His ... what did he call it—" she tapped a few fingers on the table. "Subtle body ... yeah, that's it, the subtle body still exists and moves into another dimension or something before it moves on."

"You mean to heaven or hell?"

She nodded. "The subtle body includes everything except the physical body ... you know, like your subconscious, your soul ... oh, and your ego. Those can live on."

She took a sip of tea, and her hands gripped the cup tighter as she removed it from her lips. I could feel her anxiety, feel it searing into my gut and overpowering my greatest desire not to believe her. She seemed to be struggling to remain calm, and it unnerved me even more when she dropped her voice to little more than a whisper to continue.

"I remember someone in the group asked why only certain people become ghosts, and Jack had an answer for that too. I tell you, hon, he was like a walking encyclopedia. I'd never heard him talk like that before. I felt like I was listenin' to a stranger—"

"What was his answer?" Frustrated, I thumped my hands down on the table. The silverware rattled.

She leaned back, surprised. "Answer to what?"

"As to why only certain people become ghosts."

"Oh." She reached out and spun her knife clockwise on the table, watching it circulate. "People are likely to become ghosts if they had strong personality defects while they were alive, like anger or fear or greed. People are more likely to become ghosts if they lack a faith in God or a divine maker. Or if they have a high amount of ego."

"Ego?"

"Uh-huh." She nodded. "He explained that kind of person as someone who thinks he has an existence separate from God. That to protect ourselves, we must have faith. I remember that 'cause at the time, I felt better knowin' I was safe because of my faith." She looked back at her spinning knife. "My ego's certainly in check … thanks to Mason," she mumbled to her mug.

Cassie's digression tugged at my heart, but I would have to deal with that at another time. "Who else becomes a ghost?" I asked, concerned to think that William's soul was here due to a personality defect or defiance against God.

"Well, someone who does a lot of bad things, or someone who suffered a violent death. You know, like a murder. Also could be someone who feels they have unfinished business."

Bingo. That was what I was waiting for. That had to explain William Kavanaugh's ghost—someone who feels they have unfinished business. He had died so young; of course his was a simple case of not being able to fulfill his dreams.

Wasn't it?

"So, ghosts always haunt the place where they died."

"Not always." Cassie stopped twirling the knife. "Ghosts tend to center themselves where their last source of energy was, so it makes sense it would be the place where they died. But ghosts can move by puttin' themselves into objects and people. That way they can take their center with them. That's why I remember all this so well. The thing about inhabiting people creeped me out."

Another digression. I closed my eyes and rubbed my forehead. Was I in danger of William Kavanaugh taking over my body? Was that why he was so friendly to me? But then, if he wanted to, wouldn't he have just done it already? Why spend the time being cordial? Jack had been safe with William, so why wouldn't I be as well?

"So, ghosts can be dangerous?"

She nodded. I could barely hear her next words. "Some can be downright vicious."

"But if ghosts can be mean, then how do you protect yourself?" My mind raced through possible scenarios.

"That's what one of the women asked. The best way to protect yourself is to follow a regular spiritual practice and strengthen your faith in God. A couple people in the group laughed at that. You know how some people are, 'fraid to admit that there is something bigger than them in the universe. Those are the ones who think they evolved from monkeys, ya' know. I always tell them that their ancestors may have been monkeys, but mine sure weren't."

I wanted to snap my fingers and tell her to stay on track, but I moved on. "Cassie, did Jack say how to identify if a ghost is good or bad?"

"I can't remember nothin' about that, hon. I do remember him sayin' that in order to see a ghost—or a soul, that's the word Jack used—a soul. In order to see one, you had to believe in them. They're made up of some kind of air element—"

"The absolute air element," I finished for her. I had read the term in the library earlier that day.

"That's it. The ab-so-lute air element. You usually can't see them without subtle vision, and you only have subtle vision if a lot of things come together at the same time. You know, like if you have a strong faith ... or if you have a heightened sense of death. Or if the ghost trusts you and wants to communicate with you. Stuff like that."

I could feel the blood drain from my face. A heightened sense of death like you would have if you had lost your entire family.

"Hon, are you okay out there?" Her brow furrowed as she reached across and patted my shoulder.

"I'm fine." I pulled away and grabbed my backpack. I needed to get out of there to think.

"Wait." Cassie grabbed my hand again, this time to stop me. Her grip was firm, and I had no doubt she could sling the café's large burlap coffee bags over her shoulder. It struck me that her physical strength stood in such sharp contrast to the delicate, almost fragile person she had revealed in the past ten minutes.

Not wanting to divulge my desire to leave or the turmoil in my mind, I sat back down, but remained perched on the edge of the chair, holding my breath. I blinked twice, waiting as she formulated her next words.

"I need to tell you one more thing." Her eyes dropped to the table where she adjusted her cup, spoon, napkin, then joined her hands together in one large fist.

I raised my eyebrows as though to say, "Go ahead—I'm waiting."

"Remember that ghosts can haunt objects? And that some can be dangerous?"

I nodded.

Her voice dropped several decibels. "Well, the night Jack was here and telling all these big stories about ghosts and convincing me he had first-hand knowledge, I noticed he was wearing a gold coin on a chain. I'd never seen it before, and well, Jack wasn't the kind of guy to wear a necklace. I asked him about it, after everyone else left, and he laughed. Said he'd gotten it at the house. Said it probably belonged to the ghost that lived there."

"The ghost? Jack said that? The ghost?"

She nodded. "At the time, I thought he was joking, just making some silly reference to the conversation earlier. But later, after I heard he died, I counted back. Grace, he died a few days after he put on that coin. Do you know if he was wearing it when the car crashed?"

* * *

I'm not sure what I replied to Cassie, or how I got out of there without falling. My body reacted faster than my mind was able to grasp the implications that paranormal phenomenon may have been responsible for my family's death. I couldn't breathe, like I was being strangled. I think I thanked her and offered to see her again soon.

Once on the street, I gulped for air and found my car. I climbed into my seat, wrapped my hands around the steering wheel, and dropped my head. I was four again, lost in a crowd, separated from Mom and Julie. Somehow, I was shoved back out onto the sidewalk, and Mom found me there. She marched us to the car, fell in her seat and gripped the steering wheel. I remember saying, "It's okay, Mommy." She never looked up, rasping, "Don't you understand that you are the very air I breathe? Without that air, I would die too."

I looked now at my hands on the wheel and saw hers gripping it. I sensed my chest heaving for air, but heard her breath. I saw her tears and felt moisture on my cheeks. My mother was here, in me, and I felt her willing me to continue my probe into this dark unknown.

* * *

Two hours later when I met Adriana at the towpath, I lost patience with the leisurely way she unloaded her bike. I wanted to get moving, race the trail, and think through everything I'd learned that day.

Unfortunately, her mood involved a slow ride. A smell-the-roses-along-the-way kind of ride. Once we compromised on a pace, I marveled at my new friend. Despite her obvious displeasure with our speed, she didn't pepper me with questions or push for understanding. Maybe she figured I was out of sorts and wanted to give me space to think things through.

And think I did. I replayed Cassie's comments in my head, trying to make sense of everything.

Anxious to see William Kavanaugh again, I raced along the towpath as if hurrying through the day's activities would bring nighttime, and I could talk to him.

But what would I say? "Did you kill Jack?" didn't seem like a very good conversation starter for a discussion with a potentially violent ghost. Cassie's descriptions of Jack's words to the tourists convinced me that he also had encountered William.

On the other hand, I wanted to trust my earlier instincts. William Kavanaugh had saved me from two men who, for all I know, would have killed me. Why would he save me, just to then kill me?

We headed north, toward Four Locks, the next park area along the towpath. At this point, the arching trees shrouded the landscape to my right in shadow. To my left, the wooded terrain cut a sudden drop from the towpath to the river. Bikers would call this a "heads-up moment" which demanded focus, lest you accidentally ride off the trail. Gripping the handlebars tighter, I glanced back to signal Adriana that I wanted to turn around.

Instead, something caught my eye. About twenty-five yards away, at the bottom of a shadowed ravine off to my right, stood an image that had the same distorted coloring as that of William Kavanaugh from the night before. He just stood there watching us—or rather me, and despite his deteriorated state, we made eye contact. The intensity of his stare, and the way he turned to watch me as I rode by, told me he was just as surprised to see me watching him as I was at seeing him.

I didn't register Adriana's scream of alert until a heartbeat before I plunged off the path. When her warning reached my brain, I turned in time to feel my bike soaring left, off the trail and over the edge toward the river. Two seconds after I realized I was airborne, it was over. But in that blink between seconds, I saw a tree coming at me, heard a sickening crunch, and then felt the pain.

"Grace!" Adriana scrambled down the steep hillside. "Gawd, you scared me. Can you talk?"

"Yes," I groaned. I'd had the wind knocked out of me.

"Look at you, you're a mess." By now she was on her knees beside me. "Are you okay?"

No, I wasn't okay, but I couldn't talk about it either. Fortunately, a monstrous oak tree had stopped me from soaring down to the river, but had left me with a mangled bike, scattered cuts, a burning cheekbone, bruised ankle, and wounded ego.

"Is she hurt? Do you need help?" The voice came from behind us, up on the towpath.

"We have an audience." Adriana then raised her voice a few decibels to yell, "She seems to be okay, but I think we need help getting her back up to the trail."

I heard people shimmy down the hill, so I turned to look, hoping to thank them for their trouble. The words caught in my mouth; at the top of the hill, several yards from the bikers, the ghost stood staring at me. As I watched, he nodded an acknowledgement, turned, and disappeared.

I must have lost the coloring in my face because Adriana yelled, "Please hurry, I think she's in shock."

* * *

It was an hour before I made it to the emergency room. My rescue involved being carried back to the towpath where another biker had already called the ranger station on his cell phone; then a ride in the rangers' mini-truck back to Williamsport; and finally a ride in Adriana's car to a local medical center.

The afternoon crawled into evening as doctors and nurses poked and prodded me with various instruments, technicians positioned me around cold machines, and the pharmacist filled a prescription for painkillers. I was ordered to stay off my feet and elevate my ankle, but apparently they assumed I wouldn't listen because they arranged for me to take home a set of crutches. Other than that, I should expect pain for a few days, a black eye by tomorrow, and swelling by nightfall.

Adriana took to heart the doctor's warning that I shouldn't drive for a couple hours while under the influence of painkillers, so my pleas that she return me to my car fell on deaf ears. Instead, by 7 o'clock that evening, she had taken me to her house where her family welcomed me for dinner. Their home, a spacious two-story brick house, sat on the eastern side of Williamsport.

I felt comfortable with her entire family. Mr. Baronne, retired from the Army, was a tall man with a deep Sean Connery voice and physique, and the reason the family had moved so many times. Mrs. Barrone turned out to be a twenty-five-years-older version of Adriana—equally attractive, kind, and accepting of others. As a nurse, she insisted on checking my ankle to make sure her peers had doctored me well. Adriana's brother, Corey, showed more interest in his X-box than Adriana's friend, but I earned the 14-year-old's respect when I challenged him to a game of *Guitar Hero* and didn't lose by too wide a margin.

After dinner, Adriana drove me to my car and followed me home.

By 8:30, she finally saw *Crossings* in person. After helping me climb the outdoor steps—during which we determined the crutches to be too short—she tucked me on the couch, made me a cup of tea, and began to look around.

Surprisingly, she seemed more uncomfortable with the house's remoteness than with its physical makeup, and asked me about the distance to the nearest house (I didn't know) and how good a watchdog Tramp is (the jury was still out on that one).

"Lordy, Grace, don't you get lonely out here?" She glanced out the window at the view of Williamsport's distant lights.

No. My ghost is here to keep me company.

No, I didn't say it. Will had to remain a secret unless I wanted to be institutionalized. No one would believe I lived in my own Twilight Zone.

She walked into the bedroom and whistled, "Wow, this is bigger than my room." I heard her take a few more steps, "Nice bath too." She returned to the kitchen area, her eyes darting around the room as she sauntered toward the table. I thought she was looking through my sketches, so my mind wandered until her next words took me by surprise.

"You interested in Antietam?"

My head snapped up, and I followed her gaze down to an open book on the table. It took a moment to comprehend it as one of the books that I had brought back from the library. I had left them in my backpack. Now they both lay open, side by side.

She waited for a response, but if I told her that a ghost had opened the books, she might think I had suffered brain damage. "Yes, I figured while in Rome, do as the Romans do." I laughed, much too loudly. She probably thought the drugs were making me a bit loopy. In truth, a strange pleasure blossomed at the thought that William Kavanaugh had been in the room.

"Have you been there yet?"

I shook my head.

"Good, we'll go together sometime. It's a great place to ride. That is, when you can finally ride again."

We both looked down at my bandaged ankle.

"At least everything you need is on one floor. Tomorrow, after the picnic, we'll get some groceries. Looks like you have everything else you need for now." Her eyes scanned the room again then rested on the door adjoining the main house.

She got an excited look on her face. "May I see?"

I smiled and nodded, anticipating the reaction she'd have to the old place.

She unlocked the door and thrust it open with a dramatic push, as though she expected a great surprise, but I was the one who got the surprise. William Kavanaugh stood in the doorway, looking even more pronounced and defined than the night before. His clothing and his skin were more tolerable visually, but his overall coloring remained somewhat dull. His lips were more distinct, but still drained of color, and his cheeks remained hollow, without luster. His eyes still bore a shadowed vagueness, but eye contact improved nonetheless.

I caught my breath as I waited for Adriana to scream; instead, she shivered, crossed her arms, and stepped right through him. "Sheesh, it's cold in here, Grace."

I covered my mouth to stifle my surprise. William continued standing at that spot, looking at me.

Adriana said something about a flashlight. She turned and walked toward me, missing William by inches. I pointed to the side table. After retrieving it she walked through William again and returned to the main house. On her second pass through, I again caught my breath.

I didn't say a word, but I couldn't help grinning. To my delight, William returned a slight smile.

A few minutes later, Adriana was back. "What a creepy place." She grinned. "I think I saw the Addams Family in there." She closed the door and locked it. William moved through the door and remained in the apartment with us. As had become his routine, Chubbs hissed and dashed into the bedroom.

"What's his problem?" Adriana asked watching Chubbs disappear.

I tried to focus on Adriana, but I couldn't keep my eyes off of William.

"Grace! Those drugs must have made you tired. You haven't heard anything I've said." She pouted, putting her hands on her hips. "You're so pale you look like you've seen a ghost."

I choked on my tea. "Sorry. What did you say?"

"Never mind. All that matters is that I'm going to get you another pair of crutches and pick you up at 9 a.m. tomorrow for breakfast and church. Now get some rest."

With that she left, and I was alone again with the ghost of William Kavanaugh.

Chapter 11

Neither of us spoke, as if we both knew Adriana could return without warning. Besides, the words I'd test driven a gazillion times that day disappeared, and my heart pounded in my ears, so I needed time to collect my wits. I mean, who wouldn't be a little overwhelmed with a ghost standing in the doorway!

William Kavanaugh towered there, feet shoulder-width apart, lips clamped. But his gaze darted around the room, up, down, left, right, as though assessing the terrain, before settling on me.

Anyone else would have been terrified by his appearance because he looked like a man sliding into a grotesque state of decay. They wouldn't know the transformation progressed in reverse—a figure from the past evolving into a more palatable, more pleasing …

What?

Evolving into what? Where could this lead? He would never be human again. *He would always be dead.*

At the thought, my stomach somersaulted, and my skin tingled as though invisible fingers needled it. Feeling vulnerable, I sat up straighter, unsure how to proceed and wondering how to defend myself if it became necessary.

He smiled, and in it I discerned a compassion that I could feel but couldn't comprehend.

Could he understand my discomfort?

My defenses withered. I should have remained guarded, but when everyone you love the most is dead, you aren't as afraid of your own death. It's when you have something to lose that you fear the prospect of dying. Will represented the possibility of communicating with my family, and that thought made me disregard any threat he posed.

He raised an arm and gestured toward the door through which Adriana departed.

"Your friend?" he asked, his voice resonant, mesmerizing. I suspected the palliative sound of his voice had as much to do with *my* eagerness to understand as it did his efforts. If he continued to evolve, how would I ever take my eyes off him?

I nodded. "Adriana." My voice sounded weak, so I swallowed and tried again. "She helped me get settled." With a small flourish, I swept the blanket off my elevated foot.

His gaze dropped to my bandaged ankle, and he cocked his head, as though assessing the problem.

"You are hurt."

His empathy startled me, and his kindness crashed in my head with Clay's admonishment that I grow up.

"I wrecked my bike ... my bicycle ..." *Did people in the 1800s use the term 'bike'?* I should have paid better attention in my sophomore literature classes when we read *Tom Sawyer* and *Huck Finn*, both books written in William's century.

He nodded his understanding but kept his gaze on my foot.

I watched his face as I continued my thought about the accident, unsure of how he might react: "... after I saw a ghost at the canal."

At this, his gaze darted back to meet mine. His eyes remained unreadable, but I could tell he studied me.

"You see other souls too. You have achieved strong subtle vision."

"Mr. Kavanaugh—"

"Will," he offered, as easily as if we talked at a social gathering.

"Will, did you ... did you know the man ... the ghost ... that I saw?"

The edges of his lips rose, and I swear his appearance further defined. I could distinguish the high cheekbones and the dimples I'd seen in his picture.

"No, Grace ... "

My heart raced when he said my name. The familiarity and the thought of forging a bond with this spirit terrorized me. If I continued with our interactions, I might never be the same person again. I just hoped and prayed that the effects on me would be mild rather than any of many gruesome scenarios I could imagine.

"... I do not know if I ever met that soul or not. I may have, or he could be one of millions of people who walked that same spot over the centuries."

Idiot! I scolded myself. What was I thinking? That ghosts gathered at club meetings?

"Do not be embarrassed." He brushed a dismissive hand through the air. "I must acknowledge the corn. Conversing with souls is no doubt new to you. You must feel all-overish, whereas I have encountered this reaction before. With Jack, for example."

Frustrated, I shook my head. "I don't understand what you mean by 'acknowledge the corn' and 'all-overish.'"

He frowned, and his shoulders sagged. "I apologize. Jack and I experienced the same misunderstandings at first, although I quickly adapted to his language. After spending time alone, I have succumbed to old habits. Henceforth, I will try to use the vernacular that is familiar to you, although the modern idioms remain a challenge. 'Acknowledge the corn' means to recognize the obvious. 'All-overish' suggests discomfort."

To be polite, I should have denied feeling uncomfortable, but I presumed this ghost could detect a lie when he heard it. Besides, how could anyone participate in a conversation with a dead person and not feel a little discomfort?

"My friend ... she couldn't see you. Why?"

"I could reveal myself to her, but I do not think that wise. On her own, she could not see me in a sustained manner until she learns *how* to see."

"Like me?"

He nodded. "Like you. But, be cautious. Now that you know how to see souls, you might see them everywhere. They are not used to this. Most want to go about resolving their issues in peace. They pay little attention to whether they are revealing themselves because it is rare that a living being can see them. If they know you can, they might manifest in a host of forms. Some could prove quite frightening for you. They might be wrathy that—"

He hesitated when I pinched my eyebrows on "wrathy."

"—angry, annoyed ... that you might stand in their way. In most instances, that will not be a problem. But many souls remain behind because they chose evil over good. If that is the case, they often continue practicing evil after death because they have no hope of moving on to a better world. Instead, they are condemned to eternal evil. In those situations, you could be in great danger. You must be careful to see, but not acknowledge."

Will's explanation created a hundred more questions in my mind, and I felt like my brain might explode. His words of caution and encounters with other ghosts sparked a reminder of Cassie's comment about a link between Jack and ghosts and a gold coin.

"Will!" I grabbed the arm of the couch. I wanted to believe this ghost posed no threats, but what about other ghosts? "Is that how Jack died? Did he see another ghost? I mean, soul? A soul that may have hurt him?"

Will tilted his head to the side, making me think he wondered more about my question than its answer. "I do not know, and I *cannot* know what caused Jack's death until I have passed on." His voice remained calm, devoid of emotion.

With a sinking feeling, I interpreted his answer as a lengthy way of saying, "Maybe."

"What does that mean? Why haven't you passed on already? And where is Jack? Can he tell me the answers—"

Before I could continue my litany of questions, Will raised a hand and turned his palm turned toward me—the age-old equivalent of a nonverbal "stop."

"Not tonight. You are tired. And hurt. And I cannot stay long in this place." With that, he turned back toward the old house.

"Wait!" The word popped from my mouth in a near shriek, so loud that Tramp rolled up onto his side to see what happened. In a softer tone, I continued. "Don't go. Please, Will. I'm begging you."

He turned back toward me. Before he could counter my plea, I added, "I need to talk with you. I have so many questions."

"But I can't stay in here." He gestured, indicating the apartment.

"Then I will go in there." Undeterred, I climbed off the couch.

"You should not move."

I didn't realize my bandaged ankle would weaken my balance until I fell toward the coffee table. Before I could grab support, Will removed the span of three yards of physical space and two centuries of time between us, lifted me off the couch, and hoisted me into the air. I gasped, but he didn't hesitate. He turned and strode toward the old house.

I remained in his arms for the thirty seconds it took to unlock the door and carry me to a large settee on the opposite side of the old house. I felt the comfort of solidness and power surrounding me, but without the warmth of life circulating through a strong chest and shoulders that one would expect. Instead, it felt cold, lifeless, as though the strength of a monstrous air mass supplied the power, but without the tempest or the squall. If I hadn't seen his arms wrapped around me, I'd have sworn I floated on an invisible cold mass that conformed to the shape of my body. Despite being this close to him, I didn't look into his face. It still looked deteriorated when compared to a human being, and I feared I might react and embarrass us both.

As he placed me on the settee, I shivered. He returned to the apartment. I hoped he attributed the chill to the temperature of the room and not the coldness of his form. Either way, he did not say a word as he returned with my blanket and draped it over me.

Next, he turned to a large wood box beside the fireplace, lifted the lid and removed several logs and matches—no doubt complements of Jack. Within minutes, a small fire burned, casting shifting shadows and plays of light throughout the room. He studied the flame, before gathering more logs and feeding them to the fire. The dry wood crackled.

As I watched him, I tried to calm my racing heart. I didn't want him to detect my apprehension—the remoteness of the house, the darkness of the room, being so alone with him in his sanctuary.

Or was it his lair?

Suddenly, the shadows extended like spreading inkblots as though oozing toward me. The thought made me shake, and I pulled the feeble barrier of the blanket higher.

Just as quickly, my erratic thoughts jumped to Jack again, and I pictured him relaxing on this same settee, watching this same fireplace as he and Will talked into the night. An odd comfort washed over me, and I relaxed into the realization that there was no sound but the crackling of the fire, no sight but the shadows from the flames.

With no threat to identify, I calmed, lowered the blanket and resumed normal breathing. The irony of my misplaced fears unfurled in my stomach—the house was nothing but walls and floor and furnishings, whereas the real threat was the dead man standing in front of me.

He turned from the fire and brushed his hands on the front of his pants. Bending his form into an adjacent wingback chair, he parked his elbows on its arms. His humanlike movements startled me.

"Now, ask me your questions." His tone sounded casual, as if our exchange was ordinary which, for me, made it seem all the more surreal.

"Do you have to do that?" Even as the question came out of my mouth it sounded nonsensical.

He cocked his head. "Do what?"

"Sit." I raked my hand in his direction. "In a chair. I sit because I get tired of standing or because I want to do something while I'm stationary, like eating or drawing. But you ..." I didn't know how to finish my thought: *You're not even human!*

"That's not the question I expected, but I understand your curiosity." He spoke without inflection. "No, I do not need to sit. I have no physical body, so I require no sleep or rest. I feel neither tired nor refreshed. Ever. I experience no fatigue, no pain, no remorse, no longing to circumstances today. However, I am able to remember what symptoms and emotions felt like, so most of my reactions stem from conditioning."

I must have looked confused. He brought his hands together, steepled his fingers, and continued. "For example, I remember the emotion of love because I knew it while I lived, but I would not be able to experience it now if not for my memories. And I can laugh. I discovered that with Jack. Otherwise, I am empty." He looked away and into the fire as he talked. "As for your question, I sit because I am conditioned to do so from when I lived. I am equally comfortable standing, or floating for that matter. I imagine it is the conditioning that also allows me to see and hear since I no longer have those physical capabilities."

I nodded, trying to process this information.

Before I could speak, he continued. "I also have no sense of time or distance. When I lived, we would have described such a life as in a state of limbo. I don't know if that expression is used today, but it aptly describes my existence now."

His words tugged at my heart. "I'm sorry."

He looked back at me. "Do not be. Remember, I may not be able to feel these emotions any longer, but I also can't feel remorse, so I do not miss them. Your next question?"

I smiled, grateful that he made this easy for me. "Why can't you stay in the apartment? Is it because your source of energy is not there?"

He raised his eyebrows. "You have some understanding."

"A little." *No need to explain the second-hand information collected from Cassie.*

"I learned from my interactions with Jack that my ... presence ... is hard to explain." He continued to sound indifferent, almost detached, as though discussing humpbacked whales instead of the afterlife. "Per the laws of science, I should not exist. According to today's interpretations of faith, I am ... an impossibility. A miracle. Biblical scholars would differ on that. Most people have problems with miracles, so let me address science. When I manifest, I am a compilation of different elements sustained by an energetically charged environment. The realm in which I exist and yours may seem the same as we sit here together, but they are quite different. My realm vibrates at a higher frequency due to my lack of a physical body. You have a heavier density and a lower frequency of vibration. You could say that it binds you to the earth, or grounds you. This is why we cannot truly communicate. We are on two different—"

"But we *are* communicating," I said much sharper than I intended. "I can hear you and see you. I may not understand your explanation, but that's because I haven't studied physics."

The vestiges of a smile formed again. He returned one hand to the arm of his chair and patted it. I'd seen Jack do that same thing when he pondered how to explain something.

"Perhaps that will make a difference, but I do not think so. From what Jack and I discovered, the greatest physicists in the world still cannot explain paranormal activity. You think we are talking, but I'm not saying anything because I do not have vocal chords or the physical capability to use them anyway. Just as I manifest my physical body, I manifest my answers, and with your own subtle abilities, you hear them."

I listened to every word, my desire to understand, intense, but his explanations baffled me, and he must have seen it on my face.

"Let me simplify this," he concluded. "The words and the theories that explain my presence do not exist in your world. So, human science disregards it. Humans have not determined the explanations, and they never will. The simplest way to understand in your world is to know that in classical physics, one form of energy can be converted to another. I need energy to manifest. I get it from light, heat, electronic sources, lightening storms, batteries—"

"Camera flashes."

His hesitation made me realize I'd spoken out loud, but he continued "—yes, camera flashes too. I will drain you of energy at times. You do not tire in my presence now because you are thriving on adrenaline, due to the newness of my presence. That may change after you get used to me."

I couldn't imagine *ever* tiring of speaking with this phenomenon sitting with me, but then I remembered my exhaustion after my encounters with him in the past couple nights.

Will continued. "Another source of energy is this house. This is where I experienced my last earthly energy. When I go into the apartment that Jack added, my energy is weakened. It's also not good for you because you live there. My presence will make your living quarters colder. The air will become dense and charged with electromagnetic energy."

"That's why the hair on my arms stood up my first night here. And when I played the piano."

"I am sorry about that." He shifted his left foot to rest on his right knee. "Souls can be quite curious, like the living."

I ignored the apology and focused instead on making logical, human sense of the fact that he existed. "So, if you get energy from light, then why don't you manifest during the day?"

"I can, and do at times, just as you saw a soul at the canal. But, it's not what a soul prefers. The sounds of the daylight hours are filled with the sounds of the living, and that reminds us of loss. Most of your sounds are foreign to the world I lived in a hundred and fifty years ago. The cars, trucks, television, refrigerator, coffee-maker ... it was a much quieter world when I lived. Souls tend to favor the night, and by morning we have lost much of our energy and need to replenish throughout the day. By candle-lighting we—" he saw my scrunching eyebrows again "—by *dusk* we are able to manifest again."

With his reminder of day and night, I read my watch, barely legible in the shadows. One-thirty. Dawn would arrive all too soon.

"Will, there's so much I want to know, but so little time left tonight. Do you ... do you mind if I jump around in topic? And ..." I swallowed. "May we talk again like this? Tomorrow night, I mean?"

"I am not going anywhere. I have nothing but time to offer you."

"Why? Why are you not going anywhere? Jack and Mom and Julie must have gone somewhere. They're not here with me." I tried to sound impersonal and pragmatic, but a little bitterness trickled out with it.

My question hung in the air as Will stood and moved to the fireplace. He used the poker to stir the flames into action again.

"When a person dies, he, or she, goes into what I will call another dimension. There are no earthly words that I can use, so I will have to oversimplify this."

He looked back at me as he jabbed at the fire. *Perhaps he thought I would be insulted?*

"In the dimension, you learn where your soul will go for eternity. Depending upon how you lived, you may be relegated to a place that is filled with the results of the evil that you helped create, along with all the other evil that existed on earth ... but far more horrid."

"You mean ... like hell?" I asked with more alarm than I intended. "So we *do* have to answer for our deeds while on earth? We're punished for them?"

"Yes, and no. Souls must answer for their deeds, yes. What we sow, we reap. But we're not punished *for* our bad deeds as much as we're punished *by* them, unless we have aligned ourselves with God. Whatever evil you inflicted upon others while on earth will be delivered back to you thousand-fold. Now imagine *that* evil added to the accumulated evil of all the other souls, and you can comprehend the result."

As he continued, he returned to his chair and parked one foot on his other leg. "We all must answer for every thought and deed. But, there's also the other side. If you choose goodness, if you don't harm others, if you keep your ego under control, if you have a high spiritual faith with a reverence for God, then you are destined to move on to a utopian region."

"Heaven." A warmth flooded through me at the mere thought of such a destination.

"That is what the Bible calls it. Nirvana. Kingdom come. Moksha. Pick a name. I cannot explain much about this because that is what your journey on earth is all about—to seek answers, to discover the truth for yourself, to choose to believe."

"So heaven is real." I marveled, looking into the fire.

He recaptured my attention when he uncrossed his leg and leaned forward. "Of course it's real. Did you think that death is the ending of everything?"

I shrugged, as much to ease my discomfort as to avoid an answer. I don't believe he meant to insult. I suspected he did not realize the sad state of our modern-day moral code, and how people spent more time denying death than learning about it.

"Didn't the people in your time ever question the concept of life after death?"

"Some did, of course." He drifted his back into the chair again. "Some people seemed to believe that if they denied it, and removed every reference to it ... even convinced others to follow suit, that then it would go away. But it didn't go away for them, and it won't go away for anyone else. Death is not the end. I have seen it. Experienced it. Remember that Lazarus and Christ both rose from the dead. My presence alone should tell you that death is not the end. When death occurs, we are all equal except for the decisions that we made in our lives and the destination of our souls, based upon those decisions. Unfortunately, many of the people that I cared about made the wrong choices, and I will never see them again."

He spoke with such finality, it made me anxious, and I didn't know what to say. We lapsed into silence. Only the snapping of the fire broke the stillness.

Inexplicable feelings of sadness consumed me. I understood now where Jack, Mom, and Julie were—in heaven. They'd each harbored a strong faith and a strong moral code. They'd been rewarded, and here I sat. I didn't need Will to tell me where they were, but he did anyway, as if he read my mind.

"When your family died, they entered that dimension of which I spoke. They suffered no unfinished business. No hatred. No anger. Just strong faith. They were ready to move on. They are now living their reward."

His words conjured up visions of my family together, without me. Happy. Carefree. Not even missing me the way I longed for them. Anger festered. I wanted to argue that it wasn't fair. That they might be happy, but I wasn't. That I was distraught and lonely. That there should be a statute of limitations on mourning that made all hurt end after six months. That there should be a magic switch one could flip whereby you no longer cried when you looked at your mother's picture or smelled your stepfather's aftershave on a stranger.

I wanted to scream those things, but all that came out was a weak: "What about me? I am their unfinished business. I was a child when they left me behind."

Will shook his head. "They had no choice. They could do nothing for you."

"So God took them on a whim? You're saying it's His fault?"

"Fault or blessing?" Will countered. "It all depends upon how you look at it. You can look at that as your loss, or their gain."

His words stung. Again, the old adage about two ways of looking at the same thing.

"But they left me," I murmured in a tone that I admit sounded more like a sulking child than someone in mourning.

"Grace, when one enters the dimension beyond death, one achieves a certain amount of clarity. You learn who has passed on, and with certain limitations, you can see who still walks the earth. Your family saw you. Still alive. Still chosen to continue on. They understood, far better than you do, that your work here among the living is not yet done. They could do nothing by returning, nothing but cause you harm. Your awareness of their presence as souls would have stifled your growth. They needed to move on so that you could fulfill your role here on earth."

"But what about *you*? I'm experiencing *you*, and that's not hurting me."

His gaze jerked to the fire again. *Was he avoiding eye contact?* My heart lurched, wondering if it was foolhardy to trust him. After two more disconcerting heartbeats, he responded.

"Time will tell. Life is composed of risks."

His response ... so cold, so devoid of empathy. I felt numb and confused as several emotions collided together. I was grateful for his explanations, leery of his intent, and angry that he knew details about my family that I didn't.

"I don't believe a word of that." Shaking, I climbed up off the sofa. Sprained ankle or not, I couldn't hurl my anger and accusations while reclining. I needed the strength and power of standing over him. "What's your story anyway, Will? What was so bad about your life that you've stayed here? It's been a hundred and fifty years! A lot of people died in the war and accepted it. What's *your* problem?"

He stood, hands fisted at his side, and his glare was strong and dogged, like a finger jab. "My best friend murdered me in cold blood. Right there." He pointed to the archway that led into the foyer.

He spoke with such directness, such cold candor, I gasped.

"Oh, my God!" I muttered before grasping my arms in a shudder. "Will, I—"

"And," he continued stepping toward me, "I don't know what happened to the woman I loved. I believe she is on this earth somewhere, searching for me, as I am for her. I think she knows something about my death. I need your help in finding them both before I can move on."

What he described, how he died, what he expected of me—it snaked through my mind, bleak and vicious, and poisoned my mettle. I felt myself dropping, and then everything went black.

Chapter 12

The night crawled as I suffered through fitful spurts of sleep. In a drowsy stupor, I tossed and turned, wondering if a room could be *too* quiet for adequate slumber. Tramp wasn't even snoring.

That's probably why I sensed my visitor before I saw him. I lifted my head and watched through groggy eyes as William Kavanaugh emerged from the corner by the bathroom.

Will.

Yet, he looked different. Shorter. Stockier. The hair, longer. The eyes, more penetrating. Tattered buckskins replaced his uniform, and a sword peered from behind his right shoulder, held in place by a strap that crossed his chest. Rage flared in his eyes, and the knife he held—

Knife?

I gasped and sat up.

He was gone.

I shook my head to restore logic and propped my back on the headboard of the bed. Will must have carried me here after I blacked out by the fire. And then ... *What?* Returned? For what reason? He said souls could manifest themselves in a host of different ways.

But why would *he* do that?

"Will?"

I waited.

When no response came, I decided it had been a dream and snuggled closer to Tramp, sleep still beckoning me.

I'm not sure why it didn't register with me at the time that Chubbs had dashed from the room.

* * *

The creaking of the exterior door woke me Sunday morning. I staggered to the bedroom entry in time to see Tramp traipsing from the porch into the kitchen. Behind him, the door closed and locked on its own.

A week ago, that scene would have sent chills down my spine. Today, I shook my head and murmured, "Thank you, Will. And thanks for carrying me to bed last night."

A cool breeze caressed my cheek. Then, nothing.

It would take time to get used to living with a ghost, particularly one that both perturbed and scared me. He did nothing wrong, yet our conversation from the night before made me angry, about death, and my parents, and having been left alone. May as well be annoyed with Will as anyone. After all, what could he do? *He was dead.*

Then again, what couldn't he do? I'd seen him pass through walls and hurl a man three times my weight over a balcony. His abilities unnerved me. And, how could I know his whereabouts at any given time? Had he listened to my conversations with Clay? Watched me sketch floor plans? Seen me getting dressed? I'd have to talk to him about boundaries.

"Umm, okay, Will, I'm going to take a shower now ... and ... no offense, but that's something I want to do alone."

No response.

Ugh. If anyone overheard me, they would think I'd lost my mind.

Before I could waste any more brain cells on that thought, my cell phone rang. I wasn't surprised to hear Adriana's voice, calling to make sure I would be ready at nine. She also asked if I found the crutches.

"Crutches?" I looked around. Sure enough, a new set leaned against the couch. She'd said she would bring them over, but I thought she meant this morning. I'd been distracted by Will and never locked the door. Then I collapsed by the fire long after 2 a.m. She must have returned while I talked with him, and assuming I was in bed, had let herself in. But once inside, she couldn't have missed the flickering flames through the open door to the old house.

I sagged against the wall to steady myself.

"Grace, are you there?"

"I ... yes, I see the crutches. I must have been asleep when you came by." My nerves tensed. "When did you drop them off?"

"Oh, I didn't. Clay did. See you at nine."

* * *

Two hours later, stuffed with eggs and bacon from a diner south of Marlowe, Adriana and I arrived at the church. A lovely old brick building, it sat on several shaded acres on the outskirts of Williamsport. Behind the pulpit hung a stunning copper cross; otherwise, it reminded me of the church that Mom, Jack, Julie and I attended back in Massachusetts with its standard issue white walls and wood pews. For a moment, I felt it, an invisible gravity, the tug of the family togetherness we'd shared in that church.

Then, as quickly, I remembered that on my last visit, I was required to move from my usual pew to a seat front and center, beside my family's caskets, piled high with flowers.

As my mind returned to the moment, Adriana's parents greeted me with hugs. When we sat, Mr. Barrone took my crutches and placed them under the long pew in front of us. Mrs. Barrone leaned across her husband and inquired, "Do they work better for you?"

I nodded. "Thank you for loaning them to me."

She looked surprised. "They're not mine, they—"

Before she could finish, organ music sounded from the huge pipes in the balcony, and the service began.

A few minutes into the service, a young couple walked down a distant aisle on the opposite side. I was admiring the morning sunshine gild the huge stained glass windows on that side of the church, so the couple caught my eye. To my surprise, they scooted in beside Cassie.

"They're always late," Adriana whispered. "But it gives me a chance to tease Clay."

Clay? I looked back in time to see the man's face before he dropped onto the pew. Sure enough, if you added a scruffy beard, layer of dirt, and cheap bandana to this clean-cut, well-shaven, short-haired guy, it could be Clay. The transformation amazed me. Military short hair. Flawless-cut navy suit. I found it hard to look away, and I noticed a few other women suffered the same dilemma. To his credit, he looked oblivious to the attention he garnered.

If he were a Ken doll, the woman beside him would definitely be a curvy, but petite, Barbie. Her tawny hair, cut in more layers than I'd seen since old reruns of *Charlie's Angels*, cascaded over her shoulders, casting shadows and depth that made you keep staring to figure out where it all came from. Her tanned face looked flawless.

Annoyed, I couldn't help but compare myself to her. Much her opposite, I was tall and fair-skinned, with a nondescript hairstyle in too many colors to define. At least I'd taken the time to don a dress and twist my hair into a couple clever French braids that morning. I also wore more make-up than I'd used all year, although I'd done so to hide my black eye. Adriana declared me as looking "adorable" when she picked me up. I wondered what Clay thought about his fiancé's look; I doubted that "adorable" ever came to mind, but I bet "smoking hot" surfaced a lot.

Exasperated, I turned away. Now I'd have to be polite and thank him in person for bringing over the crutches. I never did learn from Adriana why Clay delivered them. When I tried to broach the topic after our first sips of coffee that morning, she'd launched into discussion of other bike trails in the area.

The service underway, I focused on "Pastor Dale," a large man in both size and attitude. Lively and animated, he eschewed the custom of delivering a one-sided interpretation to make his points. Instead, he moved around the pulpit, asked questions of audience members, addressed them by name, and delivered a message that contained as much "interaction" as sermon.

Pastor Dale said that many people live their lives with a gnawing sense that something is missing. We too often rely only on ourselves and a logical plan to get what we want. Then we fail and don't understand why. We need to look deeper because a spiritual reality governs the universe that is as real as the physical laws we all accept and live by, like gravity. We are precarious and limited on our own, so we have to get what we need and want from outside ourselves. The more we trust and place faith in the source that provides what we need, the more we will receive it. That source is God. Going to him takes you beyond your own logical plan, providing a spiritual reality that transcends the everyday lives of people. He finished by quoting Ralph Waldo Emerson: "All I have seen teaches me to trust the Creator for all I have not seen."

A 45-minute Bible study period followed the church service, and Adriana and I joined one of two young adult groups. I relaxed when I saw Clay and his fiancé head toward the other session.

Our leader challenged us to gauge the level of our belief, but I didn't hear much. I was too busy poking around deep inside my own head. After my family's funerals, God felt as dead to me as they were. I wondered now if there is more to life than the physical world we see in front of us. Do the visible things we see and attain begin in an invisible, spiritual world, as he suggested? Could he be right that life expands with trust? And, is Will a part of that invisible world that I happened to have been granted some mysterious pass to see into?

But then, what if Will lied? What if there's nothing but a large, empty, black vacuum after death, and only a few, like him, squeak through? He wanted my help, but it sounded frightening and dangerous. What did he expect me to do—creep through haunted buildings in the black night to track down Naomi, or whomever he meant by, 'the woman I loved'? And what would I do if I encountered evil souls?

"Grace?"

I looked around. Everyone was leaving.

Adriana stood beside me, grinning. "Did you hear any of that?"

"Sorry. I guess my mind wandered."

"Wait here." She retrieved my crutches and parked them at my side. "I'll go find my parents before we head downstairs for the picnic."

I nodded, pleased with her suggestion. I was content to sit, drawn to something here I couldn't name, the sense of hope, or perhaps the mystery that the place evoked.

* * *

Within minutes, Pastor Dale walked into the room, eyed my crutches and plunked down beside me as if taking pity on me as I sat alone. He'd removed his suit jacket and rolled his sleeves into slipshod cuffs at his elbows. His jovial manner put me at ease. So much so, that when he joked about my "pensive" look during the service, I decided to be frank with him. Assuming him to be a man in touch with God, I asked if he believed in things that were inexplicable, given his belief in an invisible realm.

He smiled, looking delighted with the topic. The faint netting of lines around his mouth suggested years of joy and laughter. "I believe in miracles. That means I believe that almost anything is possible. We don't give miracles enough credit these days."

Will's use of the word "miracle" flitted through my mind. "But ... what about ghosts? Do you believe in them?"

"Certainly ..." he leaned forward and parked his elbows on his knees. "The Holy Ghost."

Huh? That wasn't what I meant at all.

"I mean spirits. You know ... like the souls of dead people."

"Ahhh." He scratched a line between his eyebrows. "Tough question. Ask ten different religious leaders, and you'll get ten different answers."

"What about you?"

"Me? Believe in ghosts?" He leaned back in the protesting chair, crossed his beefy arms, and looked toward the ceiling as though he were pondering my question. "Yes ... yes, I do. I believe spirit beings exist, such as angels and demons. But I don't believe that the spirits of people who have died remain here."

"Angels and demons? Like good and evil spirits?"

"Precisely. Angels were created by God to be faithful servants. Demons, however, are evil spirit beings who were once angels but fell from righteousness when they became Satan's accomplices. If you saw ... something, Grace, my guess is that you saw either an angel or a demon, despite the form it took."

"You make it sound ... sinister ... or dangerous."

"I suppose it could be quite dangerous if you tangle with the wrong one."

"But it's easy to tell which is which, right?" I asked, imagining the stereotype of angels with halos and demons with pitchforks.

As though he read my mind, he laughed. "Well, I doubt they'd come sporting fluffy white wings and red jagged tails if that's what you mean. There are thousands of stories of people who have been helped by angels. In each, angels took on the form of humans, but were never seen or heard from again. As if they never even existed. It only stands to reason, then, that demons can masquerade themselves as well."

My heart lurched as his comment seared through me. "So how can you tell the difference if both can take on any form they want?"

"Good question. They'd certainly be more convincing than the best actors you see on TV." He leaned forward again and raised a hand in my direction. "Your best defense? Have faith and be on guard. The Bible says the ruler of the dark spiritual world is the author of lies. It warns of the danger of seductive spirits—"

"Seductive?"

He nodded. "Charming, friendly ... the kind that make you trust them. All part of the spiritual war. They come to deceive people and draw them away from God and into their evil pursuits, through bondage."

Spiritual war? Bondage? No matter how you interpreted his words, it didn't sound like a good thing.

After that, Pastor Dale said something about happiness and our thinking becoming our reality, but I heard little of it.

* * *

When the Barrones and I entered the basement, we ran into Cassie, Clay's fiancé

Sondra, and a few people I'd never met. From the tone of the greetings, I surmised that the Baxters and the Barrones knew one another well. Cassie introduced me to her daughter, Reaghan, her son-in-law, Sidney Paness, and her identical three-year-old twin grandsons, Elias and Ethan, who scurried away after saying hello. Then, while Reaghan and Sidney exchanged greetings with Mr. and Mrs. Barrone, Cassie asked if I'd met Sondra.

I turned to look at Clay's fiancé, my first time to see her up close. Even under the unforgiving florescent lights of a sterile church basement, she looked beautiful. I offered the requisite "hello" and "best wishes" on her impending nuptials.

She returned a stiff "hello," and mumbled "thank you," then dismissed further conversation by looking away. For the first time, I noticed she exhibited a starched stiffness to the world. Or, perhaps, just to me.

As the group launched into small talk, Clay appeared through a side door. I braced myself for the requisite cordial greeting, but he merely nodded a polite hello then focused on Adriana. Draping his arm over her shoulders in a familiar manner, he taunted, "So, Ade, I scanned the feast, and I did not see your famous chocolate cake."

Without hesitation, Adriana grinned and patted his stomach. "I brought you some low-fat gelatin."

As the others carried on their varied conversations, Clay and Adriana continued to exchange jibes, oblivious to the fact that two sets of eyes were staring at them. The first set belonged to me. Their comfort and camaraderie startled me. The other set belonged to Sondra who turned from her conversation with Sidney to focus on Adriana with an intense, hawk-like stare.

"So, I see Clay's crutches work well for you."

By some sort of telepathy, everyone's different conversations ended at the same time that Cassie asked her question, as if someone lifted a needle from a record. All eyes turned to stare at me, awaiting my response.

Clay's crutches? I hadn't yet adjusted to the fact that he delivered them in the middle of the night as I conversed with a ghost; now I learned the crutches belonged to him.

I turned to Clay to thank him for the loan, but the words lodged in my throat. On his face I read anger, targeted directly at me—his eyes cold, his lips pursed. I wondered if he'd drawn a conclusion from last night that left a bad impression. I could only imagine what he must have concluded.

But what did I care? He meant nothing to me. Besides, he had entered my house without announcing himself. In that smoldering moment as we faced each other, I decided the best defense is always a good offense. "Yes, Clay, thank you so much for bringing them by last night. Once again, you do too much for me."

I could feel every set of eyes dart from me to Sondra; that is everyone's but Clay's. He kept his gaze on me and, for a nanosecond, the corners of his lips rose. *Was it possible he fought a grin?*

Just then, someone yelled that they needed help with picnic tables, and Sidney and Clay looked relieved to excuse themselves to help.

When Adriana and I were alone again, she laughed. "That was awkward. Did you see Sondra look at you? I didn't know that you and Clay knew one another so well."

I shrugged. "We don't. I'm not sure what possessed me to say that."

"Well, it was priceless."

"What about you?" I tossed her a scolding look. "You never told me you two were such good friends."

"Clay and me? We've known each other since junior high. Skipped ninth grade together, so that began our bond. We graduated together ... Sondra too, although I don't know her well. So yeah, Clay and I go back several years."

"Do you go back far enough to tell me how he got that limp and why he doesn't do anything about it?" I asked with a smirk.

In a split second, Adriana's tone changed from jovial to dead-cold sober. "Grace, you don't know?"

I leaned back, startled. "Know what?"

"Clay lost his leg below the knee when he tackled another man to save him from a bomb in Afghanistan. He limps because he's still learning how to work his prosthesis."

So much for sweeping judgments. If a vast fissure opened up in the floor at that second, I would have very happily thrown myself in it. I struggled for words as shame pulsed through me. What do you say when you've made a complete fool of yourself?

"Ugh, I'm so embarrassed," I whispered. "I didn't know. When I met him he seemed like such a redneck. And so rude. And nosy. Cassie sent him over and ..." I looked around. Too many people milled about who might overhear. "Never mind. I'll explain later." I sighed as I realized I'd have to tell her the full details of my unusual encounters with Clay.

She nodded, a smile of anticipation crossing her face. "This oughtta be good." She dropped her voice to a whisper. "Clay loves small-town life and camping, but he's no hillbilly if that's what you're thinking." She tilted her head and shrugged. "Well, okay, he can be quite the video-game nerd, and he's a little too obsessed with *Angry Birds* if you ask me, but otherwise he's a well-rounded guy ... and a bona fide hero. He plays a mean sax and reads the classics. Loves theatre. Oh, he's gone with me to the symphony, and—"

"Okay, okay," I sighed, putting a hand up for her to stop. "I get the point. I'm embarrassed enough already. I shouldn't have jumped to conclusions, but you have to understand my first impression of this guy. He looked like he'd just stepped out of a laundry basket. And painting's not exactly a job with a lot of upward mobility."

She laughed so hard she put a hand over her mouth to stifle the noise. Resting her arm on my shoulder blades, she proceeded to steer me through the basement, choosing a path wide enough to accommodate my crutches. "Would you say that law is a profession with a lot of upward mobility?"

"Of course. Why?"

"Because Clay starts law school at Georgetown University this fall. He completed most of his undergraduate degree before going to Afghanistan. Through ROTC. That's how he paid for his education. After getting hurt, he finished classes online while going through rehab at Walter Reed Medical Center. He finished in record time. Said there wasn't anything else to occupy his mind."

My shoulders slumped in defeat. I wondered if there was a dunce cap anywhere in these church classrooms that I could wear the rest of the day.

* * *

I followed Adriana through the crowd of at least two hundred people, all different ages, races, modes of dress. All of them seemed to be having fun, digging into a Comstock Lode of potluck choices—from fried chicken to taco salad to crumb-top apple pie, set out on end-to-end tables at least thirty feet long. I made small talk, calling upon any topic that kept the focus off of me and my ankle— the weather, the feast before us, the unlikelihood that either the Boston Red Sox or the Baltimore Orioles would play in the World Series this year.

When we reached the beverage table, Adriana entered into a conversation with a prim-looking woman named Latisha Gilgood who attempted to talk her into teaching one of the kindergarten Sunday school classes. I found myself eyeing the two-handed task of pouring a beverage with only one free hand, then moving everything to a table with the limitation of crutches.

"I'll hold your plate if you'll pour the drinks," a voice said from my right. "Then I'll help you to a table."

I turned to see a young man, about my height and age, who had the build of a natural athlete: no neck, wide shoulders, stalky legs and a pleasing face, topped with sandy hair.

"Thanks." I handed my plate over to him. "Punch or soda pop?"

"Punch. You look better than the last time I saw you."

Having poured both cups, I turned back to him. He knew me? Confusion must have shown on my face because he continued.

"I'm a park ranger assistant. I helped carry you back to the towpath after you crashed."

"Oh. Thanks. Not my proudest moment."

"Hey, I've wiped out lots of times. So have other people. Never in such a dangerous spot though. Most people crash near the locks. They're more focused on them than the path ahead."

"I guess you see it all since you work there."

He shrugged. "It's a job. Dad says it builds character. It's usually pretty boring, but you made it interesting yesterday."

"I'm glad I could amuse you."

"My name is Seth Rendale. Mind if I join you?" His gaze drifted around the room. "I don't see my parents anywhere. I don't come with them. I'm just here for the free food."

Once outside, we joined the Barrones at a large picnic table, but Seth paid no attention to who sat around him. With the self-importance of a teen who thinks there is nothing new to learn in the world, he proceeded to dominate the conversation for the next half hour, talking about himself. He was 17, a senior at Williamsport High, served as quarterback for his football team, and planned to study sports management in college, although he expected to coach a professional team before he was thirty. He even mentioned being adopted and said that with four older sisters, he always got his way as a child.

"Therefore," he proclaimed with the delivery of a young boy trying to act like a confidant man, "I won't take no for an answer—let's get together and do something sometime."

His words, his delivery, his sureness—all sounded so presumptuous and immature, but when I looked up to kindly tell him, "Thanks, but no, thanks,"

I saw Clay pass by a few tables away. I don't know why, but "I'd like that very much" came out of my mouth instead.

My phone number secured, Seth left to work an afternoon shift on the towpath.

I could feel Adriana's negative reaction before I saw it. Her back stiffened, and her eyebrows arched high in a look that nonverbally screamed, "Are you crazy?"

* * *

Morning turned to afternoon as the adults socialized and the kids participated in games on the lawn.

With cleanup finished, Adriana excused herself to find Latisha Gilgood. I parked in a folding chair under a huge oak tree to watch the activity on the lawn, elevated my ankle, and talked with Sidney, then Reaghan as they switched off helping their boys participate in games. Clay helped with the games too; his leg didn't seem to slow him down at all. I assumed Sondra watched him from the crowd.

Relieved from game duty, Reaghan plopped in the chair beside me, fanned herself with a coloring book from her sons' backpack, and propped her feet on a second chair. With her free hand, she massaged her pregnancy bulge.

I learned that she practiced as a certified public accountant from her home, that she was six months pregnant with their third child, and that after the child arrived, she planned to have her tubes tied "in a double-looped Boy Scout knot."

Her smile faded. "Grace, I was sorry to hear about Jack and your family. Mom and Clay were very close to Jack. I was already a teenager when he started coming around. When he announced his marriage to your mom, I was eighteen and heading to college, so it didn't faze me much. But it bothered Clay. He's been hurt a lot ..." She looked away from me to where Clay crouched on the ground, at least three children on top of him. "First with our father, then Jack, then his leg. I don't want him to be hurt anymore, Grace."

"Well, he looks happy with Sondra. I'm sure that will work out."

"Yes it will, as long as nobody gets in the way."

Ouch—that stung in a spot I didn't know existed.

"If they're meant for one another, I'm sure nobody will get in their way."

"Spoken by someone very young. Look, Grace, you seem like a lovely young woman, but Clay doesn't need any distractions right now. He needs to stay on course."

"What makes you think he'd go off course?"

She sighed and frowned, as though frustrated with my naiveté, but then offered a smile so sweet that her intent continued to remain murky.

Boy, she was good.

"Grace, Clay's life has been one of upheaval. He needs to settle down. Right here. Near the Shenandoah where he can hunt and fish and camp and do all those things he likes to do so well. It's close enough to the District that he'll be able to pick up some lucrative work as an attorney and make a great life for himself and his family. Sondra is perfect for him because she's close to his age. And, she's from the area, so she'll be content to make a home here." She looked away and, in that same casual tone, added: "She doesn't have a questionable background, and she's not running from anything either."

"Do you think I am interested in Clay? Nothing could be further from the truth. What you don't know is that he and I can barely talk. We seem to be at odds with one another every time we meet."

"Oh, I know that. That's exactly what bothers me."

I must have looked baffled because she continued.

"I was at the café twice after Clay returned from your place, and I saw his annoyance. Heard him complain about you. That's when I decided you were trouble ... no offense."

No offense? Was she kidding? "I don't understand."

She sighed in frustration and fanned herself faster. "When Sidney and I met, we took an instant dislike to one another, but our lives kept being thrown together. It was aggravating because we are complete opposites. But, as they say, opposites attract. One day we ..." her voice trailed off as though reliving a fond memory, "... well, let's just say we finally realized those feelings between us were actually attraction. It's still that way. I can be demanding and headstrong, and Sidney lets me go as far as he can tolerate, then he'll step in and rein me back on track. He's actually the rock-solid one of the two of us. He just hides it well."

What do you say when someone turns the tables on you? In no time at all, she'd gone from bossy buttinsky tossing innuendos, to seasoned sage sharing discrete insights into her personal situation.

"I've seen and heard Clay after spending time with you. Your encounters may have been brief, but he showed a lot of intensity. Being that annoyed with someone takes a lot of passion. So, either he truly thinks you are a royal pain in the—" she cut off, looking around as though remembering where she was, "—butt, or he is attracted to you and doesn't even know it yet. If he were truly indifferent toward you, why would he care what you do?"

"Clay is only concerned about me because I'm Jack's child. I'm too young for him anyway."

She eyed me before saying, "That's true."

She didn't volunteer that she was at least six or seven years younger than Sidney.

"Besides, I'm more interested in Seth."

What? Where did that come from? I was no more interested in Seth than any of the dozens of people I met that day.

"Really," she said, more declaration than question.

The awkward conversation ended when Elias and Ethan arrived to fight for their mother's lap.

As I looked away from Reaghan, I spotted three gauzy figures moving through the crowd, about a dozen yards away. Despite the bright sun that hit my eyes, they caught my attention because their body outlines suggested they were weary. Two were dressed as soldiers carrying old-fashioned muskets. The third trudged several yards away from the other two and moved in a different direction. His features were equally blurred, but reminded me of pictures I'd seen of aristocrats from the late 1700s. Despite my eyes adjusting to the sunlight, I noted all three figures remained distorted.

I gripped the chair's arms. They weren't just euphemistically "passing through the crowd." They were passing right *through* the bodies of the people in their paths.

Ghosts—each with a life, a death, a story to tell. Suddenly Clay and Reaghan were inconsequential. I forced myself to look away—Will said I should see, but not acknowledge. I slumped in my chair. This might be my destiny—to witness searching souls around every corner.

Or, as the pastor suggested, were they demons and angels in disguise?

Stifling a groan, I tipped my head back and looked skyward, wishing I were home. I'd rather spend time with death than with anyone at this picnic.

Chapter 13

I once read Robert Frost's metaphoric-laced poem about two paths diverging in the woods and his decision to take the one less traveled. Like him, I found myself at a crossroads and had to make a choice. One path involved leaving *Crossings* on a one-way ticket back to Boston. The other path, more obscure, led to independence. Though enticing, it involved many unknowns: Will, unresolved questions, maybe danger. When you dabble in death, how safe can you be? Whether angel or demon or just plain ol' ghost, Will dwelled in my house, and I needed to address that reality if I stayed.

I couldn't fathom a return to Boston, so my only option was to stay at *Crossings* and submerge myself into the life of a dead man. Finding the ghost of the woman he loved. Finding the friend who murdered him. Finding secrets that might best be left undisturbed.

The thing is, I couldn't help but wonder if all this *finding* would demand some *losing.*

* * *

By Wednesday after the picnic, I ditched the crutches and ventured to a shopping center, buying items that aided my seclusion at *Crossings*. Upon my return, I crested a ridge several miles from home and saw a distorted-looking pioneer trudge from a weathered barn toward a field of round hay bales. I tensed, wondering if I could get used to ghosts forever being a part of the backdrop of my life. And what about Pastor Dale's comments? Whether angel or demon, this ghost's intent didn't appear to involve me. So what was the point? None of this made sense. *Would I ever understand?*

I arrived home with a bundle of items: groceries, petunias, and two skirts and a dress from a closeout sale. I'm not sure what prompted the interest in girlish fashion, but my shorts and jeans didn't feel right anymore.

Also among my purchases were several items from a DIY store to make both porches more pleasurable, including throw rugs, decorative pots, wind chimes, and a wooden rocking chair. Earlier in the week, Will had said his energy was as strong on the house's porch as it was inside, so we moved the glider from the apartment porch. Despite the damage, it still rocked, but dropped lower and clicked rhythmically like the rocking chair. I assumed it would remain broken, judging by the cold greeting Clay and I had exchanged at the church. I'd be lying if I said it didn't bother me. However, with Clay I struggled to provide answers, whereas with Will, I got to ask the questions.

As the days passed, I grew more comfortable with Will, and he let me lead our discussions as we talked into the early hours of the morning—me curled on the glider, and him on the rocking chair. Despite Pastor Dale's warning about threats that charmed, I allowed Will's charisma and my curiosity to muffle concerns about demonic intentions.

Will regaled me with stories. One amusing tale involved squatters in 1907 who tried to move in. Will slammed doors and crashed china on the floor to scare them away.

I laughed. "But why? Why were you so determined to get rid of them? They might have helped you too, just as Jack eventually did."

Will shook his head. "They were not family. And, they tried to change the house. I couldn't risk allowing them to alter my source of energy."

With that, I decided to delay my decision to install Internet. I didn't mind; Will fascinated me more than the web anyway.

Throughout the 1900s, all sorts of people would venture close to *Crossings*, some just curious, others intent on mischief. As a result, Will grew more aggressive in keeping trespassers at bay, limiting their explorations to the grounds and the area near the root cellar, which he described as "beyond the hill behind the house." He never again allowed anyone to enter *Crossings*.

Until Jack showed up.

Will had identified him as family, thanks to conversations he overheard when Jack talked on his cell phone. In the same slow manner Will used with me, he revealed himself to Jack.

"When you arrived, I assumed that a young girl alone had to be Jack's daughter. Once you moved in, I couldn't prohibit anyone from visiting lest it scare you away before I could determine whether or not you'd developed subtle vision. I hope you weren't startled at the piano."

I shrugged, not wanting to admit to the mixed feelings I'd experienced.

"But I must admit, when that man Clay showed up, I wasn't sure whether I should intervene on your behalf or his."

"You saw that?" Warmth coursed over me.

"I'd have tossed the miscreant if necessary. But I was relieved I did not have to, because I did not want to frighten you."

I kept a straight face, hoping to show no reaction.

Will's voice grew serious. "But when those two buffoons arrived and threatened you, I had no choice. They would have ruined everything."

Startled, I considered this a moment. "Ruined what?"

He diverted his gaze, leaving me to wonder if he'd been caught in his own words.

"For you." His voice lacked sincerity. "They would have ruined everything for you ... for your safety."

That exchange left me feeling uneasy, and I suspected Will harbored an ulterior motive. His words from several nights before camped in the back of my mind: *"I need your help ... before I can move on."* I presumed that everything he told me was purposeful and necessary for me to know.

But why?

And, did my life hinge on all these details?

* * *

By Thursday—Friday? Time was lost—Will explained that the old house, as his energy source, just like him, existed in an altered state that humans couldn't understand. This essence extended to *Crossings'* surroundings as well, which explained why the immediate grounds around the house looked dead, as if the trees and vegetation ceased living along with him. I conceded defeat that my petunias would not grow as long as Will resided there.

As for Chubbs sensing his presence, Will said, "Cats are brilliant, dismissive, aloof creatures with knowledge and awareness that would startle and scare us if we understood them. Chubbs' sensibilities may prove beneficial to you one day."

At some point in the week, I summoned the courage to ask about the gold coin Cassie mentioned. Will remembered giving it to Jack.

"I found it by the root cellar, more than a hundred years ago. I heard trespassers, so I proceeded to investigate. They were gone by the time I reached the outside entrance. The coin was all that I found."

"Was it real gold?" I asked, awed to think of what it might be worth today.

"I saw the coin before, so yes, I recognized it as genuine gold. Minted in 1856, prior to the war. I cannot do anything with it, so I gave it to Jack. He said he would put it on a chain and give it to someone special. Was your mother that someone special?"

I wished, with every part of my being, that I could answer yes. "No."

Will cocked his head. "Not you or Julie?"

I shook my head and swallowed the lump in my throat. Something about this gold coin did not add up. Cassie seemed frightened by it. Could I trust her reaction? And who received it? Could Will be deceiving me?

I shrugged off the questions, having no choice but to forge on, regardless of any danger ahead. Even if I returned to Boston, I suspected my subtle vision would remain intact, thus revealing ghosts around every corner.

I needed to continue on this path, even if it was a one-way street with no detours.

Besides, why did it matter what lie ahead? Life seemed so tentative anyway, and I felt drawn to Will in an eerie way that I didn't understand. He touched some wellspring within me that I couldn't define, and it both excited and unnerved me. Though his manner could at times be surly and mysterious, I also found him to be gallant and intriguing.

And disturbingly dead.

* * *

On the second week after the picnic, Will and I sat indoors as a cold front passed through the area. Of course, staying in was my choice because temperature fluctuations meant nothing to him.

"For you to help me, it is important that you become familiar with my friends and their experiences during the war." He looked down at his hands as he spoke, and I could hear *and* feel the gravity of his words. "As you know, only one betrayed me, but our collective interactions culminated in my murder."

I grabbed a pillow, wrapped my arms around it, and scooted into the corner of the settee.

"Four of us became immediate friends at the university. Besides myself, there was Jubal McClain, Braxton Hood, and Fergus Lowe. Another friend from my childhood, Asa Garrett, became their friend as well, although Asa attended a different university. I will talk about each of them in turn, but let me start with Asa."

Will described a painful parting with Asa who, in 1860, left for the Virginia

Military Institute as Will headed to the University of Virginia.

"We called him 'Bear.'" Will chuckled. "By age fourteen, he was already six-foot-four, over two-hundred twenty pounds, and as strong as an ox. His parents let him journey with us to *Crossings* for Christmas. A group of us went ice-skating on the frozen Potomac. The rest of us slid across the ice with ease, but when Asa tried, he fell in. Until the war, that's the most fear I'd ever experienced. We had a devil of a time getting him out of that water. I feared that we'd lose him."

"But you didn't."

"No, but a different Asa came out of that water."

"What do you mean?"

"Before the accident, Bear ... Asa ... always stuck his nose in a book. Afterward, he showed no interest in reading. Instead, he studied things around him. Assessed the weather. Analyzed the terrain. Figured shortcuts. It was as if he parlayed his mistake of not having judged the ice accurately into a skill of logistics and tactics. His decision to attend a military institute fit him so well. Later, he left because of the war, to serve as a Second Lieutenant in the Confederate army."

"Did you ever see him again?"

Will shifted to face the fire. His next words sounded reluctant, contrite. "Twice. The first time was at my wedding. He was home, recuperating from a wound in the leg. He'd been shot at the Battle of Fair Oaks while taking water from the Chickahominy River to a dying man."

"That's so brave." I suppressed a shiver, resting my head and arms on the pillow. As I gazed into the fire, one of the logs burned through and fell with a splash of sparks.

Will continued. "I saw Bear again two months later, at the battle of Sharpsburg."

I recognized the town as affiliated with the battle at Antietam. The library books said that the South named battles after local towns while the North used the closest body of water.

Fearing that this would be the story that proved critical in Asa's life, I braced myself, took a deep breath, and whispered, "What happened?"

"We met in the midst of battle."

"Just like that?" I jerked my gaze from the fire to study him. "You didn't know he was there?"

Will stood and walked to the fireplace, poking at the embers as he talked. "Many regiments came together from all directions. It was common to see someone in the midst of battle that you hadn't seen for a while. That September, General Lee pulled about 30,000 soldiers together, on a few miles of farmland, just behind Antietam Creek.

"The night before the battle, we knew that thousands of us would die on the morrow. That night so long ago looked much like this one. Dark. Disturbing. And then a dreary rain fell. That just compounded our misery."

"It must have been awful." I shivered despite being seated by the fire.

"The next day dawned gray and foggy. It was hard to see anything. We perched on the southwestern end of the fields, with Sharpsburg to our west. The first shot rang out in the distance, and I remember praying. As I continued, the blasts moved closer. To my left. Then my right. The battle ... the explosions ... the smells of gunpowder ... the screams ... all unfolded around us, getting closer and growing in intensity. Shooting continued nonstop for hours. But the cries of thousands of wounded ... that's what affected us most."

"Oh, Will." My whisper revealed the sadness that washed over me, and I frowned, not knowing what else to offer. I imagined him on that battlefield feeling helpless and bewildered beyond explanation as he and thousands of others waited. Listened. Dreaded.

As though unaffected, he continued. "By early afternoon, the fighting shifted to the woods near us, and we were pulled in. Within minutes men were everywhere. Thousands of them. Screaming. Fighting. Stabbing. Shooting. Then, out of nowhere, two beefy arms yanked me backward, behind a breastwork."

"Asa."

"We crouched down, and for a few precious seconds, we laughed and cried and the war disappeared. We said what we could, given the noise and chaos. Asa quickly assured me that Naomi fared well, but I remember such a sad frown when he said she'd changed."

"Changed? That's the words he used? Changed?"

Will nodded. "He said he had a letter for me, from her. He'd seen her in early September before rejoining his regiment. But in the thick of the battle, he couldn't take his hands off his rifle to retrieve it. We agreed to meet up later, but then the battle pulled us back, and we separated, spacing ourselves a few feet apart. Just as I stood, a volley soared at me. We'd been well-drilled in skirmishing, so I dove to the ground. In the next second, I saw Asa lying beside me. He'd been hit. He never said a word. Just lay limp on his back, his hands clutching his rifle, a clot of blood on his forehead as large as a man's fist. Just like that. In one split second, everything changed."

My eyes misted, and I looked away again, unable to respond or even swallow. My heart ached for him and his friend. I understood the value of one split second all too well. From one second to the next my family had been there, then gone.

He continued, "Asa was lying within six feet of me, but I couldn't help him. Minie balls flew everywhere. We crouched in the range of several lines of enemy fire for about two hours. As I shot and reloaded, I kept calling to Bear, telling him to hold on. By the time I could move to him, his body twitched, and I heard an inhuman sound gurgle up from his throat. Sweat mixed with blood ... it was everywhere. I begged him to come back. For me. For his fiancé, Anabelle."

"But he didn't." My voice cracked. Grabbing the pillow again, I clutched it against my chest, took a deep breath and asked, "What about the letter?"

"As you can imagine, retrieving it was the last thing on my mind. I couldn't even mourn because the Federals kept coming. Fighting was shoulder to shoulder. Men shouted and flailed their swords, and smoke swirled everywhere. To move Asa would have been instant death. I vowed I'd come back the next day for his body, or the next, or whatever it took, but I never did because I got injured. The battle lasted all day as tens of thousands of men died or were wounded. Many on top of one another. The carnage was so bad that Antietam Creek ran red from the blood."

"How horrible," I whispered. My instinct was to reach for him, but I didn't, and instead curled my fingers into the pillow. "I'm so sorry ... for you ... for all of them."

He nodded. "It was as if those soldiers ... those men ... walked into the fog that morning, that obscurity, knowing they wouldn't come out the way they went in ... if they came out at all. In there ... in that murkiness ... that mystic unknown ... you change. Your defenses crumble, your convictions shift. Sometimes you gain perspective. Sometimes you perish."

I sat in silence, stunned by his words and feeling a disturbing familiarity to what he said. I clenched my jaw to stop the tears. If that battle had marked the end of the war, I might have been able to say, "Thank God that was the last of it." But, the war continued for three more bitter years. "How were you injured?"

"About two hundred feet from where Asa died, a volley flared, and a ball cut into my side, passing through my coat and shirt. My flesh burned, and I sank to the ground. After a few minutes and thinking I might live, I started to crawl for cover, but the pain was so overwhelming, I blacked out and awoke hours later. By then it was dark."

"But they found you and carried you to a hospital ... right?"

He shook his head. "I lay on the field all night, in and out of consciousness. I thought about dragging myself to where I'd find help, but I was so disoriented, I didn't know which way to go. The next morning, when neither side renewed the conflict, they declared truces along the line. The men who could walk started tending to their wounded comrades. By now, I scrounged enough strength to sit up, so I removed my shirt and tore it into a bandage to wrap my wound. Fortunately, it had clotted during the night. After resting a few more hours, I used my rifle as a cane and hobbled through the field, looking for water or medical care, whichever I could find first. But it was hard to navigate among the bodies and debris. I didn't make it far before I fell again.

"More time passed. I don't know how long. I remember that bodies that had been around me were now gone. I suppose they'd been taken to a hospital. I must have been mistaken for dead. I climbed back up and walked some more."

"And then you found a hospital."

"It was a few days before I secured help. I became one of the walking wounded. Thousands of us crowded the roads between Sharpsburg and the Potomac, searching for our regiments. But the army could ill afford to be slowed down by us. They didn't dare be caught north of the river, so they pulled out. We ... the wounded ... couldn't keep pace with the army, so we were left by the roadside to be picked up by the Federals."

"But that's terrible! How could they do that?"

Will shrugged. "I was one of the lucky ones ... still alive. That first night, after the battle, when darkness fell on those fields and the fighting ended, I couldn't see the death around me, and I thought the worst was behind us. But I was wrong. The darkness just brought something worse than anything your eyes could ever see—the screams and moans of thousands of wounded men begging for help. Some pleaded for water; others asked that they be shot to put an end to the pain. Many cried out for their wives and mothers. Some used their final bullets on themselves. It was worse than any sounds of battle. And what cut through me most, even louder than the cries for help were the sounds of men being burned alive. There'd been mounded haystacks scattered around the fields, and throughout the day wounded men crawled into the hay for shelter. As the battle wore on, the stacks caught fire from bursting shells. Most of the men inside were too weak to move. They burned to death. At that point, God forgive me, I was glad that Asa died a quick death."

He stopped, and again silence permeated the room. My heart was so heavy and my nerves so raw from the conversation that I couldn't move.

Finally, he spoke, and I recognized his words from the Bible. "No greater love hath any man than this, that he lay down his life for his friends."

My breath caught. The weight of his words and the visions that they evoked smothered me, depriving me of air. When I could breathe again, I curled my body tighter, craving the embrace of my own arms. For Will to have experienced Asa's death right beside him, on that gruesome battlefield with the smoke and the noise and the fear swirling about was more than I could fathom.

With further despair, I remembered that Jack's list said that "friends" died at the Battle of Antietam, meaning at least one more. I wanted to hear that story too, but I couldn't form the words to ask. It would have to wait.

I don't think either of us said another word that night.

Chapter 14

I grew so used to seclusion, that a call from Seth one evening startled me. The calendar hung by the refrigerator announced that I met him more than two weeks ago. In the interim, I'd done little more than haunt my own house.

He invited me to the carnival in Williamsport that weekend.

"I didn't call earlier because my folks and I took a trip to New England to visit colleges."

After a moment, I noticed he was waiting for a response. "Did you pick one?"

"My parents liked Dartmouth, but I'd rather go south where it's warm. You're from Massachusetts, so you should know what I mean about the cold."

"Yeah." I chuckled, sounding fake. I glanced out the window at the fading sun and wondered how soon I could talk with Will. Seth's voice brought me back into the conversation. "I'm sorry, what did you say?"

"I said, so what do you think?"

"About what?"

"About the carnival." He sounded annoyed.

"Oh, uh ... sorry. I can't. I have plans." *That was true—I planned to be with Will.* "Can I have a rain check?" *Why did I add that request?* I had no intention of ever cashing it in, and there was no point in leading him on.

"Yeah, sure. Whatever."

I clicked off the call with the feeling that Seth wasn't used to being rejected.

* * *

For many nights after hearing about Asa's death, I encouraged Will to talk about happier times, such as his childhood, hoping to delay the inevitable discussion of war.

As we talked, we created comfortable routines together. He built the fires. I set out the good china in the old house's dining room. He lit the dozen or so candles. I prepared the meals. Of course he didn't eat, but I didn't mind.

One evening, as we stargazed from the porch, I mentioned the song, *Lorena,* and how Will impelled me to play it before I'd even met him.

"Tell me about it," I urged, studying his face and hoping for some degree of intensity in his response. I wanted sincerity. I wanted to be able to trust this man. "Why did it mean so much to you?"

He parked his elbows on his chair. Not quite the passionate reaction I was looking for, but I could tell my question touched a memory.

"Naomi and I danced to it on our wedding night."

"But it's such a sad song for a wedding." I hoped I didn't sound rude or skeptical.

To my relief, he smiled. "You're right. My cousin Stephen was attempting to serenade us. He was well into the song before he comprehended what he'd done."

"That must have been awkward." I leaned back, stretching my legs out on the glider and catching sight of a shooting star.

"Indeed." He nodded, grin widening. "Jubal eased the discomfort by thanking him for the reminder of what would not happen to Naomi and me."

"You were so young." I marveled at the odds of such a marriage working nowadays.

"Couples married earlier then. But yes, we were too young. She was seventeen, and I was eighteen. We met at a university Christmas party my first year."

"How wonderful." I pictured hooped gowns, carriages, and elegance.

"She was the daughter of one of my professors and a friend of Anabelle's."

"Asa's fiancé?"

"Not yet. Engagement came later."

Before continuing, Will leaned forward and pointed out Pegasus and Orion the Hunter in the black velvet sky. He never hurried anything. Time meant nothing to him.

"Naomi was from Georgia but lived with relatives in Alexandria, whereas I considered the latter my home with relatives in Georgia. We had that in common, but not much more. We didn't know one another that well when we married. I think our decision to rush into wedlock was borne of infatuation and fear of war."

"But you loved her," I declared, my response so quick that I blushed, afraid that I sounded like a naïve romantic.

"She was beautiful and willful ... like you."

I waved a dismissive gesture. However, I wondered why his words pleased me. With a start, I shook my head to squelch thoughts of folding into his arms at a dance and reaching up to put my fingertip on the dimple that distinguished his right cheek.

"Her smile could lure a dying man to offer his last heartbeat." His eyebrows furrowed, and he stared into the distance. "She had blue eyes and hair as gold as a field of wheat. I found myself competing for her attention with another man who went after her full chisel—" He shot me with a quizzical look. "—full throttle? In earnest?"

I nodded my understanding, and he returned his gaze to the sky.

"He always got what he wanted, so I bowed out. Before long, I received a letter of encouragement from her, and we began courting."

"She must have been quite smitten with you."

"We went on picnics. Took long walks. Once, we journeyed to the local county fair where we enjoyed a ride in a hot-air balloon."

"Sounds romantic."

He didn't respond. Hoping that he would continue with his thoughts of Naomi, I didn't say more. I wanted to know everything about her, and I found myself comparing her life with mine, wondering if Will would have been attracted to me in his day.

What was taking hold of me? One minute I was leery of him, the next ...

"You must remember, it was wartime. Each month, rumor circulated that it would end within weeks, but most of us doubted that it would. We lived with the awareness that each goodbye could be our last. In stolen moments of hope, we snatched as much of a lifetime as we could into whatever time remained. We did everything with haste—fell in love, married, celebrated, died."

"And earned promotion. You moved up the ranks quickly."

"Promotions didn't always mean skill on the battlefield. Often it just meant an officer was killed and his position now vacant."

We lapsed into silence again as I thought about what Will said. Even promotions in wartime centered on death. And, because most of the war occurred on Southern soil, the realities of war proved even harsher for them.

I bit my lip before asking, "Why did you fight for the South? You didn't agree with slavery, did you?"

"Of course not. No one should live in bondage." He paused and ran a hand over his head, as though choosing how to explain the multiplicities that led to war. "For most of us, slavery wasn't even a consideration when the war broke out. It did not become a widespread moral cause of the Union effort until after the battle at Sharpsburg, when President Lincoln announced the Emancipation Proclamation. At that time, we'd already suffered more than a year of fighting."

"And you were in prison by then?"

He nodded. "Johnson's Island."

"The whole war was so ... complex. I mean, it changed *everyone's* life." I exhaled and rubbed the back of my neck.

"You can't study one isolated moment in time without the context of everything else that happened. The idea that one state or region could dominate the other did not sit well with the South. The war started, more or less, because the South was pushed into fighting to maintain its way of life, whereas the North exerted aggression in an effort to maintain a union."

"They both seemed to be right. I can understand each side."

"As could I. But in the South, pride and allegiance were particularly strong, so people favored states' rights. Withdrawing from the nation seemed like the most peaceful solution. Then, President Lincoln demanded that Virginia furnish troops to crush their Southern brethren. We became indignant. And that began what we thought would be a brief interlude in history." He paused, and his voice grew sad. "I never imagined it would be more than two nondescript sides against one another ... that it would get personal, pitting cousin against cousin. And, in my case, friend against friend."

"Tell me more about a happier time. The Christmas party."

He frowned and straightened his body as though he didn't like my request. But, he turned toward me and relinquished. "My sister Sarah came. She chose not to travel with my parents to Brazil. Instead, she moved in with my father's brother and his wife in Alexandria. The three of them came to the university to visit. That's where she met my good friend Jubal."

He cocked his head as though waiting for a reaction from me. I gestured with my hands as though to say, "What?"

"Jubal and Sarah McClain. Jack's ancestors."

"Oh my gosh! That's right—Jack's mother was a McClain before she married his father, George MacKenna. Then ... you are Jack's great, great, something-or-other uncle." I shrugged it off, deciding the calculation wasn't worth the effort, nor was the sadness I was sure to feel once I'd computed his actual age.

"That's right. I must say, however, that when I first saw Jack, I recognized my sister's eyes and smile."

"So Jubal made it through the war alive." I marveled that it was because of Jubal that I was sitting there with Will. "What was he like?"

"Of all my friends, Jubal displayed the strongest faith and friendliest disposition. I was pleased when I saw an attraction between him and Sarah."

"You and your sister were close?" Memories washed over me of the close bond Julie and I once shared.

"Very much so. But like Naomi and me, Sarah's happiness with Jubal was interrupted by the war. It wasn't until after it ended that they married. By then, I was long dead."

A cringe and a few perturbed heartbeats passed before I could say, "I'm sorry."

"Jubal was always the one to boost our morale or play a joke. Once the war started, our paths didn't cross often, but when they did, he was always on a quest for a good pair of boots."

"Boots? That's a funny thing to focus on in the middle of a war."

"Quite the contrary. Footwear was scarce. Of the dead soldiers you'd see scattered in the fields or on the side of the road, none wore a pair of boots. Not too far into the war, the Confederate army found itself half-starved and poorly clothed. We looked like a crew of hungry vagabonds rather than a regiment of soldiers. When we won a skirmish, we would search through the full haversacks of the Federal troops, snatching boots, food, candles, soap. Jubal secured enough food to stay ahead of starvation, but he was always searching for boots that would fit his large feet."

"But he and Sarah ... they enjoyed a happy ending ... right?"

Will nodded. "She gave birth to four strapping boys, all of whom later raised several children of their own. It's almost as if she and Jubal alone made up for the tragedies that befell the rest of us."

Several seconds went by before Will added, "Neither Sarah nor any of her descendants ever attempted to live again at *Crossings* after my death ... that is, until Jack arrived."

* * *

Will had mentioned two other friends: Braxton and Fergus. Accepting that it was just a matter of time before I learned more, and that I needed to know it all to resolve his death, I asked him to share their stories. We discussed Braxton one night during dinner.

Braxton Johnston Hood, Will said, was five years older than the rest of them, had already studied at the university two years, and was the most serious of the four.

"He was assigned to the three of us freshmen—Jubal, Fergus, and I—to help with orientation activities our first week of college. We were an odd lot, for sure, different in so many ways. Yet somehow we bonded through the antics and competition that first day. Thereafter, the four of us spent most of our free time together."

"What made Braxton different?"

"He was a quiet, focused man. His family was wealthy with ties to aristocracy in England. They grew tobacco on about 700 acres, in an area surrounded by large operations with many slaves."

"Did his family have slaves?" My breath caught, afraid to hear the answer.

"Braxton's father would never tolerate that."

I relaxed and took a bite of the salmon I'd baked.

Will continued. "Farming didn't interest Braxton. He preferred science. There were several sons to work the farm, so his parents agreed to send him to the University of Virginia to study medicine. Besides, Braxton suffered bad blood with a neighbor, so this seemed like the perfect solution."

"So he was a doctor? How lucky for him." Awed, I pictured warm hospitals, access to medicine, and enough good footwear to go around, unlike poor Jubal.

Will huffed a short sound of disgust. "He was a surgeon." I heard expectation in his voice and tried to read his face. When I offered no response he added, "A sawbones? I would not wish his work on the worst of my enemies."

Startled, I argued. "But he was safe. And he was trained to tend to the wounded, right?"

Will leaned forward, placing an arm on the table. "He'd never seen a gunshot wound until his first battle. The average medical student trained for two years or less and received almost no clinical experience. Before war broke out, Braxton planned to further his studies in England or Scotland where four-year medical schools were common."

I countered again. I couldn't leave it. "But he saved lives."

"He did. But the work was deplorable. Crude field hospitals were rushed together on the spot because we never knew in advance where fighting would be. Anything with a roof and four walls served as a hospital—houses, barns, stables, corn cribs."

"Poor Braxton."

Will didn't respond right away. Between his distorted features and the weak candles, I couldn't read his expression, so I waited, my eyes lingering on his face.

After a long pause, he looked away. "He died at Antietam, too."

My breath hitched, and I dropped my head into my hands. "How? How did he die?"

"I am not sure." Will stood and paced the length of the table, and back again.

"When the battle was over, the wounded lay everywhere. Anyone who could still walk helped to carry them to every shelter within miles. One such place was a shed at the edge of Sharpsburg. That night, it was in full service as a field hospital. According to Jack's research, Braxton was there, but everyone in the building was found dead the next morning."

"Stray bullets?" I offered, all the while aware it didn't make sense.

"No, from something that happened that night."

"What? And why?" I asked, spreading a hand. "Who would do that? There was already so much death everywhere."

"Jack's books say Braxton did it. A murder-suicide. But I'm certain he did not. He had too much to live for. He was in love with a slave girl named Eva. Her father was a white man from North Carolina, but her mother was a slave. Her parents died in a fire when she was six, so she was forced into slavery. Braxton's neighbor purchased her at an auction."

"That's terrible! She must have been so scared ... and alone." My mind raced. "That's the bad blood that you mentioned, isn't it? Between Braxton and the neighbor?"

Will nodded. "The neighbor was a pitiful excuse of a man. He once whipped a slave to death. Braxton confronted him, and they fought. Braxton was left with a scar on his right cheek. When the man's attention turned to Eva, Braxton feared the worst. In a private moment before my wedding, he said he intended to help her escape, and he wanted to know if she could be hidden at *Crossings* for a while."

"Like the Underground Railroad." I recalled my history lessons in school.

"Of course I said yes, but I never saw him again. I did not know his whereabouts at Antietam. That he was so close. Somehow I feel that his death was linked to mine. I don't know what happened to Eva either. I know Braxton's brother, Aaron, had married an abolitionist by the name of Savilla, so his sentiments fell with the North. They may have helped Eva escape."

Will fell silent again. By mere deduction I calculated that there was one friend left.

"That means that Fergus was the one who ... who—" My voice broke.

"Killed me? Yes, it was my beloved friend, Fergus."

Chapter 15

People say that life is made of moments—random spurts of poignant events that, when pieced together like a tapestry, form the story of your life. For most people, death would not be a central moment, but rather an event that renders the work complete.

But what if your death is so premature that your tapestry is left incomplete? So horrific that death becomes the focal point?

Every stitch that Will shared from his tapestry focused on death, but I didn't want to hear him talk about how he had been betrayed and murdered by his best friend, or that I had to find that murderous ghost.

Perhaps I used that as an excuse to delay the inevitable—his final departure. Despite lingering apprehension upon interacting with him, contentment settled within me during this time of seclusion. More than I'd experienced in three years.

I didn't want to lose this dead man.

* * *

On the Friday night after Seth called, Will and I sat on the porch. Tucked at my usual perch in the glider, and he on the rocker, I peered into the ebony night. Other than Williamsport's distant lights across the river, I saw nothing. The thumbnail moon offered no beams, no luster. Having lived in the midst of Boston for the past three years, I'd forgotten how dark the world could be. If it weren't for Will's own inherent illumination, I wouldn't have been able to see him.

"What was that like?" I asked, summoning the courage to hear the answer. "To die, I mean."

He leaned back looking relaxed. "It is different for everyone. On the battlefield, some men embraced it as a way to escape pain. Most of them, however, died amidst a sense of shock and—"

"But what about you? I want to know what you experienced."

"For me, it involved disbelief, almost denial ... then a reliance on reflex."

He spoke as dispassionately as if he described the process of hooking worms on a fishing pole. "When Fergus stabbed me, I felt a stunning thrust to my chest. I'd been wounded at Antietam the year before, as you know. But, I could tell this was different."

"Different ... how? Physically? Mentally?" I wanted details, anything to help understand the process of death and what came after.

"My physical body weakened, of course. It was damaged. At the same time, desperation hit. Then, denial. I remember thinking, 'Why, Fergus? How could you do this?' and I looked for an answer on his face before collapsing. Next, I wondered, 'Is this really happening to me?' and 'What do I do next?' I remember feeling lethargic. And dull. And yet, I let go gracefully because I was shown that an ultimate benefit waited, rather than just a dire, all-obliterating demise."

"What do you mean you were shown?" I asked, leaning toward him. "Who showed you? How?"

He rubbed his jaw. "It's hard to explain. It was ... communicated to me somehow. I just became aware."

Disappointed, I sat back, my mind scouring through all the theories and suppositions I'd catalogued through the years about death. "I've heard that when you die, your entire life flashes before your eyes. Is that true?"

"I experienced my life again, but it wasn't a *flash*. Instead, I relived every moment with a clarity I hadn't appreciated the first time. Every detail magnified. Every emotion, transparent. None of my memories were as I thought they had been. Instead, they were now as they had actually been." He paused, cocking his head, and I could sense his quest to be precise. "No pretense. No rationalizing. Just the pure, raw events as they actually occurred. I saw my mistakes and shortcomings in helping others when I could have done more. But, at the same time, I saw all the times I helped or loved or comforted someone."

"Is it like that for everyone?"

Will smiled as if he knew my real question: *When I die, will I get to relive the happy times with my parents?*

"Yes, everyone."

"So, what happened next?"

"My body lay there, on the floor, and it went still. Lifeless."

As he spoke, the chimes serenaded us, providing a haunting lullaby, and it seemed so apropos for this discussion of death. For the first time, I noticed the air smelled moist, earthy. I wondered if Will grasped this sensory experience too, or if his senses remained as still as his body became that fateful day he died.

"Something—I don't know what—told me to relax and let go. When I did, I swelled with energy and my spiritual body floated toward the ceiling. But, I could see Fergus in the room, and sadness flooded through me for an instant because he was still filled with rage."

Rage—so Fergus had killed in a rage. In cold blood. I didn't want to hear about that murderer. Not yet. "Tell me more about the experience of dying."

"The room filled with light. Several presences approached and—"

"Presences ... like ghosts? Like you?" I thought about what Pastor Dale had said. "Or were they angels? Is that what they were?"

"You could call them that. They certainly felt like kind beings, like angels. You could also call them guides. They were different than me, but I don't know how to explain it. I felt their emotions and their love for me ... and their intent. It was all good."

I wanted to argue that he should have been angry at those angels. Hadn't they let him die? Didn't he realize it was their job to keep him safe? Instead, I asked, "What happened next?"

"I left."

"You left?" Startled, I sat up and put my feet flat on the porch. "With Fergus still there, staring down at your body?"

"Yes."

"What? You just floated out the door? Why?"

"I ... dissolved ... I'm not sure what to call it," he turned his hands in a frustration gesture. "I left because other concerns took precedence. I focused on Naomi and my parents, and how my death would affect them. I needed to see them one last time."

"So the connection continued ... even after death?" I marveled, wanting to believe this true for everyone. I nudged the glider into motion. Our clacking chairs, the chimes, the cicadas—created an odd symphony in the dark.

"I started to move and realized that I still thought in terms of my earthly body. I sensed the message again to let go. When I did, my consciousness refocused from a physical to a spiritual reality, and my soul took over. I moved through walls. And, I remember mist. A fog. I'd grown so accustomed to soldiers walking into fog and emerging differently, if they survived at all, that I knew a change was underway. I couldn't see anything, but still, I kept moving. My trip to Naomi blurred. I focused on being with her, and instantly I was."

"But she couldn't see you."

"She lay in an unfamiliar bed beside a window that looked out on trees. Like the long leaf pines of the South. Her wrists were bound to the sides of the bed, and I wondered if someone had imprisoned her. Then, from outside, I heard people talking and moving. Even singing. Naomi looked so pale. I thought her ill and wondered if that's what her note had said to me—that she was going to Georgia, to be with her family to heal. I assumed she lived with relatives and proved to be such a disagreeable patient that they tied her there to make her rest."

"But you received her note at Antietam, right? That was eight or nine months earlier? You'd never communicated in all that time?"

"We couldn't. Remember, I was captured after Antietam. In prison, I could send no messages, and she wouldn't have known where to write. Today, immediate notification of a disaster or death is facilitated by those telephone contraptions, but in the 1860s we used only telegrams and letters, both of which involved considerable delay, especially in the war-torn areas of the Mid-Atlantic States."

"How awful."

"Indeed. It was agonizing to wait for word about deaths and wounds after a battle."

I nodded, understanding. But then, a memory flashed through my mind of my family's death and how that instant notification had landed me in the morgue within two hours after the accident to identify bodies. I wondered which situation was worse.

I took a deep breath and pushed the memory from my mind. "What was it like ... to see her after such a long time?"

"Confusing. Comprehension didn't come as clearly with Naomi as it did with my parents and Sarah, all of whom I saw next. Still, Naomi appeared to be safe. I imagined her waiting for me to come home."

"Did you touch her ... or try to talk to her?" My heart ached as I projected all sorts of emotions onto her. I imagined her grieving from a broken heart, thinking about Will and their future, and praying that the war would end soon so they could be together. I wondered if I could have been as patient as she. Or, would I have done the modern-day equivalent of rallying other people together to help the war cause? Maybe stormed Washington to insist an end to the madness? Surely Will had recognized Naomi's loneliness and in his death somehow tried to help her.

"Grace," he said, frustration in his voice, "I can't explain it, but by then I had no need to communicate with her. And, it would not have been appropriate any-

more. We were now of different worlds and to mix the two would only hurt her."
He shifted in his chair, a conditioned reaction to an uncomfortable conversation.

"As I watched her," he continued, "I realized that she would be fine on her own
and that each of us has to find our way. While alive, I'd always believed it was my
role to protect and care for her, but in death, I realized we were each responsible for
ourselves and our choices. I was content that we would be together again one day."

"So what did you do next?" I was surprised at the cold tone in my voice.
Could he detect my disappointment that he'd left Naomi? Sure, my real anger
centered on the whole process of death and how it prevented my parents from
communicating with me. Then again, I was relieved to hear that he could not
stay with Naomi. Perhaps my parents had no choice either.

"I moved on to see my parents and sister. My father sat on a couch reading
and stroking my mother's hair as she lay asleep beside him, her head on his lap.
My sister, Sarah, in Alexandria, kneaded bread. Seeing them left me feeling free
to transition on so I—"

"But you didn't. You came back here." I wondered why, after all that he had
seen and been through, he would choose to stay at *Crossings*.

"Yes, but not right away. You must understand Asa, Braxton, and Jubal were
like brothers to me. I knew Asa was dead, so I assumed I'd see him shortly, but I
wanted to look upon Braxton and Jubal one more time. As with the others, I
focused and saw Jubal, sitting in front of me at a campsite, studying a map. But
when I focused on Braxton, nothing happened. Remember, I didn't know at that
time, that he died at Antietam too. When I couldn't find my way to him at my
death, I realized he'd died too. As such, I anticipated seeing him on the other side.

"Once I'd seen my family and friends, everything dimmed, and I moved into
a huge swirling, black tornado. It wasn't painful or frightening. Just dark. So
much so, I couldn't see anything."

Will stood and walked to the porch railing. "Like that." He pointed into
the blackness of the night. "Then, I saw a light just ahead ... so magnetic that I
couldn't wait to get to it. When I finally did, I discovered a huge, tranquil river
and an intense peace washed over me. It was communicated to me that when I
crossed it, I would finally be home."

As though on cue, a train whistle sounded, reminding me that we sat near a
river. Will bent to rest his elbows on the porch rail and stared toward the sound.
As the blast echoed through the valley, I wondered about the contrast of these
two rivers—the Potomac, so powerful and filled with white rapids, but I pictured

the river in the dimension as peaceful, like a pond.

When the train's clackity-clack passed into the distance, I asked, "That light and that river ... that was the dimension you referred to earlier, wasn't it?"

He turned to face me, folded his arms, and rested his backside against the railing. "That's a bad name for it, but it's the only description I can offer. It's a region between your earthly and eternal homes. A passing place. No one stays. You are there for a brief period of time."

"Wow." Not my most prolific response, but words escaped me.

"Ahh, but the true 'wow' is what I saw on the other side of the river—my grandparents. I had never known my maternal grandfather, yet I recognized him there."

"Maybe from a photograph?" I offered, before remembering that photographs weren't readily available in those days.

"No, there are no earthly forms on the other side, so photographs wouldn't have helped anyway." He frowned at the puzzled look on my face. "Grace, you are not a body with a soul. You are a soul with a temporary body here on Earth. You have the soul first, and when you are born, you carry out your earthly life in a physical body. When you die, you leave your physical body here and return to being a soul, free of earthly ties."

I pointed at him. "So, you don't look like that in the dimension."

He shook his head. "Only on earth."

"So ... Souls can recognize one another ... how?"

He smiled sheepishly. "You cannot assign human understanding to what I say. There are no words or explanations in language to convey what truly happens or how this transpires. It's just something you know once you're there."

"And yet, you didn't cross."

"No."

"But why?"

"I didn't because another thing you experience is a cleansing. If you leave the earth in a violent or disturbing manner, then you have unfinished business. You have the choice of whether to move on or not, but if you move on while still having unfinished business, your eternal peace will be weighed down by an earthly heaviness. When I saw the contentment and the absolute bliss of those on the other side, I wanted it too."

"But it can never be bliss if you leave loved ones behind," I muttered, thinking, of course, of my own situation. I hated the implication that my presence would have been considered "earthly heaviness" to my family.

He cocked his head as though he didn't grasp my meaning. "I wanted to be cleansed first, of the earthliness that prevailed over my life and death. Asa and Braxton, although dead, weren't on the other side. That surprised me. They were both good men. Men of faith. I was certain they were destined for good also, so I had to believe they chose to stay behind."

I shook my head, the details I'd hungered for now causing confusion. "Well, if they were dead too and destined for heaven, couldn't you see them at Antietam where they died? I mean, you saw your family before you left."

"But they were living beings. That's the difference."

"What about from the dimension? If you can see souls that crossed over, can't you see souls that chose to stay behind?"

"Not unless you enter the dimension at the same time. This is not somewhere you stay. It is meant for crossing over. Souls go there to welcome someone home. If you have remained behind and become aware that someone is dying, you may be able to enter the dimension at the same time that they do, but then you must leave immediately thereafter, either by crossing over or returning to earth."

"But how do you know then?" My voice grew louder in proportion to my frustration. "Braxton or Asa ... or even Naomi at the end of her life ... how do you know they didn't arrive later and then move on without you being aware of it?"

"At all times in the dimension, you can see the other side. You can look into heaven and feel the happiness, and you gain knowledge as to who is there."

"But there must be millions ... billions of souls there!" Exasperated, I thumped my hand down hard on the arm of the glider. "How is it that you identified your family among that many?"

"It's hard to explain, but yes, amidst all those souls, I saw and recognized my family."

"All that stuff you described about distinguishing between souls ... that's how you recognized my family."

"Yes." His one word was gentle and affirmative.

"And ... did they ..." I swallowed. "Did they come to see me at their deaths, like you went to see Naomi?"

"Of course they did."

Disgusted with myself, I whispered, "And I didn't even know it because I was asleep."

"It wouldn't have mattered. At that moment, you and your family were irreversibly worlds apart, and they learned you would be alright."

His words were too tidy and convenient. Too perfect. I wondered again what our entire interaction was all about, and if he used these heartfelt stories to pull me toward some macabre plot he devised?

In confusion, I summoned a false bravado and decided to get more information before unleashing my anger. "You said you needed my help in finding Fergus and Naomi. What is that all about?"

He moved to pull the rocking chair close to me, sat, and reached to place his hand over mine. While the coolness of his touch startled me, the contact prompted an uncanny physical sensation. Disorientation washed over me as though something transferred into my body to take the place of my doubts. Anger gave way to acceptance, disbelief to trust. That quickly, my desire to remain receptive to him was restored.

"Grace, you're not ready yet. Your hesitations are still too strong and serve as an impassable barrier. It would be too dangerous for you."

That made no sense to me. How could it be less dangerous or frightening at any other time?

"When will I be ready?"

"You'll know when you're ready."

My immediate thought was that if helping him meant losing him, then I would never be ready. I would be content living right here with him, growing old in this house with him, then setting him free one day when time came for me to move on. *What had he done to me?*

But I didn't voice these thoughts. Nor did I ask him to tell me about the only remaining unknown—Fergus. The friend. The murderer. That would have to wait until another night.

Instead, we lapsed into silence and stared into the still night.

Even the chimes stopped their melody.

Chapter 16

The next day, I decided to explore the grounds bordering *Crossings*. The sky clouded over, breaking the intense heat from the day before, so I welcomed the fresh air. Plus, I relished the thought of sharing my explorations with Will that night.

My first destination was the root cellar. Will's description of it as "beyond the hill behind the house" was vague, but surely a root cellar couldn't be too hard to find.

Tramp and I trudged over the long expanse of the hill on the west side of the property. At this distance from the house, the lawns were green and lush with vegetation, from drifts of wildflowers to masses of dandelions under a higher canopy of scattered pines, elms and oak trees.

The incline crested at about the same height as the old house, so the hike proved easy, even pleasant; although, the distance surprised me—at least the length of a football field. From there, we descended into a small hollow from where more rolling hills rose and stretched in three directions. Several yards beyond a couple of scattered patches of thorny bramble bushes, we came across what looked like an aged, weather-beaten oak door that opened into the slope of another hill. Just then, a rabbit scampered from beneath the shrubbery and darted up over the ridge. Tramp yelped and gave me a "can't-I-go-chase-it-just-this-once" look. I obliged and unhooked his leash, knowing he'd never catch the furry creature.

Will had detected activity by the root cellar a few times through the years. That made sense; obscured by the hill, the house sat far enough away that he probably didn't become alarmed that his energy source would be disturbed.

I studied the crude entry. The angle of the door suggested that the entire cellar was encased inside the hill. No wonder Will had gone "down under" to investigate when he heard trespassers too close to the cellar. The door reached only as high as my shoulders, and the bulk of it hid behind weeds and layers of vines so thick it was roped shut. Decayed cobwebs smothered the weathered iron handle.

Curiosity overcame me and begged that I look inside. Miraculously, not much soil had eroded on the first several inches fronting the door, suggesting that through the years someone, or something—Will perhaps—had cleared away any obstructions to ensure access. Fearing snakes and rats and other creatures for which I held an aversion, I grabbed a sturdy stick from under a nearby elm tree and chopped at the vines, scooped up the cobwebs, then grabbed the handle and yanked.

Despite the rust on its hinges, the door groaned open about a foot before banging into the mounded ground and vines. Pervasive dampness and an odor of decay hit me, prompting a chill to run down my spine. I steeled my determination and ducked to inch my head inside. I had no flashlight, so visibility was limited, but the place looked to be as much cave as cellar. Hand-hewn wooden logs reinforced its hollowed-out earthen walls, and dirt composed the floor as far as the light revealed. I would have thought it empty, forgotten and left through the years to weather away, but instinct told me otherwise. Something in the air, like heaviness, discharged from within, as though the cellar had once been filled with fear or sadness. The feeling was so strong that it practically lured me to step in to find its source. However, I opted against it; not without a flashlight.

Just then I heard a noise—low, scraping—from deep inside the cavern, and despite the dim light, I saw a blur of movement toward the back where it looked as though the wall turned a corner into an area beyond view. *A shadow!* I gasped and stepped back.

Intellect counseled me that a ground creature had scurried by, but fear argued otherwise. There was no light in the back, so how could it be a shadow? And why had it reminded me of the other Will I'd seen, the one in my dream? Why would he hide from me? Or why would he manifest himself again in a different manner? Panic rushed out of my stomach and rose, scorching, into my throat. I scrambled backward and slammed the door, my heart pounding.

As if on cue, Tramp began barking incessantly from across the ridge. Between the vision I'd just witnessed and my concern for my dog's well-being, I dashed up the next slope and along its ridge toward Tramp's frantic bark. I crested another incline before reaching him.

He pranced inside a fenced grove of three spreading trees, barking at two crows that studied him with annoyance from their perch high on a top-most branch. The forest beyond reached for the grove, as if to reclaim the secluded woodlot.

My heartbeat slowed at the sight of Tramp and these creatures chattering to one another in their own language. I eased to a walk and laughed to shake off my anxiety, found an opening in the wooden crisscross fence and entered the grove. Because the sun was in my eyes, I stepped sideways to move into the shade beside me, all the while keeping my eyes on the crows. My foot struck an obstacle, and

I lost balance. As I stumbled, I broke my fall by grabbing ahold of the object itself and coming to rest on my knees. Made of carved granite, it lay low to the ground and measured only about a foot wide, a foot tall, and about three inches deep. Hardly an object that could cause much distress until one looked closer and scanned the message carved on its face.

It read: "William Alan Kavanaugh, August 16, 1844 – May 24, 1863.

For one breathless moment, I couldn't move. Then, on primeval instinct, my body recoiled as if I'd been electrically shocked. I shuddered and cried out as I scrambled backward, half crawling, half hurdling, off the gravesite. Once on my feet again, I stopped and gulped in air, willing my heart to calm down. When I felt my legs would obey me, I stepped closer to the tombstone to read it again.

Will's grave!

Six feet below my feet, the physical remains of Will lay, all but forgotten. He had lived his life and it ended, and here, as proof, sat a carved stone that represented the proverbial "stamp of finality." It was hollow comfort to me that I spoke with the man each night. His voice, his stories, his presence, all belied this gruesome symbol that others had erected for him.

Goose bumps covered my arms, and a chill chased itself down my back as I read the inscription again. My heart pounded as I thought about that fragile partition between delusion and reality.

Only your mind can produce fear...

I cried out something incoherent and ran. I just needed to be—where? Anywhere but there. Scrambling around the low hills in the direction of the house, I sprinted toward the comfortable, familiar confines of *Crossings*. As I ran, the patches of weeds, the mounds of earth, the scattering of rocks all seemed to thwart my way like snares, causing me to stumble, further exacerbating my fear.

At the bottom of the second foothill, I tripped and fell. I gasped for breath, but instead experienced uncontrolled gulping and choking, punctuated with my own sobbing.

I cried for Will, Mom, Julie, Jack, and yet I cried for no one in particular, as if the stress and the anxiety I'd harbored for the past three years were now pouring out. I'd been drowning in death all that time, and particularly this past month as I lived with it. Then, Will's stories surfaced in my mind, and more tears flowed for all those soldiers who suffered such horror during the war so long ago, many of whom lost their lives, snuffed out at far too young an age—many, at my age.

Then, my erratic thoughts returned to Will, and I sobbed even harder. He was more than *Crossings*, more than the things he left behind. I didn't want to lose him, and that thought prompted such a flood of tears, it blinded my vision, such that when his shadow appeared behind me, I scrambled up and threw myself into him, thrilled that he dared to leave the energy of the house to come looking for me.

"Grace, I heard you scream. I came as quickly as I could."

I hugged him even tighter, his arms encircling me in a strong embrace, and I cried and shuddered convulsively against him.

"You can't go," I sobbed. "I didn't know ... I didn't realize it until now ... I know you can't be with me, that you have to go ... I know you love her, but I need you ... I can't lose you."

"Grace," he murmured, "it's been hard to stay away from you too ... but I can't ..."

But he did anyway. His breathing tingled on my neck as he pulled me tighter. He kissed my cheek, working his way to my lips. I felt safe, happy—I could feel his animal warmth and smell the masculine scent of his body.

Animal warmth? Masculine scent?

With sudden dawning of something amiss, I jerked away as I opened my eyes from my fog and saw reality staring me in the face through the eyes of Clay Baxter.

* * *

At the same time that I pulled away, he stepped back, shaking his head as though attempting to make sense of what happened. Two magnets repelled.

"Grace, I'm sorry." He sighed and shook his head. "I feel it too ... like I've always known you. Maybe it's from hearing Jack talk about you ... but I can't ... I can't do this." He held out his hands as if helpless and looked at me with a "please understand" kind of pity on his face.

I swallowed back my shock. *He felt it too?* Felt what? And in that instant the truth hit me that I knew exactly to what he referred because I *did* feel it. *I felt it too!* Whatever *it* was. But it was there, and it was real, and just like that I felt my chest heaving and my eyes stinging. Yet, I managed to keep further tears at bay because, that quickly, my mind processed the rest of his words, and I wondered, why couldn't he do this? Was there something wrong with me? And what did Jack have to do with this? My heart soared in one direction, but my pride headed distinctly in another.

"I don't want you to anyway," I snapped, wiping my tears away with the back of my hand.

His shoulders jerked back, and he stared at me, mouth grim, and I could tell he was trying to make sense of my waffling behavior. He ran a hand across his head as though physical contact with himself would somehow pull comprehension from his brain. "You don't want me to? But what were you saying just now? What were you *doing*?"

"What did *you* say?" I countered, aware that I sounded more like a child than the woman he had just embraced.

His eyes searched me before speaking, trying to comprehend my rambling. I almost felt sorry for him because I knew he would read no answers or rational thinking on my face.

His shoulders dropped, and he sighed. "Grace, I'm attracted to you. Way too attracted. I don't understand what it is. But I'm engaged. This ... isn't right. And even if I weren't engaged, this isn't right."

And there it was. He'd chosen the high road—the road of truth—and answered me without ego standing in his way. I should have agreed with him, shook hands, and walked away. But pride won out again.

"Why wouldn't it be right? If we both feel the same way ... which I don't, of course ... but why wouldn't it be right?"

Before he responded, it dawned on me that Clay might be using me as an excuse to cover up his mother's relationship with Jack, and I gasped. "Because of Cassie and Jack's relationship? Is that it?"

He looked at me like I'd lost my senses, then snickered and shook his head. At another time, another place, I might have described it as a soothing chuckle, caring, even deferential. But here, in my anxiety, it rang as humor at my expense, and it infuriated me.

"Never mind," I snapped and turned to go.

He grabbed my arm. "I don't know what you're implying, but I know with certainty that Mom and Jack never had a relationship beyond high school ... other than friendship, I mean." He spoke in a slow, calm tone as if trying to explain to a child.

I jerked my arm free and cocked my head to glare at him, my non-verbals warning him not to be a smart-aleck or to taunt me. I opened my mouth to say as much, as a dozen insults and retorts flashed through my mind, but I couldn't get any words out before he continued, a wave of bewilderment creeping over his expression.

In a gentle voice he said, "Grace, I meant it wouldn't be right for us because you're young. Practically jail bait."

He must have seen confusion on my face because he continued, "You're what?

Sixteen years old? I'll be twenty-one next month. Grace, there are laws about some-one like me having a relationship with someone like you."

"That's ridiculous," I responded before even thinking. True to form, my fool-ish, stubborn ego argued against anything in my way whether or not I intended to go that way. And at this moment, I wasn't sure. "I'll be seventeen in two months. That makes me only four years younger than you. Jack and Mom were seven years apart, and they enjoyed the best relationship in the world. It's only an issue now because we're so young, but later on it won't be a problem—"

What was I saying?

"—I mean, it *wouldn't* be a problem ... *if* that's what we wanted to do ... which it's not ... at least it's not what I want ... because ... because Clay, I wasn't talking about you anyway."

His body stiffened, and he glared at me. He seemed wounded, abashed, some combination. "Then, who?"

"Who?" My voice cracked, and I bit my lip. He'd think I'd gone mad if I told him the truth—that I'd been talking about a dead man.

"Yes, who?" he asked in a tense voice, crossing his arms and lowering his chin. "Who were you talking about? You said you needed someone and didn't want him to leave. Who is it?"

"That's kind of personal, don't you think?" I huffed, crossing my arms too.

He shook his head. "No, if you care about someone, you should be proud of it."

I opened my mouth, but nothing came out. I couldn't think of any questions to ask back to dodge his probing. I knew being evasive would just prolong the uncomfortable conversation. Yet, I needed to say something. I couldn't admit that I had been distraught about losing a ghost, so I blurted out the first name that came to mind.

"Seth Rendale."

Clay inched his shoulders back even more as his jaw clenched, and his hands dropped to fist at his sides.

He blinked twice. "Seth? All this over Seth?" he asked, his tone bitter, sarcas-tic. "That's who was here with you by the cozy little fire the night I delivered the crutches, wasn't it?"

"That's none of your business."

He drew in a deep, steady breath, and I saw a vein pulse in his neck. As he glared at me, his eyes turned cold, flinty. He began to say something, but stopped and looked away instead. When he looked back, I could see that something on his face had changed, but I couldn't identify what. He nodded toward *Crossings*, his voice, flat. "I need to go. You seem to be fine now. I dropped off a new glider for you. I trust you will like it better than the old one." He turned to leave.

"A new glider? Why would you do that?"

I didn't realize I'd voiced that out loud until he stopped mid-stride and turned to glare at me.

He exhaled, his voice eerily calm. "Because Jack would want me to, and I didn't think it was such a good idea for me to spend time here trying to fix the old one. This little scene just confirmed that. Goodbye, Grace."

With that, he turned again and stalked away.

I stood there shaking, a lump in my throat, as I watched him disappear over the crest of the hill. In moments I heard a car door slam, an engine turn over, and tires cutting through gravel. I might have stood like that for hours, cemented to the ridge of the hill, if Tramp hadn't arrived, his nudge draining me of what energy I had left. I dropped onto the ground beside him, wondering what had just happened and why it mattered to me. How could it be that a man with whom I'd shared such harsh words could walk away, and all I could feel was loss and longing for the exquisite wonder of his touch?

PART III

The Thin Divide

Chapter 17

B y 8 o'clock that night, I stood with Seth beside the shooting gallery at the Williamsport carnival, sharing a funnel cake and brushing powdered sugar off my shirt.

After Clay had gone, I'd sat—sullen and sulky—on that grassy hillock most of the afternoon, trying to decide what to do. Although I could return to *Crossings* and talk with Will as usual, the tombstone had changed my comfort level, and I couldn't pinpoint why.

Death was accumulating on me again, much as it had three years ago, and I needed to be away from it, if even momentarily.

I searched for an alternative that took me away from everything for a while.

Seth became my alternative, and he seemed pleased to hear from me. The funny thing about pride is that it's selective and unveils a hierarchy of priorities that is sometimes both surprising and revealing. Pride said I shouldn't call Seth back, but an even greater pride told me I had to do damage control for my actions that afternoon with Clay.

I wanted Clay to see me out having fun, assuming he and Sondra would be there. The uncomfortable thought that I was using Seth crossed my mind, and I vowed to be frank with him about how I felt. Then, with a fresh perspective and damage control complete, I could return to Will later that night.

I had made my decision about joining Seth before I even returned to *Crossings* that afternoon, but the presence of a new oak and black wrought iron glider just to the left of the door to the apartment solidified my plan, particularly when it dawned on me that Clay had to have noticed the coziness I had created on the old porch with the other glider, the chimes, and the plants. He probably thought Seth and I were having intimate outings on that porch.

* * *

To my surprise, I enjoyed Seth's company. When I first saw him in the parking lot, I was disappointed that I didn't feel the same heady attraction to him that I had felt with Clay that afternoon, but still I was surprised at how well we got along together. I felt a sense of freedom with him.

We strolled around the carnival, rode the roller coaster, and ran into his friends from high school. We held hands twice, and I was struck at how comfortable it felt. We laughed a lot too. It felt good to be carefree, but it made me wish I could have experienced the same with Clay.

According to Reaghan, Clay and I were different. I had thought it too. But we weren't; the truth was that we were more alike than different.

The more I thought about it, the more startling the contrast became between Seth and Clay. Seth was a time that I had lost and wanted to have. Clay represented responsibility: service to country, focus on career preparation, duty to a dead father figure whose daughter unexpectedly arrived in town, devotion to a mother who practically raised him solo. Clay was a stability I longed to have in my future.

Perhaps it was thoughts of Clay that heightened my awareness, but as I stood by the Ferris wheel amidst the throng of hundreds of people, brushing away the sugar, I sensed his presence before I even saw him.

Sondra was at his side dressed in the height of fashion, standing out almost comically in a low-cut eyelet top, designer capris, and three-inch wedge shoes, against a sea of practical shorts, denim, and cotton sundresses. I suddenly felt inadequate in my jean skirt and sandals.

As it turned out, Sondra was a very good friend of Seth's oldest sister Chelsea, prompting a discussion between the two of them about Chelsea's engineering internship that summer at a Wyoming oil field. As though forgotten, Clay and I stood awkwardly by the sides of our dates waiting while they conversed. Twice, our eyes met in our efforts to be sociable, but otherwise his gaze darted to the activity and the people behind us while I took an unusual interest in the plastic plate I held, studying it, but saying nothing.

To combat the awkwardness, I offered the plate of funnel cake for the others to try.

For the first time, Sondra looked at me. "No, thank you." She forced a smile. "I don't eat grease."

I was too startled to be angry. Instead, I wondered if Sondra ever confided in Reaghan. Perhaps together they had decided I was a threat. But to whom? I began to wonder if I had imagined Clay's kiss that afternoon.

With a tone of irritation in his voice, Clay reacted. "Sondra—"

"Clay," she interrupted, "you like that stuff. Why don't you try it?" Her voice had an edge to it that made me think she was challenging him, daring him, but about what, I didn't know.

A strained silence followed as Clay stared at his fiancé.

"No, thank you." He turned to me. "I'm fine. Just fine."

Was I supposed to read a double meaning into his words? Confused, I dropped my eyes and withdrew my offer, pulling the funnel cake to the level of my navel.

Seth obviously hadn't even noticed the discomfort because he forged on, shifting the conversation to Sondra and Clay's nuptials. "Chelsea said you've asked her to be in the wedding. Have you set a date?"

"Clay," Sondra said without even looking at her fiancé, "I would like a fountain soda."

Rather than annoyance, I swear I saw relief on Clay's face. After ensuring that Seth and I didn't want anything to drink, he left to fulfill Sondra's request. I sensed that, for civility's sake, he was accommodating her request.

"No, we haven't set a date," Sondra said, picking up where Seth's question had left off. "I just haven't made up my mind, but Clay is hoping it will be this fall. He's so tired of waiting."

I pictured myself smashing the funnel cake into her face.

The ring of my cell phone interrupted my thoughts. I turned to the garbage can on my left, dumped the funnel cake, and clicked on to hear Aunt Tish's voice.

Clay returned just as I clicked off the phone.

"What happened?" He handed the fountain soda to Sondra, but kept his gaze on me. For one horrified moment I thought he was going to reach for me in front of the other two, but the concern in his voice prompted Sondra and Seth to turn to me also.

Seth quickly put his arm around me and feigned a closeness we hadn't yet developed. With false familiarity he said, "Grace, baby, what's wrong?"

Too shaken from the call to shrug off his arm, I spoke in little more than a whisper, "My Grandma Sadie had another stroke. The doctors said she probably wouldn't make it until morning. Aunt Tish said I should meet her in Philadelphia as soon as possible."

* * *

Escaping the carnival should have been a simple matter of saying goodbye and leaving. Instead, it turned out to be an emotional, ego-charged encounter among four people, each with a different agenda.

"Now?" Seth pouted. "You're leaving now? Can't you wait and leave later?" He must have sensed the collective disapproval of the other two because he shrugged and muttered, "I mean, she's dying anyway."

On both sides of me, I caught the negative reactions to his comment. To her credit, Sondra groaned and shook her head to let Seth know his words were inappropriate.

Clay, on the other hand, was more direct. He stepped into Seth's personal space, without having given the effect of moving at all. Despite his war injury, there was something almost feline in the way that guy moved. He put his face mere inches from Seth's, locked eye contact, and said, "Seth, Grace doesn't need your selfishness right now. What she needs is your help. So man up and figure out what you can do to make her life easier."

Seth hiked up his shoulders. "This is none of your business, Baxter. I—"

Before Seth could finish, I squeezed between the two of them.

"I'll be fine." I didn't have time for this argument or their locker-room behavior; I had already switched into automatic and was plotting the tasks I had to take care of before embarking on my trip. "Thank you both—"

"Drive her home," Clay commanded to Seth.

Seth's head snapped back indignantly. "But—"

"That's not necessary." I sighed.

"—her car's here," Seth countered, his voice sounding angry. "Why don't you just back off?"

"Clay, stay out of it," Sondra said, annoyed.

"Sondra, don't—" Clay started, never taking his eyes off Seth.

"Yeah, who does he—" Seth countered loudly, puffing out his chest.

"Clay, don't tell me—" Sondra began in a seething tone.

"Stop it!" I yelled at the colliding voices. My voice sounded a little hysterical, so I took a deep breath and exhaled slowly. All three sets of eyes stared at me, as well as several sets from passersby who had now stopped to see what the commotion was all about. "Look, I'm fine. Seth's right, my car is here, and I need it anyway."

"Someone should drive you." Clay's voice was now one of take-charge practicality, less emotion.

"No, it's too far. I might be there for several days," I contended, more than a little annoyed. I was perfectly capable of handling this situation on my own.

Clay didn't respond but looked directly at me. He was used to taking charge, and I could tell he was trying to formulate a response or a plan to handle this unexpected crisis. Then, as if some unseen signal had passed between us, he nodded acceptance of my words. His shoulders eased.

"What about Tramp and Chubbs?" he asked, ignoring the fact that he was revealing personal knowledge between us.

He must have read on my face that I had completely forgotten about them because he solved the problem before I could even think of options.

"Leave your key under the door mat, and I'll pick them up. Between Adriana and me, they will be in good hands."

From the side, I sensed disapproval from both Sondra and Seth.

When I looked into Clay's face to say "thank you," I caught my breath. For an instant, I thought I saw there the same tenderness that I had seen that afternoon before I had pulled away from him. I wanted to throw myself into his arms again, just for a minute, just to feel his strength, but I was acutely aware that Seth was watching closely, and he was supposed to be my date for the evening.

In a gentler tone, Clay continued, ignoring the others. "It's no problem. I didn't mention this earlier, but Jack spoke of Sadie Gallagher often. Did you know he would stop to see her on his way to or from Boston?"

I shook my head and never lost eye contact with him, but inside my heart sank. Another tidbit about Jack that I never knew.

"Despite her paralysis, Jack somehow communicated with her. I feel like I know her too." As he spoke, my eyes filled with tears. He reached out and touched my arm, and all the splendor of his embrace that afternoon was in his fingers. "Be careful on the drive—" he suddenly seemed to be aware of the other two. Their pooled gaze cut like a guillotine between us. He dropped his hand and stepped back. "—we'll watch the place for you," he finished in a neutral tone.

And yet here I sat, my Volvo headed east, on my way to still more death. I felt apprehensive about going. Grandma Sadie hadn't been able to talk in years. She probably wouldn't even recognize us, if she were cognizant of anything at all.

After packing my backpack, I had gone in search of Will in the old house. By then it was going on 10 o'clock, certainly late enough in the day that he could manifest himself. He responded immediately. Perhaps it was because of the urgency in my voice, but for the first time, he seemed to float hurriedly down the stairs toward me. Always before, when time was not of the essence, he would make a semblance of walking much as a living person would. The shock of seeing his form glide toward me brought back the horror I had felt that afternoon when I found his tombstone. In that instant, he seemed very ghostly to me—a ludicrous thought, considering that he was a ghost.

He must have read distress on my face. "Are you hurt? What happened?"

I was more than willing to attribute my reaction to Grandma Sadie's death. When I told him what had happened and what my plans were, his reaction startled me. He nodded his head and asked, "Is she a pious woman?"

"I dunno ... yes, yes I guess ... given the way mom talked about her... I guess so."

"Wonderful. How wonderful for her. Remember to pray for her. It helps to ease the transition into her next life. Be safe." With that, he turned to leave.

"Wait! Will, I may be gone for several days."

He turned back. "I understand. Even with automobiles, it's somewhat of a trip to journey that far."

"No ... I mean ... I will miss you ... talking with you, I mean."

He cocked his head and stood silently looking at me. More than any time before, I was annoyed that his face remained distorted such that I could not read his expression. Before I could verbalize my feelings, he added gently, "I will be here when you return. You must go and enjoy the celebration."

His use of the word celebration would register with me later. At the moment, however, I was focused on his disappointing, nonchalant demeanor.

I was hurt—I admit it. I wanted him to say more. But what?

"What if I don't return?" It wasn't a challenge, just a question.

"You will." He reached out and rested his cold hand on my cheek.

Then he turned and faded into the walls.

Chapter 18

By 2 a.m., I stretched out on a lounge chair, just outside Grandma Sadie's room at the Jefferson Hospital. Nearby sat Aunt Tish with Uncle Phil, Sadie's sister Elizabeth, and Elizabeth's daughter Sharah.

The conversation proved tolerable for the first few hours after my arrival when we settled into the spacious visitors' lounge.

However, once they exhausted the memories, the foursome focused on me. Between the things Sharah said and Aunt Tish's awkward glances, I deduced that my aunt had exaggerated the details of my summer venture. Sharah's comments and praise made my physical location in West Virginia sound more like Washington D.C., and my project to refurbish *Crossings*, a venture akin to a formal summer arts program. As a result, I avoided details in my answers, lest I incur my aunt's wrath.

Just before dawn, I tired of being the topic of conversation, so I excused myself. Something—I'm not sure what—drew me back into Grandma Sadie's room.

She looked at peace as she lay on the small bed, eyes closed, arms at her side, unaware of my presence. Despite her yellowed coloring and her age, Grandma was still an attractive woman. Her hair was still thick and more auburn than gray, her wrinkles were soft and inconspicuous, and her lip definition hadn't faded away like I'd seen on so many senior ladies. A gold chain encircled her neck and disappeared under the folds of her hospital gown. To her right lay a worn Bible; placed there I assumed, by a friend or perhaps a nurse, certainly not the family. The movement of the heart monitor signaled life, but no doubt she was taking her final breaths in these last hours of her life.

My throat tightened. Mom should have been there to say goodbye to her mother. Then again, I wouldn't want Mom to go through this heartache. I suspected that no matter what your age, losing your mother would be painful. I, for one, had learned that it's an ache you never get over; it's just one with which you learn to live.

Beside the lone window in the room sat several oversized chairs. I pulled two together, plopped down, and stretched. I intended to take in the city lights before the dawn drowned them out, but my eyes kept drifting back to my grandmother. My mother's mother. She'd already experienced her first stroke when my mother died, so Grandma Sadie never had an appropriate chance to say goodbye to her daughter. I marveled now that—assuming Will spoke the truth—they would be able to say "hello" before the day ended. To think that she clung to life here in the room with me now, but that tonight, tomorrow, sometime soon she would be gone forever, well, it ranked as one of those finalities about death that I always had a hard time grasping.

As I stared at her, I thought it sad how little I knew about her. Perhaps that's why it bothered me so much that people in West Virginia shared things about Jack that I'd never known. I had wondered if that meant he harbored some kind of a secret life. Perhaps the simple truth was that I'd never taken the time to learn more about his world. Or Mom's. Or Grandma Sadie's.

These thoughts filled me with desire to go to Grandma Sadie's bed, take her hand, and ask forgiveness for being so selfish. To tell her I regretted not having known her better. To ask her to hug my family for me when she moved on.

But doubt stopped me—the process of death that Will described sounded so absurd.

With a sigh, I turned to look out the window. The first rays from a butter-yellow sun illuminated Philadelphia in a dim glow, casting a harsh light on the rigid lines of the city's landscape. I looked dispassionately at towering buildings and saw instead a crop of tall elm trees set against the backdrop of blue-ridged mountains. The wide expanse of the Ben Franklin Bridge as it ushered scores of vehicles across the Delaware River brought memories of the unadorned Cushwa Basin Bridge that deposited me at the crude road leading to *Crossings*. And the pedestrians hurrying in and out of Au Bon Pain on Chester Street below, crossing each other's path with no sign of recognition, contrasted with the *Time Out* and the small handful of people who would be there at any given time, all of them more inclined to talk and linger than to rush through as these folks did.

I closed my eyes to picture Williamsport and *Crossings*. I wondered where Tramp and Chubbs were at that moment.

Most of all, I wondered *who* they were with.

* * *

When my cell phone rang, I awoke with a start, wondering when I'd fallen asleep. Before hitting "send" I noted the time—9:05 a.m.

Adriana's perky voice came over the line. Home now in Williamsport, with her boyfriend Darius visiting, she expressed sympathy about Grandma, and asked when I thought I'd return.

"I don't know," I yawned. "The doctor thinks Grandma will be ... passing ... today." I cringed. *Could I say these things within earshot of my grandmother? What's more, was she still alive?* With relief I noted that the heart monitor still reacted to her heartbeat.

"Grace, I'm sorry I can't be there for you."

"Don't be silly. How did the auditions go?"

"Great! I earned first chair ... that's like first place. I'm going to have a busy semester with all these concerts, but that's okay. The exposure will be great."

"Ade, that's wonderful. I look forward to hearing you play."

"Grace," her voice soared from exuberant to serious in two seconds flat. "Tramp and Chubbs are here with me."

I laughed. "Yeah, I'll bet that one surprised you."

"Helloooooooooo, are you kidding? You could have blown me over with a feather when Clay showed up with them this morning. He looked exhausted. Said he and Sondra ran into you and Seth at the Carnival. Did Clay offer to take care of them? Just like that?"

So that was the story he gave her? Of course he left out the fact that we exchanged words at *Crossings* yesterday afternoon.

"Yes, but I'm not surprised he brought them to you. I could tell Sondra didn't like his idea. He must have decided that he'd have no peace with her until he put them in someone else's care."

"I don't think Clay is worried about making peace with her anymore."

"What do you mean?" I groaned, picturing Clay lecturing Sondra on her behavior at the carnival. Would he be so gullible as to believe she would just agree to change her ways?

"They broke up last night. Clay says it's over between the two of them ... for good."

I felt my entire body react to the news—my head jerked back, my mouth fell open, my hand flew to my chest, I may have gasped ... or not because I think my heart and voice stopped in tandem. I began to sweat; my mind went fuzzy, and I almost fell off the chair. Then, every part of me re-activated and kicked into overdrive—heart, mind, adrenaline, sweat glands. Adriana may as well have said that Williamsport disappeared into a large fissure in the earth over night.

"Hello? Grace, are you there?"

"What? Yes. I'm here." My heart pounded with such loud reverberations that I could hear them echoing in my throbbing temples.

"Oh, thought I'd lost you. Anyway, I feel bad for Clay, but I'm sooooooo happy about this," Adriana continued without taking a breath. "After he came back from Afghanistan, they were never the same. It seemed like Sondra held a grudge about him getting hurt ... like he's to blame. She is such a ... a ... "

"She's a witch."

I thought I heard Adriana snicker, but, true to form, she did not reciprocate the mud slinging.

Still trying to compose myself, I asked, "So, who broke it off?"

"I don't know. He distinctly used the word, 'we' as in 'we broke up last night.'"

"What happened?" I tried to sound—*to be*—detached. For good measure, I even forced myself to yawn again. I wanted to feel indifferent.

"He said that they'd grown apart and wanted different things."

"Well, that's the perfect textbook breakup line."

"Uh huh. But he'll tell me in time. I'm just so glad to have him back that it doesn't matter to me why it ended. You wait—now you'll be able to get to know him too. You'll love him."

Ouch.

She meant "love him" in the figurative sense, I know, but still, her words made me cringe, and I almost felt guilty, although I wasn't sure about what.

"Hey, you never did explain that little scene between the two of you at the church."

"That? Oh, it's nothing." I didn't want to talk about my interactions with Clay over the phone. "Ade, I just have a few minutes. Can we talk about all that when I get home?"

"Sure. You've got a lot going on right now. Don't worry about Tramp and Chubbs. Clay wanted to come back and get them this afternoon, but I told him I'd keep them. His apartment ... over Cassie's garage ... it's not very big."

"Is it alright with your family if Tramp and Chubbs stay there? Because if not—"

"Don't be silly," she chided. "In fact, Corey volunteered to walk Tramp ... day and night. He thinks that will catch the attention of the ladies. And Chubbs's just fine. My dad is kind of fascinated with him. You might have a hard time getting him back."

"Your father's fun."

"I know." She laughed even louder. "This morning we saw a guy named Holland Greer pulling out of that road that leads into your house. Dad said he's the sort of guy that follows you into a revolving door and comes out first."

Holland Greer! On Whistle Ridge Road? My discomfort radar sounded alarm. "You saw Holland Greer leaving my place?"

Adriana hesitated, and when she spoke, her voice sounded guarded, curious. "I don't know if he was at *Crossings* or not. Is something wrong?"

"There are no other houses on that road. He had to have been back at my house."

"Maybe he'd turned around," she offered, although her voice suggested she didn't believe it either. "He *is* a Civil War expert, you know. We saw him on the History Channel once talking about Antietam. And he's always searching for artifacts. That whole area around the Potomac, and especially your house, was in the middle of all the stuff that happened during the war. Maybe he came to visit to talk about the house."

"Before 9 o'clock in the morning?" I spewed, annoyed, but I regretted my tone. Poor Adriana was just the messenger. "Sorry. You're probably right. I'm sure it's nothing."

But it was something. I just didn't know what. Mostly, I fretted over Will, and concern grew in my gut.

* * *

As I clicked off the phone, Aunt Tish came into the room.

"I thought I heard you talking. Was that Kate?"

I shook my head. "My friend, Adriana. She's watching Tramp and Chubbs for me." I needed Aunt Tish to be able to trust me, so I figured the less said, the better.

"Sounds like you've made a nice friend." She pulled a chair close and sat, curling one sandaled foot beneath her, then brushed a piece of lint from her signature bohemian-style outfit of ill-fitting linen. She'd topped her ensemble with the "love beads" she had purchased in New York City the afternoon that John Lennon of the *Beatles* was assassinated.

"I'm glad you've moved on from that airhead Kate, but I hope this Alexandra person—"

"Adriana."

"Whatever ... I hope she's the one who's not originally from that area." She sighed, flipping loose tendrils of frizzy hair from her face. "Perhaps instead of socializing, you should be working on your designs. It's the only gift you've got."

That's not true. I can communicate with ghosts.

"Yes, I am."

"Good, good. That's good." Satisfied with my answer, she assessed my physical traits.

"You slept for a few hours." She huffed, leaned over to lift lank strands of hair from my eyes, then rattled off her observations: My hair looked atrocious, I'd lost too much weight, I should have packed better clothes, blah, blah, blah.

This from the woman who wore wrinkled linen and whose hair frizzled out three inches from her head.

"Sorry." I meant for sleeping, but if she thought I meant for her list of my shortcomings, then that was fine too. "Did I miss anything?" I used my head to point in Grandmother's direction.

"Not much." She exhaled and sat back, apparently giving up on my hair. "The doctor checked in while you slept. Lordy, he's quite the talker. I'm surprised he didn't wake you. Maybe he thinks a lot of conversation helps justify his exorbitant fees."

"What did he say?" I stretched, trying to work out the kinks from the awkward way I'd been sleeping.

"That it was up to the insurance companies how much—"

"About Grandma," I interrupted gently. "What did he say about *her?*"

"Oh, that. Mother's heart is weakening rapidly. He doesn't think she will live through the day."

"I'm sorry."

"It's okay. Mother had her own backward way of viewing the world, but she was a good woman and lived a good life, I guess. You know that she and I haven't been close through the years. Tracy understood her best, but still when it's your mom, it hurts." She startled then, as if she remembered to whom she was talking. "But you know that." She waved away her discomfort with a flick of her wrist.

I looked out the window. I wouldn't talk about my sweet, precious mother. Not here. Not with her. Not in this context. The relationships Aunt Tish and I shared with our respective mothers were as different as night and day.

"You doing okay? We didn't get a chance to talk alone when you arrived." Aunt Tish's kindnesses were generally startling and always short-lived. A wolf in sheep's clothing.

"Yeah, I'm fine." I smiled, then looked at Grandma Sadie and added, "All things considered."

She followed my gaze. "Aunt Elizabeth will have a hard time with this. I'm glad you didn't volunteer your actual whereabouts this summer. It would just give her more to stress about."

I'd lived with Aunt Tish long enough to know that she wasn't concerned that my location would give Elizabeth more stress, so I let it go by.

A taut silence fell. Tiny ticks of uncomfortable time.

Then, Aunt Tish leaned forward and placed a finger under my chin. "You look oddly worse and yet strangely better."

"I'm happy, Aunt Tish. I'm working on the house, and playing piano, and biking with Adriana. The fresh air is clearing my head. I found a great café, and I've met some nice people." I'd already voiced these same details to her on the phone, but I needed to say it in person, too.

"Like Seth? Wasn't that the name of the young man you went out with last night?"

I shrugged. "He's okay."

She raised her eyebrows. "No vibes?"

"He's fun. But he's just a friend."

She smiled and relaxed. "Good. Just don't let him know how large your trust fund is. I imagine that would be a real attraction to those kinds of people." She pulled another chair close, kicked off her shoes, and elevated her feet as I was doing. Just when I thought she had refocused, she offered more: "A local boy with small dreams and cloistered experiences isn't your kind, Grace."

What about one with experiences in life-and-death situations on the other side of the world?

I took a deep breath before responding. "I won't let anything or anyone get in the way of my dreams."

She squinted her eyes and studied me again, and I sensed she was trying to come to a decision.

"You really are ahead of your years, aren't you?" she asked derisively.

I shrugged. "I'm different, that's all. I guess I had to grow up quicker than my friends."

"Well, you do make sensible decisions. I don't agree with your thinking and your philosophy most of the time," she complained, "but I can work on that this fall."

"Sounds like work." I chose a vague answer so as to protect my plans of staying in West Virginia. She didn't know I had no intention of returning to Boston. Best to hold off on that conversation. Jack had tried to teach Julie and me that timing was everything, and I finally appreciated that lesson.

She nodded and said what I'd been waiting to hear. "Grace, you'll understand if I delay my trip to Marlawn—"

"Marlowe." I followed my firm correction with a sweet smile. *Don't intimidate her.*

"Whatever." She rolled her eyes. "You'll understand if I delay my trip? This," she swept the hospital room into a gesture, "will put me dangerously close to the deadline for the open house at the Lockwood Gallery."

"I understand," I said and managed to contain my joy.

* * *

By noon, the entire family gathered in Grandma Sadie's room, chairs pulled close to the bed, Sharah collecting sandwich orders. In the interim, the doctor had visited and told us what we already suspected: "anytime now." Thereafter, the tears flowed again, as Aunt Tish, Elizabeth and Sharah secured time alone with Grandma to say goodbye, each in her own way, given that Grandmother couldn't respond.

This meant that I, alone, had not yet said goodbye. But the others did not know that; I could tell they assumed I had done so during the night while they talked in the lounge. I dreaded goodbyes, especially one so permanent.

Once again, I questioned my faith in everything Will said. Perhaps there were ghosts and nothing more. Perhaps the ghosts existed only because they died horrible deaths. What did that mean for Grandma Sadie? No dimension, no heaven, no anything? What could I say to her? *So Grandma, good luck with that nothingness you're headed into. Your good choices were a waste of time.*

"Grace?"

Uncle Phil's voice brought me back to the present.

"Oh, sorry."

"The doctor asked you a question," Aunt Tish said.

I hadn't even noticed the doctor's return. I glanced up and saw a man in his early fifties, medium height, pale face, and a tired look in his eyes. He wore the stereotypical uniform of a doctor—white lab coat, polished shoes, stethoscope around the neck.

He cleared his throat. "I was curious as to what you hoped to study in college?

We can always use good doctors."

The heart monitor eliminated the need for a response. It switched from emitting a steady beep to an accelerated blip, to a long, single tone. While the rest of us held our breaths, the doctor placed his stethoscope on Grandmother's chest. A nurse hurried into the room. Seconds ticked by before the doctor frowned and looked up. "She's gone."

After a few initial nonsensical sounds of surprise, no one said a word, as though we were shocked, despite having had ample warning. It was as if we each tried to grasp this change, this concept of death, and were giving acceptance time to kick in as we took one last look at this woman who'd been a part of our lives for years. Several of us reached out to join hands.

A second nurse entered the room and proceeded to remove plastic tubes. The doctor turned to the first nurse, who grabbed Grandmother's chart. "Time of death is one seventeen p.m."

So that was it. From one second to the next, a heartbeat stopped. Life then death. I closed my eyes. It niggled inside me that I should say some kind of a prayer. "Grace?"

Before I could respond, I heard a collective gasp from the others.

I opened my eyes to see everyone staring, in dropped-jaw incredulity, not at me, but at Grandma Sadie.

My breath trapped in my throat, and before I even turned my gaze to her, I knew—just knew—that my grandmother had spoken to me.

"I don't believe this—" Elizabeth squeaked.

"Mother! Oh my God—" Aunt Tish whimpered.

"Doctor?" Uncle Phil stammered.

Grandma Sadie feebly lifted her arm a few inches as though reaching toward me. I hurried to her and wrapped her hand in both of mine.

"Grandma, I'm here." Tears flooded my eyes as I moved my ear to within inches of her face.

With her free hand, she feebly reached under the neckline of her gown to grab at the chain. She pulled, easily severing it, and dragged her fist to my hand, depositing an object onto my palm. Without breaking eye contact, I closed my hand. The object felt cold and flat and round. I knew, without even seeing it, that she had placed Jack's gold coin in my hand.

She spoke two words that, later, I would look back and identify as the instant when my world changed, with a complete and irrevocable shift, and headed in another direction.

She whispered, "Trust Will," then closed her eyes to welcome death.

Chapter 19

My memory of the next few minutes is a blur, but I recall everyone around me reacting, trying to apply human logic to the most unusual death they had ever seen. Uncle Phil mumbled something about incompetent medical staff while the doctor swore he'd never seen anything like this in his twenty-six years of practicing medicine. The nurse dropped into a chair and grabbed a magazine to fan her face as Elizabeth wailed over Grandma Sadie's body. Aunt Tish and Sharah busied themselves rationalizing their way through what Grandma had said.

"No, no, it wasn't 'trust will.' She must have said 'trust *His* will,'" Aunt Tish snapped.

Sharah agreed. "Yes, that must be it. She always had a rather religious side to her."

"Of course," Aunt Tish further reasoned. "It only makes sense that Mother would reach out to Grace since she is so young and gullible. Mother wanted her to trust His—" she bopped her head toward the sky, "—will, His word, and all that stuff."

"Definitely," Sharah agreed.

Their distorted rationalization complete, the two congregated with the others. The confusion about what had just transpired proved more than ample reason for them to pull together, as though a pool of gawkers could make better sense of it than each could individually. Their opinions matched, and they differed. Grandma Sadie died twice or she hadn't. Her heart stopped and started again, or it didn't. The coin could be real gold, or it couldn't. Someone should find out if she'd been able to talk all these years, or they shouldn't.

As I listened to the six of them trying to find logic in something only blind faith could explain, I watched Grandma Sadie's soul rise from the bed. I must not have seen it ascend when she first died because I had lost my belief in everything Will had said. This meant she must have left, met him in the dimension, and returned.

Her words, then, to "Trust Will" changed everything. The wires coiled around my heart broke free. Anguish had overtaken me in increments, first through loss, then through its many aftershocks. But the truth is that sometimes all a person needed was someone to remind her of hope, of a reason to keep on going on.

I would never be the same again.

I felt an infusion of such joy, it nearly lifted me off the floor. Tears trickled down my face. The first happy tears I spilled in more than three years. As Grandma rose, I could feel the burdens lifting from *my* shoulders and from *my* life. Will was right. And, he cared enough to have gone into the dimension to greet my grandmother. She had come back to change my life forever, and now she would journey on to a monstrous greeting from my mother. *My mother! And Jack and Julie!*

Even through my tears, I could discern the definition of Grandma's soul so much better than Will's. Could I attribute this clarity to the fact that I had changed? Or, did the newness of Grandma's death play a factor, whereas Will was centuries old? I couldn't wait to get home to be with him.

As Grandma Sadie rose, I remembered Will voicing confusion right after death. Knowing that the others could not see her soul and paid no attention to me, I blubber-whispered through my tears, "It's okay, Grandma. It's all good."

She smiled and moved closer. "Of those to whom much is given, much is expected. Use your gift wisely, Grace. I love you."

My chin trembled, and I clamped my lips together, almost undone by the love she radiated. I nodded because there was no need to say more. As she faded away, I sensed that in a few blinks of time, she would see my family on the other side of that river calling, "Look! Look! Here she comes!"

* * *

With the discussions going on around me of the details of Grandma Sadie's burial wishes, I headed to the large stone church I'd seen from the hospital window.

For an hour I sat in that church, enjoying its privacy and sacredness. I prayed for Grandma Sadie. I talked to God. I chattered to my family as though they sat beside me. I emptied my heart of three years' worth of angst. I thought about Will and, for the first time, truly accepted that I had to return home to set him free. I wondered how I would find the strength to face the "dangerous and frightening" situation he had said it would take to help him. With that thought I added a new affirmation to my self-talk: "I will fear no evil, for Thou art with me."

* * *

That evening, we checked into a hotel on Walnut Street and in the morning attended a small chapel service at the Emerald Lawn Assisted Living Facility where Grandma Sadie spent her last years.

By early afternoon, the family tackled the onerous task of emptying Grandma Sadie's room. We each selected a keepsake. I chose a beautiful cross that Elizabeth pulled from Grandmother's jewelry box. Dangling from a long platinum chain and encrusted with small white pearls, it measured two inches in length. By 5:30 p.m., I hung the cross from my rearview mirror and tucked a newly purchased box of chocolates for the Barrones on my front seat.

With a contented sigh, I headed home.

* * *

"Oh my gosh, Grace, these are amazing." Adriana bit into her fourth chocolate. She'd carried two pieces from the house where we left the rest of her family, haggling over what few caramel-centered pieces remained in the box. "You didn't need to do this."

I placed an annoyed Chubbs on the back seat. Tramp had already bounded onto the front seat, immediately forgiving my absence and his removal from our new home, but Chubbs—in true cat-like obstinacy—still rejected my attention.

I pulled Adriana into an embrace. "It's the least I could do. You are the best friend a person could ever have. Thank you."

She must have been startled by my candor because she broke the embrace to look me in the eye. "Are you okay, Grace?" She tilted her head, studying. "You seem different."

I felt a tiny smile playing at the corners of my mouth, and I darted my gaze away. Where to begin? It would take hours to explain—hours I didn't want to spare tonight.

I looked back in time to see her roll her eyes and grin. "Never mind. Just tell me when you're ready."

What had I done to deserve such a good friend? "Thanks."

"But I still want to know what happened at the Carnival with Clay." She grinned as she walked me around to the driver's side. "And I mean *soon*."

"I promise. Tomorrow. Okay?"

"Sure." She stopped and smacked her forehead. "Clay asked me to let him know when you got home. I'll call him—"

"No!"

She stared at me, wide-eyed. I calmed my voice before adding, "Not tonight, okay? Wait until tomorrow to call him."

She frowned. "You know, you both sure are acting weird. And that's funny because you two are so much—" She broke off. Comprehension blossomed on her face. "Oh my gosh! You two *are* so much—"

"Whoa." I raised both hands and pulsed my palms at her. "We can talk about all this tomorrow. Just ... please, don't call him tonight."

A few seconds ticked by, and then she nodded, still staring at me as she tossed the last chocolate piece into her mouth. I pictured her mind working, racing, trying to second-guess what I might say the next day.

I tried to refocus her thoughts. "Biking tomorrow? At Antietam? If it's still okay for me to use your mom's bike ...?"

"Sure, sure," she muttered, although, given the caramel clamping her teeth together, it sounded more like "Sore, sore."

"I'll pick you up here at one o'clock," I yelled as I pulled away, heading home to Will.

* * *

The timing could not have been better. As I crossed the Potomac, the sunlight dropped rapidly behind the distant mountains. I'd made it to *Crossings* by candle-lighting to see Will. With a start, it hit me that my heart had set up permanent residence here. *Home.* The word swelled in my mind. Home was the wind rattling the chimes on the deep porch and me curled on the swing. Home was a crackling fire and Will sitting in a wing-backed chair regaling me with stories of a long-ago era. Home was Tramp and Chubbs and my piano and cooking in my own kitchen. Home was where history came alive.

Home was *Crossings*, and I determined to *never* let it go.

Once inside the apartment, I moved too quickly to situate my pets, spilling dog food, then water, then slipping on both as I hurried to the door leading to the main house, all the while yelling, "Will! I'm back!"

Just after my butt made contact with the floor, I heard Chubbs hiss and dash into the bedroom. Only one thing could raise his dander—I looked up to greet Will.

Instead of speaking, however, I gaped in stunned silence.

A different Will stood before me, one of perfect clarity as if I'd finally removed bottle glasses. No distortion. No deterioration. His skin, a fleshy color. His cheeks, rosy. He had beard stubble, and green irises in almond-shaped eyes. Hair straddled a lean, strong face and brushed his shoulders. For the first time I noted tattered, unkempt clothes, his waistcoat threadbare, and his boots scuffed, how he must have been dressed when he died.

Yet, despite rugged, strapping features and an intelligent countenance, he looked careworn for one so young. No doubt war could be blamed for the signs of premature stress on his body. His eyes, however, belied his war-torn appearance, reflecting innocence, as though untouched by the experiences he'd collected.

"Welcome home." His voice, crisp and distinct, he held out a hand to assist me off the floor.

He appeared so different, so real, so male, that my face warmed.

Had he always looked at me with such intensity and appreciation?

Joy cut through my discomfort and I shrieked, "Oh, Will," as I scrambled off the floor and threw myself into him.

The hug was brief, long enough to feel his cold form and to remember that despite his different appearance, he remained a non-being, a soul. *A ghost.*

"It went well." He stepped back. "I spent time with Sadie."

In one smooth movement, I squealed, laughed, and bowed my face into my hands. "Will, she died and then came back! It was incredible. You should have seen everyone's faces. She reached out for me and held my hand. She came back to tell me to trust you, and then she gave me the gold coin that Jack had given her—" I broke off when I noted, from the grin on his face, that he already knew. "You saw her before *and* after she gave me the coin, didn't you?"

He nodded. "I was fortunate to meet her."

"So you were there, in the dimension, when she crossed over."

His smile grew. "Your mother is beautiful."

As though someone flipped a light switch marked "tears," my eyes glazed over.

"You saw her?" My question came out part whisper, part plea.

"Yes. Her. Jack. Julie. Your father and your grandfather, Patrick. Your great grandparents. It was an incredible homecoming."

I dropped in the nearest chair, shaking, overwhelmed. "It's all so hard to fathom," I said, wiping away tears.

"I know." He crouched down beside me like a baseball catcher and took my hand. His touch was cool, but still I warmed inside. "They're happy, Grace, and they're together. They want you to live your life. Now, come. Let's make a fire and talk about it."

I let Will lead me toward the old house. Just as I opened the connecting door, someone called my name, rapped on the exterior door to the apartment, and walked in.

I turned to see Seth, dressed in his park ranger attire. I had no chance to close the door to the old house or prepare myself to have Seth and Will in the room *at the same time.*

"Hey, Grace!" Seth glanced around, oblivious to Will's presence.

My peripheral vision caught Will's body posturing protectiveness toward me, a habit ingrained from long ago. "Seth!" I blurted to let Will know I recognized our unexpected guest.

Will's body relaxed, but his voice revealed annoyance. "He let himself in."

"I see that," I gave him my best "don't-make-this-awkward" look.

"You see what?' Seth moved across the apartment toward me.

"I said ... I see ... you ... I mean, it's good to see you."

"Oh, I'm glad to hear that." Seth grinned and relaxed. "After the other night I was afraid ... well, never mind. I'm glad you're back. I saw you crossing the Cushwa Basin Bridge. Thought I'd follow you over."

By now he'd reached me and planted a quick kiss on my lips.

"Should I throw him out?" Will inclined his head in a conspiratorial manner, and then circled Seth, assessing him. His countenance darkened again, as though a black tide coursed through his body. "In my day, a man could get horse-whipped for taking such liberties."

"Stop that," I whispered to Will.

"Sheesh, it was just a kiss," Seth complained. "What's the big deal?"

Given that he thought I spoke to him, Seth's comment was justified, but his resentful tone surprised me. He pulled back and turned his attention to the apartment. "Wow, this place is drafty."

"I didn't mean the kiss," I took his elbow and led him away from Will. "I meant stop ... standing in the draft ... and instead come over here and sit by the table ..." I turned and shot Will a pointed look. "... where there will be *no* draft."

"Is this your boyfriend?" Will asked, ignoring my nonverbal plea and following us to the table. "I'm not comfortable with him. He doesn't seem to fit you."

I caught myself before responding out loud to Will. Instead, I shook my head at him and turned my attention to Seth who was settling into a chair facing out the front window, toward the river.

"Nice view. The place is kinda vampirish, but the view is great."

"Seth, I just got home, and I'm really tired. I was going to call you tomorrow."

"That's okay. We don't have to go anywhere. We can just sit here and talk."

"Not seasoned in taking hints, is he?" Will stood behind Seth, facing me as I sat down at the opposite side of the table. I suspected he rooted himself there so that he could thwart Seth in case things got out of control. "Were he a true gentleman, he would leave."

His complaint overlapped with Seth's comment: "Grace, I want to talk about that Baxter chump."

Before I registered Seth's question, or the tone in his voice—angry, determined—I responded, out loud, to Will. "He is a gentleman."

Seth hitched his head back again, looking indignant. "How can you call that jerk a gentleman? Pushing his nose in where it doesn't belong? Now I hear he and Sondra have broken up. Is that because of you? So, who's it going to be, Grace? Me or him?"

"Who is he talking about?" Will asked, his gaze glued to the back of Seth's head.

They both talked at once, such that when I blurted, "Clay," to Will, I cringed. It wasn't the answer I had intended for Seth. This prompted them both to repeat Clay's name, but whereas Will nodded and said, "Clay" in an "ah-yes-I-remember-him" kind of way, Seth said it with disgust.

"Clay?" Seth repeated, pounding the table with his fist and standing up. His chair tumbled backward behind him. Startled, I sprinted out of my chair. He paled and his hands fisted at his sides. "You led me on, Grace."

I opened my mouth, but nothing came out. I couldn't think. Seth turned red, and Will swelled in darkness again, preparing to step in if things escalated. Memories flashed of Henry and Greasy Jim flying over the side of the porch. I didn't want Seth to suffer the same fate. I had to get him out of the house quickly.

"Seth, wait," I stood and came closer to him. Will moved in too. "That's not what I meant. I really enjoyed being at the carnival with you. Honest. I think you're a ... great guy. I want to spend more time with you. It's just that I'm not sure about things at the moment."

Seth's eyes searched my face, no doubt trying to determine if I meant what I said.

"I'm sorry, I can't talk right now. Can we get together tomorrow night, and we'll talk about it then?"

As if he sensed my determination, he nodded and stalked to the door, leaving an atmosphere of tension behind. It struck me again that Seth wasn't used to not getting what he wanted.

I followed him to the door. As he reached for the knob, he turned.

"Meet me at the *Time Out,* tomorrow night." His voice was demanding. "Seven thirty." He hesitated, exhaled a deep breath, and softened his tone to add, "My treat."

As he exited onto the porch, he grumbled, "You oughta turn some heat on in there."

Chapter 20

An hour later, seated by the fire, Will and I exhausted our conversation about Grandma Sadie. For the first time, Tramp joined us, as though anxious not to be separated from me again. He curled into the open angle between our seats.

"I'm not sure—" My breath caught as I looked up to see Will's smile. Despite the shadows from the fire dancing across his face, he looked so handsome and *alive*. I wasn't used to this clarity, nor how it made me feel. I wished I could touch him, trace the curve of his chin, the arch of his brow.

I couldn't stop myself from saying it: "Will, I love you."

He reached forward and placed a cold hand over mine, his eyes searching my face before frowning. "I love you too, Grace."

"You're so ... amazing ... and brave ..." I moved forward also, our faces a few inches apart, and babbled in one long breath. "I've never met anyone like you. Can't you stay here with me? Won't you at least consider it?"

He smiled, and with his free hand, reached out to tuck a lock of loose hair behind my ear. "Your life won't progress until mine ends."

"But—"

"Shh, Grace, someone special is out there. Perhaps around the corner, and you don't even know it. But as long as I'm here, you cannot move on with any aspect of your life. Education. Relationships. Nothing."

I looked away, and silence fell, sad and melancholy.

After a moment, I looked back, guessing the obvious. "So it's time?"

He nodded. "But, I will always be with you." He sat back and dropped a hand to stroke Tramp's fur. My fickle dog leaned into the sensation, not caring—or seeing—the source of the pleasure.

I understood Will's intent; that he would always be watching over me, from beyond. And, given the cycle of life and death through all recorded time, how could I expect more than that?

Resigned, I wiped away a lone tear and inched back, too. "So, we need to talk about Antietam."

For a couple heartbeats, he looked as though he would counter my comment with a suggestion to wait until later. Then, he nodded. "Where did we leave off?"

I swallowed the ache of my sadness. This was the beginning of our goodbye. "What happened after being captured, up until the time of your ...?" I made a vague gesture with my hand.

"Death."

"Yes ... that. Tell me how you came to be with Fergus again. Then you can explain what I need to know to find Asa."

* * *

After limping off the battlefield, he wandered into the outskirts of Sharpsburg. "In every direction, thousands of men lay dead, or mangled and bleeding. Many of the wounded crawled in any direction they thought might provide shelter or help. Others searched for friends or helped to haul away the wounded. And, of course, there were scavengers robbing the dead and the *almost* dead of anything worth stealing."

"Oh, Will, it must have been awful."

He nodded. "I was wounded and disoriented, so I wasn't much help. After several days I got medical care in a barn and recuperated in the home of a local judge. As soon as I could, I left and sneaked through the countryside, hoping to move south of the Potomac River to rejoin my regiment. I tried to cross the river by stowing away on a merchant boat, but the Federals nabbed me. I was transported to a prisoner-of-war camp at Johnson's Island on Lake Erie. It was September, so the weather was tolerable. But, by November, winter set in. We were surrounded by miles of a monstrous, ice-cold, lake. The buildings had no insulation and the temperatures dropped below zero. Each man had just one thin blanket. We Southern boys weren't used to such weather."

Just the thought made a chill chase down my spine. "How did you stay healthy?"

"It wasn't easy. Sickness was common. The camp was also overrun with pneumonia and fever. Every day, men dropped from scurvy or dropsy or infected wounds. Some of the injured suffered rotting limbs covered with maggots. The smell was unbearable. By this time in the war, medical supplies were scarce, so our men suffered agonizing deaths."

"What about Fergus? From Jack's chronology, you found him at Johnson's Island."

"He arrived mid-February, two weeks before I saw him."

"Why did it take so long?"

"More than a thousand prisoners crowded on that island. And, the Federals kept Fergus in solitary confinement at first because they suspected him of being a spy. That could have meant execution."

"Oh my gosh!" My thoughts raced. Weren't spies admired for risking their lives for the good of the cause? How could such a steadfast personality have later murdered his best friend? "What happened? How did he go from being a spy to ... to—"

"He was a smuggler, not a spy." Will frowned. "I learned much later that Fergus wasn't loyal to anyone except himself."

"So, he stole from the North and smuggled into the South? Wouldn't he have been considered more of hero than a smuggler?"

"He also stole goods from his motherland and delivered them to the North. Once word of that surfaced, the Federals set him loose in the camp. They knew his worst punishment might come from the other prisoners since he'd deserted and aided the enemy."

"So ... he was a traitor?"

"More like an opportunist. He didn't recognize sides, but rather opportunities that would serve him."

"But you forgave him?"

"I didn't believe the rumors. Smuggling didn't fit the character of the man I'd known."

"What happened to change him?"

"I don't know if he changed or if I just never knew the real Fergus. Then again," he said, plowing his free hand over his head, "we all changed through war."

"Did he say why he turned to smuggling?"

"When I first found him at the prison, he suffered from fever so he spoke quite freely. He'd been reported missing in June of 1862, so he hadn't attended my wedding. We assumed he'd been killed or captured. So, to find him there was such a blessing. But, as I nursed him back to health, I learned how much he'd changed."

I curled my legs onto the settee and hugged them, bracing myself for the story.

"The Confederate States were building sleek ships to outrun the Northern Navy. Depending on the goods and the final destination, soldiers sometimes worked alongside the Navy to accompany the cargo."

"Fergus received one of those assignments?"

Will nodded. "This opened his eyes to the bounty he could make. I think his intentions were honorable at first, but then a wealthy man in New Orleans offered him eight thousand dollars to defect and oversee the transfer of a load of cotton to England."

"That must have been a lot of money in 1862."

"Indeed. Before the war, Fergus never expected to make that much in two or three years. Now he was making thousands by moving freight up and down the Atlantic seaboard. Nails, salt, iron, morphine, opium, anything that would turn a profit."

Will rose and paced as he talked. Tramp turned and rested his head on my chair, and I picked up the task that Will had abandoned.

"Because prices soared in the South," I said.

"Salt rose from one to fifty cents a pound in less than two years. Iron prices escalated from $25 per ton to $1,500. Even the lowliest crewmember could earn upwards of $5,000 per trip. You can see why the opportunity enticed Fergus."

"How did you keep the other prisoners from harming him? Didn't they hate him?"

"Rumor spread, yes, but within a month we escaped."

Will interrupted himself by stopping at the fireplace and poking the embers back to life. He remained there, staring as he continued, as though watching his memory in the fire.

"It was March. I'd never experienced such cold. Despite the temperature, Fergus recovered his strength. One night, the guards huddled indoors. I suppose they thought no one would be foolish enough to attempt escape under those conditions. You see, we had just two routes to freedom. One, to head south three miles across the frozen lake, toward the mainland. The other involved journeying north across thirty miles of broken ice to freedom in Canada. On this particular night, the moon was full, so visibility worked in our favor. Fergus said he was leaving. That he couldn't stand it anymore and didn't want to die in prison."

"So you left with him?"

Will continued staring into the fire. "At first I said he was crazy. That he'd fall through the ice to certain death. But then I realized that to stay there meant a slower, more agonizing death. So, yes, I went with him."

"But how? What did you do?"

"Fergus pulled a sack from his back and showed me a bundle of food, two pistols, and two Federal jackets. By the light of the moon, Fergus must have been able to see my confusion. He laughed and said, 'I have connections, brother.'"

"And just like that you left?" I gasped, thinking of how frightening it would be to walk on ice across miles of deep water in the dark.

"It just happened. We had no possessions, so leaving was easy. The promise of food and warmth, and seeing Naomi lured me as much as thoughts of freedom. And, I couldn't let him head out alone. So, we hurried to the shore and headed into the darkness and the bitter wind."

"How horrible! Three miles over ice? How did you do it?" I marveled that the lethal depth beneath them concerned them less than living a slow death on the island.

He parked the poker and returned to his chair.

"With just enough light from the moon, we crossed that ice, sometimes walking, sometimes floating on large chunks and paddling with a tree branch we dragged along. It took the entire night."

"It sounds so dangerous."

He nodded. "Foolish too, in retrospect. But I kept moving. Better to die attempting freedom than be shot for loitering outside my prison block."

"But the lake is a wide open space. Didn't people on shore see you arriving?"

"As morning dawned, fog rolled in. The perfect cover."

"That was lucky."

"Perhaps, but before reaching land the fog worked against us, moving in when we were still a half mile from shore. We scrambled to move faster, knowing that once it surrounded us, we might become disoriented and head in the wrong direction. Just when hope faltered, a fog horn sounded and guided us to shore."

"That's incredible." I exhaled in relief, imagining their joy at touching shore. "You must have been exhausted."

"We headed south on foot in a blinding snowstorm, sleeping in barns and abandoned buildings along the way. After three days of little progress, Fergus traded one of his pistols for two old horses and a bundle of food. Then began a long and arduous journey back to Marlowe. All along the way troops and patrols guarded roads and any accessible or navigable points. With no other options, we forged new paths through the mountains.

"After several weeks, we came across an old farmhouse on the outskirts of a town in Pennsylvania called Everett. We were retched hungry. The farmer saw us coming and grabbed his gun. We weren't sure what we would encounter. When we got close enough, he smiled, dropped his gun, and said, 'I'se beginning to think I'd have to make another plan. Wasn't spectin' de uniforms. Com'on, they be awaitin' fer ya, and ya look hungry.'"

"What did he mean by that?"

"We didn't know and didn't care. If it meant a good meal, we were willing to pretend to be anyone."

"So you went with him?"

"We followed him to his house where he spoke to a woman—I assume his wife—in a language I strained to understand. Jack guessed it to be Pennsylvania Dutch, such as certain German settlers spoke. As the woman cooked, the old man led us into his cellar. He shoved away a large partition, and there huddled two adult Negroes ... I guess the proper term now is African Americans ... a man and woman. The woman clutched a small child. The farmer introduced them as Isaac and Sally. It was easy to deduce that they hoped to escape to freedom via the Underground Railroad and that they expected us to help."

"What happened then?" I'm sure my eyes were as wide as nickels.

"We helped, of course. Fergus saw it as an adventure, and I thought it was the right thing to do. We stowed them in a hay wagon and followed the farmer's crude map to a place called 'the Grove,' near a town called Bedford. It was slow moving in that darkness. And yet, in the clouded moonlight, I caught a glimpse of the baby and its skin looked more white than black. I must have reacted to what I saw because Isaac quickly asked that we keep moving."

I sighed, feeling relief for Isaac and Sally. "They must have been grateful. All they had was one another and their child."

"No doubt."

"Do you think they headed to Canada? It must have been so hard for them with no money."

"That destination was our guess as well. But, surprising to us, they weren't penniless. When we turned to leave, Isaac followed us to the door and thanked us with a gold coin."

My heart raced.

He nodded. "Yes, I assume it is the same gold coin that I found by the root cellar and which Sadie then gave to you. It bore an identical vintage. I remember that Fergus looked startled ... like he recognized it. He snatched it and studied it closely and murmured, 'eighteen fifty-six.' Then he pocketed it, and I never saw it again. I assume he lost it by the root cellar at some point after killing me."

As Will talked, I pulled the coin from my pocket and stared at it.

"Many people touched this coin." I marveled, thinking about the role it played in the lives of Isaac, Sally, Fergus, Jack, Grandma Sadie. "But how did the couple get it, and why would they give it to you? Didn't they need it for food and shelter?"

"I don't know. All I can assume is that they had more of it."

More! Memories of Greasy Jim's and Henry's demand for gold soared through my mind. "But where did they get it?"

"I don't know, Grace. The war changed everything, so nothing surprised me. All I wanted was to get home to *Crossings*. Get my bearings. Find Naomi. Figure out what happened to my regiment. So we left and a week later reached *Crossings*."

"Was anyone else here when you arrived?"

"I thought I would find my cousin Edmund and his mother—my mother's sister Lila—but I did not. After Edmund lost an arm at Pittsburg Landing he returned to Marlowe and moved into *Crossings* to recuperate with my aunt's assistance. I wanted to ask them if they'd heard any word from Naomi, and whether Braxton managed to help Eva escape."

I listened in awe to these details that Will shared, knowing that today we could find our answers easily with phone calls or check on the Internet. "So, the house sat empty?"

"To my disappointment. But Fergus seemed happy about it. Almost immediately, he excused himself. At that time, the property had a couple sheds out back. He said he was going to search for supplies. I built a fire and found letters on the dining room table. One was a dispatch warning Edmund and Aunt Lila that Lee was moving north, through the Shenandoah Valley. It was already a week old, so I assumed the troops would pass through at any time, and that my relatives relocated into town to be near other family."

"And you were determined to join your regiment again? Even after everything you'd been through?"

Will sank back in the chair. "It was my duty to present myself and either fight or convince my superiors that my tenure deserved to be over." He shrugged. "Truth is, if I'd known Naomi stayed in Virginia, I would have journeyed to her, but I suspected that she'd gone to Georgia."

"But you knew the Army wouldn't release you. They needed every man they could get, didn't they?"

"That's why Fergus turned pale when I told him of Lee's impending arrival." Will propped a foot on the opposite knee and picked at his boot.

"He didn't want to join the troops again?"

"I looked up as he entered the foyer and saw the strangest expression on his face. Mud covered his boots. I remember thinking that odd because the ground was dry. His countenance differed too, and he looked anxious. I read him the dispatch. When I finished and saw his reaction, I knew he had no intention of joining the troops. When I asked about it, he laughed. Called me a fool. Said I lived in a dreamer's world. That the South would lose, and that to continue fighting meant certain death. I didn't want to lose him again, so I told him that Naomi and I wanted our children to grow up knowing his children, and Braxton's. Remember, at that time, I didn't know who was dead or alive."

"How did he respond?"

"He laughed. Said Naomi was not the woman I remember, and that Eva was gone."

"Gone? What did he mean by that?"

"I don't know. When I pressed him to explain, he turned to leave. I grabbed his shoulder, only intending to stop him. He jerked and shoved me away. As I stumbled, he grabbed a sword that I now noticed he wore on his back. He cursed and said I knew too much."

I gasped. "What did you say?"

"I was shocked. He called me a fool again and said Naomi wasn't waiting for me anymore."

"Asa said that too." My voice was a whisper.

He nodded. "Then Fergus said, 'Goodbye, my Captain,' and plunged the sword into my chest."

My hand flew to my throat. For a full minute I sat there in silence, trying to comprehend it all. The fire crackled, but all I could think about were Fergus's final words.

I took a deep, calming breath. "I would think that despite his deranged state of mind, he would want you to know why he was killing you."

"As I fell, my being swelled with the need to know. I'd nursed him back to health and helped him escape from prison. It was so shocking that Fergus would kill me after all we'd gone through."

"And that became your unfinished business."

"Yes."

"And that's why you think the letter from Naomi, the one that Asa carried at Antietam, will tie together all the pieces?"

"It's the only place I have to start."

"So, I must go to Antietam, find Asa, and ask him about it."

He nodded. "But chances are Asa may not have read the letter."

"And if he didn't?"

194

"Then he might tell you what happened to it. Remember, he died, and I know he has not passed on."

As I pondered the task before me, Will excused himself to retrieve one of the Civil War books from the apartment. He placed it onto my lap, opened it to a detailed map of Antietam, and pointed to a spot on the lower left near the Hawkins' Zouaves Monument.

"To the best of mine and Jack's estimation, Asa died right there, around the area where this statue has been erected. If you can locate that, you should be able to find Asa."

"Was that Jack's next step?"

Will nodded. "Yes, but it was a full moon, and he couldn't wait any longer on that visit due to work commitments ..." Will's voice trailed off, and he smiled, "... and promises to his girls to get home as soon as possible."

"But what is the problem with finding Asa during a full moon? Wouldn't that make it easier to see your way?"

"Your visibility would be better, but a full moon also makes conditions better for the souls that remain behind, and that's not a good thing."

At my confused look, Will continued.

"A full moon provides optimum energy for souls. It's the night when the divide between life and death is thinnest or weakest. Souls are more likely to walk the earth and act out their torment or their deaths. It might be more gruesome than what you could tolerate. It would also be more dangerous because their energies are heightened in whatever state of mind they held upon their deaths. If they were evil, or angry or caught up in a killing spree, that could be dangerous for you. These souls are not just manifestations. They can touch you, which means they can hurt you too. It's possible that evil souls could try to take over your body in order to finish whatever foul thing they planned at the time of their death."

Demons. Spiritual warfare. I tried to stay focused. "So I can't go now because we're just two nights from a full moon."

"That's correct. We should wait at least two weeks to be safe."

"We?"

"Yes, I will go with you. I will transfer my center to the gold coin and you can carry it. The coin is an original from the 1800s, and it already carries energy from *Crossings*."

"You mean, you will ... *haunt* ... the coin rather than the house?" I cringed at my use of the word haunt. "Sorry."

"Do not apologize. The term is more correct than not. And yes, that's what I mean."

"But isn't it risky for you to leave here?" I leaned forward and clasped my hands. I could feel anxiety building.

"Yes. Quite dangerous, in fact. The coin might be lost or stolen, or even seized by another soul, so we must be careful. You should also be aware that my strength would be weakened."

I didn't like his answer. After all this time, I loved this man, this soul, this ghost. Despite all this swirling through my mind, I remembered our purpose for going. "But if Asa gives us answers, you won't leave right then, will you?"

"No, I will depart from *Crossings*. In the interim, I recommend visiting Antietam during daylight so that you can become acquainted with it."

"What if I see Asa during daylight? I mean, I've seen other souls. Can't I talk with him then?"

"You must not do that. Tourists might see you. Besides, we aren't having a simple conversation with Asa. We are asking him to relive his last moments of life, so he will need his full energy. He will have that only at night."

I told Will my plans to go biking at Antietam the next day. With that knowledge, he stood and put another log on the fire, signaling that we would continue talking and that he wanted to prepare me as much as possible.

I just wondered if any amount of preparation would be enough for what lie ahead.

Chapter 21

B y eight o'clock the next morning, I awoke from five hours of sleep as refreshed as if I'd slept for ten. My thoughts centered on Antietam, and one o'clock couldn't arrive soon enough.

Tramp and I headed out for a long walk. When we reached the lawn, the train whistle squealed, reminding me of the river and the canal beyond it. I decided to move our walk to the Canal towpath, where I hoped to sharpen my ability to communicate with strange ghosts by talking with the soul I'd seen there. If I could converse with him, then I'd feel better about talking with Asa in a few weeks.

My first stop, however, was the *Time Out*. With Tramp tethered in the shade beside the café, I enjoyed a cup of coffee with Cassie, who, of course, drank tea. After a heartfelt exchange— her expressing sympathy for my grandmother's death, me apologizing for the many times I stretched the truth about Aunt Tish's whereabouts—I showed her the gold coin that Grandma Sadie gave me. I left out any mention of Will and ghosts and Grandmother's brief return to life.

She studied the coin. "So Jack's death was an accident. Nothin' weird or paranormal. I hope you're right. Course, I know that doesn't make it any easier for you."

"I'm fine now," I replied with the comfort that it was at least mostly true. "I know I'll see my family again."

"Yeah, it's the *not* knowing that'll kill ya'." She frowned at her cup.

I was certain she wasn't trying to turn the focus back on herself. In fact, if I asked about Mason, I figured she'd shrug it off, even though his disappearance hung like a veil over her life, distorting her perspective. I suspected she'd spent the past several years imagining all the possibilities of what had prompted him to leave: a mistress, a secret family, illness, financial disaster, the allure of freedom on a Pacific island. The best way for me to help her was to stay on topic and let her talk in her own time, so I continued: "I need to finish a few things that I've started. Then, I'm going to correct a few mistakes I've made, and finally move forward."

Cassie looked up. "Does 'move forward' include my son in some way? Are you the reason he and Sondra broke up?"

Her question caught me off guard. As I stammered, she laughed.

"Honey, Clay is such a good man. I don't think a mother could be more proud than I am. But he's hurtin' right now. Sondra's demands have left him feeling raw." As she spoke, she returned the coin to me by sliding it across the table.

I didn't want to have this conversation, so I muttered, "I understand."

"He doesn't know you're back, does he?"

"I hope to talk with him tonight or tomorrow, after I've taken care of a few other things." *Best not to explain that I planned to talk with Seth first.* I picked up the coin, hoping to use it to refocus the conversation. "Cassie, I'm certain my family's deaths were an accident. I believe this coin was associated with good things. That it even helped slaves escape to freedom in the Underground Railroad."

"What makes you think that?"

The voice came from our right, causing us both to startle. I turned to watch Holland Greer reach for the coin.

"May I?" he asked without waiting for permission. Before I could respond, he pulled the coin from my grasp. With his free hand, he retrieved a pair of gold-rimmed spectacles from the pocket of his blazer and perched them on the tip of his nose. The glasses made him look quite studious, and I remembered that Ms. Bealle at the library described him as a historian and a researcher. I don't know why I couldn't get past the thought that he was equal part snoop.

"Excellent condition. Quite impressive," he murmured as he inspected the coin. "May I inquire as to where you got this? And, what makes you think it has anything to do with the Underground Railroad?"

My thoughts raced. I couldn't lie anymore, but I didn't want to raise his curiosity such that he would explore the grounds of *Crossings* again. As long as Will remained there, I didn't want Holland Greer near my home. Most of all, I balked at his impertinence.

"And you are ...?" I quipped, to remind him that we'd never officially met.

His eyes darted to my face, and his thick gray eyebrows peaked upward. In that reaction I read that he was rather confident that I already knew his identity.

"My apologies," he replied, offering a bow of head and sweep of hand. "We have not formally met. I am Holland Greer, and I am a historian. My specialization is the Civil War era. Including Antietam. In fact, I'll be filming an interview there this afternoon. So, you see, I am quite interested in relics from the past. I heard you mention the Underground Railroad, and that naturally would place this coin at the time of the War Between the States."

I didn't like Holland standing over me, and his deep, charismatic voice compelled listeners to pay attention. The whole effect intimidated me, so I stood. As I thought he might, he assumed I stood to shake his hand, so I did.

As we clasped hands, Cassie excused herself, mumbling something about getting back to work. *The second time she'd scurried away because of Holland.*

"I'm Grace MacKenna."

"And, you have moved into the area?"

"Somewhat, yes."

His eyebrows peaked again.

"May I inquire as to where you got the coin?" He repeated his question with as much patience as I assumed him capable of displaying.

"From my grandmother. She lived in Philadelphia, so it's hard to tell where the coin was before that."

"Indeed." He handed back the coin, and his eyes burned into mine, almost as if he tried to read through them into my mind. "I guess we'll never know. In fact, it's safe to say that there's not a *living* soul who could tell us the secrets of this coin ... wouldn't you agree, Ms. MacKenna?"

My body tensed. I blinked and pondered his double meaning. Before I could stop myself, I fell into his trap. "What do you mean by that?"

"Nothing more than the fact that it has been almost 150 years since these gold coins first circulated."

"I don't think it's pure gold—"

"Oh, but they are, Ms. MacKenna. Fourteen hundred and sixty of them were minted in 1856 in Dahlonega, Georgia. They were uncirculated when seven hundred fifty of those coins disappeared ... right after being minted. The coin you hold in your hand is worth about thirteen thousand dollars. Multiply that times seven hundred forty-nine, and you would have almost ten million dollars in gold."

I couldn't breathe. The coin sat like a boulder in my hand. The air thickened around me, and the walls of the *Time Out* squeezed in.

"Ms. MacKenna, as a historian, I—"

"I'm sorry, but I have to go." I needed fresh air. *Quickly.* "Maybe we can talk at another time."

A dark annoyance crossed his face, but he caught himself and responded, "That would be delightful."

I grabbed my backpack and headed for the front door, all the while feeling his eyes sear into my back.

My smooth getaway, however, was anything but. As I neared the door, I heard the bells jingle and looked up to see Reaghan, Elias, and Ethan enter. The twins broke free and scurried in search of their grandmother, leaving me alone with Clay's angry sister.

"Grace." She frowned. "What are you doing? Clay's not here."

"I didn't come to see Clay. I came to—"

"See my mother. Causing a fight between Clay and Seth didn't work, so now you're honing in on my mother?"

I flinched from the antagonism in her voice. "What are you talking about?"

"Everyone's gossiping about it. Clay and Seth fought over you at the carnival. In *public!*" She stammered, as though this were on par with having stripped naked and run through the streets.

"There was no fight, Reaghan. I'd just learned my grandmother was dying. That caused a difference of opinion."

"Yes ... well ... I'm sorry to hear about her. But, Grace, because of you, Clay and Sondra have broken their engagement."

"Reaghan, I can't help what Clay does," I countered. Still aware of Holland's eyes on my back, I wanted to get out of there, sandwiched, as I was, between two colliding storms. "I'm sorry. I've got to go. I want to be your friend, Reaghan, but if you want to know more, you should talk to Clay."

With that, I proceeded past her toward the door.

"You should know that I'm calling your aunt today and making her aware of everything that's happened."

Fear gripped me, and I swirled around. "Why would you do that?"

Reaghan pushed back her shoulders. "Grace, you're a minor. Everyone knows you're living alone. Your guardian needs to know what you're up to. I think she'll be quite interested in your little scene at the carnival."

"Reaghan!" Cassie's voice cut through our glare. She walked toward us, staring at her daughter. I couldn't help but notice that Holland was gone. I wondered if he heard the part about me living alone. "Stop it. *You're* the one that's making a public scene."

"Mother, she is—"

"—none of your business."

"It *is* my business when her actions hurt my brother."

"Don't you think that's for him to decide?"

Just then, the twins came running from the back. Both women took on a new posture, exchanging a "we'll-continue-this-later" kind of look.

"I have to go," I murmured and pushed through the door. It would do no good to stay and talk with Reaghan.

On the street, I retrieved Tramp and headed to my car, hoping my last two encounters didn't foreshadow what was to come with the Canal ghost.

Chapter 22

When I arrived at the Canal, the time read half past nine. Tramp and I reached the towpath in seconds.

The distance from the parking lot to where I'd seen the ghost stretched about two miles, so I had time to steer my mind from what happened at the café to what I wanted to say to this new soul.

All the preparation and thinking was for naught, however, because by the time I reached the ravine where I'd ridden my bike off the cliff, I forgot the script in my head.

Off to my left, the land dropped dramatically. Halfway down the steep hill I could see the oak tree that stopped my plunge toward the river. The bark bore a few scuffmarks where my bike had made contact. I shivered at the memory.

I looked around, but saw no one else on the towpath.

I will fear no evil ...

"Hello." My voice was weak. "Are you here?"

No response. I took a deep breath, leashed Tramp to a thin tree, and stepped off the towpath into the ravine.

"Please. I am able to see you. I want to talk to you." I continued moving, scanning the landscape around me. It grew darker due to the heavy canopy of trees casting an umbrella-like shadow. My palms began to sweat when I realized I could no longer see the towpath. I continued talking out loud. "My name is Grace. Please let me talk to you." By now I'd taken a couple dozen steps into the thicket. "I'm the person who crashed ... on the bike."

"Yes, I know."

The voice came from my right. The hair on my neck reacted before any other part of me. I swirled around to see the ghost. And yet, my surprise at hearing his voice paled to the amazement that washed over me when I saw him standing only ten feet away.

We stood there for a long moment, staring at one another. Too startled by the clarity of his presence, I found it hard to talk. He was a distinguished-looking man, late-forties, with a full head of dark hair and thick beard stubble. He wore jeans and a short-sleeve polo shirt with a Ralph Lauren insignia on the left breast pocket, and it hit me that his death was more recent than Will's.

I swallowed and broke the silence in little more than a whisper. "Hello. Thanks for talking to me."

"You have subtle vision," he drawled, a slight hint of a Southern accent, not uncommon in the area, I'd discovered.

"Yes."

"And you're not afraid."

"No." Okay, I was a little scared, but I couldn't let him know that.

"You were hurt when you soared off the cliff?"

I blushed. "My ankle bruised, and I got a black eye, but they both healed quickly."

He put a hand on his chest. "I'm sorry I startled you. I was surprised that you could see me."

"It's not your fault."

"I usually can mingle freely among the hikers on the towpath." He gestured in that direction. "People look right through me. The most I ever hear to suggest that they're aware of my presence is complaints about pockets of cold air." He frowned. "They always attribute it to the river or the trees overhead. After all this time, I'm still not used to being around people and not even being seen."

I felt a tightening in my throat. "That must be hard to get used to."

He shrugged. "My choice."

I found comfort in the fact that I knew what he meant: that he *chose* to stay here rather than move on.

"My name is Grace."

"Delighted." He nodded. "It fits you. I am Jarrod."

He raised his hand and stepped toward me, but just as quickly stopped and dropped his hand. "I'd shake your hand, but it might be rather—"

"Cold."

"Ahh," he nodded. "You've experienced this before."

"You're only the second soul I've talked with."

He cocked his head as though this information peaked his interest. "And the first?"

I gave a sweeping gesture toward the river. "Over there. In an old estate."

"Are you sure he ... she?"

"He."

"Are you sure he is safe and won't harm you?"

"As sure as I can be ... given the circumstances. In fact, I'm going to help him resolve some issues, so he can move on." I inhaled sharply and bit my lip. Perhaps it wasn't wise to reveal this information.

He looked pensive. "Is that possible?"

"I don't know yet. I'll have to get back to you on that."

He nodded. "Please do."

The silence stretched, awkward and stilted, and he looked down. I couldn't read his face, and I couldn't think of any of the questions I'd intended to ask him.

After a while, he looked up and asked, "How can I help you?"

Embarrassed, I shook my head. "I'm sorry. I don't need your help. I guess I'm ... using you. I wanted to make sure I can talk to other souls before ... before ... doing certain things to help him."

"Because you must do this to set him free?" He looked as though he pondered this. "So, you're becoming a sleuth of sorts for lost souls."

I hesitated. "Perhaps." *Best not to share details.*

"I imagine your parents aren't sure how to respond to this."

"They're dead. I'm on my own."

He frowned again. "That's not good. Children need their parents. But now I understand why your vision is so acute."

I heard a familiar buzz and realized my cell phone announced a text message. I pulled it out and read Adriana's text message: "Meet at eleven?" I typed in "OK" and pocketed my phone again.

"That's my friend. Texting. She wants to meet me earlier than I thought."

He didn't say a word. Just nodded. I wondered if he even understood what cell phones and texting were.

"Thank you for talking with me."

He didn't respond, just stood there staring at me as I turned to go.

After I'd taken a few steps, he spoke. "Will you come back again? I want to hear how your venture turns out."

I turned back and shot him my warmest smile. "Yes ... yes, I will."

He nodded. "God speed."

I nodded, not sure what to say to this. His invoking God into the conversation, no matter how clichéd his choice of words, reminded me that this man, like Will, harbored a unique and poignant past of his own, and his soul waited for a remarkable and interesting future, none of which I knew anything about. But now wasn't the time to ask questions. Adriana was waiting.

I turned again and headed toward the towpath. I could feel his stare until distance and thick vegetation separated us.

Chapter 23

"There's something spiritual about this place," Adriana said as we left the Antietam National Battlefield Visitor's Center to retrieve our bikes and start our riding tour. "Can you feel it?"

If only you knew!

Adriana and I planned to follow the battlefield's eight-and-a-half-mile path through to completion. I determined that Asa died on a post located between the tour's last two stops, ten and eleven.

I tried to prepare my emotions as we unloaded our bikes. If Adriana, with no subtle vision, could feel the presence of spirits, I wondered what the next couple of hours would hold for me since I could *see* and *hear* souls.

My answer came at the first stop, outside the Dunker Church, about a half-mile west of the Visitor's Center. On the day of the battle, fighting unfolded around the little whitewashed building, and that night, it served as a makeshift hospital for the wounded.

As we neared the entrance, two souls emerged, looking weary and distraught, one wobbling with the aid of a long cane while his friend, head bandaged, helped him along. They clomped from the left side of the building toward the west woods. Two more souls sprawled inside on wooden benches; one lying on his back, moaning, the other silent and looking shocked. He held a blood-soaked cloth to his stomach.

Although I avoided staring, lest they discover I could see them, my throat tightened, and I wondered if I'd ever get used to this. I didn't bother to hope that they fared well in the building; the fact that I saw their souls meant they died there.

I kept my eyes on Adriana, the fine hairs on my neck bristling. She shivered and brushed her arms.

"Let's get out of here," she said.

Back in the sunshine, Adriana's cheery demeanor returned, but for me, the trip remained dismal. For the next several stops, I saw six more souls, scattered over the cornfields, propped against trees, leaning on fence rows—each wounded, scruffy, dejected, pitiable. I ignored them and focused on the path.

As we rode, I thought of my latest conversation with Will. He said that most of the souls that remained here would not reveal themselves fully during the day. He proved correct in that the souls I saw looked dull and darkened. Others, he warned, would manifest without thinking, or because they wanted to get attention if possible. Only once, however, did I see a soul walk right through one of the other hundreds of tourists that walked, biked, and stopped to read placards and monuments. When the lady jerked her gaze up, in the way one does when reacting to an unexpected breeze, the soul stumbled away, coughing and chuckling.

As we reached stop eight, Adriana braked. "Grace! This is the Sunken Road. Bloody Lane, remember?"

Indeed, I did. From the moment the film described the spot as an "open grave" for hundreds of the dead, I anticipated the lane would prove disturbing. Union troops had encountered Confederates posted along this old sunken road, and for almost four hours, fighting raged. In the end, the Confederate soldiers lost and bodies fell on top of bodies, in some places as many as three and four layers, according to the film. After the battle, "Sunken Road" took on the legend as "Bloody Lane."

As my eyes scanned its stretch, I counted five wandering souls. If that many appeared now, in daylight, what might the nighttime bring?

"It's so sad," Adriana whispered, looking at—but not *seeing*—a poignant bit of history.

I agreed but averted my eyes, making a mental note not to come near the site when Will and I returned to talk with Asa.

At stop nine, we neared the battlefield's observation tower that stands at the opposite end of Bloody Lane. A small group of people gathered near its base. Once we moved closer, we could see four people huddled around a camera that pointed at two gentlemen in sport jackets.

"Look!" Adriana said. "It's Holland Greer. He must be filming something for a television segment. Let's watch."

With no time to kick myself for not having shared with her the details of my morning encounter with Holland, I followed, being as quiet as possible so as not to disturb the recording. We stopped about eight yards to the right of the film crew, parked our bikes, and inched closer.

An interviewer held a microphone to Holland's mouth as he explained how the fighting had unfolded at Bloody Lane. His voice again struck me as charismatic, almost hypnotic, and I could understand how he attained a reputation as a good interviewee. The sound of his voice entranced me such that I didn't even pay attention to the details of *what* he said, so I jumped when I heard a different voice, off to my left. Its lilting tones reminded me of a thick brogue, with its soft vowels, hard consonants, and almost musical inflection. "Himself got it wrong again. Don't sound a bit like no Christmas song."

I turned to see two souls, standing about six feet from me, glaring at Holland. Startled, I whipped back to face forward, too afraid that I might make eye contact with them. Wondering what disturbed them, I tuned back into the interview.

"Yes, Chuck, that's right. Their chant was Gaelic. It sounded much like the fa-la-la chorus in that old familiar song, *Deck the Halls.*"

"Tweren't no chant," the first soul complained. "It be a battle cry, ya' pathetic idiot."

"Ayeh," the second soul shouted, "it be Fág an bealach. Clear the way, ya' fool!'"

"Yes, that's right, it was a Scottish brigade," Holland answered to another question.

"Blimey," the first soul shouted. "We be Irish, ya' twit, not Scottish!" His voice seethed with disgust, and in my peripheral vision I saw him blacken with anger.

"That's not true!" Why I thought I should intervene I'll never know, but before I could stop, I'd opened my big mouth.

Silence fell, and all eyes focused on me—the camera crew, the dozen onlookers, the duet of angry souls. Adriana gasped. Holland scowled at me, clenched his jaw, and fisted his hands. The two souls moved into my peripheral vision and studied me with curiosity.

I had no defense but the truth. "They were Irish." My voice sounded weak. "Fág an bealach," I dragged it out, emphasizing each syllable, "was their battle cry." I butchered the accent, but I figured no one would care. Embarrassed, I added, "It means to clear the way."

"Ayeh," the second soul murmured, elbowing his buddy. "D'ya s'pose the colleen 'ears us?"

They edged closer, but I steeled my focus on Holland and his crew. My thoughts jumbled, wondering how I could conduct damage control. Just when I thought Holland would explode, he surprised me.

"Why, yes, that's right, young lady," he said in that smooth, convincing voice of his. "Thank you for sparking my memory. This particular brigade *was* Irish." He chuckled, then motioned for the interviewer and cameraman to focus his way. "Let's tape that segment again."

I had to hand it to him; Holland was a smooth operator. I had contradicted the man in front of a camera crew, correcting him on a topic of which he purported to be an expert. Everybody makes mistakes, but I wondered how it could be that a scholar and historian of his reputation could make such an error. I had absorbed every detail of Will's stories like a sponge, and I couldn't imagine depicting his life with such carelessness.

Right or wrong, the damage—both with Holland, and the souls—was done. He returned to taping his segment and the souls calmed, although they regarded me with discomforting interest.

"Come on," Adriana said. "Let's go."

I followed, anxious to put some distance between the two souls and us. The spot where Asa died was at least a mile away, and I was confident they wouldn't leave their energy source to follow me.

As we departed, Adriana laughed, but it sounded contrived, as though it masked worry or discomfort. "What happened back there? You almost freaked out when Holland made that mistake."

"He's wrong." I glanced back and pretended to look at Holland, but instead, the souls watched me. "He wasn't accurate in his details. You can't do that. It's a disservice to those who actually fought here."

We arrived at our bikes, and rather than climbing on, Adriana stopped and looked at me. She smiled and it looked genuine. "I didn't know you were such a history buff."

I shrugged. "I didn't either."

* * *

The next several stops involved long stretches and steep hills, so that by the time we reached Harpers Ferry Road between stops ten and eleven, I convinced Adriana that I needed to stretch.

She sat down on the side of the road to re-lace her shoes as I headed into the pasture. A path led to the Hawkins' Zouaves Monument that stood off to the right about two hundred feet. An obelisk in shape, the narrow, four-sided, tapering monument reached well over fifteen feet in height and peaked with a pyramid-like cap at the top. I looked around and spotted three souls, two moving and one sitting. I recognized the man on the ground from the group picture taken at

Will's wedding. *Asa!* I almost shrieked with excitement but caught myself at the thought of Adriana a short distance away. The thought flicked through my mind that this couldn't be more perfect and that I should talk to Asa now, but he would not have full strength and Adriana might think I'd lost my mind if she saw me converse with the air. I needed to wait for Will. Besides, giddiness bubbled in me at the vision I conjured of a reunion between these two friends.

Before I could decide my course of action, I heard Adriana behind me, reminding me about our schedule for the afternoon.

* * *

By six o'clock, we sat in a little sandwich shop in Sharpsburg, plotting our next outing. That's when Aunt Tish called and changed my immediate plans.

"Grace," she yelled, "what in the world is going on? I got a call from someone named Reaghan Paness, and she said—"

She recounted the conversation, stressing blow by blow how it made her feel, how it embarrassed and angered her, and how inconvenienced she'd been in devoting time to the call. The key parts of her harangue that registered in my mind, however, included: today was Wednesday, her gallery show was Friday night, she would be here Saturday, and I should pack my things because I'd be returning to Boston with her.

In three days!

"Aunt Tish," I interrupted her. "I'll have to call you back." I hit "End" to sever the call, lowered my hand to my lap, and from beneath the table turned off my cell phone. I met Adriana's gaze with as much normalcy as I could muster.

"Everything okay?" she asked, hesitant.

I steadied my voice, hoping to sound convincing. "Aunt Tish and her crisis du jour."

"What's up? You look worried."

I want to be alone to think.

"I need to clear my head, that's all. I think I'll go for a drive. Maybe back to the battlefield."

"You don't have to go that far to—"

"Your performance is at 8 o'clock, isn't it?" I hoped the distraction would take her focus off of me.

It worked. She read her watch. "Oh! I have to go."

Chapter 24

Twenty minutes later, Adriana and I reached Williamsport. She spent the ride plotting through her limited time before the performance and asking about Aunt Tish's call. I waved it off and redirected her focus onto her evening plans.

After leaving her, I steered the car west, back to Antietam. Somewhere between Aunt Tish's snarls and her threats, I had panicked that I was running out of time. I had to see Asa that night, but if I told Will, he would try to stop me. He'd been adamant that we could not conduct our visit during a full moon. I had no choice. I had to risk it.

Before I even rehearsed what I would say to Asa, I reached the battlefield. While biking earlier, I learned I could not park near the statue, or drive onto the property after dark. Yet, I needed to approach Asa under the cloak of night, lest any tourists see me and deign me half-crazed. So, I parked on a remote side street edging the southwest side of the fields. My cell phone read 7:15, almost two hours before sundown. I turned it off and settled back in my seat to wait.

Next thing I knew, I awoke with a start, shrouded in nightfall. I'm not sure how I fell asleep, given that my mind churned with so many worries: Aunt Tish's impending arrival, encountering Asa during a near-full moon, hoping Will would understand this change in plans, my need to resolve his murder. Then again, perhaps the stress alone made me shut down. I turned on my cell phone. Multiple messages waited to be heard. Ignoring them, I focused on the time: 10:35 p.m.

I took several deep breaths to steady my nerves. Meeting Asa didn't concern me as much as anything and anyone else I might encounter. Willing myself to refocus and take action, I removed Grandma Sadie's cross from the rearview mirror, draped it around my neck, said a prayer, and climbed out of my car.

The wall of darkness startled me, and the lane on which I'd parked struck me as a dividing line between good and evil. Behind me, the pallid lights of tiny Sharpsburg glowed, thanks to a few streetlights and scattered porch lamps. In front of me stretched a wall of nothingness, vast and endless from right to left. Who knew there were a hundred shades of black?

From where I stood, I'd have to walk southeast for about a quarter mile. I just hoped that my eyes would become better acclimated to the obscurity. The bright moon overhead would make my plight easier, but if what Will said proved true, that same full moon that provided comfortable visibility, would also bring frightening possibilities. He said I might encounter souls that are "much more likely to act out their torment." My palms began to sweat.

As I stood there trying to steady my breath, my legs feeling battleship heavy and rooted to the ground, I began to see that even a wall of darkness has shadows and degrees of tonal difference. *Could there be things in those shadows waiting for me?*

With a deep breath, I stepped off the street and into the past.

* * *

I walked about two dozen steps before seeing the first souls. A group of three soldiers dragged by, propping one another. They moved, heads bowed, staring at the ground, a look of defeat and despondency on their faces. I continued as they passed, so they would not know that I could see them. Besides, I dreaded stopping; if I did, I might not move again.

The three soldiers' departure did not open a clear path for me. Instead, it was as if they were curtains being opened on the first act of a play that involved a mass of characters. In front of me, figures moved about, their twisted forms and stretching shadows scattered across the long hillside, each having been exiled from their families and homes and now seeking release from their own purgatory.

Oppression seized me, and I was filled with an overwhelming desire to shut down. I shook, almost vibrated steadily like a tuning fork, and grappled with staying focused.

By now I'd begun descending a hill, so the momentum kept me moving forward. Though I locked my head in a forward position, my peripheral vision spotted souls strewn everywhere across the cavernous Aceldama, in all manner of positions, from staggered walking, to lying face down, to clawing their way toward some imaginary respite that I suspected they would never reach.

So intent on reaching the statue and blocking out the scene surrounding me, I didn't see a particular tragic-looking soul until I stepped into him. I felt coldness on my ankles, and I erred by looking down. When we made eye contact, he whooshed to his feet and, with a shrill laugh, yanked a blood-soaked bandage from his chest and shoved it toward me. The blood spurted from his heart onto my chest. I froze, stymied in my tracks, and opened my mouth to scream, but nothing came out. The soul howled with hysterical glee then dropped to the ground with a wail. As he fell, I realized another soul had slammed a rifle over his head. I watched as the second one tossed the rifle and jumped on the first soul. The two fought as though I wasn't there. After staggering a couple dozen steps away from them, I fell to my knees and gulped in air. Shaking, I reached up to touch my shirt where the blood landed, but it was dry. *I was alive and not part of their world.*

After a moment, I climbed back up and continued, fighting off the urge to run lest I attract more attention.

Here and there, I slipped or tripped on the uneven terrain of the field, but moved forward, step by determined step, hoping that I looked as though I believed myself to be alone on the field. Most of the souls moved about in a manner that made me believe they manifested their life after the battle, but a handful of other soldiers wielded their rifles or knives as though the battle was yet to unfold. It struck me that as the moon moved higher in the sky, I would see more of this behavior. Will's words came rushing back: *acting out their torment … re-enacting their deaths … more gruesome than what you might be able to tolerate.* I regretted my haste in not waiting to bring him along.

At one point, a group of four soldiers stood in my path, and for the first time, I could hear the noises of the battlefield—canons booming, rifles blasting, swords striking, bodies falling, and men calling for mothers and sweethearts. Those sounds mixed with wails of agony, shouted curses, crackling fire, and demented laughter.

Then the smells hit me too. Putrid odors of rotting flesh, fecal waste from men and horses, the stinging smell of gunpowder, the foul scent of un-bathed bodies.

I tightened inside as the world closed in around me. My stomach ached, and the air in my lungs tasted vile. I needed to get past these four souls in my path before I emptied my guts onto the ground. If I veered to the right or left, they would know I could see them. I had no choice but to plow forward. Taking a deep breath, I stepped through them. Despite my concern, they didn't demonstrate a single vestige of reaction as I trudged on.

I continued for about a dozen steps before dropping to my knees and heaving up my dinner. That's when I acknowledged that I was hanging onto my world with urgent desperation.

* * *

As I reached the monument, my heart pounded out of my chest. I pressed my body into its cold granite, cherishing its solidness and inability to change with the moon. When the sun rose in the morning, this granite structure would still be standing here, unaltered, and I found comfort in that.

I didn't stand there long, however, because I didn't want my back to the activity unfolding behind me. I turned, hoping to get oriented. The moon accommodated, casting a teasing light bright enough to reveal the shine of blacktopping on the Harpers Ferry Road to the west. Between the location of the road and the statue, I factored Asa at several paces to my right.

That same moonlight helped me ascertain he was no longer sitting in the same spot. Discouraged, I wondered if I'd have to move among the souls, searching faces to find him. It's hard to act casual when you're standing on a battlefield in the middle of the night. It's even harder to assess the familiarity of a face without looking into its eyes. Still, with the security of my back against the statue, I scanned the field, trying to look relaxed.

If the energy of the souls around me hadn't been affecting my thinking, I might have had a clearer mind and might have talked myself out of what I did next. As it turns out, however risky, it proved to be the right thing to do. I called out, "Asa Garrett, may you rest in peace."

What was I thinking? I'm not sure, except that I'd come too far to give up now, and that Aunt Tish's impending arrival stood between Will and his freedom. Perhaps saying Asa's name would garner his attention. As for the part about resting in peace, I hoped that would signal to all other souls that I believed Asa to be dead and gone. Anywhere but on that field at that moment.

From off to my left, I heard a throaty chuckle, then, "Someday. God willing."

I turned and stared into the moonlit shadows, spotting him about twenty paces away. He sat scrunched on the ground, knees bent, his rifle perched in an upright fashion with the barrel pointing up. I locked gazes and moved toward him. He looked surprised, as though he had answered without expecting to be heard.

As I crossed the distance between us, I took note of at least two other souls watching me.

Even when I reached Asa's side and dropped down beside him, he didn't speak. *Was he startled that I singled him out, or afraid to trust the budding notion that I might be seeking him in particular? Or, did something else disturb him?*

As I fell forward, my knees touching ground, I took a deep breath and braced myself for the conversation to come. *I will fear no evil.*

"Asa Garrett?"

He didn't move. Didn't respond. Just sat there studying me, like he intended to determine my intentions, as though they were written across my face in ink.

"William Kavanaugh sent me."

He jerked, sitting taller in the chest.

"Will?"

Just one word, but I heard an odd combination of a deep bass voice and heightened curiosity.

I nodded. "Yes, Bear ... Will sent me." At my use of his nickname, his eyes widened, and the edges of his lips lifted into a slight smile.

He continued studying my face for several heartbeats before saying, "How ..." His voice died away, and instead of finishing the question, he shook his head.

"I have subtle vision. I can see and hear souls."

Although I almost whispered that revelation, my voice must have carried through the still air because the two souls watching me inched closer.

Asa saw it too. He looked up at them and tilted both his head and his gun to the left, in a "move along" gesture. The two moved as Asa indicated but stopped to watch us after they'd gone about five yards.

"Where? Where have you seen Will?"

Again I could hear in his voice the dichotomy of a deep voice mixed with a soft caring. That, coupled with his long, beefy body, made me think of him as a gentle giant of a man. His friends had been right to call him "Bear." I relaxed a bit, and instead of kneeling, I sat my butt on the ground, hoping he would take that to mean that I trusted him and didn't plan to run off.

"At *Crossings*. I'm related to one of Jubal McClain's descendants, and I've inherited the estate. I met Will there."

"Jubal," he said, speaking more to his gun than to me. "Jubal survived the war."

"He did."

Asa nodded and looked back at me, a look of satisfaction on his face. "When he passed years later, I saw him on the other side. With Sarah. And his family."

"And yet you didn't join him?"

"I couldn't." He gazed beyond me with that same look I saw in Will's eyes when he talked about the past.

"Why not? Because of Will? Because you couldn't deliver the letter from Naomi?" I hated being so direct with him, but the souls around us unnerved me. The rest of the battlefield, including Bloody Lane, spread out in front of me, and from that wall of blackness, the noise intensified—laughing, cursing, screaming, rifles and canons blasting, swords clashing, horses galloping. I just wanted to get whatever information I needed and get out of there. I could always visit Asa at another time, when the moon waned.

With one hand, he laid down his rifle and rubbed his temples and forehead, like he wanted to make sense of information or pull answers from his head.

"Will saved my life once."

"Pulling you from the icy river."

Asa looked at me. "How could I move on before I helped him? His wife trusted me with a letter. She said it was urgent. That Will should get it as soon as possible. But I died before I could give it to him. I failed him."

My eyes misted, overwhelmed by this man's love for his friend. Before I could console him, before I could determine if it was *possible* to console him, he continued.

"Did he make it? Did Will survive the war?"

It was a simple question with a simple answer, an answer that addressed 150-year-old information, yet my body tensed, bracing to deliver bad news as though both parties involved belonged in the current era.

"He lived for eight more months. The Federals captured him. Here. Outside Sharpsburg, and sent him to prison. He escaped and made it back to *Crossings*, but was killed by ..." I caught myself. No need for Asa to know their friend Fergus betrayed them. "By someone."

Asa's shoulders slumped, and he dropped his head. "So Will never got his letter from Naomi? Did he ever see her alive again?"

"No, and he hasn't seen her on the other side after all these years. He thinks she may be lost somewhere here on earth searching for him. He asked me to come here and find out what the letter said. Do you know, Asa?"

I concentrated on his face, blocking out all other sound.

"I didn't read it. It wouldn't a' been right. Now I wish I had."

"Did Naomi give you any idea what it said? Did she seem in good health? Did she say if something was wrong or if she was going anywhere?"

He looked away again, into the past. "She seemed agitated. Unsettled." Asa propped his elbows on his knees. "But she was a new bride and missed Will. Maybe she feared for him. For that matter, we lived in the middle of a war. In a world of agitation. It was the norm, not the exception."

I slouched in defeat. "Oh, Asa, how am I going to tell Will?" I dropped my head into my hands, my arms propped on my knees. We must have looked like a set of defeated bookends.

"Braxton may have read the letter."

"What do you mean?" Startled, my heartbeat quickened with guarded optimism, and I inched closer. Braxton died at Antietam too, but Will never mentioned that Asa and Braxton interacted that day.

"After I died, I saw Will bending over my body. His anguish as he cradled me. He didn't even think about the letter, just kept holding me and begging me to come back. But I couldn't. You have to tell him that. I couldn't come back."

He looked so anxious to get my assurance, I nodded with exaggerated movement. It was all I could offer. Tears festered so close that if I spoke, I would sound like a blustering child.

"I tried to comfort him, but he couldn't see or hear me. Then he had to skedaddle because the fighting grew intense. As I watched him go, I received insight about what would happen next. I felt the need to go to my family before I crossed over. After I saw my dad and my brother, I had a choice of whether to move on or not."

"In the dimension?"

He raised his eyebrows, looking surprised. "I couldn't leave. My mom had already passed away, and I saw her on the other side. She wanted me to cross and join her. But I couldn't. My work wasn't done here. I'd let my friend down. I waited ... but Will never came back. Then as time ... months, years ... went on, I never did see him in the dimension or on the other side. He was a good man. Humble. Pious. He would have moved onto that heavenly realm, I'm certain. So I reckoned he remained here on earth somewhere, just like me. Trying to solve something. I couldn't move on without him, knowing he was still tied to his earthly life."

"But what about the letter? Did you see what happened to it?" I didn't bother asking why he thought Braxton may have read it. Braxton was long dead now. What good would that do me?

"That night, under the cover of darkness, stragglers started rifling through the pockets of the dead and wounded, before the medical crews got to the bodies. One scruffy ole' guy from another regiment ... Hardin ... Hardin Flinch or Fluke, something like that ... He picked me clean. Got my picture of my ma, my pouch of tobacco, Will's letter, even my four-leaf clover. And he was a Rebel, no less."

From behind me, off in the distance, I heard the piercing cry of "Fág an bealach," then a whole new round of screams. I flinched and addressed Asa with more urgency than I intended. "What happened next? Did you see what he did with the letter?"

"I followed him, but he didn't make it too far. Turns out he bled from a chest wound. The medical crew loaded him on a wagon and hauled him to one of the hospitals in town." Asa waved a hand toward Sharpsburg. "Hardin died before the doctor could even tend to him."

As Asa talked, I wracked my brain trying to figure what this had to do with Braxton, and then it hit me.

"Braxton was the doctor!" I delighted in my ability to connect the dots of his story, but just as quickly grew weary, remembering Braxton was no longer available to us.

"That's right. I'd met him before. He was a friend of Will's. We fought at Fair Oaks together. I also saw him at Will's wedding. He's a good man. I watched him in that shed," Asa motioned toward Sharpsburg again. "He tried to keep track of the names of the dead so that their families could be notified. Before Hardin's body was hauled away, he searched the man's pockets—"

"And found Naomi's letter," I blurted. "Did he read it?"

"Not right then, but I figured he would later. I could tell he was surprised to see Will's name on the envelope. His face grew pale, and I guess he thought the presence of the letter in this stranger's pocket meant that Will had been killed."

"But he didn't read it there?"

"He couldn't. There were hundreds, maybe thousands of men that needed his help."

"So what did you do?"

"I left. I had to. The building was so far from my energy, from where I died. But I came back the next day."

His voice trailed off, and I didn't think he would continue, so I prompted him. "And?"

"Braxton was dead."

I groaned and put my head in my hands again. I don't know why I was surprised by this revelation. Will told me that Braxton died there. In fact, Will said that Braxton was accused of murdering several people in the building before killing himself.

"How did he die?" My words came out in a choked whisper.

"I don't know. His soul was there but the letter was gone."

"Did you talk to him ... I mean, his soul?"

Asa smiled, the look on his face telling me that I didn't quite understand how death worked and how souls interacted. "No, there was no need. No hope at that point of helping Will. Of getting the letter to him. Braxton was now tormented with something greater. His own unfinished business."

I must have looked confused because he added, "We don't talk and socialize after death the way we did before we die. We have no need or desire to do so. At least not here, in this limbo. Now on the other side, it's another story altogether."

"So," I exhaled, trying to piece the events together in my mind, "if I can find the building where Braxton died, I may be able to find him, and to find out what the letter said."

"It's possible."

I glanced back up the hill, toward Sharpsburg. The souls scattered across the field exhibited more energy, their noise and activity intensified.

"Asa," I leaned closer to him. "I'm afraid. What if any of them ..." I pointed my head in the direction of the more boisterous souls, "... bother me?"

"I'll accompany you to the top of the hill. Most of them are too busy fighting to pay attention to us." He moved to his feet in one fluid movement. "From there, it's just a short walk to the hospital. I think it's just an old shed now."

"You're certain it's still there?"

"It's there. I can see the corner of it from here ... in the daylight." He frowned and looked down at the ground. "I can't go the whole way with you, though. There may be curious or agitated souls in that area that aren't preoccupied with fighting, and if they see you walking with me, then they'll know you can see them too. It might be dangerous for you. You must act as though you can't see them at all."

"I understand. Will explained that too."

I stood, and Asa smiled, searching my face. "That Will, he always could pick the prettiest girls."

I looked down, hoping the moonlight prevented him from seeing me blush. I turned to start our journey, but his next words stopped me.

"Please tell Will I did all that I could. Will you tell him that for me? And tell him ... well, tell him that he was always a brother to me."

So moved by his request and the gentleness in his voice, I forgot for a moment that he wasn't a living being. I reached out to touch his arm, but he was unprepared for my action so my hand dropped right through.

"It's alright. I forget it too sometimes. And for that matter, I'll probably fade away by the time we reach the top of the hill. Without an energy source to take with me, I'll lose my strength."

"I understand. I'll come back after I—"

"No." He shook his head. "There's no need. I won't be here."

"I don't understand." I panicked, wondering how in the world I'd tell Will I found then lost his friend.

"As I fade away, I'll be crossing over."

"Oh my gosh!" I threw my hands over my mouth. "That's right. Your concerns are now finished. You've relayed what you know, and you've done all you can. You're moving on to ...to—"

"The afterlife? Yes, I'll be moving on. My family is waiting."

My whole body tingled with emotion. "I promise I'll do everything I can to get Will there as soon as possible," I blubbered, moistness stinging my eyes. I shook, overwhelmed at the thought that this man was on the precipice of stepping into an eternal bliss, leaving all his earthly cares and horrors behind.

"Thank you, Grace."

"God bless you, Asa."

Asa smiled. "He already has, Grace. Wait 'til you see it. It makes every bit of living worthwhile, all the strife and angst we go through here on earth. We are rewarded for standing strong. And for our choices. You will see that yourself one day." He reached out his hand for mine. This time, I felt a cold solidness.

We stood there a moment before the movement of other souls made me aware again that we weren't alone. Anxious, I looked around, wondering if they would be angry that I helped to set one of them free.

"Will they care?"

He looked around and nodded. "They'll care. Those who are destined for a better eternity will wonder how they can get a jewel like you to help them too. Those slated for eternal damnation will care the most because they have no hope."

I still marveled at this thought. "All because of their choices."

"And their beliefs. Now come. I'll go with you to the hilltop. By the time we crest it, I will be gone. Please tell Will that I loved him like a brother."

"No." I turned and, through tear-filled eyes, shot him a mischievous grin, my way of letting him know that I anticipated them being together soon in the afterlife. "Tell him yourself."

Asa grinned.

Chapter 25

The shed stood beside an empty lot at the end of Burnside Bridge Road, the nearest house at least forty feet away. Abandoned, it looked like it suffered a century of ill repairs, before being left to rot forever. A narrow splash of gray paint under the roofline suggested the building once garnered some attention. A DeKalb corn sign rusted above the shed's crooked porch roof. A weathered wagon wheel rested to the right of the door.

I tried to focus on the shed, but I couldn't stop thinking about Asa. He'd faded away as we walked. It was too overwhelming to comprehend, his departure a reminder that he belonged to another time, another world.

I took a deep breath and stepped onto the porch, anticipating what awaited me on the other side. The moon shimmered, just two nights away from being full, so I expected activity within.

Sliding the battered wooden latch to unlock the weathered door, I gave a gentle push and watched as it drifted back two centuries, revealing a horror so surreal that no book, no movie, no historian ever had depicted the real butchery and despair of this war.

Before I could take in the entire scene, a stench hit me, and I placed an arm over my mouth, trying to breathe through the fabric of the sleeve. It didn't help, so I abandoned the effort and suffered the foul air. Good thing I'd already lost my dinner in the past half hour.

Once again, I regretted my decision to sleuth during a full moon. As Will had warned, the souls reenacted the night of their deaths. It was as if I'd been sitting in a quiet room and turned on a cheap, grade B horror flick that shattered the calm, except that this time, the good guys sawed the bodies apart.

The connecting fiber of the scene in front of me: blood. It ran non-stop from ceiling to walls to dirt floor where it puddled on the uneven ground. To my right and left, five men lay on boards or leaned against blood-soaked feedbags. One man looked dead, his body rigid and bloating, but the others were in varied states of shock: each bled, one cried, one whispered a prayer, one begged the surgeons to save his life. I wondered if Hardin perched here, the letter tucked in his pockets as he waited for care, or if his body had already been removed.

Hoping to restore a sense of reality, I moved my gaze from the immediate scene to the rear of the building where a door stood ajar. Though a huge pyramid of objects blocked the path leading from the exit, I could still see the stars. The view, if even for a brief respite, helped to ground me, to remind me that I could return to my safe life after this. I stepped into the building.

Just ahead of me, two men—each holding a saw—stood working at crude operating tables made of doors perched atop old-fashioned pickle barrels. These two, covered in blood, reminded me more of butchers than surgeons.

The surgeon to the right looked too old to be Braxton, so I focused on the other man. If not for the glasses, I would not have recognized him from Will's picture, due to the endless blood that ran from hair to feet. Two other men flanked each end of his table, holding down a patient that screamed in agony.

In that instant, Will's description of surgical procedures came to mind, and I hoped that this poor fellow suffered no drastic consequences. But then Braxton laid down his saw, grimaced at the stained cloth he stuffed where his surgical tool had been, and picked up an object about the size of a French baguette. With a wallop in my stomach, I recognized it as an arm. Braxton turned to his right and tossed the arm onto the pyramid just outside the door. For the first time, I saw that it was composed of severed limbs. His frown and beleaguered countenance made me wonder if the horror of this task had long since destroyed any hope he ever courted of easing his patients' suffering.

A man dressed in the plain clothes of a civilian entered the building. The slush of his footsteps reminded me, again, of the bloody ground. With his right hand, he held a cloth over his nose. In his left hand dangled a lantern, and in the crook of his arm draped about a dozen folded, tattered cloths.

"Where ya' want 'em?" he asked of the men standing by the tables.

As Braxton removed his glasses and wiped them free of blood, the other surgeon pointed to a hook dangling from the ceiling over Braxton's table. The man laid the sheets on a stuffed burlap bag, hung the second lantern, and left.

When Braxton replaced his glasses, he scanned the room as if he were triaging the patients. In that brief scan, we locked eyes.

Before this, I'd never understood the depiction of someone as "brooding"—as in how antagonists in science fiction novels were always odd, brooding characters—but now I did. Braxton bore a sad, woebegone demeanor, as though all hope was lost. His pitted face bore thick eyebrows atop carbon-black eyes with deep shadowy circles under them. In contrast, his skin looked pasty and unhealthy. Today, he'd be mistaken for a gloomy, shifty, aloof computer nerd who didn't get enough sun. The result of the contrasting extremes of dark and pale made for an intimidating soul.

A chill fingered its way down my spine as I watched him step away from the table and move in my direction, stepping through a soul lying on the floor. His gaze never faltered.

He stopped about three feet from me and scrunched his brows. At this close distance, I saw the scar on his right cheek.

I took a deep breath. "Braxton Hood?"

I learned in that moment that it's nigh to impossible for a "brooding" individual to show surprise. Instead, the single suggestion I received that he was startled by this turn of events was the way he shook his head as though telling himself, "This can't be."

"William Kavanaugh sent me. My name is Grace MacKenna."

"You can see," he said, not in surprise, but rather as an assessment, a deduction.

"I need to talk to you." My eyes darted around the building. "Alone."

He hesitated then glanced back at his patient. Perhaps he realized, too, that his efforts were both futile and about 150 years too late, because he gestured toward the door. "This way."

I hitched my breath and followed him into the darkness, to the side of the building, eerily aware that he once was accused of losing his mind and murdering every person within.

From the battlefield, the sounds, the smells, the smoke and gunpowder in the air hit me all over again. I guessed it to be near midnight.

"You are not safe here." He scowled. "You should return at another time."

Had he been ready to re-enact the murders?

I closed my mind to the thought. "It has to be tonight. It's hard to explain."

"Will sent you?"

So discomforted with this man, this soul, I ignored the explanations that I had shared with Asa and got to the point. "Will has not passed on because he's trying to solve his murder and the whereabouts of Naomi. We need to know if you read the letter that was carried into this hospital in the pockets of a man named Hardin."

"Who murdered him?" he asked his tone as calm as if he had asked the time.

I inhaled, bracing myself to deliver the answer. *Did I dare say it? I'd heard of honor among thieves, but was there a bond among murderers too?* "Fergus Lowe."

By the light of the moon, I saw his jaw clench in response. "I read the letter. Naomi was with child and returning to Georgia to be with family."

"A child!" It came out far too loud and prompted two bedraggled souls on the street to look my way.

Braxton frowned and motioned for me to move deeper into the shadows. My heart beat faster, but I followed.

"Will never knew he had a child," I whispered.

"Naomi also expressed her wish that Will *not* come home to her. She loved someone else."

My heart sank. "A 'Dear John' letter?"

He looked at me with confusion.

"Never mind." I shook my head, trying to make sense of it all. "So she went to Georgia. Did she go with this other man? Who was he? Did she say?"

"No. She was vague. And cruel. I don't think Will knew her that well."

"What happened to the child?" I blurted before remembering that there was no way Braxton would know the answer.

"I do not know, Ms. MacKenna. I died here that night."

I swallowed hard. A high-pitched wail from the distance cut through me like a knife. "I have to go."

I turned to go, but he reached out. His cool presence touched my arm.

"Will you let me know when William passes?"

The thought of returning to talk to Braxton repulsed me. He was an enigma—caring doctor, brooding murderer. Still, I reasoned that I could return on a less graphic night; definitely when the moon was a mere thumbnail.

"I'll try."

"I did not murder these people."

"Then who—"

"I do not know for certain." He removed his glasses and rubbed his temples. "I was shot first and fell unconscious." He studied my face then restored his glasses and continued. "By the time I died and rose from my body, everyone around me was dead, and their souls either moved on or were searching for release."

"I'm sorry." I wrapped my arms around my waist.

He nodded, looked down and up before saying, "The only way I will ever know is if someone like you witnesses my death."

To say I was horrorstruck would be an understatement. Was the man suggesting I stay and watch his death?

I backed away, shaking my head. "I can't ... I'm sorry ... I can't do that."

He didn't react.

"I have to go." I kept moving backward.

He didn't move, but watched me retreat. "Be on guard. The last time I saw my wife, she was with Fergus. I paid him a king's ransom in gold to secure her freedom. If what you say about him is true, it might explain why I never saw her on the other side. Perhaps she suffered the same fate as Will."

By now I had backed into the street. "I'll ... let you know about Will."

I turned and could feel his eyes sear into me until I disappeared from his view.

* * *

In this sleepy little hamlet of Sharpsburg, the houses were scattered, dark, closed up for the night. No cars passed on the streets; no bars burned the midnight oil. If not for the bright moon and the occasional porch light illuminating my way, I would have lost my sense of direction.

I feared encountering angry souls, but forced myself to walk–not run–down the dark street to my car. I made nonsensical deals with myself to refocus my mind and combat my anxiety. If I could just make it to that corner, then I'd be okay. If I could reach that road sign, then I could breathe again. If I could make it past that repulsive soul by the rose bush, then I'd find my car without incident.

I was so concerned about being nabbed by an errant soul that when I rounded the corner and heard my name being called, it took me a second to recognize the voice.

Clay!

He stood about fifty paces away, beside my car. When I called back to him, he turned and sighed with such relief that I picked up speed and ran as fast as I could, right into his arms.

I should have been embarrassed by the nakedness of my delight in seeing him, but all I could think was that it felt right. He hugged me tight, and I hoped his contentment equaled mine. One second of this told me I could spend a lifetime in his arms.

Too soon, he pulled back, his hands anchored on my shoulders. In the moonlight, I watched his eyes probe mine, and I assumed he wanted answers: why I was there, why I shook, and what my intentions were in embracing him with such delight. I didn't have answers for any of those questions.

Instead of seeking explanation, however, he murmured, "You're trembling," and pulled me back into his arms. "Adriana stopped at the café. She was worried. She asked me to come look—"

"Is that why you're here?" My voice sounded desperate, and this time, I pulled back.

"What? Yes ... no." He dropped his grip on me. He stepped backward and rubbed the back of his neck with one hand. The look of a man in turmoil. He studied me, his shoulders sagging. "Yes, she asked me to come here, but I would have come anyway, Grace. Crimeny, I've been waiting for you to get home from Philly. When you left, I felt so ... well ... blast it, I don't know what I'm trying to say here. I—"

"Me too." It came out much softer than I intended.

His chest pulled back and he stood erect, frozen in place. "You too? You too what?"

"I feel it too."

"You feel ... what?" He looked like he was afraid to trust what I said.

"Between us. I'm not sure what it is, but I know it's something. Something I'd like to ... explore."

"But I thought you and Seth—"

"He is my friend. I enjoy his company, but that's all. He's just not ..."

"Not what?" Clay stood rigid as though bracing himself for the worst.

I shrugged. "Not you."

His shoulders dropped again, and he studied me with burning intensity. Then, the corners of his mouth rose into a smile. "Well, good. I'd hate to feel this alone."

Just as my heart stopped and my knees began to melt, he pulled me into an embrace. His lips glided over mine as though they were exploring, searching for the best spot or right approach before getting serious.

"Grace," he breathed, "you've been driving me crazy." His mouth found a sensitive spot beneath my right ear that sent all sorts of sensations through my body. I slumped against him, thankful for the size and strength of his body, otherwise, I'd have fallen to the ground. He embodied everything I'd ever associated with the idea of a strong man, a man's man. I could imagine him wrestling a bear in the wilds or building an empire on Wall Street. He epitomized rock-solid security, and I couldn't get enough of it.

His hands moved down my back and, reaching my waist, pushed me tighter against him as his kiss deepened. When I reached up to pull him closer too, he tensed. With a moan, he pulled away, holding me at arm's length.

I opened my mouth to protest, but before I could, Clay continued. "I feel like I've known you all my life. But the truth is, I haven't."

I said nothing. I was dazed. The last thing I wanted was to end the embrace.

He continued, hesitation in his voice. "Good things take time. I want us to take our time." He lifted my hand and kissed it. "I want to do this right."

He read the reaction on my face and said, "No, don't look at me that way." He pulled me into his arms again. "Let's find somewhere to talk. I want to tell you what I'm feeling. And, I want to explain about Sondra—"

"What's going on here?"

It took a heartbeat for my mind to register that a third voice, an angry voice, had interrupted this poignant moment. Clay and I pulled apart to see Seth step from the shadows into the moonlight.

"Baxter, you're quite the Casanova, aren't you?" he smirked. "I don't think Sondra's engagement ring is even cool yet."

"Seth, don't," I pleaded.

"This doesn't concern you," Clay said to him. Clay looked calm, but his voice conveyed a mixture of both authority and annoyance. "I saw you in the café. You heard Adriana talking. You can see Grace is fine, so you can go home and not worry."

"Just who the … Look Baxter, for your information, Grace and I had a date tonight, so you're the one who needs to go home."

Our dinner date! I'd forgotten. I stepped toward him. "Seth, I'm sorry. Things changed today, and I—"

"Stop lying, Grace," he shouted, turning to me. He fisted his hands, his voice rising, and his words rushed together. "You forgot our plans, didn't you? Well? Didn't you? Why don't you just be honest? I don't like being led on. I—"

"Seth, that's enough." Clay's voice remained steady, but commanding. "Let's go back to Williamsport and talk."

Seth ignored him and continued spewing accusations and vitriol, but I didn't hear another word he said. My attention was diverted by a soul that popped up out of nowhere. It was misshapen, grotesque, its extremities gnarled and exaggerated. Claws protruded from mangled arms, and its head rolled and turned backward as if it were otherworldly. Just as I registered fangs and a tail, it squealed in delight and moved in to study Seth.

Will's words came rushing back, that during a waxing moon, evil souls "could try to take over your body in order to be able to finish whatever foul thing they planned at the time of their death."

"Seth!" I screamed. "You have to stop."

Clay shot a startled look at me. I remembered that he could not see the soul and, therefore, might misunderstand my plea. He must have thought I felt threatened because he moved toward Seth.

"No, Clay!" I grabbed his arm and looked back just in time to see the soul step into Seth's body.

Seth swayed, and his eyes shot wide open. He howled a screeching wail like a wolf in pain. His body rose into the air, shook like a ragdoll being abused by an invisible hand, then slammed down on the ground, lifted and shook again.

"What's happening to him?" Clay yelled, fear and frustration lacing his words. He spread his arms, like he was bracing to help if he could snatch the chance. Seth must have looked, to Clay, like a rug being shaken by an invisible giant.

Without warning, Seth's body careened into a wood fence that edged the road before dropping motionless to the ground.

Clay ran to his side. "Grace, call 9-1-1."

By now, Seth lay quiet on his side, his left leg bent and twisted sideways. In the dim light I could see saliva trickling from his mouth, and blood from his nose. His eyes were closed, but I could hear a deep, raspy inhuman-like breathing issuing from his mouth.

"Clay, we have to help him!" I paced as I waited for the 9-1-1 call to go through.

"We can't move him." Clay crouched down to feel his pulse. "His back might be damaged."

An ambulance arrived within minutes, although it seemed like hours. While we waited by his side, Clay talked to Seth, but he just lay there, breathing unnaturally. Once in a while, he uttered a guttural sound, but otherwise, he remained still.

We followed the ambulance to the hospital in our separate vehicles, then waited for an hour while the staff worked on Seth. His parents arrived prompting a whole new round of questions. Our answers were vague because we had nothing to offer.

The doctor told Seth's parents that, other than running tests, nothing else could be done that night, although he suspected Seth might have had a seizure.

I knew in my heart the doctor was wrong. Seth had been possessed by an angry soul, a demon. But how could I explain that to a doctor, a man of science? I wrestled with what to do until I visited Seth's room while his parents filled out paperwork.

He looked so calm that I wondered if I had been seeing things. I reasoned that although the soul had been there once, it wasn't anymore. Seth was being nursed for the damage, and that was all that mattered. He would be okay.

"Come on. He's fine for now," Clay said from behind me. I hadn't heard him follow me into the room. "There's nothing else we can do tonight. Let's go home."

Home. I liked the sound of that. I also liked that I faced a twenty-minute drive ahead of me, alone in my car, so that I could figure out how to tell Clay I wasn't staying home. I intended to leave for Georgia before he and I could even talk about us.

I prayed that he would understand.

* * *

Thanks to traffic lights and a heavy foot, I reached *Crossings* ahead of Clay. Once inside, I yelled for Will as I doubled Chubbs' food and water.

When Will appeared, I talked non-stop as I whirled around the room, stuffing my backpack for a long road trip. "I need you to place your center in the gold coin. Hurry! Clay will be here soon. I don't have time to explain. You have to trust me on this. Aunt Tish is on her way. We have to leave now. I talked with Asa tonight. Long story—sorry. He led me to Braxton before he passed over … Asa, I mean … Braxton hasn't passed over yet. But he read the letter! Braxton, I mean, not Asa. He said that Naomi was going to Georgia." As I rambled, I moved in circles, grabbing one item after another for the trip. "Will, I'm so sorry, but she was leaving you. But there's a child! You're a father! Naomi was pregnant. We have to go to Georgia to find her. We have to find out if the child lived." I stopped when I saw the astonished look on his face.

"A child?" he said, a note of awe in his voice.

My shoulders drooped, and my backpack dropped to the floor. "I'm so sorry. I wish we could talk about it, but there's no time right now."

Lights whipped across the room, and I heard a vehicle skid to a halt. The apartment wasn't near as soundproof as the old house.

"Clay's here." I held the gold coin in my hand toward Will. "Please."

For one heartbeat he looked at me and I could tell he wanted to talk before taking this step, but that he knew he had no choice.

"Keep me close." He stepped forward into my hand and disappeared. The coin vibrated, and much like the rippling effect in a river when a stone breaks the water, the aftereffects reverberated through my body, so that I grasped a chair to steady myself.

I hadn't yet fixed the coin's chain, so I shoved the coin into the front pocket of my jeans, intending to keep it as safe as possible.

I could hear Clay on the steps. I picked up my backpack and kissed Chubbs. "Be a good kitty while I'm gone. I'll be back in less than two days, or I'll have Adriana pick you up." Then I grabbed Tramp's leash and headed to the door, hoping to make it outside before Clay entered.

"Come on, Tramp." Voicing the invite was redundant; Tramp had jumped to attention when he saw me pick up his leash.

I opened the door to find Clay reaching for the handle. The weariness of the past several hours gave way to a warm smile, and I could see an expectation on his face. But then he took note of the backpack on my shoulder and the determined look on my face as I stepped onto the porch and locked the door.

He frowned. "What are you doing?"

"I'm sorry. There's something I have to do. I'll explain later. In two days. I promise. I need you to trust me on this." I kissed him quick on the cheek and walked past him.

He grabbed my arm. "Wait a minute! Where are you going?"

"It will take hours to explain. There's something I have to do, and once that's done, I can be normal. We'll talk then. I promise. I just have to go now."

He looked baffled, but who could blame him? He ran his hand over his head as if he knew that arguing with me would be futile.

"I'm going with you. We'll talk on the way." He grasped my elbow and steered me toward the steps.

"You can't."

"I can't?" He stopped and because he held my arm, Tramp and I stopped too. "Why not? Who are you meeting?"

"No one. Well, no one right away." I sighed. "It's complicated."

"Try me." He wiggled his fingers in a "come on" gesture.

I took a deep breath and looked into his eyes. Could I tell him about Will? In that split second as I contemplated how I would explain the situation, I reasoned that the explanation would sound crazy. He would think I lost my mind.

"I can't right now. Please, you have to trust me."

In the moonlight, his eyes studied me. "Fine." He steered me forward and down the steps. "You can explain later, but I'm not letting you head out alone this late at night."

Things moved too quickly for me to decide whether I dare have Clay accompany me on the trip or not. I have to admit, I wanted him to come. He represented security. On the other hand, I didn't want to lose him, and if he thought I'd lost touch with reality, he might walk away.

"Get in my truck," he said. "I'll drive."

His "truck" was a safari green Land Rover Defender and it looked like it could handle any terrain but would not be as easy on the gas as my SUV. I hesitated. "It's rather far. I think I should take my car and go alone."

He ignored me. "Get in, both of you."

I decided it would do no good to argue, so I opened the door for Tramp to bound in back, while I dropped into the front.

He put the key in the ignition. "Where to?"

"Georgia."

He stopped, leaned back, and looked at me. "Georgia? As in the *state* of Georgia? That's a ten- or eleven-hour drive!"

I grabbed my backpack and the handle of my door. "This was a bad idea. I'll take my car. I'm sorry, I'll just meet you when—"

"No." He reached across me and pulled my door shut. "I'll drive. But this had better be good, Grace."

Chapter 26

"Okay, start talking," Clay said once the waitress filled our cups with coffee. We had pulled into a busy convenience area that made its money servicing the drivers on the Route 95 corridor.

"It's going to sound crazy."

"I'm sure of that. Why don't you start by telling me where we're going?"

"A town called Screven. If it's still there."

"Never heard of it."

"It was there during the war."

"The Civil War?"

I nodded. "I'm not sure it's there any longer."

He shrugged it away. "We'll find that out soon enough. My iPad's in the truck. It's easier to use for searches than a cell phone. You can research while I drive. So, why there?"

How to answer him? Several thoughts raced through my mind. Before I chose one, he said, "Don't think about it, Grace. Just say it. Why Screven?"

"I can *see* things." My response sounded almost like a plea, a request for approval.

"You mean things that aren't there?" He furrowed his brow and sipped his coffee. "You asked about that at *Crossings* when we met."

"No, things that *are* there. Things that no one else can see."

His gaze never faltered, and he showed no surprise. "So that's why your aunt made you leave Boston?"

"What? No, she doesn't know about this."

"So it started …?" he raised his eyebrows.

"When I moved into *Crossings*."

"Prior to that?"

"Nothing."

The waitress returned, placed our orders on the table, and left.

Clay watched her go then looked back at me. "Did you know that Jack experienced a presence at the house?"

"I did after I got there. But I didn't know that you knew. Why didn't you tell me that first night?"

"I didn't want to scare you. I'd never gotten the impression it was anything to be concerned about. Jack talked to mom about it, but didn't say much to me. When he did, he was vague. He'd say, 'There's more out there than we can see, Clay.' He'd often quote Einstein, that we still don't know one thousandth of one percent of what nature has shown us."

"Sounds like Jack."

"His point was that we're not even sure about ninety-nine percent of what exists."

We lapsed into silence for a moment, and I suspected that he, too, was thinking about the man that brought us together.

I reached across the table to touch his hand. "Thanks ... for not acting like I'm crazy."

Our eyes locked, and I felt like I was gazing into a crystal ball, hoping to find my future there, rather than just understanding. He wrapped his hand around mine. I decided on the spot that if the man spent the next fifty years holding my hand like that, it still wouldn't be enough.

"Adriana told you how I injured my leg?"

I nodded.

"She told you I saved some men?"

"She said you were brave. She's really proud of you."

As if embarrassed, he leaned back and shook his head. "Courage isn't pure, Grace. It keeps company with fear and doubt." Then he leaned in again, locked his blue eyes on me, and lowered his voice. "My point is that I also lost a man. Terrance Green. He died from the blast. But I swear to you, Grace, he appeared to me that night. I know I wasn't dreaming. Terrance looked as real as this table." Clay released my hand to pound the marble top. "He said to me it was alright. That I did all I could and that he was ready to move on."

I blubbered something inane about how it must have affected him.

"I told you once, anything is possible," Clay said. "I'm not saying I'll understand everything, but I'm going to keep an open mind. I believe in miracles."

* * *

For the next two hours, Clay drove and I explained everything. Clay never interrupted, just kept his eyes on the road and let me talk, although at times I noticed his hands gripped the wheel a little tighter.

After another rest break, I took over the driving, and Clay pieced together our collective knowledge. As it turns out, Cassie had told him about the last night she had seen Jack, when he talked about ghosts. Clay admitted that, at the time, he questioned whether Jack was playing a joke on her. Now, with my story to back up hers, he didn't know what to think.

Somewhere in southern South Carolina we saw a sign announcing Savannah as thirty miles ahead.

"Pull off there," he said with a yawn. "We'll figure out where Screven is, then get some rest."

"Rest? We can't stop."

"We've been up night and day. It's not safe to drive when we're so tired. We'll get a few hours of shuteye, then hit the road again."

At Exit 109 we found a wooded rest stop. While Clay walked Tramp, I found his iPad in the back and logged on.

"You find it?" Clay said when he returned to the back of the truck, rear door open, where I sat, legs folded beneath me, iPad on the floor.

I nodded. "Screven is in southeast Georgia, about forty-five miles from the coast and thirty-five miles from the Okefenokee Swamp.

"That's about two-to-three hours." He leaned on the bed of the truck, feet on the ground, and read his watch. "It's almost four now. We'll get there in the dark. We may have to wait until morning to talk to anyone."

As he talked, I opened a search engine and typed, "Screven, ghost."

"Maybe we can figure this out on our own." I smiled, reading the results of more than twenty thousand hits.

"What'd you find?"

One entry announced, "ghost sightings." I clicked on it. "It says here that Screven is the home of a famous ghost light, or 'spooklight' as the locals call it. It's a bouncing orb of light seen for over a century at a railroad crossing on Bennett Road. The light moves back and forth like it's being carried. It often appears after a rain or after a train goes by." I looked up. "That's got to be it. Will mentioned that he heard a train outside Naomi's house."

Rather than matching my enthusiasm, he frowned and turned his gaze.

"What's wrong?"

"I don't know. I told you I'd keep an open mind, but this is just so …" He threw his hands up in an exasperated gesture.

"Hard to believe, I know, but you believe *me*, don't you?"

"I believe that you believe it. That you've experienced it. But other than that, I just don't understand in what form. Most people would think this is crazy."

"But you're not most people." I heard the hope in my voice.

Before Clay responded, I felt a vibration in my pocket, as though Will had listened to our conversation and moved within the casing. I pulled out the coin, and it stopped moving.

Was Will trying to tell me something?

I reached for Clay's hand and pressed the coin into his palm.

His eyes registered curiosity, until it vibrated again. I could see it move as it lay on his hand. Clay gasped and cupped it with both hands, as though he thought it might move enough to fall. "Whoa ..." he whispered, never taking his eyes off the coin.

When he gazed up again, I must have looked stricken because he said, "Grace, what's wrong?" He put his free arm around me and pulled me close even as he gingerly held on to the coin.

"You have no idea," I sniffed, "how good it feels to finally share this with someone."

* * *

We slept for three hours in the back of Clay's vehicle. He lowered the backseat, creating a makeshift bed. It was lengthy enough for us—Tramp too—to spread out. With the aid of sleeping bags Clay kept in the car, we settled in for a long nap, me curled against him, his arm over my right shoulder. As it turned out, bunking in the back of a Land Rover opened my eyes to all sorts of realizations: that camping can be fun, that comfort is sometimes a state of mind, that no amount of money could purchase such a perfect moment, and that I was falling in crazy, irrevocable love with Clay Baxter.

Chapter 27

With a little help from employees at a convenience store, we found Bennett Road. It was unpaved, but wide enough for two-way traffic. After driving a half-mile and passing nothing but a forest of tall pines, the railroad tracks appeared. Clay pulled into an open patch beside the road and turned off the car. The store employees had said the train would roar through at 1:15 a.m. My cell phone read twenty minutes past midnight. The creepy darkness and stillness brought to mind campfire stories of hook-handed psychopathic killers who attack young lovers in cars, always in remote locations. *Like this one.*

Clay broke the silence. "I feel ridiculous. We're sitting here waiting for a ghost to show up, and we'll probably get mauled by some swamp creature instead."

"Stop it." I threw an empty paper cup at him and laughed, although I sounded more nervous than amused. "There are no such things as swamp creatures."

"Are you serious? They're as real as ghosts," he quipped, but then his smile faltered, and he shook his head. "I just have a hard time with all this." He banged his fist on the steering wheel and looked away.

I bit my lip. The time ticked close enough to the train's arrival that Will could make an appearance without losing much of his strength. "Do you want more proof?"

He looked back at me. Despite the limited lighting, I saw his eyes narrow, heard skepticism in his voice. "What do you mean?"

I pulled out the coin and talked to it. "Will, it's almost time for the train. Can you join us?"

Before I finished speaking, the coin vibrated, and Will appeared in the back seat, stroking my dog's head. Tramp looked around to see where the pleasure came from. Finding no source to lean into, he continued leaning into the strokes.

"You heard everything?" I asked, looking at Will.

He nodded.

I looked back at Clay in time to see him gazing at Tramp then back at me. His face belied the open-mindedness of which he spoke, but I remembered he could not see Will.

"Everything," Will affirmed, his eyes studying Clay. "I trust this man. What would you like me to do?"

I put the question to Clay. "Ask Will to do something."

"You're kidding, right?" Clay's head darted around again as though he searched for something he was supposed to find. He even turned and leaned into the back seat to search. If Will hadn't been a ghost, they would have butted heads.

"Anything. Just ask him."

His sigh said he would tolerate this game ... for now. "Okay ..." He pointed to objects sitting on the console, "... move that CD case."

Will re-positioned the case, unzipped it, took out a CD, placed it in the player, and turned on the car. In an instant, music serenaded us. After a few seconds, he turned it off, and we sat in silence again.

Clay sat frozen in place, eyes wide, facial muscles taut. To him, it must have looked as though things floated in mid air.

"Will, how did you know how to do that?" I asked, impressed.

"Jack's television. Quite an amazing invention. The interpretations about history are notoriously wrong, but the automobile scenes are educational."

* * *

With little time to spare, Will and I discussed how to approach Naomi as Clay sat there looking dumbfounded. In short, I was to remain in the car guarding the coin while he handled everything. I relayed the plans to Clay who, after having listened to my side of the conversation, called defeat by splaying his hands in the air as though to say, "You're in charge because none of it makes sense."

I sat back in my seat, nerves on edge, but comforted by the notion that we had a plan.

* * *

But, plans change.

Overcome with exhaustion, I closed my eyes, knowing that, when the time came, the rumbling of the train would rejuvenate me and provide me with enough time to collect my wits to prepare for Naomi's arrival.

Instead, Clay's shrieking voice woke me. "What is she doing? She's going to get killed!"

I followed his gaze to the track and blinked in disbelief. A little girl staggered on the tracks, about fifty yards away. She looked petite and gaunt, as though she hadn't been eating right for years. She wore an ankle-length, pale summer dress, ratted and loose-fitting, and her feet were bare. Her long black hair fell in an uncontrolled tangle below her shoulders. Her right hand held a lantern, and in that instant, I understood the reason for the "spooklight." She looked forlorn, desperate. When she neared the crossroads, she staggered off the track, dropped to the ground, and placed her neck on the rail.

"It's Naomi, manifesting herself as a child," Will said. He now stood outside my open car window.

Naomi?

"What's she doing?" I heard panic in my voice.

"She was happiest as a child," Will said, his cool composure the antithesis to the horrified reaction from Clay to my left. "She's reenacting her death, to end it at a happier time. You may not want to watch."

"Get up! Get up!" Clay urged.

"You must stop him," Will warned. "She will know you are here."

The ground trembled, announcing that the train drew near.

"She's crazy. She'll die!" Clay bellowed to no one in particular. Then through the open window he yelled, "Stop, don't do it," as he grabbed the door handle in an effort to get to her. I sensed his heightened adrenaline, his fear for her, his intention to save what he thought was the life of a breathing little girl. If the scene hadn't been so terrifying and unexpected, Clay would have seen that the girl exuded a spectral aura and that her long ratty gown was a style from the 1800s.

At that moment, I remembered Will's remark that under the right circumstances, anyone could see an apparition.

"Clay, no!" I gripped his arm with both hands and every bit of strength I had. "It's Naomi. She's not real. She wants to re-enact her death."

He froze, startled. "What? No! Let go—"

"She's already dead. You're looking at a ghost."

The train roared closer as if a monstrous beast bore down on us.

Clay tried to wrestle his arm from me as he yelled, "It's not a ghost. I can see her. I can't see Will. Where is he anyway?"

Will urged, "You must stop him."

I whimpered as I shrieked, "You have to believe me. You can see her because

241

she's using all her energy for this one moment. To live her death again!"

He stopped and stared at me, looking lost in confusion, as though wanting to help someone he believed was about to die, but trying to reconcile that such a response could put us in jeopardy.

He yanked his arm away from me, and I fell over the console, as he said, "No, I can't take that chance." Before I could stop him he jumped from the truck and bolted toward Naomi.

I screamed. "Will, stop him!"

In the next few seconds, so much happened that, years later, I would often think back on it and wonder how I had been able to absorb it all. In the confusion, Naomi looked up when she heard Clay yell, and I saw on her face the instant she realized we could see her. Clay raced toward her, no sign of a limp, just pure determination to save a life. But Will was faster. He scooped up Clay and tossed him like a ragdoll into the undergrowth of palmettos and long pine needles beneath the trees, just as the train roared down the track, its air horn blasting. I roped Tramp's leash over the emergency break and jumped out of the car. With no time to look away, we watched as Naomi's body severed from her head. Her body twitched and rolled, and the head flew into and through the train. If I weren't so worried about Clay, I'm sure I would have retched on the spot.

Keeping an eye on the roaring train and the decapitated body, I ran to Clay's side. He lay on the ground, but leaned up to watch the cars pass Naomi's body. He held one arm as though it had been injured in the fall, but I was rather sure that the look of horror on his face trumped any pain he experienced from an injured arm. I dropped to the ground to cradle him.

Before the tail end of the train passed by Naomi's shattered body, her headless form stood and stepped into the train, disappearing on the other side. Will still stood at the spot where he had caught up with Clay, and he watched her go, his body erect, his feet braced, as though he expected her to return.

As the last of the train roared by, the sound died away, leaving behind a shocking silence. Naomi stood on the other side of the track facing Will, her head and body intact and reshaped into that of a mature young woman. Lantern in hand, she stared at Will. Their sullenness, their smoldering stares, their physical distance—all reminded me of two duelists prepared to bring a vendetta to a close in the most heinous way.

I don't know if it was shock or fear as Clay and I crouched there on the ground, or an astute awareness that we were in dire danger, but neither of us said a word.

Clay couldn't see Will, but his silence made me think he finally believed and maybe even understood that Will was dealing with Naomi.

She spoke first. "William." Two simple syllables, yet I'd never heard such pain and turmoil wrapped into one mere word. Her voice sounded pitiful, heartbreaking, and I wondered if Braxton had told the truth about her.

"Naomi," Will said with marked gentleness. "Beautiful Naomi. We lost that future we dreamed so much about."

She didn't react, just stood looking at him, her face devoid of emotion.

Beside me, Clay shifted. I remembered he might be in severe pain, so I moved to support him, as quietly as possible.

But, I wasn't quiet enough. A stick beneath me cracked. With no trees to block the moonlight, Naomi's eyes flicked to us before returning to Will.

"Friends of yours, William?" Her tone changed to one of annoyance, further emphasizing that we dealt with the ghost of a deranged woman.

"Where'd she go?" Clay asked in a hushed, startled tone.

Upon hearing Clay's observation, fear seized me. Why would she want to hide her appearance from us? Of course she didn't know that I could still see her, but I had to assume she wanted the upper hand by hiding her appearance from him. *But why?*

Will ignored her question. "Naomi, what happened that drove you to this? I know the war hurt—"

"You know *nothing.*" She spat at him, the pitiful, frail girl replaced with the scorn of a maniacal woman. "You think the world is good and fair and you fought for honorable causes. And where did that get you, Will? You died in poverty and filth, fighting for a life that wasn't even worth coming home to."

Again, Will ignored her. "I thought we loved—"

"I loved Fergus!" She shrieked. "Not you! But before the war, you were going to do better in life than he was, so I betrothed myself to you. I thought the war was a whim. That it would be quick. But it wasn't. So what did you do? You turned your back on everything we wanted to fight for some ridiculous noble cause. But not Fergus! He knew how to capitalize on the war, so I took him back." She laughed. "You poor, stupid fool. All that time trying to come back to the woman of your dreams, and she snuggled in bed with Fergus! While you slept on a soggy field, we slept on satin sheets."

Will's fists clenched, but he showed no other signs of a reaction. My heart ached for him.

He spoke, his voice calm. "It must have sickened you to discover that you were carrying my child."

Will was trying to bait her. I'd spent weeks studying him, cataloging his words, his habits. I'd learned enough to know that he chose his words here with care, to get at the truth, to determine if the child was his.

"Yes, curse you!" she said, and the particles that formed her body swirled and blackened as though she filled with rage. "Fergus and I only had one month together when I found out I was several months with child. We both knew it had to be your child. We hated you."

"So you came to Georgia to have the baby with family."

"Yes! And Fergus was to come for me after it was born."

"But he never came."

She dropped her guard and whimpered. "No. He never came." She thrust her shoulders back and raised her chin. "But I knew he was alive. I heard stories about him. Living our dream, spending our gold while I lived in poverty. I wanted to find him, but that child stood in my way!" She hissed, but her voice sounded like a bundle of old knotted ropes, ready to unravel with one tug.

"What happened to the child? Who raised him?"

"No one! I killed him!" She shrieked, breaking into demented laughter and flailing her hands toward Will. "With my own hands, I killed your son. Just the way you killed my dreams!"

Her eyes darted over to Clay and me, then back to Will. She cackled and sauntered toward him. "So it's my turn to destroy your dream, isn't it, sweetheart? It would be justice if you didn't make it to your little heaven and instead had to stay here in this hell with me." Once at his side, she reached out and drew a finger across his cheek. "Where's your energy source, sweetheart? Hmmm? Are they guarding it?"

With the speed of a hungry serpent, she appeared at my side. I didn't even see her move. She studied me as if I were the ghostly one, the curiosity. I was so scared I couldn't move a single part of my being.

"She's pretty, Will. But you two are so different. She's so *alive*, and you're … not. Perhaps I should make her join us, then you'd be stuck in your own hell forever, wouldn't you?"

Somehow I sensed Will urging me to remain still and quiet. Clay couldn't see her, though he must have sensed my panic because he moved to stand, but then fell back instead.

Naomi bent over to look into my eyes, her face mere inches from me. I tried to look through her, but she had placed herself in my line of vision and to dart my eyes away would have told her what she needed to know. Instead, she tried another tactic.

"What can you see, pretty thing?" Suddenly, snakes crawled out of her mouth and eyes. A substance—blood?—oozed from her nose.

"It's not real," Will said to Naomi, but I knew it was for my benefit. "Even if Grace could see you, she'd know these tricks aren't real."

Naomi changed back to herself and stood. "Well, then she'll know this is real."

She gripped my neck, squeezed and lifted me into the air. I couldn't breathe and began flailing and gasping. I struggled to grasp from my neck two hands that weren't even real, whereas the murderous, invisible grip cutting off my air was all too real.

Clay screamed my name and crawled toward me.

"Naomi, let her alone!" Will ordered and appeared at our side. "Your fight is with me."

She tightened her grasp and smiled. Will leaped on us. Her grip broke, and I fell to the side, landing on my hands and knees, taking in deep gulps of air.

"Grace!" Clay crawled to me. "What's happening? Tell me where they are, how to fight!"

But there was nothing Clay could do. How can you fight invisible enemies?

I turned to see Will and Naomi, swirling, surging, changing sizes and forms. At one point, their forms stretched and expanded, and they towered over the tall pines, shrinking low to the ground like snarling animals. The air whirled around us as though we hovered in a wind tunnel. The trees reacted to the squall, bending to the ground from the force of the air funnels then jerked back to bend in a different direction. Branches snapped; twigs and leaves flew everywhere. Clay pulled me against him and tucked my head into his chest.

Naomi had anger and hatred and evil on her side, so her maneuvers and her violent movements were her familiar territory, but for Will they were a foreign concept. It looked as though she might be able to subdue him.

And then something snapped in me. I reached that point where the life force had taken over, and my body followed along. Before I had time to think, I leaped to my feet against the gale, grabbed the cross that hung inside my shirt and raced toward the tumult, my movements primal, adrenaline-driven. I thrust the cross into the air and cried, "Please help us! Save us from this demon, this evil. Send her to the abyss …"

As I rattled on, the scene before me died a quick death. Will and Naomi returned to their original forms. The wind calmed. The silence returned.

Naomi dropped to her knees and cried, "No, no, no!" She looked possessed, insane. "Lucifer help me," she wailed in the most piteous plea I'd ever heard.

In an instant Will stepped to my side, carrying Clay. He looked at Naomi with such sadness, I wanted to put my arms around him, but sensed that the cross was saving us, and that I needed to keep it raised like a fortification between her and us.

"Naomi, I'm so sorry for you." Will didn't say what for, but I assumed he meant for the eternal hell that she had created for herself. He turned to me. "Walk backward slowly. Keep the cross high."

I did as he directed. He put Clay in the backseat, and we climbed into the front. With one hand I started the car, never dropping the cross. By now, Naomi raised her arms toward the sky, begging for a release that would never come.

I drove with one hand, never lowering the cross until we pulled from Bennett Road onto the highway. In the next town, Jesup, I stopped at the Wayne County Hospital along Route 84. The emergency room doctor diagnosed Clay with a slight concussion, a dislocated shoulder, and a broken ulna bone in his left arm.

Several hours later, with his arm in a sling and his body filled with painkillers, Clay slept in the backseat as Will sat beside me in the front, heading home.

"Naomi and I used his energy to manifest ourselves." Will once again studied Clay. "He will sleep for hours."

"What will happen to her?" I asked. She was a product of her own making, a product of her choices, but to leave her there in that pitiful state seemed so brutal and unfeeling.

"She has two choices now. Remain there or move on to her own hell. There is nothing we can do for her now."

We decided Screven would have a spooklight indefinitely, given her two options.

* * *

The drive home proved uneventful. Between my adrenaline and my thoughts, I drove six hours in what passed like two. When the sun crept over the horizon, Will excused himself and returned to the coin.

Somewhere in southern Virginia, Clay roused and we stopped for coffee and food. I took Tramp for a long walk before starting out again. Clay remained too groggy to talk much, let alone drive, so I again took the wheel. My plan was to get home, say goodbye to Will, and get a good night's sleep before my aunt arrived the next day.

Imagine our surprise when we pulled into *Crossings* and saw several cars parked on the driveway, while, from the porch, four sets of eyes watched our arrival. I looked up to see Aunt Tish, Michael, and two police officers.

PART IV

Shifting Shadows

Chapter 28

While Aunt Tish shrieked at me for having disappeared, Michael kept shushing her, and Sheriff Barnes—a beefy man who smelled of tobacco and spicy aftershave—focused on Clay. He must have known Clay because his tone harbored an apologetic awkwardness when he spoke: "Son, I'm real sorry about this, but I'm afraid I have to arrest you for the attempted murder of Seth Rendale and—"

Clay's face registered shock, while I voiced it. "What are you talking about? Clay didn't do anything. Seth was fine when we left."

"Grace," Michael murmured, snaking an arm around my waist and pulling me toward him. "They don't think this Seth kid is going to make it."

Fear struck me like a padded fist. "That can't be right!"

The sheriff raised his eyebrows in a warning to keep quiet. "We've had an APB on you and … well, Clay, I got a report that your car was spotted crossing from Virginia into Maryland … and now here you are in West Virginia. This means you drove a minor over state lines … and this lady," he gestured a thumb toward Aunt Tish, "seems to think it was for nefarious purposes, so—"

"What?" I sputtered. "That's crazy. And, Clay's not even twenty-one yet anyway. You can't—"

"Yes, I am." Clay turned to me and frowned. "Yesterday was my birthday."

I blinked. "Why didn't you tell me?"

"We were kinda' busy. It just never came up."

"So," the sheriff continued, admonishing us again with his eyes, "if Mrs. Rosenburg still wants to press charges, then I'm afraid we'll have to—"

"Of course, I do!" Aunt Tish bellowed. "My niece would never have gone off on her own volition—"

"Mom, stop. You're not helping the situation," Michael growled.

"I *did* go of my own free will," I said. "Clay insisted on coming to protect me, not—"

"Enough!" the sheriff yelled, and everyone's colliding voices grew quiet. "Now then, Ms. MacKenna?"

I nodded.

"I'll need you to come to the station. We have a few questions about the night of the attack. Clay?" He motioned for Clay to turn around. He and the deputy spent an awkward moment clasping handcuffs on a man who had one arm in a sling.

As I watched them leave with Clay, Will emerged at my side.

"You must take me to the hospital right away," Will said. "If the soul that entered Seth is still in him, his life is in jeopardy."

Dumbfounded, I nodded as I tried to absorb it all. I felt the vibration of Will's return to the coin where it sat in my jeans pocket. I did the only thing I could think of to do. I cried, "I'm going to the hospital," then bolted down the porch steps and to my car, ignoring Aunt Tish's thunderous warnings to stop.

* * *

I hurried to the hospital. A nurse told me Seth's parents wouldn't return for a while, so I sneaked into intensive care. Placing the gold coin on Seth's heart, I watched it vibrate as Will transferred into Seth's body. I backed into a corner and prayed that Will would have enough strength to fight Seth's demon and that he could do so before a nurse returned.

Seth writhed and twisted in pain and issued guttural noises that I feared could be heard in the hallway. Just as a nurse burst into the room and ordered me to leave, Seth grew quiet, blinked open his eyes and strained to sit up. His skin was pale and his arms shook as he moved, but the change was startling. The nurse's jaw dropped, and she just stood there, stymied by what she saw. She was so distracted that she didn't notice me moving in and grabbing the coin where it had fallen to Seth's side.

If the nurse could have seen the soul that emerged from Seth, I bet she would have fainted. Will looked normal enough, but the other soul was a fright—puckered skin pulled away at spots from a diseased-looking skeleton beneath, and claws replaced hands. Moving through the wall, he exited into the hallway. Will grabbed my elbow and ushered me out to watch him stagger down the corridor. When I suggested he might possess someone else, Will disagreed. "He can't harm another being without returning to Sharpsburg, his main source of strength. And, he has such little energy left, he will have to cross over. He failed in his mission to prolong evil."

By the time the soul reached the nurse's station, he began to fade.

"But couldn't he find his way back into Seth?"

"No, Seth is not the angry person any longer that he was when the soul attacked him. I think you'll find that Seth not only recovered, but came through all this a different person as well."

"Why would he be different?" I whispered, aware that the medical staff eyed me. I put my hand on the side of my head to make it look as though I covered a Bluetooth headset.

"Life and death experiences will change you. Miracles too." He smiled. "You know that first-hand."

And indeed, Will was right. The Seth that left the hospital that same night—after what doctors called a "near miracle"—told a deputy who'd stopped by that Clay wasn't responsible for any ill will. When pressed for the name of a culprit, Seth shrugged. "I lost control. That's all."

As for Clay, the sheriff released him, but told him that Tish Rosenburg was pursuing a restraining order against him and that, as a precaution, he should stay at least fifty feet away from me. I learned this after leaving the hospital and visiting the jail, missing Clay by minutes. While I'd been racing to Georgia, Aunt Tish had been talking with legal authorities. She wanted an order by law that he could not come near me until I turned eighteen years old. A year and three months away! Furthermore, the sheriff advised him not to use phone, cell, or Internet to communicate with me in any manner.

* * *

Somewhere in the midst of all these developments, Michael found me. Aunt Tish had instructed him to return me to *Crossings* immediately, but instead he kept me company until I felt ready to return. We grabbed a soda outside a convenience store on Canal Street and sat on a dark curb talking.

As it turns out, Michael's company had presented him with a choice of positions in either of their offices in Seattle or Bethesda, Maryland. He'd flown back to the states on Thursday and had intended to surprise me. "I chose Bethesda," he said. "It's a 45-minute train ride from your place. I figure we can live here for a while."

Aunt Tish arrived early, he said, due to a fire at the gallery. He promised to convince her that I could stay there with him, and that he should be my guardian. "Just tell her that she can keep her monthly payments from your trust fund if she'll let you stay. She'll be happy to do that once it dawns on her that she gets the money *and* doesn't have to spend any of it on you. That is, assuming you want to stay at that house. If not, we can go to Seattle—"

"Oh, Michael!" I grabbed him in a bear hug. "Thank you. Yes, I want to stay here. *Crossings* is my home now."

He snickered. "It's kind of a cross between Modern Ghoulish Cool and Early American Creepy, eh? Hey, once we open our own firm, we'll make it our first restoration project."

He referred to our plans of owning an architectural firm together, him overseeing the civil engineering and construction, me handling the design. But in that instant, my mind swirled at how I had changed.

I took his hand. "We'll refurbish *Crossings* together, but I'm not going to study design anymore."

His eyebrows lifted. "So what's your future hold now?"

I grinned. "It's provincial," I said in a tone imitating my aunt.

"Try me."

"I want to study history education. I want to be a teacher and a historian."

He stared at me, and I wondered whether he would try to argue. He must have decided my decision was irrevocable. "Sounds like we have a lot of catching up to do."

I smiled. "You have no idea."

He cleared his throat. "This Clay guy ... he's ... *special* to you?"

Tears surfaced as I repeated: "You have no idea."

* * *

After returning to *Crossings*, I journeyed south with Aunt Tish and Michael to an all-night diner because Aunt Tish couldn't "tolerate that disgusting apartment."

While she lectured, I remained quiet, catching key phrases: "ashamed of you," "ungrateful little girl," "like your mother," "wash my hands of you," and "on your own, missy." Other than that, I heard buzzing.

I think I stole her thunder by not arguing. She was my guardian, and I needed to honor and respect her. But that didn't mean I had to accept her abuse. I attempted to show her respect by keeping quiet.

She gave up when she grew hoarse, so Michael pitched his idea about the two of us remaining at *Crossings*.

He was right. Despite her anger, she loved the idea of the money in Boston without me as part of the package. She also accepted the notion of Michael becoming designated guardian, as long as it didn't interfere with her receiving the stipend, and only after she made a snide comment about the fox guarding the henhouse. We remained quiet as if we both understood that she needed to strut her power over me by making a huge show of coming to the decision on her own.

With the decision made, she established the rules: I had to sign up for public high school or join a home school network with Michael overseeing the effort; eight-thirty was my curfew, and I had to have the phone company install a land-line phone in the apartment so that I could call her each night at 9 p.m. from that number; and at all times I would answer my cell phone when she called.

With our new agreements intact, we returned to *Crossings* where Aunt Tish climbed in her rental car and left to find a room at a hotel in nearby Hagerstown. Michael crashed on the couch.

I headed into my room, closed the door and turned on my cell phone. About a dozen messages had accumulated during the past three days. I ignored them and called Adriana.

She yawned "hello," then squealed, "Grace!" when she heard my voice. "Clay was here. He told me about being arrested and you two going to Georgia. The police told him to stay away from you. What's that all about?"

"Ade, can we talk tomorrow? I feel like I've been up for days. I just wanted to call and say I'm here and that I'm sorry for being so flaky lately. I'll make it up to you."

Her voice grew somber. "Clay is leaving. He said if he sees you or talks to you, that you might be forced to move back to Boston. The only way he knows how to stay away from you is by leaving."

I fell onto my bed, still clutching the phone. Just when I thought I had no energy left, I discovered I had enough to feel my heart breaking. I had lost our relationship before I'd even found it. He was leaving, and I never had the chance to tell him how I felt. He was doing what he felt was best for me. How then, could it feel so wrong?

"Grace? Are you there?"

"When is he going? And where?"

"He's leaving in the morning. He has an uncle that lives in Lexington, Virginia, about three hours south. He's hoping to go to law school there at Washington and Lee, instead of Georgetown."

Three hours. No goodbye.

We ended our call with the promise to talk tomorrow.

It would be at least an hour and hundreds of tears before I could compose myself enough to deal with the biggest life change of any of the cast of characters that had entered my life—my final goodbye to Will.

Chapter 29

While Michael slept on the foldout couch, I lit the lantern and crept into the old house. Latching the dividing door with a gentle tug, I turned to see Will standing by the piano. As always, his rugged, good looks took my breath away.

He spoke first: "I cannot thank you for all that you have done."

The lump in my throat prevented me from responding. As if he understood, he moved to within two feet of me and continued. "You know I must leave now. My business is finished here, and I am anxious to meet my son."

I nodded, too overcome with emotion to say anything. Finally, I managed a deep breath. "I don't want to say goodbye."

"Then don't."

He spoke so tenderly that it took all my strength not to throw my arms around him and beg him to stay.

"I will see you again, so there's no need for goodbye." Confusion must have registered on my face because he added, "In about eighty years."

That's when my tears started.

He lifted my hand and brought it to his cold lips. "My beautiful Grace. I'll meet you by the river."

I choked on my tears and feigned a smile. "You promise?"

With his free hand, he brushed my cheek. "I'll be there to greet you with open arms. Your mother will have to wrestle me for the first hug."

I gulped, trying to catch my breath, and let the tears flow freely. The visual he created of seeing my mother overwhelmed me, and I couldn't think of a coherent response.

He continued. "Meanwhile, do something for me?"

"Anything." I wiped my eyes and almost mustered enough conviction to sound convincing.

"Enjoy your life. You only get one. Use your gift, but be cautious with other souls you encounter. And remember, life's not about what you're dealt, but rather what you do with what you're dealt. Like a deck of cards. It's about your choices.

The biggest choice being to believe and trust in God. And you do. And because you do, I am finally able to move on. No words can express my gratitude."

I gulped again and choked back more tears. "You just did."

He turned to look away, and I thought he would disappear. I gasped. "No!"

Instead, he walked to the corner cabinet and picked up his wedding picture. Returning, he placed it in my hand. "Look at it from time to time. Remember me."

I gulped back a choke and tried to smile. "You got it."

"I like this one because it reflects a happy day in my life, despite what happened to Naomi. But there are other pictures, too." He pointed to the cabinet.

I followed his finger and something caught my eye, a picture I had never noticed before. I walked to the cabinet and picked it up. "Will, who is this?" I turned to look at him.

He moved closer to see and frowned. "That's Fergus. Why?"

Fear gripped me, and I looked away to hide my reaction. "N ... nothing." As steady as I could manage, I returned both pictures to the shelf. With a deep breath, I focused on Will again. "I will miss you so much. You've taught me so many things."

"Do not cry, little one," he said, his tone, tender. "I will see you again."

We hugged, one of the longest hugs I ever experienced. Then he stepped back and, just like that, he left my life.

My whole body felt battleship heavy as grief consumed me. I left the old house and stumbled back to my bed where I collapsed, too bewildered to cry anymore. Finally, when I had no strength left, I fell asleep.

It would be days before I entered the old house again, but when I did, I moved straight to that corner cabinet, picked up the picture of Fergus and looked at the man whose soul I had seen just weeks ago in my bedroom and in the root cellar.

He still remained ... somewhere ... at *Crossings*.

Chapter 30

I learned several things the next afternoon: that misery *does* love company; that drenching rain can further deflate an already miserable mood; and that I'd been a selfish friend, out of touch with the people I cared about, such that I was embarrassed to learn that while I'd been chasing ghosts, Adriana's boyfriend Darius had broken up with her, and she'd lost first chair for the fall concert series at her college because they granted a late audition to a new transfer student. What's more, Cassie had gone out on her first date since Mason's departure, and it had not gone well.

"All I could talk about was Mason," she said, slumping over a cup of tea. "I asked Nick to bring me home early, and that's when I heard about Clay."

We shared our sorrows around a table at the *Time Out*. When Adriana and I had arrived, Cassie took one look at our forlorn faces and hung the "Closed" sign on the door. It didn't take long for the patrons already in the café to take the hint. Their discomfort won out over their stubbornness and, in short time, we found ourselves alone. Cassie raided the kitchen for anything chocolate and poured us each a cup of soothing herbal tea. Coffee wasn't even mentioned.

As we talked, all three of us red-eyed, the gloomy weather outside reflecting our mood, it struck me that we shared a kind of collective mourning. Here sat the three most important women in Clay's life—his mom, his BFF, and, if I had my druthers, the woman he loved, although I'd lost my chance to develop that. So, when Cassie mentioned Clay's name again, sadness overtook the room like a fog. If not for me, they would both have Clay there to talk to, to boost them as he had done so many times in their lives. I sank even deeper in my chair, and the three of us studied our cups, not seeing anything, as the gray rain pelted against the windows.

Adriana broke the silence, her voice bearing a chipper tone that rang false: "Dad always says that to be upset over what you don't have is to waste what you do have."

Cassie and I shot her a glance as though to say we couldn't believe she had just said that.

"What? At least we have one another." She shrugged away her awkwardness. "I'm just saying." With a frustrated look on her face, she picked up the chocolate syrup bottle and poured a large puddle on her triple-chocolate cake.

Appropriate or not, her comment goaded us into conversation. This time the topic centered on me, and we talked about Clay's warning from the police, my new "house rules," and my new guardian. Both Cassie and Adriana voiced interest in meeting Michael. From there, conversation steered back to Clay again and how much we'd miss him. When I muttered something off-topic about ghosts and demons, both Cassie and Adriana stopped me short.

"No!" they yelled in unison and flicked their palms toward me as though they'd talked beforehand and practiced their responses.

They glanced at each other and grinned.

"Sorry, Grace," Cassie said. "I'm not as brave as you."

"Me either," Adriana agreed. "I'da been out of there a long time ago. Talk about anything but that. I don't want to be afraid to visit you, so don't even suggest the idea of anything creepy."

I nodded. "I'm sorry it's been so crazy. Clay was helping me to resolve a lot of things, and my aunt didn't like that very well. Now he has to change his plans because of me."

Cassie leaned over and pulled me into a sideways hug. "Hon, my son would have changed his plans because of you even if he *had* stayed. Right, Adriana?"

Adriana bobbled her head yes and giggled. "Yeah, it took me a while to see it, but he fell hard."

"Reaghan saw it too." Cassie directed her comment to Adriana.

I groaned. "She'll never accept me now."

"Who knows? She might be fine with it," Cassie said. "If Clay's not here, then he's not around you. Don't worry about her, hon. She's my daughter, and I love her, but she has her own issues to tend to."

While I appreciated Cassie's comment, I couldn't help but be concerned. I added a talk with Reaghan to my growing list of things to do. Also on the list: start restoration on *Crossings*, establish routines with Michael, and register for school. And, I faced a series of unresolved questions that I needed to investigate: Was Fergus haunting the grounds of *Crossings*? Why was Holland Greer so interested in me? Did the gold coin play a role in all this? Was that part of the gold Naomi had mentioned? Was I dealing with ghosts, or angels and demons? And did it matter?

* * *

Gossip spread like fire around Williamsport about the young quarterback from Williamsport High who almost died, but then made a "miracle recovery." The grapevine concluded that Seth's "injuries" occurred while he and Clay Baxter settled some long-standing disagreements. Rumor placed him at the local Food bank helping to distribute goods while scuttlebutt whispered that he volunteered at the hospital. Adriana's brother Rory announced that Seth "acted weird," these days while Cassie shared that Seth had patronized the *Time Out* several times hoping to catch me. I spotted him in church with his parents while I sat with the Barrones, but he left right after the service.

Therefore, I wasn't surprised when I answered a knock at my door one morning to see him standing there. Michael still slept, so I suggested we sit on the porch. We perched on the glider as Tramp bounded down the steps.

I sensed an immediate change, a maturity that I hadn't expected would develop for years. He sat without fidgeting, talked without getting agitated.

"Look, Grace, I'm not sure what happened back in Sharpsburg and then at the hospital, but I know you had something to do with it."

I took a deep breath, wondering if he would talk about the accident or the recovery. He chose the latter.

"Some *odd* things happened as I woke up in the hospital. And there you stood. You didn't seem at all surprised by my ... unusual ... recovery." He leaned in, studying my face. "You know something that the medical staff doesn't, don't you?"

I looked down at my hands folded together in my lap, trying to think of a response.

He didn't wait for an answer. "I thought so. Will you teach it to me one day?"

Startled, I stared at him for a few heartbeats before responding. "Yeah. One day."

"Good, good. And thanks for what you did. You're a good friend."

I had no response. I wasn't good at compliments, particularly those I didn't deserve. If Seth hadn't been seeking me out in Sharpsburg, he wouldn't have gotten hurt in the first place.

I roused a smile. "You look much better."

He grinned. "I feel great."

I studied him. "How so?"

His gaze jerked toward the river, toward Williamsport. "I'm not sure. It's like a lot of stuff has been removed. Anger. Jealousy."

"Anger about what?"

He blushed and grimaced before he spoke. "About Clay, for one. You have to understand, Grace, for years I've been compared to him. He was a quarterback in high school, too, and senior class president. Big man around town. Could do no wrong. Then he came home a war hero. The town worshipped him. Meanwhile, I became the quarterback, and it always seemed like I was compared to Clay and came up short. So when you entered the picture and … well … it's obvious you chose him … I just had a hard time with that."

I searched his face for signs of rivalry, but I found none. When I didn't respond, he continued. "I heard he left town … and why. I'm sorry."

I nodded, the lump in my throat preventing any other response.

"I want you to know I'm here for you. As a friend. I understand how you feel about Clay. I can't say I like it. I'll probably try to change your mind, but I promise to respect your feelings." He hesitated then extended his hand. "Friends?"

He had such sincerity in his eyes, and I *felt* so grateful that he made this easy, that I couldn't help but ignore the hand and instead gave him a quick hug. "Friends."

"Thanks."

"You're going to be busy this fall," I said, hoping to change the subject, "between work and football and all these volunteer things I hear about."

"I've dropped football."

"What? Should you do that? I thought you wanted to major in sports management in college."

He took a deep breath and locked his jaw, looking determined, sure of himself. "No, I'm going to study medicine. I'm looking into a pre-med program at Johns Hopkins."

"But that's here in Maryland. What about heading south where it's warm?"

He shrugged. "It's not that important anymore. I need to focus on getting into medical school."

"That's quite a change in plans." I marveled at the difference in the young man beside me.

He looked at the river again, but I suspected he was seeing into his future. What he said next reminded me that we all want answers to the riddles of life, death, God, good and evil, angels and demons. "Grace, the doctors said I almost died, and yet they can't explain why I didn't. I want to explore that, the role miracles play in science. How often does divine intervention occur and under what circumstances? Are the answers ignored because they don't fit neatly into scientific explanations?"

I looked away. I didn't want Seth to think I laughed at him when the truth was I relished in the fact that Will's soul—my angel—had changed Seth's life too. My mind flittered back to Will's comment that the dimension and heaven were not places up high, but rather existed all around us, just in different vibrations, and I wondered if Will could hear Seth's conviction.

Just then a draft of cool air brushed my cheek, but the trees and wind chimes stood still.

* * *

The night before the moon waned to its weakest state, Michael called to say that he planned to join his new co-workers for a Friday evening in Georgetown, and that he'd be home by midnight.

His plans meant freedom for me, so I secured his okay to carry out an errand once done with my requisite check-in with Aunt Tish.

Phone call complete, I said a quick prayer for strength, put Tramp in the car, and headed to Sharpsburg. I figured the timing was perfect—early enough in the night that Braxton would have full strength.

When I reached the porch step that led to the old shed, Braxton emerged through the door. Given the weakened moon, I assumed there was little activity inside the shed, but sighed relief that he came outside anyway.

"Ms. MacKenna," Braxton said, bowing his head, his cold, aloof demeanor still obvious. He gestured to the porch floor as though to say, "Please sit."

I complied, and he reclined his form beside me, our feet parked on the ground. Tramp sniffed the ground off to the side, oblivious to the soul beside me.

I said, "I wanted you to know—"

"That Will has moved on. Yes, I know."

Startled, I looked at him, and in that instant I made a decision. I had been apprehensive about this meeting for more than a week, wondering how I would tell Braxton that Will *was* free but then *not* follow it up with the offer to help set him free too. Braxton scared me. His demeanor was dark and gloomy and brooding compared to Will, and he drained me, whereas I'd always been able to maintain my energy with Will. Braxton's murder was especially odious, and it frightened me to know that helping him would involve *watching* his murder. Once again I recalled Pastor Dale concluding that ghosts might be angels and demons. Braxton didn't strike me as angel material, so did that make him a demon? And what were the secrets that dwelled within him, secrets that I would have to cultivate to resolve?

Yet, when Braxton acknowledged Will's passing before I even mentioned it, I remembered that Braxton could communicate with Will in the dimension. Perhaps Braxton would be my link to Will. In that instant, I decided that if Will trusted him, then I would too.

Before I voiced the offer, Braxton said, "Thank you for helping my friend." His voice was flat, devoid of the warmth that accompanies gratitude.

"He was my friend too. That makes you my friend as well." I hoped he didn't sense that I disliked him. I swallowed. "So, I will help you too, if you want."

His deep-set eyes studied me. "I'm afraid that my story is a little more gruesome and involved than Will's." In the shadows carved by the barest of moons, he appeared ten years older than the twenty-five years of age that I calculated him to be.

I broke eye contact and studied the ground. His gaze penetrated and scared me, even though I tried to believe that he posed no danger. "Your story involves Fergus too, doesn't it?"

"Not my murder, but perhaps that of my wife, Eva. But I *do* believe my murder is linked with hers. Do you want to hear the story tonight?"

"No," I said louder than I intended. "No, I don't have time tonight. Maybe not for several weeks. It may be hard for me to get away for a while ... and, well, I need a little time to prepare myself. But, I will come back."

He continued studying me. "I understand. Thank you."

Even his "thank you" sounded cold, stoic, so I ignored it. "Braxton, I need to know something ... I have reason to believe that Fergus's soul may still be at *Crossings*. If that's true, might I be in danger?"

His jaw tensed, and he looked toward the street. "I don't know. That's part of what we'll have to uncover. I know that he used *Crossings* for all sorts of purposes, but he limited himself to the root cellar because he could hide things ... even people ... there."

"Things ... such as gold?"

Despite his chilling demeanor, my question surprised Braxton. "Yes, gold was involved. It sounds as though we have much talking to do to piece together what we know."

I nodded, but said nothing.

"Be careful, Ms. MacKenna. My guess is that if you stick to the house and avoid the root cellar, you will be fine. Fergus never liked the house much because he was jealous of Will. If Fergus experienced his death at *Crossings*, I have to believe it occurred in or near the root cellar. If you saw him in the house, and he didn't harm you, I'm guessing he has little strength there."

"That's good, I suppose," I said, my voice little more than a whisper.

"But we do have a problem." He locked his eyes on mine. "Resolving my death may require that you spend considerable time in the root cellar and its maze of tunnels."

Tunnels? I felt a headache coming on, but then thoughts of Will flicked through my mind. Even if Braxton were able to deliver one message from me to Will, it would be worth the risk.

"I understand." I stood. "Goodbye for now. I'll try to return in a month or two."

I didn't wait for his reply before retrieving Tramp and walking away.

Chapter 31

Cassie, Adriana, and I found such comfort in one another that we continued our teatime a few nights a week, after Cassie closed the shop, and, of course, after I checked in with Aunt Tish.

For each gathering, I drove to the café, until on one night when Adriana picked me up, and she met Michael.

I was used to Michael being a Don Juan with the ladies, but I wasn't ready for the attraction that struck between these two. He stood straighter; she twirled her hair around a finger. He insisted on giving her a tour; she acted like she'd never been there before. He stared like a child being presented with a new sort of candy bar; she returned an adoring expression. They ignored me, laughed at inane remarks, and agreed they'd look forward to getting together.

I steered Adriana out of the apartment, but she wore a silly smile and remained quiet as we journeyed to the *Time Out*. I decided to talk to Michael about his intentions with this particular friend. She'd been hurt enough already.

When we arrived at the *Time Out*, I didn't notice at first the unlocked door or the flickering lights. It wasn't until we let ourselves in that the blind-covered windows and the burning candles grabbed my attention.

"What's going on?" I asked, looking around. "Where's Cassie?"

When Adriana responded, she sounded distracted. "I don't know. Wait here, I'll check in the kitchen."

Within seconds of her departure, music swelled from the speakers perched above in the shadows of the exposed beams. With a start, I recognized the tune as Eva Cassidy's *Songbird*.

The floor creaked behind me, and I whirled around.

Clay!

He was so handsome and smiled at me with such warmth that I broke into tears. He stepped forward, and I thought he intended to embrace me. Instead, he reached out, took my hand, and brought it to his lips.

He gestured to an open space on the floor. "May I have this dance?"

I couldn't talk. In fact, I could hardly see through misty eyes. He must have seen it too because, as we swayed to the music, he kissed my cheeks to remove the moist signs of unhappiness.

Neither of us spoke as we leaned into one another and let the words of the song express what dwelled in our hearts. I marveled at this man's memory for what I'd said about songbirds.

The song ended, and Anne Murray's *Could I Have This Dance for the Rest of My Life?* poured through the speakers.

A third song began, but even if my life depended on it, I could never recall the title. I was too focused on the man in my arms. He kissed me. Gently, like I was a rare china doll. But that lasted for only about fifteen seconds before the kisses intensified. I wondered if it was possible to inject a hefty supply of tenderness into the moment to make up for the long months ahead.

All too soon, he pulled back and frowned. "I have to go. Your stay in Williamsport's in jeopardy if we're caught together."

"No! Please don't leave yet. Clay, I … I …"

He planted his hands on the sides of my face and directed my eyes to look into his. "I love you, Grace. I know that now. But we both need to move on."

"What? No." I blubbered.

"It was selfish of me to arrange this with Mom and Adriana, but I had to see you one more time. Dance with you. Say goodbye. Your aunt was right … you are too young to tie yourself to one—"

"No, no I'm not too young—"

He put two fingers on my lips. "Listen to me. I want you to move on with your life. I'm going to be busy with school. You have a gift. I'm not sure what it is, but I want you to use it. Then fifteen months from now, we'll talk again. We'll see how things stand. How we both feel."

"Nothing will change," I said with the naiveté that every young person mutters in situations like this.

He kissed my hand again. "Goodbye, Grace."

He turned and exited through the back.

I sank to the floor and sobbed.

Chapter 32

I don't remember anything from the time Clay left until I found myself in bed that night. Somehow Adriana brought me home and put me in bed. All I remember is lying there wondering how I would carry on without him. How could I foster a future without Clay?

While Michael slept late the next morning, I walked along the Canal with Tramp. I intended to follow through on my promise to Jarrod, the Canal ghost, to let him know how things had turned out with Will. Going into the visit, I'd had no plans whatsoever to offer to help resolve his death too, but something he said changed not just my mind, but my entire life.

I found him deep in the same ravine where I'd talked with him earlier. A huge smile lit his face, almost as though the goodness of his soul revealed itself there. The difference between Braxton and Jarrod startled me.

"Ms. MacKenna! Such a pleasure." He cocked his head as though assessing me. "You have succeeded in your mission."

"Yes." I smiled, his cheeriness warming me. "William Kavanaugh has passed on."

"Ah." He clasped his hands together, although his actions produced no sound. "A job well done. Congratulations. You must be a very special young lady."

I looked down. "You're pretty unique yourself, Jarrod … err, Mr ….?" I shot him a questioning look, intending to use his more formal name as a sign of respect. I figured that would make him feel special. Imagine, instead, how he made me feel with his response.

"Jarrod is fine, but since you're my friend now, call me Mason." He bowed. "Jarrod Mason Baxter at your service."

The last thing I remember is grabbing a tree branch as I sank to the ground, never once taking my eyes off of the soul of Clay's father.

The End

Look for the sequel in the Crossings Trilogy, *Edging through the Darkness* ...

EDGING THROUGH THE DARKNESS

Sequel to *Crossing into the Mystic*

By DL KOONTZ

Prologue

In my experience, death is never final, and good-bye is not forever.

The dead can return to life and occupy the same space as living beings, just on different planes. Sometimes inexplicable circumstances come together and open a door between the worlds, allowing living beings and the souls of the dead to interact.

But perhaps I'm getting ahead of myself. I should explain that not *all* souls remain behind; just those whose demise is unexpected, perhaps violent, as in a horrific fire or an accident.

Or, in my experience, *murder*.

I witnessed it first-hand. When I escaped Boston to move, alone, into *Crossings*, the house I inherited from my stepfather, I befriended the soul of William Kavanaugh, a handsome soldier from the Civil War. By the time my "subtle vision" matured, I could see Will just as he looked more than a hundred and fifty years ago when he walked the earth as a living being.

What's more astonishing is that I conversed with him. We spent many evenings discussing life, friends, pleasures …

… and murder.

You see, when there is enough energy to warrant it, ghosts can seem as solid as anyone. That can be good or bad news, depending upon the ghost—or "soul" as Will taught me to say—you encounter.

Okay, I must confess that I cared more for Will than mere friendship. Fact is, I loved him. At least, I loved him enough to let him go and isn't that the real test of unconditional love?

If so, then consider me twice blessed because I also fell in love with a living man, Clay Baxter. However, thanks to my obsession with helping Will, the tide of tolerance turned against me, and I had to let go of Clay, too.

But all this belongs to another memoir. What I want to share here are the tragic events that transpired in the weeks after Will and Clay left my life.

It was a time of incredible revelations as my subtle vision continued to mature. Chief among those revelations? That mankind lives in a physical, tangible, material world, but it is influenced by an invisible, intangible, spiritual world.

A pastor I befriended suggested that the ghosts I see may be angels and demons in disguise. As you can imagine, it's the demons that are concerning. They know where we are, but only a few of us with vision can discern where they are.

Sadly, those forthcoming weeks also became a time of mourning for us—"us" being my cousin and friends from the local town of Williamsport—because one of us all too soon would suffer a tragedy within the confines of *Crossings*.

But again, I'm ahead of myself. Let me first return to where I left off in my earlier account, the moment when my whole essence veered off course.